Battle for the Second Realm

When Magic Awakes – Book 2

Petra M Costa

First published by Busybird Publishing 2021

ISBN
978-1-922691-14-9 (paperback)
978-1-922691-15-6 (ebook)

This is a work of fiction. Any similarities between places and characters are a coincidence.

Cover image: Petra Costa
Cover design: Kev Howlett, Busybird Publishing
Layout and typesetting: Busybird Publishing
Editor: Scott Vandervalk

Busybird Publishing
2/118 Para Road
Montmorency, Victoria
Australia 3094
www.busybird.com.au

This book is dedicated to my dad. A man that created art using his bare hands – his medium was stone, his creations breathtaking.

He taught me that strength is something that comes from within.

And that if you harness that strength, there's nothing that can stop you.

I think the strength was his, but he may have gifted a little bit to me.

Love you, Dad. Love you, more!

Contents

Glossary of terms   i

Prologue I   vii
History of the Magic Wars

Prologue II   x
Thirst for Knowledge

Home Life   1
In the Book   10
Search Pattern   13
Finding One Amongst Many   24
Networking   30
Here There be Dragons   45
Fragments   58
A Field of Blue   73
Aftermath   90
Who Knows?   97
Mirror, Mirror   109
Greedy Tome   128
Connections   145

Dark Net 161

Contagion 179

Ascension 190

Control 209

Finding the Dreamer 229

Supply Lines 244

Cutting Ties 259

Motivations 280

Interference 289

Growth 302

Agendas 323

Entrapment 344

Fallout 370

Imprisonment 383

Camouflage 397

Transformation 419

Resolution 446

Epilogue

Epilogue 450

Family Ties

Prologue

Prologue 457

Brother of Mine

About the Author

About the Author 461

Glossary of terms

28 and always – A bedtime saying that means 'I love you without limit, always and forever.' It has also become a maxim for the bonded warriors.

Anarcus – see *The doll*.

The barrier – A magical barrier created to separate magic from the world. The barrier was reinforced when the doll was imprisoned, in an effort to keep it forever bound. Each great use of power weakens the barrier further.

The blood (aka The chosen) – A line of magic-wielders that are true to the source, the power that creates and binds the world. Michael, Dana and Ashley are the current generation of the blood.

The bonded – see *The sleeping warriors*.

The breach (aka The rift) – A tear in the magical barrier created to separate the wilder forms of magic from the world. The breach is allowing power to seep back into the world. Any great use of power widens the breach further. Magical creatures are drawn to the breach since their powers are enhanced by the magic that seeps through.

The burden – The task of guarding *the doll* and maintaining the spells that bind it. The burden is passed down through bloodlines. The burden was first given to Trevlor, and the task now sits with Michael, Dana and Ashley.

The chosen – see *The blood*.

The covenant – A magical contract that prevents the faeries from engaging in battle directly. If they use their magic to destroy, they will be stripped of their magical protections.

Disciples – Those loyal to the doll who are willing to affect its release.

The doll (aka Anarcus) – A creature of great power that was bound centuries before by *the chosen*. The doll is a manipulator of dreams, and it feeds off minds as well as blood. Its goal is to merge the *first plane* and *second plane* so it can be in full control of both.

The dreaming plane – see *The second plane*.

The emblem (aka the crest) – A circle made of branches representing the tree of life, in amongst which rest a dragon. In the dragon's tail, it holds a sword, poised ready to strike, or to fall. The emblem is found on the cover of *the gypsy book,* on the warrior's sword, or as images on gypsy wagons throughout history. Nicola and Sarah wear pendants with the crest. Michael, Dana and Ashley have recently been gifted with jewellery that hold the same crest. The symbol is said to offer protection.

The faerie – A group of magical creatures that live in a land that can only be accessed by magic. Historically, the faerie are the teachers of the magic-wielders.

The faerie realm – The home of the faerie that can only be accessed through magical means. A place of sweeping bridges and high archways.

Fire sprites – Small delicate creatures that resemble the faerie and control the element of fire. They have hair and eyes of fire and talk in cracks and pops. They can be any colour.

The first plane (aka The first realm) – The waking world. The physical plane.

The gypsy book – An ancient book currently in Nicola's possession. An old reference book that is passed down from generation to generation. The book works on a transactional basis: when someone asks the book a question, if it is able to answer it takes a fragment of memory as payment. The book contains fragments of every mind that has ever used it.

The rift – see *The breach*.

The second plane (aka The second realm, the dreaming plane, the realm of dreams) – The second realm is complex with various levels, one being the void, the place where dreams have yet to form. It also contains the dreamer's quarters, the place where people dream. Injuries sustained in the second plane can transfer over to the first plane.

The sleeping warriors (aka The bonded) – Magical warriors created by the source. Created from the blood of *the chosen*, mixed with the land they are sworn to protect. There are fourteen warriors who ride fourteen horses. They have a bond that allows them to speak through a mindlink. They are bound by a magical compulsion to obey those of *the blood*. They are sworn to protect the source and those true to it. The sleeping warriors can only be summoned by those of *the blood*. One of their number was lost thousands of years ago. Michael is the first mortal to become a member of the sleeping warriors.

The source – The power that creates and binds the world. Magic is a facet of this energy. The wilder aspects of this power are locked behind a barrier that took the magic-wielders generation to create. These barriers are weakening. The weak points are referred to as *the breach* or *the rift*.

Trevlor – A mage's apprentice who was the only magic-wielder to survive the doll's binding. He was gifted with his master's powers, along with his memories, as his master died in his arms. He was the first of *the blood* to take on the burden of maintaining the binding magic around the doll. It is his memory of this moment that Nicola relives when she first accesses *the gypsy book*. This fragment of Trevlor's memory later takes possession of Nicola's body.

The void – The first place entered when magically transported into the second plane. The void holds the matter from which dreams are created. It will actively obstruct entry or manipulation by a conscious mind.

Water sprites – Small delicate creatures that resemble the faeries and that control the element of water. They sing beautifully and speak in a 'pipping' voice that humans cannot understand. They are usually blue or green in colour.

Weeping women (aka white women) – Pale-faced women, with thick, dark ropes of hair. They have elongated features and gaping mouths that attach to the back of the neck of their victims and drain their life force. They are a natural enemy of *the sleeping warriors*. The weeping women remain insubstantial until injured, and then gain more substance.

Wild magic (aka wildfire) – A form of powerful magic that is almost impossible to control since it requires the balance of order and chaos within the mind. The wildfire has the ability to create as well as to destroy, and it usually turns on those trying to use its powers.

White women – see *weeping women*.

Prologue I
History of the Magic Wars

The histories tell us that there were three ruling classes of magic-wielders, humans able to harness the powers of the elements.

Some sought enlightenment and chased knowledge for nothing more than the satisfaction of understanding. They looked to the heavens, they looked within, and they looked deeply into the fabric of the universe to unlock its secrets.

Others used the knowledge they had gained to lead. For whom better to create a map for the future than those that understood the seasons, those that could control the humours within the bodies, thereby lifting the curse of ailments that had plagued humankind for time immemorable.

The final group sat in contemplation, listening to the universe as it spoke to them, allowing its power to flow through them taking a shape and path of its own design.

War broke out between two of the more powerful groups. The land was twisted as fire was pulled from deep within its core; the oceans rose and deserts formed as water became a weapon; creatures living in the shadows fed on the energy spilled in the conflict. With their power and influence, the battle was set to rage on for centuries.

Until the third group intervened.

They had sat and listened as the universe cried, watched on as the destruction and misuse of the source of all energy threatened to be drained beyond any ability to recover. They listened as the whispered words of the divine asked for aid.

And they responded, allowing what remained of the source to guide their hands. They created a divide, a system of barriers to prevent free access to the source. Creatures that had been born of the shadows were bound. Layers of existence were formed to keep the worlds separate. And then slowly and methodically, they siphoned away the energy that the other magic-wielders were using so mercilessly, protecting the energy and depriving the heretics of their power.

Faced with disconnection from the source, the two warring factions united, looking to destroy this third group. And it is said that this is the moment the faeries came to the fight, battling to protect the source. No more feared opponent had ever been encountered.

Although the process took centuries, those protecting the source prevailed.

As a final safeguard, a band of warriors were created. From the blood of those true to the source and from the earth of the land they were sworn to protect, they were raised. Sent into a magical slumber. Tasked to monitor the system of barriers created to keep the world in balance, to serve those true to the source if they were called upon. Bound to serve.

It was said that the power of these warriors rivalled even that of the faerie.

And we pray that the extent of their power has not become exaggerated over time as it is also said that the forces exiled to the shadows would not rest easy, and that a day would come when they would again rise and seek out those who had imprisoned them.

Their first objective to exact their revenge against those who had wronged them.

Their second: to destroy the barriers that separated the worlds.

Prologue II
Thirst for Knowledge

Nicola looked down on the rough circular hole that the wild magic had created in the quiet suburban street. The blast area resembled some kind of war zone with shattered concrete, rubble and dust-laden smoke spreading over more than a ten-metre radius. Soot-covered faces emerged through the haze. The hiss of broken pipes and the steady tick of cooling metal were the only sounds to break the uncomfortable silence. Chunks of broken concrete were moved aside by the firefighters desperate to clear the area. A few of them nimbly scaled the network of pipes and steel that lined the inside of the crater.

Two men remained, kneeling in the mud that had formed at the base of the hole, slowly getting soaked by the water leaking from ruptured pipes. A pale white arm, remarkably untouched by the chaos at the bottom of the crater, was lifted as the firefighters searched for a pulse.

Urgency seemed to enter the scene as the men who'd scrambled to the surface ran back to the edge of the crater, handing down portable resuscitation equipment.

Who had she missed? She'd tried to protect everyone.

Nicola ran through the faces she knew surrounding the hole and mentally ticked off Michael, Ashley, Dana… All were safe. She couldn't be sure, but the firefighters all seemed to be accounted for, and the person who lay struggling for life wasn't wearing any protective clothing or uniform. When the firefighter in charge reached up to grab the resuscitation gear, Nicola caught a glimpse of the owner of the pale unmarked arm.

Her own unblinking blue eyes stared back.

She had been the one unprotected. She had been the one exposed as the wild magic tore through her. She couldn't remember when her consciousness had left her body, but she'd been in this position before and she knew what she had to do.

Her heart had stopped once before during a gruelling ten-hour surgery and she'd awoken to the disorienting experience of looking down on her own body. The surgeon, controlled and purposeful, had methodically gone about the task of resuscitation.

Nicola knew at that time, as she did now, that mere moments mattered in this one instant more than at any other time in her life. She instinctively knew that panic, if allowed a foothold, would literally kill her.

She stilled her mind, found her focus. She needed to be as controlled as the surgeons had been years before. With calculated calm, she forced herself to become *more*.

More what?

More solid.

More real.

More tangible.

The words mattered little; it was the intention that mattered. She needed to refocus her being. She could not allow herself to dissipate. With only her thoughts to ground herself, she found the gentle pull of her body. Once sensed, the connection grew with a kind of weight and she allowed herself to descend. Resisting the uncomplicated comfort that surrounded her, she embraced the complication of self, knowing that now wasn't her time.

Her mind flinched as it re-entered her body. The restriction of flesh felt claustrophobic, but she'd known what to expect and she stretched her senses out to regain contact with fingers and toes. As her consciousness poured through the empty vessel that was her body, she encountered unexpected resistance.

Pathways were being blocked! Areas that should be empty had already been filled. Nicola felt a moment of panic.

Was she too late? Had she been out of her body too long? Was the damage too great? She struggled for composure and felt the resistance flex; her hold on her own body was forcibly pushed outwards and her grip weakened. Trying to regain focus, she searched for any mental or physical handholds that could help her anchor herself. Desperate to find a way to pour around these blockages, Nicola sensed the other's presence too late. As the pathways and avenues that led into her body were being barred against her, Nicola recognised the mind behind this unexpected expulsion.

Trevlor had taken control of her body.

Nicola was losing cohesion. Knowing the fight for her body had been lost, her mind raced for a solution. The wild magic linked so intrinsically to the physical plane wasn't available to her, and she felt her clarity of thought diluting, distracted by the images of her family before her, so bright, so complex, so engaging. She almost became lost in their light. There were so many points of brilliance surrounding her, each begging her attention. She found her mind split in a myriad of directions.

How different everything looked now that the connection to her body had been severed.

As she felt her consciousness drifting down the many paths before her, whispered voices accompanied her journey.

Need to see.

Need to know what happens.

She never went this far last time.

Need to know.

NEED the answer. The voices were one from many, and a prickling of annoyance disrupted her gentle journey into dissolution. Irritated by the chorus of thought, Nicola's focus became drawn to the susurration that surrounded her and she tried to understand the many voices, tried to understand what they were talking about. *Need the answer. Will never get another opportunity. Need to know.*

NEED.

THE.

ANSWER.

What answer? What opportunity? The greedy hunger in the words was almost obscene in its blatant need. A prickle of recognition. She had encountered this single-minded thirst for knowledge once before, when she'd been on the receiving end of an unwavering, unforgiving transfer of information. And wasn't she now paying the ultimate price for the answers she'd received then.

As Nicola focused on the whispers, the sounds shifted to include the rustling of pages. The questing, hungry voices faltered as Nicola recognised an opportunity. She remembered the dry, dusty feel of the paper, and she mentally traced the now familiar symbol with her mind's eye. As the symbol clarified in her mind, Nicola felt herself being pulled, as if she were nothing more than metal filings drawn towards a magnet. What remained of her was rushing towards her own home, to where the gypsy book lay, sitting in an upstairs cupboard, shoved into the back corner of the highest shelf. Put there specifically so that no-one would accidentally come across it.

With each layered detail of remembering, her scattered thoughts gained weight and descended, not towards her own body but towards the greedy pages of the book.

The book lay open, pages turning as if blown by a strong wind, restlessly flicking back and forth, the dry rustling sound of the pages mixed with the voices in her head making thought almost impossible.

She had no idea whether the book could support life, but when needs must, the devil drives. Nicola hesitated for a moment resisting the magnetic pull of the book, but with little other choice available to her she allowed herself to flood through its pages. There was a moment of resistance, and then the cover slammed shut, encasing her in pages of memory.

Home Life

Michael needed to walk, needed to move. There was no solace to be found in his home. He wasn't certain if it was the absence of his mother's calming presence or the fact that her body now harboured the mind of a deranged mage that was causing him so much difficulty. Probably both.

He listened as the faeries planned how they were going to track down his mother's soul. The process sounded so simple, so academic. Michael knew days before the worried looks and the noncommittal responses that they were not finding the tracking as easy as they had made it out to be. Michael told himself for the hundredth time that he would know if his mother were truly gone. He would sense her absence. But an increasingly disturbing thought kept creeping into his mind, disrupting his certainty.

Would he really know if she was gone?

Didn't every person hoping for the return of a loved one convince themselves that everything was okay because they still felt a reassuring presence? That they still expected them to walk around every corner.

He'd been brought up to believe that nothing could separate them. Nothing. Not even death. That was what Michael's mother believed – but it was easy for her. She'd always sensed the presence of those who had passed. Nicola said she mourned the ability to pick up the phone to someone who'd passed and tell a funny story. She missed the ability to reach out and offer comfort or receive it in turn, but she never lost her connection to the individual – this connection she claimed to retain. She'd often joked that the spirits liked to vex her with moving things around the house or hiding them so completely that no amount of searching would find them. Only when Nicola had finally called off the search, always with acknowledgment to the individual whom she believed had moved them, would the items appear, and in the most unlikely of places. Shoes on kitchen benches. Books in the bed or under the covers, even after the bed had been freshly made. Things impossible to reason away with a logical explanation.

Michael wished he possessed his mother's certainty. He needed her presence; he needed to see his mother looking back at him through her dark blue eyes, not the demented gaze of the unhinged freak that strode around their home as if he were some kind of overlord, wearing his mother's body like some cheap suit.

The faeries' most recent discussion about their progress in finding his mother had been the tipping point. Azuradien and Malcarielle had arrived at their family home, appearing as nothing more than petite humans with slightly pointed ears. The wings that only appeared in the human realm when the faeries became agitated or enraged were nowhere to be seen. The progress of the faeries, or lack thereof, in finding his mother was causing a great deal of anxiety amongst his family.

When Azuradien, the faerie king, with his white hair and long flowing beard that spoke of authority and wisdom, stood at the kitchen table to explain how another string of options that had been put forward with supreme confidence now had to be scratched off the list, Michael felt emotions a little more intense than anxiety.

As proposed initially, his mother wasn't inhabiting the mind of another person or animal living nearby. They'd searched at least a two-kilometre radius from the house, saying any farther was unlikely to be fruitful either. Dana had stormed out of the room upon learning this, always comfortable expressing her emotions in public.

When the conversation turned to life forces, potential hosts and long-term viability, Michael too had had enough.

How had it come to pass that in less than a week his mother had gone from only being 'lost' to now being less than 'viable'?

They were talking about her as if Nicola were merely a specimen in a jar, something that might simply cease to be. The faeries' lack of empathy, their basic inability to grasp the slowly escalating desperation that he and his family were feeling, was creating more tension than any of them could bear. Michael would have appreciated the agitated appearance of wings, the lifting and swirling of their long hair as their distress caused the air currents to swirl around them. But the faeries stood before their family, having returned to their default position of being the teachers in this situation, and lectured them on *life forces*.

The faeries, with their thousand-year lifespan, appeared to lack awareness for the abject fear that Michael and his family were struggling to keep at bay. He hated them a little for their detachment. What did the faeries have to fear? They could run back to their ethereal kingdom, protected by their spells and enchantments, live their long, untroubled lives and sit back drinking tea, contemplating the great mysteries of existence. Meanwhile, Michael and his family had to deal with the simple fact that the clock was ticking. If they didn't find Nicola soon, she would be lost forever.

Michael's family might be the ones destined to protect the world from the evil of the doll Anarcus, but they were a family first and right now that was all that mattered. Forget the lives that were being consumed by the doll's manipulations, forget about it all. His family was only functioning because there was still a chance.

Michael took in a shaky breath and wiped at his eyes. The faeries continued to drone on, discussing life forces and time frames. Michael couldn't listen any longer. He pushed away from the table. With forced control, he returned his chair to its correct position. With shaking hands, he dug his fingers into the fabric of the chair and fought the instinct to hurl it at the faerie king and his aloof daughter – and their dispassionate discussion.

There was no doubt Michael hated them right now. Hated them for their long, impervious lives. And he hated himself a little too because in that moment he would do anything for his family to have long, impervious lives.

So, before his emotions could get the better of him, he drew his shoulders back, prised his fingers off the chair and walked calmly towards the back door to find his sister. He was determined that the faeries would see none of his pain.

Dana was striding around the back lawn like a caged lion, glaring angrily when an obstacle forced her to change direction. Sheba followed at her side, tail down, head lowered, her eyes searching every corner of the yard. For a large black Doberman, Sheba was doing an excellent job of looking small and vulnerable. The agitation in both of them was palpable.

Michael sat at the edge of the lawn, outside of their circuit. He didn't want to be the object that got in their way. But he sat close enough to feel part of them rather than separate, knowing that Dana would come to him when she was ready.

It didn't surprise Michael that his older sister's powers manifested as her having an affinity with animals. Sheba was the family dog, but everybody knew she was really Dana's. Dana just had a way with Sheba that was more than a standard owner-pet relationship; they shared emotions, even personality traits. His big sister might be small for her sixteen years but she was no shrinking violet; she was always intimately in touch with her emotions – and she wasted no time bottling things up, you always knew where you stood with Dana.

As Michael waited, he absently plucked at blades of grass. He'd always been the more patient of the two of them. They might look like twins with their dark blond hair and olive skin, but their personalities couldn't be more different. So Michael sat and waited for Dana to burn some of the negative energy off.

It didn't take long for Dana to circle around the yard and then sit down beside him and let him know the full extent of her outrage. The fear for their mother was etched into her face. The inability to act in any meaningful way was eating her up inside.

* * *

'Why the hell have they been wasting time searching animals around here?' Dana said. 'Don't you think Sheba and I have already done that?'

Michael didn't answer her – he knew her well enough to know it wasn't really a question.

'If she was in some other body, she would have made her way to us by now. She would have found a way to communicate with us. She wouldn't just sit around having tea or eating bugs or whatever the hell it is they think she would be doing. She wouldn't be doing that! She would come home. Mum would come back to us!' Dana wiped a tear away angrily and continued her circuit of the backyard.

'Even around school, I haven't found any sign of her,' she said.

'I know, Dana,' said Michael, almost under his breath. 'The bonded are searching the second plane, but there seems little point. Titan would be able to find her if she was over there.'

'He hasn't found a trace,' said Dana.

Even in death, Titan still watched over them. Animals didn't have the same distinction between life and death as humans did. Sheba's brother had simply moved from one plane of existence to another when he passed away. Now Dana could reach him too – it was one of the few perks of their new-found powers.

Sheba paced beside her whining softly. Realising the stress she was causing the dog, Dana reached down and stroked her head, then she sat next to Michael and pulled up chunks of grass and threw them across the garden.

'We're thinking too laterally. We need to think like Mum, not like *them*!' A piece of lawn with roots and soil attached flew across the garden and hit the window. The faeries, still calm and unaffected while they sat around the kitchen table, turned and looked at Dana as the *thud* drew their attention. The clod of soil had disintegrated on impact; a shower of soil scratched its way down the glass. Dana defiantly glared at them. She knew her gaze held all the raw emotions that she was struggling to contain. And she didn't care.

Michael and Dana's father, who was sitting inside with the faeries, glanced at Dana through the glass and slowly looked away. Dana saw the fury in his eyes, and smiled. She might not be the one who had to bring the faeries to account for this situation. Only one person she knew could build a rage anywhere near her own, and that was her dad, Joe. With southern Italian heritage, Joe had near-black hair and dark olive skin. He was also an emotional stereotype when it came to how he reacted to difficult situations. He did not go from zero to one hundred. With Joe, there was *only* zero and one hundred. Dana almost expected to see the flicker of fire near him.

The faeries had better come up with something more than 'extended radii' or their father was going to explode. She felt no lessening of tension, knowing Joe shared her frustration.

Her hands still trembled, so she reached for more grass. She needed to unleash some of her anger before it turned into the fear she knew was really at its core.

'We need to think outside of the box, Michael! She's not in an animal. Please trust me on this. We would know.' Sheba had laid down next to Dana, occasionally pawing at her leg as if trying to remind her of her presence. 'If I didn't sense it, Sheba would, and she'd find a way to let me know. Michael, we would know!'

* * *

'I'm hearing you, Dana.' Michael wrapped an arm around his big sister, knowing that now was the right time to offer comfort. He couldn't read Sheba like Dana could, but the Doberman's head was now in Dana's lap, occasionally stretching forward to nuzzle her hand, no longer fretting and pawing at her leg. He didn't need this confirmation though; he knew his sister well enough to know her anger was fading and all the uncertainty of their situation was bubbling up to the surface. Michael felt Dana relax slightly as her head settled on his shoulder.

'But where, Dana? She wouldn't go into a random stranger. She just wouldn't do that, no matter what the cost. She might have piggybacked into one of us. I truly want to believe that if she could, she would have known we were here for her. But…' Michael shrugged, and Dana's head shifted slightly, moving with him rather than pulling away.

'You're right, but what else is there? If we listen to these faeries, there's nothing, no hope…. They're so wrapped up in their own view of the world that they refuse to look for alternatives. And they've lived for centuries, so they believe they're right. We just don't have the time to convince them otherwise.' Dana was plucking at the grass again and it was coming out in clumps. Michael dropped his arm so he could look into her face.

'Could she be in something… electrical?' Michael asked with some hesitation. 'Thoughts are electrical currents, right?' It even sounded farfetched to his own ears.

Dana stopped the slow destruction of the area around her. 'I know how it sounds, but in the movies, in video games, they always transfer to something electrical.' Michael knew he was rambling but couldn't stop. Dana hadn't responded. The only sign that she'd heard him was her sudden stillness.

'Dana, do you think she could have transferred to something electrical or not?'

'Dana?' Michael asked again. Dana seemed lost in thought. Her eyes were no longer staring through the window. Instead, they were roaming from side to side, her brow furrowed so much like their mother.

Dana took another long moment to consider things then turned to Michael. 'That's not such a stupid idea. But how could we find her? We can't just boot up our computers and search for mum.exe!'

'No. But we can try talking to them again, get them to think a little *new age*. The faeries must be able to search for energy spikes, energy drains maybe, I don't know, something.' Michael was on his feet and walking towards the back door before Dana had time to drop the grass she was holding.

Dana threw the clump haphazardly to the side, dusted her hands off, and reached into her pocket and pulled out her phone. She paused as she examined the device, laughed at her own ridiculousness, and followed Michael inside.

As Dana walked, she dialled her cousin. 'Ashley, family meeting. We need you over here.'

In the Book

She existed. She must because she thought, and didn't that mean she existed? Wasn't that the big philosophical debate? She didn't know. She no longer had any point of reference. She had no form, no body, no sense of self. She had only consciousness, tortured consciousness. Bombarded with innumerable versions of herself, she was awash in a tide that would not relent.

A hall of mirrors lay before her, infinite reflections reaching outwards in a never-ending kaleidoscope of refracted colour. Each polished surface held the face of a different person, looking back at her with scorn and anger. Each of these tormented souls wanted a voice, wanted to be heard, and if she let her eyes lay on an image for too long, their consciousness would consume her and force her to live through their eyes.

But it was impossible to turn away when you had only a memory of form. You couldn't close eyes that didn't really exist.

She forced her focus to move on; she had looked upon the man with brown hair, hazel eyes and strong jaw for far too long. She tried to move her attention to another panel, another likeness, but she was already too late. With a spinning sense of vertigo, the man's tormented gaze dragged her back into the mirror, to experience his life as her own.

He stood before the bowl of water, trying to clear his mind. Until his mind achieved the clarity of the crystal-clear liquid in the bowl, he would be unable to scry.

A white-hot streak of pain tore across his back, the sound of the whip cracking reaching his ears a moment after the pain. He refused to let his knees bend. If he reacted to the whip, his master would strike again. He distanced himself from his body, focusing only on the bowl before him; the waters swirled, and an image started to emerge.

Focus.

He dropped to his knees when the next blow fell, but he registered this as only a change in perspective. The colours dancing on the water's surface gained structure, purpose. A scene was forming, clarifying as his mind dropped farther into the cool liquid. He used the rhythmic sound of his own blood dripping to the floor to give a deeper aspect to his focus.

Water was liquid.

Blood was liquid.

They both flowed.

The image in the bowl revealed more detail. He now saw the outline of one man standing above another.

A dull crack and his body fell forward as the next more brutal blow landed. He ignored the sounds of his own ragged breathing and tried to steady the bowl that he had set to rocking. His shaking hand succeeded only in spilling more of the precious liquid. The image in the water wavered as he saw a man drawing back his arm, twisting his body to strike another. The victim knelt, bleeding profusely, his back torn open by a score of wounds. As the blow fell and he watched the victim crumple, he heard his master's words echo from behind him as well as from the water.

'IGNORE YOUR BODY AT YOUR PERIL. YOUR BODY SUSTAINS YOUR LIFE.'

She felt the agonising pain rip through her back as the last lash of the whip fell. The image of the man shimmered. She saw him mouthing the words AT YOUR PERIL as the vibration of the mirror intensified. The face of the man became a blur moments before the mirror exploded out in a shower of fractured images.

She didn't flinch, didn't turn away. She knew a mirror would still stand before her and a new image would take its place.

Once again she was surrounded by thousands of reflected faces, trapped as if suspended in the middle of a crystal, every facet reflecting a different part of her personality. Every time she caught the gaze of another of the faces, she would experience a moment of life – sometimes painful, sometimes joyful – but always as if it were her own. The problem was that she was so many people.

Lost in the maelstrom of memories, her eyes caught those of a black-haired young girl and she was pulled into her dark gaze. There was a moment of panic as the girl reached towards a book.

Search Pattern

Michael had sent out the mental call. Ashul was on his way to him, having completed another sweep of through the second realm. The bonded were methodically working their way through the realm, section by section. It was like looking for a piece of plane wreckage when you had no idea where the plane had gone down.

Michael could already feel the distance between them diminishing. It was amazing how quickly he'd gotten used to having an internal radar that enabled him to feel and track his connection to the bonded. When the sleeping warriors had woken, he'd been so wrapped up in the torment the doll inflicted upon him night after night that he never questioned their existence, nor the code that bound them.

The code was now his. By accepting the link that Smoke had offered him, Michael had accepted the bonded and all the tenets that bound them. Michael was sure that this should trouble him. Maybe at some point in the future it would, but right now he only cared about getting his mother back and the bonded were doing everything in their power to make that happen. So although he knew this was the wrong reason to embrace the link, embrace it he did.

Michael had always felt the need to protect those around him, those who were vulnerable. It was just how he was built, how he had been raised. So he was quite familiar with the motivations that drove the bonded. He understood how the sleeping warriors thought. Of course, there was a huge distinction between wanting to help others and being magically compelled to help just a few – the defining difference being free will – but Michael doubted any of these warriors had yet to be truly forced to comply. The bonded warriors were driven to fight evil as it came into the world, returning to their rest only when danger had passed. Michael believed that these warriors would fight evil in all its forms regardless – it was just how *they* were built.

Michael didn't know what was going to happen to him when the bonded finally stopped the doll. The strange quirk of fate that found him offered a place amongst the bonded, amongst the sleeping warriors, did not come with a detailed contract or operating instructions. Somehow, for Michael, destiny and choice coexisted regardless of the fact they were fundamental opposites. The path that had been chosen for him just so happened to be the same path he would have chosen for himself. Michael didn't question these things, didn't see any point in arguing about free will just to be contrary. When Smoke had lowered her head to Michael's hand, he didn't think *destiny,* he didn't think *free will,* he really didn't need to think at all. A wonderfully intelligent, proud being had stood in front of him and offered him friendship, and he had simply accepted. Ancient pacts and magical bonds were secondary considerations. *After all, didn't all friendship come with some baggage?*

Smoke was now part of him – she understood and shared Michael's need to find his mother. *Stay resolute. Your thoughts are clear. The faeries have their own measurement of time, though it may not always keep pace with your own. Ashul will support you.* With her thoughts, Michael could also feel the intolerance that burned within Smoke. She viewed the faeries as allies, but not as equals.

Michael drew on Smoke's emotions and some of her strength since they were almost his own, and marched towards the house, determined to be heard, knowing that Dana was only one step behind.

As they stepped into the house, the sound of raised voices confirmed that their dad had finally exploded. An argument was already underway.

* * *

'We do not have the time for this. Have you seen her today, Azuradien, really seen her? She's fading. You need to get him out of her.' Joseph stood clenching and unclenching his hands. His face a mask of anger, his voice lowered so as not to draw unwanted attention but still menacing in its intensity.

'We are expanding our search; we have our strongest…'

Joseph slammed his hand into the bench and although sparks did not fly, Michael noticed all digital clocks in the room flicker, and the lights dimmed briefly.

'Well, maybe your strongest just aren't good enough. Or isn't it important enough to you to save a mere mortal.' Dana had now wrapped her arm around Joseph's waist, and what in any other pair would seem reassuring; in them, it looked nothing less than menacing.

'Joseph, we treasure your wife, we would do anything to save her.' Malcarielle looked towards her father for support. 'Please understand this is not a usual occurrence.' Her emerald-green eyes had dimmed to a swampy grey over the last week, and dark circles ringed her eyes. If not for the almost translucent skin and the constantly shifting hair, she would look like any normal tired teenager, not the hundred-year-old forest faerie that she was. Azuradien, her father, still a king in this realm, looked concerned – but he was not intimidated.

'We are working tirelessly, we are doing all we can—'

Ashul strode into the room and interrupted Azuradien's carefully chosen words. He bowed briefly to Azuradien and Malcarielle, then to Joseph, kissed the back of Dana's hand then wrapped Michael in a bear hug. If not for his demeanour, you could have mistaken Ashul for one of Michael's teammates. He stood at around six feet with ash-blond hair and the build of a midfielder. His age would be put at around eighteen until you actually looked into his eyes, then you would have to question your first impression. The way he held himself spoke leader; his eyes were all soldier, eyes that had seen too much.

'We have also found no trace.' Ashul's cold blue eyes searched the faces of all present and silenced any argument with the intensity of his stare.

'Do any here question my intentions?' asked Ashul. 'Are my motives suspect? Are those of the bonded?' His steely gaze demanded attention. 'No, then let us stop this bickering. Michael, you have an idea.' His gaze locked onto Michael's. And with nothing more than a casual nod from Ashul, all attention shifted to Michael.

'Ah… well, I was talking with Dana…' Michael hesitated, never one to enjoy talking in front of a group. 'And well, we need to think outside of the box, think like our mum.' Michael paused, hoping Dana would jump in. When she didn't, he continued, 'Mum wouldn't jump into another person, so just cross that off the list. She won't read text messages off our phones, so possessing another person, just no, she wouldn't do that.'

'There may have been no other choice available to her,' Azuradien interjected in his scholarly tone.

Four voices replied in unison: 'There is always a choice.'

It was no surprise to Michael that his dad and Dana had spoken these words; they'd all heard them a thousand times. Nicola destroyed many a carefully crafted argument with that one phrase, usually accompanied by an irritated hand gesture, silencing any further justification. But that Ashul viewed the world in the same simplistic terms, with the same black or white mentality did surprise him. He wasn't certain why. Maybe he'd just assumed with all of their experience, the bonded warriors would have a shades of grey approach to morality. Ashul just indicated for Michael to continue as if they had all spoken an undeniable fact and this kind of simple truth did not require further discussion.

At this point Aunty Sarah, Uncle Brent and Ashley walked into the room. Michael's aunt did not stop to say hello, did not smile in her usual friendly manner. The look on her face indicated that she'd heard enough of the conversation to be annoyed.

'No need to stop on our account.' Sarah said with a carry-on gesture of her hand. 'We caught the general gist of the conversation as we walked in. Michael, you were saying?' Her words were clipped and it was only as her eyes turned to Michael that any warmth entered them.

Michael nodded his agreement and continued on, 'Thanks, Aunty Sarah. Well, as I was saying, she's not in a person. It wouldn't have been an *acceptable* option, so stop looking there. Forget your searches and expanded radii. Pointless!

And Dana is confident that she has not entered an animal, so unless you want to scan all the insects in the area, forget that too.'

'Dana, your powers are new and unexplored. You can hardly be sure of this?' Malcarielle tried to take some of the sting out of her words by laying a hand on Dana's arm. Aunty Sarah placed her hands on Dana's shoulders and gave Malcarielle a slightly raised eyebrow that said *everything*.

'Yes, I suppose you are right. I don't have your experience, just learning my skills.' Dana was studying Malcarielle's hand as if she were waiting for them to be lifted before she continued. Then, realising Malcarielle had no ability to read the room, Dana raised her head until she was looking Malcarielle directly in the eye. 'But Sheba has been a dog her entire life and she would sense it if Mum was piggy-backing in any animal in the area. And before you ask, yes, we have checked. Double-checked, triple-checked. There's no animal in the area showing any signs of distress. Quite the opposite. They're showing nothing but relief now that the doll is no longer in the area. Because, yes, we have checked that as well. And before you question the integrity of that piece of information, I will point out that the animals were aware of the doll's presence before you faeries even came into the picture. While you were holed up in your underground fortress, the animals were trying to warn whoever would listen. Well, I'm listening now, and no animal is harbouring my mother's spirit.'

Dana was shaking slightly by the time she'd finished. Malcarielle had taken a step backwards. Through all of the emotions swirling around the room all could feel Ashley's support for her cousin. Each of the family had their own magical gifts. Ashley's gift was her emotions. She could sense what others were feeling, transfer her own feelings onto others and basically amp up people's emotions if the mood took her. And sometimes even when it didn't. Ashley had always been one of those people who could change the mood of the room just by walking into it. Her emotions were infectious. As the barriers keeping the wilder aspects of magic separated from this world broke down and more and more energy flowed through the rift, her powers increased. She was wasting no time in broadcasting her feelings to the room: both in her support for Dana and at her annoyance and frustration at the faeries' lack of urgency.

Ashul nodded his acceptance of her views as if she'd spoken them aloud. 'So, fair Dana, where does that leave us?'

Ashul maintained his stoic demeanour. He was a warrior looking for more information; frustration, desperation, annoyance – these emotions would just get in the way. He always remained focused, detached. Michael could sense through their bond that Ashul felt all of the same emotions and more, but he locked them away so they did not impact his decision-making.

'That leaves us everything else,' Michael announced. He held his hand up before anybody could speak. 'We need to look for energy spikes, energy drains. We need to look in both realms because I'm pretty certain a spirit could reach both. We need to consider modern technology. Could she have used a computer, maybe even the PlayStation? I don't know, but we need to look for the energy, not the soul. One will show us the other. Mum may be hiding. Have you stopped to consider whether that thing wearing her body like a glove is looking for her?' Michael paused, allowing the impact of his words to sink in. 'If he destroys her, then he can stay as long as he likes.'

'Actually, he cannot,' Azuradien interjected. 'The body will not survive long without its true soul!' Azuradien stated this in a matter-of-fact manner that made Michael grit his teeth. These few unconsidered words had increased the tension in the room tenfold. It wasn't only the concept behind the words, but more the lack of any attempt to soften the blow that gave them their sting.

Joseph stepped towards Azuradien, electricity running across his knuckles. 'You say that again and I will fry you like I did the eels.' Brent closed the distance between himself and Joseph and placed a restraining hand on Joseph's shoulder.

Michael was more concerned about Aunty Sarah. She was mumbling to herself and wringing her fingers. Michael couldn't understand any of the words, but it sounded to him like she was repeating the same phrase over and over again.

Malcarielle finally began showing some sign of distress. She hovered a few feet off the ground, her near transparent wings beating against her back. Her golden hair blew around her face like some kind of avenging goddess. A nimbus of energy bathed her in an emerald glow. It looked like all hell was about to break loose.

'Bonded.' Ashul spoke so quietly that Michael barely heard him. The slow drumming of hooves steadily pounded away in the background was something they all could hear.

'Hush,' Aunty Sars mumbled. Her fingers continued to move as if she were trying to undo an invisible knot. 'Just hush for a moment, I'm thinking.' Aunty Sars was a quietly spoken woman and even though she'd barely raised her voice, all talk in the room ceased. Michael watched her hands for a clue as to what she might be thinking about. Her nimble fingers were his aunt's strength. She had saved his life weaving a binding spell around the doll, and again when she'd protected them from poisonous smoke that threatened every living thing within its radius.

Michael had a great deal of respect, but little understanding of his aunt's strange powers. When her head dropped towards her chest, Michael took a quick step backwards. He held his left arm protectively in front of his sister. Michael could sense his aunt drawing from the energy that surrounded them all. The fine hairs on the back of his arms stood up and the air felt laden with a strange, static charge. If he had the eyes to see such things, he was certain her aura would be glowing with a light to match Malcarielle's.

After what felt like minutes, the strange charge in the room built to the point where Michael wondered whether a click of the fingers would create a spark. He held his breath for good measure until his aunt lifted her head and threw her hands out as if she'd come to the most amazing of realisations.

Above everybody's heads now shimmered a fine web of iridescent interconnected threads. Where Ashul stood, the network appeared to twist and spin in a fine silvery tapestry that had thin cords snaking around Michael. A more complicated network of lines connected to Dana, with radiating threads linked to everyone else in the room. Only the faeries had no direct connection to Ashul.

Ashul mentally told the bonded to stand down. The network pulsed with a flare of light, and then returned to its former more delicate state with the ripple of Ashul's energy slowly dying off around the edges. One moment, the iridescent network reminded Michael of a spider's web, the next moment a complicated dream catcher. Threads delicately twisted around all of them and he looked on in awe as more colour shimmered onto the web. Green where Malcarielle stood. Blue around Azuradien. The colours merged to a bright turquoise where the faeries' energies combined. Traceries of their colours shimmered around all of them, with Michael momentarily surrounded in green. Malcarielle gasped, and her thread faded from the network.

'Can you do that? Can you dim your flow?' Aunty Sarah asked. Malcarielle's cheeks now flushed with colour for the first time in days. 'I am not dimming my flow, just removing it from your grid.'

'Ah, I see that now.' Aunty Sarah twitched her fingers. The green returned for a moment. Sarah nodded to herself as more green threads surrounded Michael, and then with a casual gesture towards Malcarielle, the green flared before fading once more.

Azuradien stepped forward, his hand hesitantly reaching towards the fine network of interconnecting strands. 'May I?' He turned towards Sarah, his expression a mix of wonder and trepidation, finger poised a centimetre from the nearest strand. This combination of emotion changed his bearing immeasurably. He no longer commanded the room: he appeared surprised by what he found in it.

Azuradien ran one of his long fingers delicately over the silver strand shimmering nearest to him. 'This is truly an amazing array that you have created, Lady Sarah. I wonder if I knew not of the sleeping warriors would I still recognise this thread as one of the bonded.' He stepped through the web without disturbing its structure. The strands terminated on one side of his body and reappeared on the other side, unaffected by his forward movement. He plucked at the elaborate cord of twisted strands that emerged from Ashul's shoulders and disappeared through the ceiling. 'Darmead. Bellisan. Each of the bonded can be clearly identified. How did you create this?'

Sarah seemed puzzled by the question. 'Azuradien, have you not taught us to feel the flow, to recognise energy and draw on it when we need to?' She looked towards Joseph, then Brent to see if she had missed something. 'This is just a graphical representation of what I feel.'

'But Lady Sarah, it is more than that…'

A flicker of red pulsed on one of the outlying strands of the network, and Azuradien drew his hand from the web and stepped backwards. The pulse flared brighter and shot out to surround Ashul.

With strands of light twisting to encapsulate Ashul, the room turned as one as Trevlor strode into the kitchen. Although the mage possessed his mother's body, nothing residual of his mother's warmth remained. Michael saw only cold hatred burning from those blue eyes. Every small twitch of tightly held muscles confirmed for him that his mother was no longer in residence. With the same hand that his mother had used to push hair back gently from Michael's forehead, the mage dismissively swiped at the network. The intricately interconnected threads dissolved.

'While you talk of choice, the enemy has *chosen* to gain strength. While you play like children, children are being consumed. You think me the enemy. Your own weakness is the enemy!' Trevlor threw up his hands and a new network appeared suspended above their heads. This network was made of cords of fiery red that spun at an ever-increasing rate until the individual threads became a blur. As the movement slowed, the cords descended, tightening until they enveloped Ashul.

'You! You think you have choice.' Trevlor's lip twisted up into a condescending sneer as he barked out the words. 'You forget yourself. Forget who created you. Forget what you are. I am OF THE BLOOD. You will do as I command! Gather your bonded, we go to the second plane to seek the doll!'

Finding One
Amongst Many

*inds of fire swirled around her head. She saw the skin on her
own outstretched hands blackening, yet still she drew on the
strange power that ignited in her core. The men who had killed her
family — who had driven them like cattle into a canyon outside of
their remote village and casually lit the bonfire — stood hooting like
animals as they threw her family into the inferno. They cheered as
the flames caught on clothing and rejoiced when the first head of
hair ignited. They savagely thrust spears at anybody attempting
to escape.*

*She saw a man younger than herself run forward. He was
surrounded in a nimbus of pale light as he pushed past a dozen
villagers, chanting as he ran. An arrow pierced his left shoulder,
but fuelled by some inner power, he ran on. His arm hung uselessly*

at his side. His feet were kicked out from under him, and the arrow was driven through his body as he hit the ground. He tried to push himself up. She could just see his face through the swirling smoke that surrounded her. The faint light that shone from him started to fade. With the head of a spear driven through the centre of his chest, pinning his body to the ground, the light finally died.

Her rage built and the strange force that burned within her intensified. The screams of her people fanning the internal fire until the flames in her core eclipsed those that surrounded her.

The ground beneath her cracked, and lightning rained down from the sky to join with the flames in a dance to the death. Where the lightning struck, the flames were consumed and extinguished. The twisted branches and burning debris of the bonfire fell into deep fissures now scarring the earth's surface, radiating out from where she stood. Finally, her rage reached a point of release, and flames of her own creation shot from her blackened hands. Waves of force flew in concentric circles, obliterating everything they touched. And just as the circles of power were about to reach the desired target, her power failed her. The rage-filled energy fell back towards her, collapsing in upon itself, and the wild magic snuffed out like nothing more than a candle flame.

The fire that had blazed so unexpectedly inside of her was gone. Left with smouldering skin and hands that had fused into black misshapen claws, her heart beat on, and she had no choice but to listen while her village, her family, were slaughtered around her.

'You cannot play with wildfire,' she heard a voice whisper in her mind. The image of the white-haired, green-eyed woman with blistered skin blew apart into a million fragments. As each shard flew towards her, reflected from countless perspectives, she saw a blackened misshapen hand reach towards her. She didn't feel threatened, nor did she feel comforted. She felt only sorrow.

Why should they not pity her? They had their faces; they had their memories; she stood alone, even while surrounded by others. But were they other, or were they she? She no longer knew.

She found herself unable to focus, but she knew it was her mind – not her eyes – that had become blurred.

Each encounter left her a little more disorientated, left her mind more fragmented. Her thoughts traced patterns of memory, looking for connections, praying for meaning, constantly skipping from one image, one sound, to another. Her hands tingled with remembered pain. She flexed her fingers and found they could move; she reached towards her back and found no blood. She rubbed her ankle and found no chains.

Hadn't there been chains? No, it was the gentle rocking of a boat she remembered.

And she swayed with a rhythm that existed only in her mind.

But it all only existed in her mind, and wasn't that the frightening part? The mind numbingly, terrifying part? This place was just a construct, a projection of her mind created to cope with some trauma she couldn't remember. She had no hands, no ankles, no blood. How long before her mind no longer existed, before the lapses became a slow dissolution into nothing. Not long, she suspected. The images were taking longer each time to clarify.

Where once she'd been fearful of catching the mirror's gaze, now she sought the connection. The moments of memory were intense, often painful, but they were coherent, structured, and she preferred this structure to the fog her mind was slowly dissolving within.

Reflected faces blurred in front of her, a constantly shifting kaleidoscope of images. She tried to focus on some aspect of each face, a curve of a nose, the arch of a brow – anything to make an image clearer. A hundred different faces flashed before her: black hair, white hair, brunette, blonde, male, female, but the gazes eluded her and faded to be replaced by another indistinct countenance.

In the vertigo created by the spinning images, her mind reeled.

She forced stillness.

A pale face resolved on the silvery plane in front of her and she focused on the slight bump on the bridge of the nose, expanded her gaze to include the pointed chin. She kept the spinning vertigo at bay and took in the laughter lines around the edge of the eyes, the frown line on the brow and the denim blue eyes that looked back and held her gaze.

The hum of machinery surrounded her, the rhythmic exhalation of equipment trying to keep her body alive. She could taste the harsh chemical flavour of the anaesthetic dripped into her bloodstream. Pipes ran from her mouth to the machine that hissed in the corner of the room, and other pieces of equipment were being pushed closer to where she lay.

None of the details really mattered. She could feel the connection to this part of her life weakening. Her mind expanded, taking in more than the controlled urgency happening beneath her.

She was more than the girl lying on the table below, she now realised. Her gaze expanded to take in details that the singular dimension she had lived previously had not revealed. She was more than just a patient, a girlfriend, a sister, a daughter. As her consciousness expanded, so too did the link to the girl below diminish, and with this dissolution came the realisation of the finality of the event that was occurring. She was not ready to die. She wanted to remain the patient, the girlfriend, the sister, the daughter. So she focused on these very things, the things that defined her. And with each thought, each remembrance, her mind gained weight and descended.

She heard the beep of her heart resume.

With an electronic beat filling the room, the resuscitation equipment was pushed aside. After a time, she was wheeled into a room where other patients lay connected to similar machinery. The beeping and the steady hiss and suck of assisted breathing was not exactly comforting, but it was better than the alternative.

Amidst the electronic reminders of life, her spirit lay in a thin layer over her body, unable to find a way back inside, draped like a dust sheet thrown over furniture no longer in use. She saw the people surrounding her as a rainbow of shifting colours, mesmerising in their complexity. Her attention drawn to the stunning intricacy of each individual's spirit, and when her bed was moved to another room, she almost found the effort required to make this shift too difficult. The movement created currents of energy that blew against her and lifted her back into the nebulous ether, lessening her hold. With a determination that came from years of fighting illness, she narrowed her focus and strove to ignore the colours that made up the delicate fabric of existence.

She forced herself to hold on.

As they wheeled her body into this new room, a fragrance that spoke of safety, comfort, love and so much more enveloped her. She smelt her mother's perfume and lay unable to do anything other than watch as her own hand was lifted into her mother's confident hold.

Her mother stroked the back of her hand, as if nothing was amiss. Her face showed the signs of her worry and she constantly glanced at the monitors beeping hesitantly in the corner. But still her mother continued to trace intricate patterns up and down the back of the hand held firmly in her own.

She focused on her hand, tried to concentrate on the sensation of fingers running lovingly against skin. Tried desperately to remember the simple feeling of being touched. And with each stroke, the sheet of her consciousness became more form fitting, grew tighter, more responsive, until it was nothing more than skin.

She was back inside the hall of mirrors.

The image in front of her looked back. The denim blue eyes held her gaze reflected from a thousand different angles.

She waited for the vibrations to start, for the resonance to magnify until the image fractured and exploded out in a scintillation of shards. But this time, the image did not waver.

The eyes stared back. An eyebrow lifted in bemusement, waiting for the penny to drop.

Nicola had found herself.

Networking

Michael searched the faces surrounding him for some insight into what was happening. The red cocoon of energy descended and tightened around Ashul. Michael saw his friend's eyes harden and his shoulders tense. He was pushing against the web that now held him bound.

'This is beneath you, Trevlor,' Ashul said. 'You have forgotten the path if you think that this is required to make me serve.' Ashul shrugged his shoulders and the net flickered and dissolved around his feet. 'I have not forgotten my path. I serve those of the blood of which you are one. But I also serve those in this room. They are of the blood and their tie is the strongest as they retain their connection to the land. I can deny your will if they so command it!'

'Can you now?' Trevlor gestured towards the network of threads lying dormant at Ashul's feet. The fibres twitched and twisted up one leg and then another, all too reminiscent of Sarah's binding of the doll. When the threads reached Ashul's face, the network flared and dissolved into his skin, a fine tracing of red writhing just below the surface. 'You will come with me, because you are bound.'

Michael stepped forward to help his friend, but Azuradien's hand was like an iron grip on his shoulder. He spoke quietly so that only Michael could hear. 'We can do nothing.'

Trevlor walked towards the warrior. 'Do you wish to test this?' The red pulsed under Ashul's skin. It appeared as though Ashul's own veins had been replaced by Trevlor's web. 'You can try, but I do not think you will like the result.'

'Get that stuff out of him!' Michael struck Azuradien's hand away and stood beside Ashul, wondering if he could punch Trevlor when he wore his mother's own body.

'Hold!' Ashul commanded, and Michael drew back.

Confident in his victory, Trevlor intensified his attack. Ashul dropped to one knee as the red veins thickened and burned under his skin. Ashul almost looked to be made of lava encased in a layer of skin, and that at any moment the liquid fire would burn its way through the thin membrane that contained it.

'Ashul, please don't fight this,' said Dana. 'Trevlor is right in that we need to consider the doll. People are still being harmed. Please! Don't fight him over something we all agree on.' Dana's voice broke on the last word. She threw a pleading look in Ashul's direction. A small nod from the warrior made it clear that Ashul would comply.

Dana took in a ragged breath and then turned and backhanded Trevlor.

'You would possess him too if you could, wouldn't you? We need no reminders of what is right and what is wrong while you stand in our kitchen.' Dana's lips trembled, but her eyes challenged Trevlor to push things further.

Trevlor touched the cheek, red from the force of Dana's blow, and took a step in her direction – the distance between them now mere centimetres.

'You dare!' Trevlor hissed in accusation. His hands raised as if to strike back. Before Trevlor could take a breath to continue, a shimmering network of energy rose to encapsulate Dana. Electricity danced across her skin from head to toe: sparking and snapping but seeming to harm her in no discernible way.

'No Trevlor, *we* dare!' Joe was now standing at her side. Electricity hissed across his shoulders. The standoff continued for a couple of moments until Sarah stepped forward and broke the moment.

'Ashul, we can handle things here.' Sarah moved towards Ashul and placed her hand on his arm. Michael had noticed a tracery of blue that had flickered into existence above Ashul's head when the situation grew tense. His aunt must have as well for she removed it from her network with a quick flick of her fingers. They didn't need Trevlor to be further provoked by Ashul's continued defiance. Almost too casually, Sarah continued, and said, 'You go with Trevlor and see what the doll is up to, but you're not to engage.' Sarah looked around, uncertain whether her words were enough to overrule Trevlor's command. She didn't have to wait long for confirmation.

'I hear and I obey.' Ashul nodded formally towards Sarah. 'Trevlor, I will await you in the second plane.' Ashul tilted his head gratefully in Dana's direction then turned and walked away. He was visible for two paces before he faded from view, leaving a tense group of people behind him.

* * *

Michael looked from one face to another, wondering what was going to happen next. The crackle of electricity had left the room, but all knew it could return in a second.

In the end, it was Trevlor who broke the silence. 'Fools. You forget the doll is your enemy. I have suffered at Anarcus' hands, you have not. If you had, you would join with me and think of nothing until It is destroyed.' Despite the calm in Trevlor's voice, some kind of insanity burned behind his every word.

'Trevlor, you are but a fragment of what you once were'. Azuradien reached towards Trevlor tentatively, careful to offer no offence. 'No longer whole, no longer balanced. We could help you, if you were just to allow it.'

'Help yourselves!' Trevlor strode from the room, forcing his way past Joseph with a jolt of electricity of his own.

* * *

Michael had received instructions from Ashul to join him in the second realm when and only when Trevlor had left the house. Michael had some difficulty explaining his need to follow Ashul to his family, but Aunty Sarah felt the impact of her command on Ashul, so she'd some understanding of the compulsion that drove them.

Those of the blood are connected to the bonded. When Sarah had asked Ashul to monitor the doll, the force of her command was something she would have felt as a tangible weight inside her mind. If Michael were to accompany Ashul, in theory he could either reinforce or overrule Trevlor's, or his aunt's, command. But Ashul was the leader of the bonded, and Michael was duty-bound to obey his orders over all others.

Michael believed that his family were oversimplifying things and didn't yet grasp how interconnected everything

33

was becoming. Sure, technically he was of the line of magic-wielders that served the land, passed down through his mother's side of the family. The sleeping warriors, the bonded, as they called themselves, had been created by his ancient ancestors to protect the land whenever there was need. And when there was no threat, they were to rest and await the call. All pretty simple: those of the blood created the sleeping warriors, the sleeping warriors served the blood through some form of biological imperative. All good! Until you throw into the mix the fact that the sleeping warriors recently had a position vacant and Michael stepped in to take on the role.

So now he had a place in the troupe, one of fourteen bonded warriors, who rode on fourteen magical horses, destined to protect the land, obeying the wise command of those of the blood.

But, and it was a pretty big *but*, Michael was also of the blood. *Could he command the bonded?* His family thought *yes*. Ashul thought *yes*. Michael wasn't so sure. Ashul was the leader of the sleeping warriors, and Michael believed that this trumped everything. Michael hoped he'd never be in a position to find out. Feeling the force of the command, but with no way to confirm its true source, Michael did what he did best. He stopped thinking, and just acted.

Once he was sure that Trevlor was nowhere near his family, Michael returned to the second realm. He no longer needed to be asleep to reach the dreaming plane. From the moment he became one of the bonded, he could feel the second realm like a cool wind blowing against his skin. The suggestion of limitless expanses always tingled against his fingertips. He had only to concentrate and the barrier between worlds thinned, allowing him to simply step through.

The second realm contained more than just the dreaming plane. It was a world of many levels, most of which were beyond his ability to even comprehend. But the void was where his first step always took him.

This place held many 'glorious' memories for him: the doll's torturous nightmares, his own thoughtless stupidity, illusions of betrayal and fear that had nearly cost him his sister and cousin. He had allowed his fear to rule him previously, to control his actions just for one moment, and in doing so Michael had endangered his family – that, he couldn't accept. He had changed since that night. Something within him had broken, or maybe more aptly, something within him refused to ever break again. Either way, he would never run away again, not until every person he loved was safe.

You are too hard on yourself; you knew not that they needed you. Smoke whispered softly in his mind, so intertwined with his own thoughts they were sometimes hard to separate. *My thoughts will always be the wiser.*

Michael ignored this last comment – he was pained by how much like his mother Smoke sounded. To distract himself, he asked Smoke a question. 'Were you with me even then?'

Becoming one of the bonded meant accepting your horse as being part of yourself. Smoke was his better half. Her thoughts merged with his own, her strength was his. She compensated for his shortcomings. *You have strengths of your own; the exchange is and will always be even. And yes, I was with you even then. You have ever walked through my dreams. At first, I did not recognise you for what you were. Why would I? Never has a beloved been lost. I had spent centuries half of what I was meant to be. But you would not let my mind rest. As the doll stirred and we started to wake, you became like a magnet that drew me forward. I believe I would have found you even if the call had not been made.*

Michael stopped to take in what she'd said. He'd never asked her about the rider that was lost – he knew only of the hurt the loss had caused her. At some point it was bound to come up, but he wouldn't cause her undue pain just to satisfy his curiosity. *Now stop your prevaricating – the void will react to your hesitation.*

Michael hated the void. The first landscape he always encountered during this shift across realms was a bleak, grey nothingness. A vista that defied any kind of explanation because there was so little to explain. It held a hushed expectancy. It read your thoughts, drew on emotions, used any kind of reaction as stimulus for change. The air always felt poised, caught between what it was about to become and the memory of what it had once been.

Michael knew the theory. The second realm was the ethereal plane, the place of dreams and nightmares. It was not governed by the rules of the first realm, the physical plane. Nothing here was fixed. The mind of the dreamer imposed its own physics: time, gravity, light, sound – all arbitrary concepts. There were no equal and opposite reactions. Gravity only existed if the dreamer imposed that belief on the grey template.

But the second realm was not just a place waiting for the dreamer to inhabit when off in the land of nod. That was just one of the many layers held within this world. The second realm was also a place where the minds of the initiated could wander. He now fit into this illustrious category even though he did not feel in the least bit enlightened. He had met no other people in his wandering within this realm. The doll, Michael's family and… Marcus had been the only individuals that he'd come across.

There was power here, and all sorts of otherworldly beings existed in this realm, sustained by the energy that thrummed through the very air of the place. There were also entities that used this place as a hunting ground, feeding off the dreamers as well as the native inhabitants of this realm.

Michael was here now with the bonded to track the doll. He hoped any other creatures would continue to stay away.

'Michael, you followed only after Trevlor had left?' Ashul queried him. The warrior waited in the second realm astride Lightning, a magnificent black stallion, who was a hand taller than Michael's own mare, Smoke. The horses were perfectly still and listened to what was being said as well as to what was not.

'Yes, that's why I took some time,' Michael said. 'When Trevlor went outside, he stood on the fence-line to Marcus' house and he just stared over. I thought the doll might be back and that this whole visit to the second realm was pointless. But after watching their house intently, for no reason that I could see, he just snapped out of his trance, spun on his heels and vanished.' Michael was feeling nervous. Smoke snorted her frustration.

'What do you make of this?' Ashul asked.

'I have no idea what to make of it.' Michael let exasperation seep into his words. 'But I know it's weird. He's completely fixated on getting the doll, so why spend so much time just staring over the fence?'

'Because there is something of interest to him over that fence.' Ashul eyes continued to scan their surroundings.

'No shit,' Michael muttered under his breath. He squinted to see if he could make out any of the bonded in the distance.

Ashul had sent the other bonded out to form a protective perimeter while they waited for Trevlor to arrive. They instinctively faced in opposite directions: Lightning and Smoke stood a metre apart, leaving Ashul and Michael a safe distance to draw their swords if required.

Michael decided to focus on their current situation. 'What are you expecting?' he asked.

'There is nothing that I can safely exclude,' Ashul said. Michael wondered if he was kidding. And some of this must have passed through the link they shared.

'We are in the second realm; anything can exist here. If it can be imagined, it is possible!' Smoke snorted on Michael's behalf.

Be calm. He means not to be allusive. He means only to prepare you. Smoke said this as a private message into Michael's mind, then she continued with a more public form of commentary, *Michael, there are many aspects to the second plane. Some believe that it is where all worlds were born.*

Now it was Ashul's turn to snort.

Smoke barely paused, before continuing. *Our leader has no time for such esoteric philosophy. The dreamers, as you have learned, create a self-protecting cocoon around themselves to prevent contamination, although, of course, when the dream is powerful enough there will always be some seepage. When the dreamer leaves this place to return to the first plane, the void ensures the return to a neutral state. You have battled the void before and know of its strength. The dreamers do not walk where we now stand. That is another level. This is the place for the mystics, the initiated, the spirit, but it is also for many other beings, ones that cannot live in the first plane.*

Michael knew Smoke had much more to tell him. She always held a certain tone to her thoughts when a subject required due consideration. But Michael didn't need the detail, he was already jumpy enough. This place might as well have a sign saying *'Here there be dragons.'*

He kept scanning the rolling grey mist surrounding them, searching for any sign of the bonded on the perimeter. He was able to sense them, yet unable to get a visual.

The jingle of Lightning's tack when Ashul turned to speak to him made Michael jump. 'Where is Trevlor? We cannot remain in one place for so long. The void senses our presence and it will try to suppress it,' Ashul said as way of explanation.

In the short time it had taken Ashul to speak, almost in response to his words, the surrounding mist began to thicken. Michael felt his breath fogging around his face and his hearing deadened. The beating of his own heart became louder than the sounds of the horse's movements. Smoke shifted restlessly beneath him, systematically lifting one hoof then another. Wisps of vapour were twisting their way up each of her legs. A quick shake and the vapour dissolved, but within a few seconds the cold air began to coil again.

'We know our purpose,' said Ashul. 'Look for any signs of disturbance or tampering. Anything that may suggest the doll's presence. Trevlor will just have to catch up to us.' Looking through the mist, speaking to the riders that hovered just beyond the eyes' ability to see, Ashul issued his command.

'Bonded, ride!'

Smoke automatically fell alongside Lightning's left flank. They didn't ride hard, but as Michael had experienced before, it felt like great distances were being travelled. Wind whipped past his ears and the atmosphere felt thinner, almost less dense somehow. This light, airless quality made breathing difficult. Michael sucked in short, fast breaths of air, but this was almost to be expected in the void.

Uncertain whether it was their speed that had caused this change in the air's density or simply the void's acceptance of moving objects, Michael continued on. He scanned left and right, all around him was the same bleak, uniform grey in every direction. The rolling mist-like quality had fallen away as soon as the horses gained some speed, allowing Michael to catch glimpses of the other riders. Where one minute he could see at least five other riders, the next Lightning was barely visible in front of him. Leading him to surmise that although the mist was not coiling around them in vaporous swirls any longer, it was still present in thin translucent sheets that impacted his ability to see clearly.

Michael took in a deep breath, finding on his left the air felt heavier, easier to breathe. He sucked in one breath after another in quick succession. This helped to knock back the slight light-headedness that often accompanied a ride in the void.

The air continued to rush past Michael's face – they hadn't reduced their speed but for reasons that Michael didn't understand the air was noticeably easier to breathe when he turned away from the group. It didn't have the thin quality that made him feel like he was riding at altitude. The thin air wasn't unpleasant as such, he just liked having a clear head. He expected dogs travelling with their heads out a moving car's window would feel the same kind of relief when they brought the faces back inside.

Michael shifted his weight ever so slightly to the right and Smoke dropped back, moving until she flanked Lightning's right shoulder.

Ashul turned, perplexed by his activity and he gave Michael a questioning look.

Darmead, riding Ember at Ashul's right, also seemed puzzled. Michael just took in another deep breath – and once again the air was thin, almost insubstantial. There was a definite disparity, so general buffering couldn't be the cause. Michael eased back towards his original position and Smoke responded, this time with an annoyed shake of her head. Ashul raised his left fist and the bonded drew up to a slow stop.

'What ails you, Michael? I can hear your panting behind me. Do you want me to stop so you can smell some nonexistent roses?' Ashul swept his hand around dramatically, indicating the never-ending expanse of nothingness that surrounded them.

Michael ignored the rebuke.

'Why is the air heavier on the left of us? Even now when we've stopped, I can still feel the difference.' Michael took in a deep breath and steered Smoke farther to the left. 'Back there it was like breathing in a sauna. Thick, heavier, easier for me to breathe.' Michael pointed back over his left-hand shoulder.

'I perceive no difference,' Ashul commented, but a frown now creased his brow. He sat forward, testing the air. After a few moments of non-verbal communication, the bonded agreed that the air did indeed have a different density in the direction Michael had indicated.

In a world with no visible signs to guide them, a change in the air quality seemed like as good a thing as any to ride towards.

* * *

Aunty Sarah confirmed with a casual flick of her wrist that Trevlor was no longer in the immediate vicinity. The complicated network of individual strands again hung over the room. Malcarielle's green light and Azuradien's blue, each pulsed independently but merged at points, indicating some kind of interconnectivity.

'Can you be sure he's gone?' Dana asked, rubbing at the back of her hand where the knuckles were still tender. Her uncle noticed her wince from the other side of the room. Brent was pulling out a jar of ointment from his jacket pocket as he navigated his way towards her, skirting around the outside of the network as he did so.

'I know him now. I can say with a high level of confidence that he's no longer in the first plane.' Sarah was walking around the room, tweaking a string on the network here, examining a line there.

Brent reached Dana's side and lifted her hand, gently rubbing the cream into the swollen knuckles.

'This cream may make you a little drowsy,' said Brent. 'Why don't you try to get some sleep? We'll call you if we spot anything.' Dana heard his words but responded with only a nod. There was no way she would sleep while her brother rode around in the second realm hunting the doll. But the mention of sleep gave her a sudden thought.

'Aunt Sars, why doesn't Trevlor need to go to sleep?' Dana asked. 'How is he able to just flip over into the second realm?' Dana stood off to the side of the web, while Ashley, on the other hand, remained transfixed, tentatively reaching to touch the network.

'Trevlor has great knowledge,' Azuradien said. 'The knowledge of a master. He can choose where he walks, much like the sleeping warriors can. The more cognisant exposure one has to the second realm, the easier the journey becomes. You too will be able to make this journey soon.' Azuradien walked over towards Ashley while he was answering Dana's question. He bent forward to peer closer as Ashley gently touched each strand. 'Amazing, isn't it? These are more than just a graphical representation. I am not sure what… but they are much more.' Azuradien watched Ashley as if curious of what she would make of her mother's network.

'But how can we use it?' said Joseph. 'My son is off searching for the doll, my wife is still lost, and all we have is a GPS of the people that I can see just by looking around the room. No offence, Sarah. But how does it help?'

'Joe, can you give me some charge?' Sarah asked.

'A charge? What? Why?' Joseph was looking around, hoping somebody would speak some sense. Brent had placed the jar of ointment back in his pocket and moved beside Ashley to examine the network more closely. After a moment he looked up and shrugged.

'Don't direct it at me or the network.' Sarah moved to stand beside Joe, pointing at the threads of incandescent light that flowed within her web. 'That's just energy, Joe. I'm trying to track it. I want you to draw in some energy like you did when protecting Dana.' She stepped back to give him some room. 'And watch the "GPS" as you do.'

Joseph only hesitated for a moment, and then sparks of electricity danced across his shoulders.

* * *

The network flared as Joseph drew on the electricity flowing around him. Since he'd come back from the faerie realm, he could perceive a low current that hummed just below the surface of all things, at all times. When he focused on the sensation, he could make himself a conduit.

Forcing the current to his will, sparks arced from one finger to the next, racing after each other until they became a blur. His hand became encased in a white glove of electricity. Joseph held the charge for a moment and then flicked it towards the kitchen sink. It sparked across the metal, following the line of the taps and then faded away to nothing. The water sitting on a rinsed plate left to dry hissed and evaporated. A small crack now ran across its edge.

Sarah's network pulsed as the energy shifted around Joseph, tracking the arc of the electricity towards the sink. There was a brief moment of intense light that cut off as suddenly as it had appeared. They all blinked trying to clear the afterimage from their eyes.

'This network can pick up energy spikes.' Sarah looked right at Joseph, trying to gauge his reaction. But Joseph just continued to stare. He'd seen more than the spike.

'Oh, more than that, Sarah.' Joseph was now transfixed by what, only moments before, had seemed to him like nothing more than a fancy light show. He finally smiled. He'd seen the light flare on Sarah's network as he drew energy from the ether, saw how the colour surrounding him had brightened and intensified, but he'd also picked up the fading of the light in the base network in his vicinity. A base network that he hadn't perceived until the colour was drawn from it.

He looked more closely, now that he had something to focus on. He saw for the first time the way each person drew from this base network. It was like a dimpling on the surface of clear water, the pattern raindrops make. But in this instance, without the rain. Was he seeing the source? Or, more accurately, was he seeing them draw from the source? And if he was – and he was pretty sure that was exactly what he was seeing – then it was also evident that they drew on this underlying universal energy just by being alive. And if that was the case, he had a way to search for Nicola.

Seeing everyone's puzzled expressions, Joseph explained, 'It also picks up the drain.'

Here There be Dragons

They continued to ride through the grey void. Searching for a near imperceptible change in the air quality was easier than Michael would have thought. Sniffing around at the air initially had caused a return to his light-headedness, but Smoke made it clear that the horses would take it from here. The horses, now aware of the ever so slight disturbance, had a greater feel for the air density and were better able to sense the void's resistance.

As long as they were in motion, any significant change to the void should be as a result of something other than themselves. Logic suggested that if the void resisted intrusion, it resisted *all* intrusion and that if the doll were active in this realm, the very thickening of the air could be a way of tracking its position.

Time was different in this place. So when Ashul called a halt, Michael had no actual idea as to how long they'd been riding. He knew only that a wind had picked up, gusting around their heads, making the ride somewhat unpleasant. The horse's manes whipped about, stinging hands and necks alike.

'Ware, bonded!' Ashul yelled. 'We have company!' The increasing howl of the wind almost snatched the words out of his mouth, though the mental command that accompanied his words was clearly heard by all.

'What am I waring? I don't see anything!'

As if Michael's question had been the catalyst, the air thickened and darkened before them and a vortex of cold vapour appeared where before there had been nothing but grey void. Michael felt Smoke's muscles bunch beneath his legs as the horse resisted the pull from the spiral of dark air.

'Fall back, we are not to engage!' Ashul yelled over the howling wind.

Smoke responded, kicking off in the opposite direction and came to a sudden halt as another vortex appeared in front of Michael. His sword cleared the scabbard with a crystalline note that sung with the voices of the faeries. The swirling layers of mist cleared for a moment and Michael saw a dozen more small twisters forming. He knew the option to fall back had just been taken off the table.

The buffeting of the vortices as the air swirled and twisted made it difficult for the horses in the air. As soon as they kicked off from the ground, the air currents hurled them in differing directions. Ember came close to striking Bellisan in the head and Lightning, the strongest of them all, veered to avoid the collision. His strength alone kept him from being caught by the edge of the vortex. The turbulence in the air was forcing the horses back towards the ground.

Michael didn't know what the vortices signified, but he knew it was more than just an extreme weather event. Something was coming. A tickle of fear played at the back of Michael's mind. *Would they be able to fight if they had been commanded not to?*

Whatever was approaching had no care for Michael's thoughts.

Shadows formed, coalescing in the centre of each maelstrom, the darkness swarming under and over itself in constant, restless motion. The light-quality in the air dimmed and an oily mist coiled out of each vortex and coated the horses with a slick film.

Tears poured down Michael's cheeks as trickles of the greasy liquid ran into his eyes, burning them. He tried to blink the sting away, but his vision only blurred. Dragging his hair back, wet with the mist, Michael ran the back of his hand across his face, trying not to think about exactly what it was he was wiping from his eyes.

The bonded reined their mounts back into a tight circle. A difficult procedure since the horses' footing was being eroded as the substance of the void was sucked into the whirlpools. As the spinning intensified, the howling of the wind became a high-pitched wail.

Patches of light were appearing, not because the shadows were dissipating, but because the darkness was being drawn in and forced to have form.

Michael jolted into action when a large, segmented tail whipped out of one vortex, centimetres from his face. Smoke twisted away from the strike, saving Michael from the blow. She managed to avoid hitting any of the other bonded, but it was a close thing.

The rest of the bonded were engaged in similar efforts to dodge the barbed points of the tails now slashing through the air, stabbing towards the bonded then disappearing back into the centre of each vortex.

Darmead's mental warning the only thing that saved him. Michael twisted to the left, avoiding the tail that flew towards the centre of his back. Smoke sidestepped to the right, giving Michael the room to spin left. He brought his sword around in a two-handed sweep and severed the tail as it swung around for another strike. Michael centred himself just as a sharply clawed, multi-jointed arm nearly knocked him from Smoke's back. Only Smoke's quick footwork kept Michael in the saddle.

'A little fucking help here!' Michael cried out as another tail flew past his face, this one aimed towards Ashul.

Michael barely managed to bring his sword around in time to slice through the tail, but he felt the blow in his left shoulder and knew he was already slowing down.

The severed tip of the tail blew apart into thick fragments that were sucked back towards the nearest vortex to reform. Michael chanced a glance over his shoulder. He felt the bunching of Smoke's muscles and barely perceived her instructions to hold on.

Smoke reared and struck out with her front hooves as Michael turned back.

A baleful reptilian eye peered out of the mist in front of him.

And, as if a spell had lifted, all of the bonded erupted into a frenzy of activity.

Darmead had a crossbow slung across his arm and fired into the vortex in front of Michael. The bolt struck one of the sinuous multi-jointed claws, but then disintegrated. The eye staring at Michael didn't blink but continued to watch him, taking his measure.

Ember moved in precise circles, reacting as quickly as her rider. Darmead's bolts flew systematically into the centre of each vortex, leaving nothing but swirling black sand where segmented reptilian body parts had been before. Bellisan and Flint had a more hard-headed approach: Flint charged in, reared up then brought his huge weight crashing down on the tails where he could, while Bellisan swung a battle axe in a sweeping arc from left to right clearing a path for other bonded to follow. But their efforts seemed futile to Michael. Where one claw was destroyed, another reformed, all the while the constantly spinning air churning the shadows into more sinuous tails, more brutally powerful claws – always with that one cold malevolent eye watching on.

'To the air, bonded,' Ashul commanded. Almost as one, the horses kicked off the ground and galloped upwards in a tight circle, just out of reach of the creatures lurking in the vortices. The constant changing winds were making this a dangerous endeavour.

'What are they? Our swords and arrows are having no impact!'

'Not so, Michael! We are hindering their birth. Once each vortex draws enough energy, a Bezenhart will be born. If so many were to spawn at once, we would have a difficult time of it. I cannot believe the doll has gained this much strength so soon.'

'Okay, so what do we do?'

'We are not to engage.'

'No way am I leaving those things to spawn so they can creep into my dreams!'

Ashul paused for a second. Michael couldn't understand the delay. There were barbed tails flying at them, creatures ready to spawn, but Ashul was keeping his thoughts to himself. His hesitation was making Michael nervous.

'Okay, so what happens if we jump, flip back into the first realm? Leave these things be?' Michael had to ask. He trusted Ashul. If the warrior's instruction was to return to the first realm, Michael would obey.

'They would complete their birth cycle and track you in this realm as well as in the first.'

Michael's reaction to Ashul's words could be felt by all of the bonded. He had no intention of allowing these things to follow him home to his family. Before Michael had time to voice this view, Ashul's posture changed and the mindlink opened.

'We fight. We must prevent their birth.' Ashul's command held all the authority expected from the leader of the bonded.

Michael's head was spinning and the sound coming from below them now sounded like a washing machine revved up to a full spin-cycle. He didn't think they had much time.

'What's our strategy?' Michael asked, trying to keep his voice level. The sound coming from below them was playing on his nerves.

The bonded each drew their weapons and each weapon glowed with a bright blue light.

'Our life force is the weapon, but we can only maintain the charge for a limited time.' Ashul was smiling. 'We don't normally need long.'

Michael was mentally running through all the weapons he would have access to if he were playing a video game and cursing his lack of options.

A long-segmented tail pierced the air within millimetres of Bellisan's left ear, the horse's constant sidestepping the only thing that caused the tail to miss.

The howling of the wind pounding against their ears faded and the silence was pregnant with menace. The birthing cycle was almost complete. Multi-limbed creatures were waiting in the middle of the vortices waiting to step through, pushing against a thin membrane that was already torn in places and which wouldn't hold them for much longer. Michael was only able to see clearly through these rips but the creature in front of him stood upright on what appeared to be two legs. The creatures were so heavily muscled it was hard for Michael to tell but he was sure he could see more than four arms sprouting from a barrel like torso.

Ashul was first to strike. Lightning rode straight towards the nearest vortex, sparks flying as his hooves struck the ground. Ashul rode with his sword held before him like a lance. With a quick flick of his wrist, a snap of energy flew from his sword towards the nearest Bezenhart, hitting the creature in the chest. Its body lit up with charge and for a moment Michael could see inside the creature. Dozens of chitinous monstrosities writhed within the Bezenhart intestines. The black skin bulged where heads pushed eagerly for release.

'No! No way!' Michael screamed as Smoke rode towards the nearest vortex, striking the ground next to Lightning. Michael reached without thought to his left shoulder. As the Bezenhart before him ripped through a final layer of birthing membrane, Michael fumbled for the trigger on the weapon he'd pulled from his back. His hands found a comfortable grip and he squeezed. He was just as surprised as those around him when a purple blast of energy spiralled out of the end of the weapon. The energy blast rippled out and around the nearest Bezenhart, slowing its movements to almost a standstill.

Michael kept his finger on the trigger. He could feel the weapon in his hand heating up and knew he would have to swap this weapon out soon. Michael had somehow drawn a gun from a video game he played into the second realm. The blasts were slowing the Bezenhart as they ripped their way into existence, but it was not killing them.

With the Bezenhart being almost frozen, Michael was better able to take in the details. No longer shrouded in the shadows of the birthing membrane, the blast from Michael's weapon had temporarily paralysed the creature in the act of stepping through into the second plane.

The towering monstrosity shimmered before him with oily scales a purple so dark they were almost black. It had five arms hanging from a circular collarbone structure that supported shoulders so muscular they looked deformed. The arms were multi-jointed, having two, maybe three elbows with hands with more joints and fingers than any creature had a right to have. The body and tail were part scorpion, part crab, but the head and neck made Michael think *dragon*.

Once these things got free, they would be very agile and very quick. To top it all off, their intestines housed dozens of crab-like creatures, crawling over each other in their eagerness to escape. Their barbed heads pushed constantly as they sought release. The Bezenhart's skin was almost transparent under the pressure of their probing skulls. Michael had no idea what kind of anarchy would reign if the things inside the Bezenhart tore their way out into the open.

'Michael, sweep that weapon over the group,' said Ashul. 'Keep drawing the energy from around you.' Ashul held his sword ready to defend Michael if needed.

'Ashul, my weapon is about to overheat!' Michael kept his voice low, making sure the bonded heard him through the link. 'Darmead, shoot the creatures that are frozen, infuse your shots with your power.' Michael wanted to add that this strategy was based purely on his experience playing a video game, but the bonded wouldn't understand the concept, and they would all know soon enough anyway if it worked. So Michael kept his mouth shut.

This time, the bolt that flew from Darmead's crossbow flared with fire. When it sunk into the creature's chest, a network of flame spread through the Bezenhart, igniting its flesh as well as the parasites crawling through its intestines. The creature dissolved from within, flames flickering across an oily liquid all that remained once it was gone.

The weapon in Michael's hand now glowed orange. When it turned red it would overheat and become unusable, Michael didn't think he had time to wait for it to cool down. He eased off on the trigger, using small bursts of fire to target the Bezenhart starting to regain some movement. The attacks from the bonded seemed to have more of a destructive impact on the Bezenhart still partially paralysed.

'Clockwise on my mark!' Michael didn't have the time to explain that the make-believe weapon he held was drawn from an arsenal in his imagination gained through years of video-game play, the details and limits to its functionality defined by the makers of the game. This particular gun might have unlimited ammo but it would overheat and require a cooldown if not used sparingly. The bonded – being trained warriors – were ready to capitalise on any advantage found during battle. They didn't require explanations, just instructions.

Once Michael shot each creature with a short burst of fire, the bonded set to work with a frenzy of sparking hooves, crossbow bolts, metal balls and flaming swords. The fighting was in close quarters, all bonded having returned to the ground, but there was no confusion – they worked as one. Each Bezenhart burned and then dissolved, leaving only an oily stain to mark its demise.

They continued this process until only one creature remained, this one the largest of them all. Michael's weapon had finally become red hot, but he held on, not wanting the deformed dragon to know his weapon was temporarily useless.

The bonded responding to Michael's mental warning. All of their weapons remained at the ready. Light still flickered across blades and bolts but each had dimmed to conserve energy. The sinuous neck lifted the reptilian head to its full height and the scorpion tail poised high, weaving back and forth with a hypnotic rhythm, ready to strike. Its eyes found Ashul, and its neck contorted. Michael feared the creature was about to disgorge the parasites squirming within, agitated now beyond measure. But the creature did not spew forth the contents of its innards; instead, it forced words to come from a mouth designed only for ripping and tearing.

'We are but the first of our kind to be raised. Anarcus has promised us this! You will not succeed this time, bonded!' The Bezenhart spat this as a curse, slurred and malformed, yet the condescension was still conveyed. Scorn dripped from each syllable.

'You believe the promises of a liar. Anarcus is using you merely as fodder.' Ashul spoke as if to a child. 'What reason have you for this attack? You are no match for the bonded. You know my words to be true.'

'This time it will be different. We have allies.'

'Yet it is you that Anarcus has sent to certain death.' Ashul spoke with patient calm. 'What point is there in you being raised if you throw your life away so cheaply. You were more than this once.'

'We are more than you know ALREADY!' As the final statement crossed its curled lips, the Bezenhart slashed viciously across its own abdomen and released one last curse.

Ashul had kept the beast talking just long enough. Michael squeezed the trigger as dozens of scurrying creatures swarmed towards the horses, each scuttling over the other in desperation to get closer. The purple beam of energy that blasted from Michael's gun slowed the creatures, but the ones underneath remained protected from the paralysing light. They grew as they ran, with a wet crack, tails sprung from their abdomens, each dripping a clear liquid.

'Fall back! Fall back!' Michael cried. 'I need room.' Sweeping the weapons-fire to the left then the right, Michael sprayed the mass of chittering atrocities. When all were frozen, the horses strode forward and crushed them under their flaring hooves like the bugs they were.

Michael breathed a sigh of relief as he tried to ignore the wet crunch as Lightning finished off the last of the Bezenhart spawn, but his relief was short-lived as cackling laughter reverberated around him – laughter he knew to be that of the doll Anarcus.

* * *

In a room full of fragmented mirrors, Nicola stood surrounded by the tortured stare of so many fractured personalities. She dared to hold each gaze for only a second. She had found herself in amongst these lost fragments but retained hold of her true self only through iron will. Her world constantly threatened to dissolve. Each identity had a memory, a history that they needed to share with her.

And there were so many memories here. Once gazed upon, there was no release until she had lived through their memories as if they were her own. Nicola had found herself through nothing more than blind luck. Her own stolen memory was as eager to share as the others.

She understood the nature of the gypsy book better now. On the surface, it was merely a collection of spells, incantations and magical folklore, an encyclopaedia of knowledge passed down generation to generation. But the gypsies of Europe had not been aware they had another older culture hiding amongst them. The last of a long line of mages known only as 'the blood' had hidden themselves in plain sight amongst many gifted cultures throughout history. The gypsies were just one of many who unwittingly provided cover. Where there was true magic, the blood would likely be hiding. These magic-wielders hid themselves, vowing never to enter the politics of the time. They watched and waited for moments in history where balance needed to be restored. As good fortunes would have it, the wait was often long and, as a result, a way to retain knowledge was required between the decades. Words would never be able to capture the nuance of the power they needed to document. The sheer magnitude of the task required that they think differently. So they created the book. A way to capture thoughts and emotions as well as the words.

The book was a repository of recollections, of knowledge. But the gypsy culture bled into the workings of the book and its nature changed. The book became transactional. An exchange occurred each time knowledge was sought. The book searched the mind of the person seeking assistance for a moment from their past that provided insight into the greater mysteries of life. Each treasured piece of memory held the full history of the individual's experiences up until the point of capture, but only the emotions of that one moment. And this is how the book became dangerous.

In the initial conception of the book, it could be added to by anyone with the knowledge of its workings. If the information was worthy, the book would store the 'data' for future reference, recording the thoughts and emotions of the donor. But as people accessed the book in extremis more and more often, the overriding emotion stored within the pages was desperation. So the book became desperate with an almost compulsive desire for knowledge – a hunger.

So Nicola found herself surrounded by these fractured souls, each clamouring to be heard. The book's own desperation drove each fragmented shard of personality to share is history, believing themselves to be whole but unable to move forward because their emotions were locked in one small moment of time.

Inside the book there were times of quiet where the mirrors held only Nicola's reflection. This was when she redoubled her efforts at control, knowing from her experience of battling pain and dizziness that when she relaxed she was at her most vulnerable. She'd fought hard but knew that she was losing the battle. Almost all the mirrors now contained faces that were not her own. She'd been trying to avoid the gaze of the young man with pained hazel eyes, but everywhere her eyes flicked, his image appeared. He dropped to the ground as the lash fell against his back, flesh torn. Nicola flinched, feeling the pain as her own.

'I know you; I already know your story!' Nicola was forced to look into the bowl of water in front of her with an image hovering just below the surface. She could not stifle a scream as her back was torn by another blow. She tried to retain her sense of self as the memory enfolded her.

'I know you…' she whispered as the image in the bowl started to clarify.

'You are not me…' she pleaded. The water took on an oily quality and the face of the young man appeared in front of her. She nearly lost her tenuous grip of her own identity when the image in the bowl suddenly screamed, 'A little fucking help here!'

Fragments

Nicola looked through the mirror in front of her. The image of the hazel-eyed man had dissolved, replaced by the horrific scene of her son being attacked by some reptilian hybrid. The perspective she was seeing was strange to her. She was viewing the whole thing from what felt like ground-level with an oily haze that never cleared completely. Shadows kept rushing towards her, obscuring her vision. A wickedly barbed tail shot past from her left and she screamed a warning. Michael reacted faster than she'd ever seen him move before. The tail dropped to the ground when he severed it with a massive two-handed sword strike. Ashul looked back over his shoulder and nodded his thanks.

The moment the tail hit the ground, more shadows formed over her vision and she could see nothing but writhing darkness. She felt a moment of panic. She was losing her connection to Michael, but she had no idea how that connection had been formed!

A quiet voice whispered from beside her, 'Did you learn nothing from my pain?'

Nicola was too scared to look away from the shifting image of her son. The shadows coiled and spun, threatening to obscure her view of her son completely. She could hear a strange high-pitched whine. Forcing her mind to calm, she tried to look through the shadows, compel the image in front of her to clarify.

'Are you calm? Are you focused?' the quiet voice asked from the surrounding mirrors.

'I'm as calm as I can be under the goddam circumstances, and I can assure you, I am bloody focused! Now help me or shut the hell up!' Nicola hissed at the hazel-eyed man watching from all bar one of the mirrors.

'If you are truly focused then—'

But Nicola cut the voice off before it had the chance to finish. 'If I'm focused, then the image before me is true!'

A hundred hazel-eyed reflections nodded at her response.

In the mirror the darkness took form. A multi-jointed arm reached forward, followed by another then another. The tail waved menacingly behind the body of a creature; a strange chittering sound accompanied its movements. When it reached its full height, the air surrounding it cleared and Nicola could see Ashul raise his sword. The room of mirrors exploded into white light. Then as the light faded, ripples flowed through the creature's body, like sparks of electricity lighting it up from within.

Nicola now understood the source of the strange sound. When Ashul's power hit the scorpion-like creature, its intestines had lit up. Crawling around its insides was a mass of smaller monstrosities restlessly swarming over one another, producing the constant scuttling. She watched on as the larger creatures moved out of the whirlpools surrounding her son. Nicola threw herself against the mirror, but it was like slamming into solid rock. She tried again but every effort produced the same result – she accomplished nothing.

'You have no body, so stop acting like you have one. You are only thought. Look with your mind's eye!' And Nicola saw currents of energy flowing through the scene in front of her. Ashul and Michael had become so interconnected it was hard to discern where one finished and the other began. A fine tracery of energy spun around them all. Michael was surrounded by gossamer-thin threads, each covered in a strange beading like droplets of dew on a spider's web. This mist of energy settled on the network's threads where it was then absorbed. Nicola blinked in wonder when she realised her energy was flowing through the mirror. The droplets of liquid were acting as a kind of conduit to Michael.

'Is that all I am now? Mist? A bit of static?'

'You have reached him, which in itself should take years of training, outside of this tome,' Hazel-eyes replied calmly. 'From inside, it should be impossible.'

'It's not enough!' Nicola sobbed. The creatures stepped forward to attack. She felt helpless as she again tried to pour herself through the mirror, but only a light blue haze drifted up from the ground. 'Static is just not enough.'

'But it forms lightning, does it not?' asked Hazel-eyes, his voice coming from all around her.

'Yes, it does.' She scanned the myriad of reflections that surrounded her. 'But only if there's enough of it!'

Nicola wiped away every image of Hazel-eyes with the sweep of her hand. She now saw Michael from the different angles. If she had been inhabiting a body, in all likelihood it would be vomiting. The blue mist around Michael intensified so that he sat on Smoke surrounded by a cloud of energy – her energy. Nicola had to shake her head. A laugh escaped her tightly clenched lips when he reached over his shoulder and grabbed a gun that only exist in the realm of video games, a product of someone else's rich imagination.

Her smile faded as she took in all that he faced.

Allowing her energy to seep through the mirrors, Nicola marvelled at the speed with which her son moved. She had feared for him when he became a bonded warrior, and the reason for her fear was being played out before her. Watching him now though, she understood he'd always been destined to become one of the bonded. He moved just like them. He understood when to lean back and allow a crossbow bolt to fly past his shoulder. When to roll to the side as a sword swept the air where his head had been moments before. When simply just to duck. But most importantly, he knew when to strike.

Nicola moved to place her hand against the glass surface in front of her as the last writhing creatures were crushed under the hooves of a horse. When her fingers touched the cold surface, the images of her son shattered around her. The sound of breaking glass was not enough to drown out the doll's laugh as it echoed around the chamber.

She had only a moment to register shock before the shrieking laughter stopped and the connection to her son was lost.

* * *

Something was happening in the second plane. The network that Sarah had created was flaring with activity. Michael's thread was easy to differentiate among the mass of colours that flickered across the web, even though he was not present in the first realm. Distance didn't seem to make a difference. His energy signature remained delicately wrapped around each one of the family to varying degrees but Dana could see she was the most strongly connected.

When the first signs of activity shot across Sarah's network, no-one could work out what was going on. The network showed only the first plane. But Michael's connection to them was still clear to see. His blue thread that ran around and through Dana pulsed. Joseph's thread flared with the same muted shade of cobalt. Michael was drawing energy from them, Dana could feel it. But with the help of Sarah's network, she could see it.

'Sarah, can we expand this to include the second plane?' Joseph asked. His eye roaming over the connections.

Sarah reached forward and gently placed her fingers around the threads of blue surrounding Dana, while simultaneously wrapping her other hand around Dana's wrist. A glow crept along the threads stopping only when Michael's connection to them terminated in mid-air.

Sarah seemed unsure how to continue. She tilted her head, first to one side then the other. She nodded to herself, and with a few deft flicks of her fingers, a secondary network appeared, hovering above the original. It made Dana feel like she was looking at some futuristic heat map.

Dana recognised the blob of cobalt blue that was Michael sitting amongst a group of other energy signatures. This map that Aunt Sarah had created might look like a Hollywood version of heat vision, but Dana knew it mapped energy patterns. Rather than seeing changes in temperature, they could see differences in energy fields. There was an underlying base energy that swirled under the whole construct. Colours blurring where energy fields merged.

The bonded appeared almost as a singular entity. The individual parts were recognisable, but they flowed and intertwined so freely it was hard to view them as anything other than 'one'. For no reason that Dana could explain,

Michael was easy for her to separate from the others. He was unmistakably unique to her. Amongst all the twisted patterns of light before her, she didn't need to follow the threads running through her to find where her brother appeared on the grid. She just recognised him as soon as he appeared.

The constantly shifting mass of energy that represented the bonded was surrounded by swirling vortices that drew in the light. If Dana had been looking at a map of the stars, she would have associated the spinning patterns as being that of a black hole by the way the base energy was being sucked towards the centre of each vortex. But this was no abstract representation of the heavens. She didn't know what she was looking at, but she felt the muscles in her shoulders tense in response to these unexplained spirals of darkness. Dana leant forward, drawn towards the dark spots, trying to perceive what they might represent.

Azuradien placed a restraining hand on her shoulder. With a quick shake of his head, he conveyed his concern, and Dana took a step back. With the speed of a striking snake, one of the dark areas flared up and cords of black shot towards each of the bonded. The hairs on Dana's body stood on end. She didn't need to look towards Azuradien for confirmation. There was no doubt in her mind that Michael was under attack.

'Dad, we have to help him?' Dana searched the faces surrounding her, hoping for some reassurance.

Quick to take charge of the situation, Azuradien spoke with the authority of a king. 'Send him what energy you can! Sarah, can you use this net of yours to funnel additional energy, use it as a conduit?'

'I don't know how,' said Sarah, her voice rising in pitch and her hands trembling. 'I feel resistance. I don't understand.'

'Calm, be calm.' Azuradien had moved so he blocked

Sarah's view of the network, forcing her to look him in the eyes. 'He is in the second plane, you are not. The resistance you feel is in your own mind; it is aware of the divide.' Azuradien placed a reassuring hand on Sarah's shoulder.

'We do not have time to bloody well go to sleep, Azuradien. Give us some practical advice.' Joseph was crackling with the energy he'd absorbed in response to the threat. Blue sparks arced across his knuckles, sparking from his fingertips.

Dana turned to the windows where Sheba was scratching against the glass sliding door, desperate to get to her. The dog's ears were down, the whites showed at the edges of her dark brown eyes, and a black stripe of raised fur ran down her back. With her hackles up, Sheba looked like every overly aggressive image of a Doberman that had ever been posted online. Even through the glass Dana could hear the deep rumble of her growl.

Dana pulled the door open. Sheba shot through the gap, her feet scrambling against the polished wood of the floor. Then she sat in front of Dana, her muscles quivering with the tension running under her skin, but apart from that she was as still as a statue.

'I have a link to the second plane! Titan's on his way to Michael.' Dana placed her hands on either side of Sheba's face, cradling her head gently even though her hands shook with the same nervous energy that coursed through the dog, Brown eyes stared into the depths of brown eyes and the connection was made.

'How long, Dana?' Sarah asked as a thick spike of darkness thrust towards Michael. His energy became a blur of blue as the black spike was severed. Scattered fragments ran back towards the vortex from where the spike had been spawned.

'He is having to fight his way through. Dana's eyes closed for a second. Dark shapes, sharp claws, too many arms!' Her lips curled back from her teeth. 'He still has a way to go.'

* * *

Joseph was the first to notice the subtle change around Michael – likely due to being more attuned to energy fields and how they behaved. The bonded still radiated brilliant blue and Michael was shifting amongst them, a fast, fluid mass of energy, a shade slightly darker than that of his brethren. The more Joseph looked at this strange network of energy, the more his brain could interpret what he saw. Splashes of colour resolved into clear images of each of the bonded.

He recognised individual horses now as well. Lightning, true to his name, radiated a sparking energy. Smoke was more insubstantial, but she still exuded her own elusive strength. Each rider shared the characteristic of their horse: Michael was all shifting, rolling energy, whereas Ashul was all sharp angles. But Michael's signature was subtly changing. A faint wash of denim blue had appeared, almost like a lens filter over Michael's signature.

Joseph continued to try to interpret what was before him. When he focused on the spinning vortices, he got impressions of sharp, chitinous multi-jointed tails. A strange purple glow flowed out from Michael, unlike the other energy running over the network.

'Are you guys seeing this? What the hell is that purple energy, it's coming from Michael?' Joseph was met with head shakes and shrugged shoulders.

'That energy pattern makes no sense,' Azuradien said as he moved closer to the network. 'It does indeed appear to originate from Michael, but he is somehow absorbing multiple sources of energy from the second realm. This just shouldn't be possible.' Despite his earlier warnings, Azuradien had moved to within inches of where the black vortices spun.

'Stop telling us what's impossible and start giving us something we can use.' Joseph looked towards Sarah, 'Sars, any idea…?' Before Joseph could finish the question, the purple light started to strobe, disappearing from the net then flaring back into life. Each time the purple light flared, a second later a swirling vortex blew apart.

'I know what he's doing,' said Dana. 'Michael's using that gun from his video game. Watch the pattern. He's running hot, so he's using small, fast bursts.' Dana sounded almost dumfounded.

'Dana's right,' said Ashley. 'He even has the bonded attacking when whatever they're fighting has been slowed down. He uses that damn tactic in the game all the time. And it's working. No more spinning black holes of darkness.' Ashley chuckled quietly to herself.

Joseph knew that the girls were right. As soon as it was pointed out to him, it became hard to miss. How had Michael been able to get hold of a make-believe weapon?

'Okay, I think we should get them out of there. Azuradien, how do we contact them?'

Before Azuradien was able to answer Joseph's question, a new darkness appeared on the network hanging suspended above their kitchen table. This dark thread of energy appeared on the far edges of the network, but it was not accompanied with feelings of dread or apprehension. It was like the shadow cast by a friend as they reached down to help you up. This new presence held warmth, affection, succour. A halo of shimmering amber light surrounded the shape as it moved rapidly.

Titan hurtled towards Michael, sped on his way with a hefty dose of energy from a terrified sister and her best friend.

* * *

Michael watched as the grey of the void absorbed the last oily pools of Bezenhart remains. The bonded sat motionless as the doll's laughter echoed around them. Even the horses made no sound. Every ear tried to pick up the dying traces of the doll's mockery, trying tried to pinpoint the location of the next attack.

'Bonded, back into defensive positions! Ware Anarcus! Ware the doll!' Ashul drew himself level with Michael and spoke barely above a whisper. 'How do you fair, Michael? That weapon of yours required a great deal of energy. Are you able to continue the search?'

'Do we have any choice?' said Michael. His ears were straining to pick up the first whisper that might indicate the approach of the doll. He didn't feel comfortable with the sudden inactivity. 'I think the doll is just playing with us. It's around here somewhere, watching. Ashul, you know its ways. Why did it expend so much of its force for no real advantage?' Michael sounded muffled. The void was already trying to suppress their presence.

'Michael, talk not of this here. My question remains: are you able to continue?' Ashul's eyes were running over Michael's face as if looking for sign of injury.

'Ashul, what the hell? I'm fine. Can we focus on what to do next? Because I can feel the air thickening around me, and I don't want to stand around and wait while the void starts playing with my mind.'

The air already had a syrupy quality, and Michael's ears had detected a change in the air pressure. He pinched his nose to try to equalise his eardrums but couldn't achieve the required pop. At this rate, he wouldn't even be able to hear the doll if it crept up behind him.

As if sharing his concern, Smoke shook her head and lifted each foot slowly and deliberately, shaking off the thickening shroud of the void. The other horses were moving around restlessly, repositioning their hooves, as if uncertain of their footing.

Michael was thrown back in the saddle as Smoke reared up. The horses had sensed something. Michael had never seen them react in this way before. *I do not merely sense something, Michael, there is something under my hooves. Something seeking release.* Smoke's thoughts rang clearly in Michael's mind. He felt her muscles bunch as she prepared to jump. He had the reins firmly wrapped in his hands; his own legs were tense, gripping the saddle tightly. But rather than launching into the air, Michael felt Smoke slip backwards. The ground beneath her was degrading. She tried to reposition her hooves but could find no purchase. Where before there had been solid ground, there was now a pool of thick mud. The substance of the void was crumbling around the edges of the pool, like an ice shelf breaking away, except the structure of the void was dissolving, being consumed by the ever-spreading quagmire that was all that remained beneath Smoke's hooves.

In seconds, Smoke's legs had been consumed up to the hocks. Her front hooves pawed at the ground, trying to find something to leverage against. Michael kept his grip on the reins and jumped clear of Smoke's back, not wanting his weight to force her to sink farther. Finding himself on firmer footing, he threw his weight backwards in an attempt to help her pull free. With about a 500-kilogram weight variance, Michael was acutely aware of the futility of his efforts.

Most of the other horses had managed to jump free of the sucking ground and now circled warily around the edges of the mud pit that had formed. Three other horses struggled in the darkening sludge, but Smoke was being pulled under at a faster rate. Michael was being dragged forwards, his feet sinking into the stinking mud. He had already lost the feeling in his fingers as the reins tightened around his hands.

Release your grip, Michael, Smoke said softly into his mind.

'Not on your life.' Michael hissed back through clenched teeth. The sulphurous odour that wafted up from the mud burned with every breath he took.

Michael slipped and fell to one knee, the mud swallowing his leg with a wet sucking sound.

'This is not the void's doing. Michael, release your hold.' Ashul had jumped off Lightning with a rope in his hands. One end he tied around Michael's waist, the other he knotted securely on the pommel of Lightning's saddle, but he was unable to do anything further because of Michael's continued grip on Smoke's reins. The other horses had managed to break free, but Smoke was now submerged to the flanks and her front legs were struggling to break away from the hungry grip of the mud.

'Another rope, throw me another bloody rope,' Michael yelled, and he caught the one that Darmead threw. He was forced to release his hold on the reins when Smoke sunk deeper again. As the mud slid up past her flank, Michael thought he saw movement from more than just the horse. But once he'd made the decision to release Smoke's reins, he'd also committed to his chosen course of action. Able to anticipate Ashul's next move, Michael turned and cut the rope tied around his waist before they could attempt to pull him free.

Michael jumped towards Smoke and wrapped his arms around her front legs. The extra weight forced her legs under the surface and Michael took one final stinking gulp of air before the wet embrace of the mud enveloped him. The exultant scream of the doll's triumph was barely heard above Smoke trumpeting her distress. Her head was so close to his own face, but the sound was deadening as the thick filth filled his ears.

Michael felt a moment of panic. If Darmead pulled back now, Smoke would be lost. But the bonded heard his mental concern and waited for Michael's mark to pull. Ashul already had another rope secured so he could plunge in after Michael if he lost contact. All this Michael sensed through their link.

Smoke was keeping her thoughts to herself. Michael kicked at the thick branchlike obstructions that threatened to tangle around his legs and focused only on securing a knot around Smoke's foreleg. They would only get one shot at this and if his knot did not hold, then Ashul might not be fast enough to save either of them.

Something hidden under the shifting surface of the quagmire had tangled around his legs and was pulling Michael down. He forced his mind away from his legs and whatever he'd gotten snared on. He needed to concentrate on his fingers: this knot had to hold!

Michael's ears rang and red flecks passed across the black of his vision. He desperately needed air. He'd already been oxygen deprived when he jumped into the mud. One brief gulp of air couldn't sustain him for long.

With his eyes screwed shut and his jaw muscles aching from the force required to keep his teeth clenched, Michael doubted he could maintain his composure for much longer. Even though he feared suffocation, Michael was more concerned that reflex would force his mouth open and he would take in a lungful of the disgusting ooze.

With one last twist, Michael signalled for the bonded to pull. He anchored himself to the rope as he felt the slack of the line grow taut.

Ashul hadn't waited for Michael's call. He could feel Ashul fighting his way through the mud near him. As Michael's head cleared the surface, he shook the mud from his eyes, but could still not interpret what was going on in the churning quagmire around him. There were just too many arms. Even if every member of the bonded had jumped in to save him, it would still not explain the number of limbs thrashing around him.

Ashul was beside him with one arm hooked around the rope, the other wielding a short dagger, slashing at the many hands attempting to drag him back down. The tangled obstruction wrapped around Michael's ankles now made sense. He scissored his legs and broke free of the grip that he now understood to be some creature's hands. Revolted, Michael continued to kick, needing to get away from whatever was trying to drag him down.

Darmead wasted no time. As the line pulled taut, Ember steadily stepped backwards, and Smoke soon had her front legs on solid ground. Michael only had his upper body free of the mud's embrace – but there was no time left – and he grabbed the dagger stored in a sheath strapped to his left leg. Following Ashul's' lead, he stabbed at the hands trying to drag him under. The soft flesh yielded easily to the blade, releasing more of the same noxious odour permeating the thick liquid. The bonded had their weapons drawn, but Ashul commanded them to hold.

'Steel! Use only steel! Use none of your powers here.'

The questing hands were slow and attempted to draw away from the cold kiss of steel, flesh scorched where the blade touched, reduced to charcoal when the blades stabbed deeper. This had made them wary, and their reticence to engage further made it easier for Michael and Ashul to clamber free. They emerged covered in thick, dark stinking muck. Michael wiped what he could from his face, but he still felt contaminated. It was a weird testament to his upbringing that he felt more put out by the revolting crap dripping off him than by being attacked by the intestinal parasites of a seven-foot scorpion dragon.

'If I am correct, they are Nachzehrer and they are very dangerous. Bonded, use no weapon that will generate light. Steel will harm them. Create no shadows!' Amongst the other bonded, Ashul was recognisable purely by his cool, blue eyes shining through the mask of filth that obscured the rest of his features. He seemed completely unaware of the mud dripping off his face.

The bonded moved into offensive positions with their swords drawn.

With a muffled whump, the pit in front of them erupted into a mass of writhing limbs. Thick trails of brown slurry poured from the mounds of bodies striving to extricate themselves from what had once been a quagmire but was now more like a shifting geyser of human flesh. The doll rose forth from the filth, lifted upon the shoulders of the rotting corpses. The black of the doll's skin was paler with the mud that coated its body, and clumps of mud dripped from its stringy hair. It reached down, resting a taloned hand upon the nearest Nachzehrer head. Even with a body that suggested weakness – its joints swollen and deformed – the doll exuded nothing but strength.

Michael raised his sword and made ready to defend himself, feeling like he'd been dropped straight into a zombie apocalypse.

A vice-like grip encircled his left leg and he felt himself being dragged backwards. He stumbled and came close to losing his footing altogether.

Michael spun and brought his blade down in an inelegant chopping motion. Expecting to see another reanimated corpse, his confused mind shouted *hellhound* until he recognised the sleek, shining black coat. He realised with less than a second to spare that Titan had a hold on his leg and was trying to drag him away from the danger.

A Field of Blue

The tinkling of shattered glass showering down around her was an almost magical sound. After being exposed to the concussive blast as the hall of mirrors spectacularly exploded, Nicola's ears should have been ringing. Yet, they weren't!

Her skin should have been pierced and lacerated by a thousand shards of glass. Yet, she was unblemished!

She had no body, only one of her own imagining, yet still her heart ached. She could barely breathe through the sobs that racked her frame.

Tears ran down her face, joining the shards littering the floor, yet it was all fabrication.

'You were the lightning.' Hazel-eyes gazed at her from the mirrors that had reformed around her.

'I was the static. My son was the lightning!'

'Together, you are quite the storm.' Hazel-eyes chuckled.

'The doll banished me so easily.'

'The doll was not even aware of your presence. The conduit closed because, with your aid, your son was able to destroy his foes.'

'You heard the doll's laughter; it has something worse planned for him. And I am locked in here slowly losing myself, unable to reach out to him.' Nicola felt depleted. She maintained the falsehood of her body purely from habit. She knew no other way to view herself. If she didn't focus on the details, she would be nothing more than a captured memory, trapped in the pages of the damn book.

A green-eyed woman with striking white hair and scarred skin spoke next to Nicola. 'You are more than you know, but you must be careful with the power you use. It cannot be replenished,' she said. 'You cannot access the wild magic without your body. You cannot access the source from the confines of this book. You are limited to the energy you brought here with you.'

'I would happily give you some of my energy,' said Hazel-eyes. 'It is stale and without inspiration, but I would give it to you in thanks for breaking me out of the memory loop that is this book's curse.' Hazel-eyes looked at Nicola with gratitude in his eyes. 'You have released me.'

'I don't understand. I only experienced your memory, nothing more.'

'The book's purpose is the acquisition of knowledge – it is a greedy tome. Once it has the fragment of our soul that contains the knowledge it desires, the fragment is filed away for a time when the knowledge may be of use. Thus, you released Trevlor, just as you have released me. You called on his knowledge and got a little more than you bargained for, I would think. Do the voices of the masters still ring in your head?'

'I didn't call on your knowledge,' said Nicola.

'No, you did not,' said Hazel-eyes. 'But because of your unique circumstance, you have relived a number of memories which included my own fragment of knowledge. Experienced them all as if they were your own, learning all that our experiences have to teach. Understanding a little of what motivates each fragment. In doing this, you freed us, and thus we can converse if we now choose. We can move outside of the limited loop of our memory. Therefore, we become less of a fragment with each interaction we have with you and each other. The less a fragment, the closer to whole we become. A different whole, no doubt, but you will never understand the hope this small growth gives us. For, this I would gladly share any energy I can. You have but to ask.'

The hundred different faces nodded their agreement. 'You have but to ask.' The weirdly discordant words bounced around the chamber with a surprising level of synchronicity. The depth of emotion each voice struggled to convey was being magnified exponentially by the vast array of personalities that echoed the sentiment, creating a force that reverberated through the mirrored hall of her creation.

The faces in the mirrors looked to Nicola for that outlet. Each and every set of eyes held the same hope.

Nicola recognised them all.

She'd lost all sense of her own identity when she'd been bombarded with the ceaseless memories of others. Her mind became a maelstrom of uniquely distinct personalities, and that process would have eventually led to insanity. Luckily, she had come across her own fragment when her mind could still recognise itself. This moment of recognition had given her something to hold on to, something to focus upon. The thought of being caught in a loop, forced to repeat what in most instances was a traumatic life experience without hope of changing the outcome in any way, felt like something dreamt up by Dante.

'I have memories of the masters singing in my head. I also have yours, luckily recognisable as being other than my own. But these other "fragments", are they still trapped in some loop?'

Hazel-eyes responded, 'They are still trapped.'

'That cannot be allowed.'

'I had so hoped that would be the way you felt. The others would be likewise grateful. You could have enough energy to survive in here.'

'I cannot survive in here without my family.' Nicola's eyes again welled with tears, which she hastily brushed away. Looking around with more certainty, she said, 'Regardless, in the short term I need to find my son—'

Before she'd completed the sentence, every mirror became a window looking out onto a different vista. The hall of mirrors expanded to accommodate all the released fragments, the shades of the people they had once been. Each shade stared intently into their own mirrors in search of her son, switching through one view then another at an extraordinary rate, with the ease of children channel-surfing.

'You could have thousands more to aid you,' Hazel-eyes commented as he flicked through multiple views: blank grey glimpses of the void, sometimes rolling with fog, other times clear. On occasion, a glimpse of a shape could be seem moving amongst the fog but more often than not his mirror returned to a hazy view so obscured it was like looking through mud.

'I will free them, but first I must make sure my son is safe,' Nicola said. 'The doll is baiting them. The attack from those creatures made no sense.'

A small girl stepped forward, swaying as she walked. She had either spent her life at sea or she had a similar medical condition to Nicola's own – the vertigo she suffered from had forced Nicola to make tiny adjustments to her daily routine, right down to the way she walked. When you had been dealing with it for as long as Nicola had, you became accustomed to reading similar patterns in others.

'I know a little of the doll's ways,' the girl said. 'It was my family's burden to maintain the wards that kept the doll bound. I had that thing whispering in my mind for years until the doll was stolen from us.'

'Are you Kitty? I've read your diaries.'

'Aye, I am Kitty. If you have read my diaries, you know the revenge the doll inflicted upon my family as punishment for its imprisonment. Babes born misshapen and deformed, my father beaten to death, the men coerced by the doll's false promises. *It* finds weaknesses. Even the most noble of men have a fault that can be exploited. Your own son guessed as much, knew himself that the doll was gathering information rather than committing to a full force attack. He is wise beyond his years.'

Nicola didn't know whether her son was wise, but he knew how to gauge an opponent's actions. Michael had been playing team sports all his life and could sense when he was being manipulated. It was this skill that made him such a good midfielder. Nicola kept these thoughts to herself; she'd been watching the attack, and she'd come to the exact same conclusion.

'Kitty, what do you think it wants?'

'I saw that your son is one of the bonded. There is no way to predict the extent of his power. The doll could be testing, not only your son, but also how having a mortal as a bonded warrior impacts the strength of the group. It would need to know many things before it commits itself – it has too much to lose. Never has it been closer to its goal.'

'Will you help me, Kitty?'

'Aye, course I will help ye! Look to the one you think of as Hazel-eyes. He has already found the doll. I can smell its stink from here.'

* * *

Joseph watched as Titan flew through the layers of the second realm, breaking down the distance that separated him from Michael. With the speed Titan was moving he would get to Michael soon, which was a relief because Joseph could perceive something new building in the second realm. His eyes shifted back and forth across Sara's network, trying to read more from the intersecting glowing lines than was immediately apparent. He could see a suggestion of a bulge in the underlying topology. It was difficult to view the map in anything other than three-dimensional terms, but he had to keep reminding himself it was something altogether different.

'Sarah, Azuradien, what is that?' Joseph pointed towards a section of the map that was pulsing and undulating. If distance meant anything on the map, the weird undulation was close to Michael and the other bonded.

Joseph saw Sarah's network as a complex energy grid. The grid created a kind of supportive lattice for the twists and turns of intersecting energy signals to lie upon. Joseph perceived each separate entity as a node of their own. What he was looking at now was more like a boil on the skin of the network, the underlying grid bulging. Under this skin of the network, he could see multiple energy markers, each intertwined in a way similar to the bonded.

'There appears to be a disturbance of some kind,' Azuradien offered.

'No, it is more than that, father,' said Malcarielle. 'There is something pushing through. Could it be coming through from another realm?' Malcarielle had been standing quietly to the side.

'Another realm?' asked Brent. Alarm started to build within the room.

The substrate of the network split, and Joseph watched as a mass of energy encased his son.

'My god,' said Ashley. 'How many are there?'

'There is one. They are only one,' said Dana, standing with her hand on Sheba's neck. 'Titan is with Michael, trying to get him out of there but Michael doesn't understand the danger. They're like ants: Titan sees them as one organism with many parts.' Dana dropped in front of Sheba so she could look into her eyes again.

Dana's breathing slowed. Her eyes seemed to be looking beyond the dog in front of her. Joseph was beginning to get worried. Her breathing was so shallow. Before he had a chance to intervene, Dana took in one ragged breath. 'I can feel Michael.'

'Send him all the energy you can!' said Azuradien. 'Quickly!'

This call for speed was unnecessary – Joseph could already see the complex amber hue of Dana's energy pouring towards Michael now that a link had been established.

'Can you tell him to get out of there, honey?' Joseph asked. 'Can you tell him to flip back home?' Joseph knelt at Dana's side and allowed his energy to flow towards his son.

'It doesn't work that way, Dad,' said Dana. 'I wish it did, but it doesn't.'

A myriad of colour now flowed around Michael's imprint on the network. Joseph was finding it difficult to separate one energy signature from another.

'Dad.' Panic entered Dana's voice. 'The doll is there. Oh jeez, the doll is there with Michael.'

Joseph was searching through the web, desperate to find the doll so he could rip it out of existence. He knew the net didn't work in that way, but he wanted to give it a red hot try regardless.

He was the first to perceive the faint wash of denim blue energy that rose from the same tear in the network that had spewed forth the undulating mass now surrounding Michael. This same indistinct energy had appeared before, energy that had the ability to change Michael's own signature even so slightly.

This blue haze moved like a blanket of fog and was undeterred by the other energies that moved around Michael. It slipped towards Michael with slow, resolute purpose, finding him in the chaos and condensing around him, contracting until it encased Michael like a second skin. Michael still remained fluid, but he appeared more compressed somehow.

Joseph focused on Michael, trying to block out all other activity. He knew that Michael was under a new assault, but his energy signature seemed strong – even buoyed somehow, as if he were using this new energy to reinforce his own. Although Joseph knew that this was not the right analysis, he couldn't quite grasp what he was seeing. 'Azuradien, Malcarielle,' he said, 'what's that new energy surrounding Michael?'

Azuradien was first to answer. 'He is drawing power from the void, drawing from his connection to you.'

'Yes, I can see that. But the mist – the denim blue mist—' Joseph realised what he was seeing as soon as the words left his mouth. Michael wasn't feeding off the energy: the energy was nurturing him, protecting him.

'Nicola?' Joseph whispered under his breath. In the few short seconds since it had appeared, the blue haze grew so intense it almost obscured Michael completely. Joseph reached towards the static that surrounded Michael, but before his fingers could make contact, there was a sharp snap and the charge was released. The blue charge dispersed, and he wished he knew how to keep the energy from dissipating, but he did not have the knowledge to do so.

* * *

Titan dragged Michael away from the doll.

The bonded had formed a semicircle on the very edge of the mud pit. From within the pit, the detritus-covered hands of the corpses clawed away at each other, dragging at the solid ground where the bonded stood firm.

Some bonded remained on their mounts and still were firing arrows as a decomposing head pulled itself clear of the seething mass. Other bonded stood with swords drawn, chopping at any hands that found purchase.

The doll remained above the horde under the mud, casually stepping from head to shoulder like a cattle dog running across the backs of sheep. It seemed to relish the caress of the mud as it slipped and slid, mud dripping from its hair, its fingers, its face, moving in an almost dainty fashion with a slow smile lifting the corners of its mouth and making no effort to wipe the mud from its skin.

Michael felt the pressure on his leg ease. Titan was at his side, throbbing with energy from the first realm. When Michael placed his hand against the dog's head to reassure him, he could feel his sister's thoughts. Anger. Outrage. Concern. All of these emotions were accompanied by a flood of energy. Michael stepped towards the doll. His fingers maintained the gentlest of touches on the scruff of Titan's neck until he reached the edge of the pit, and then he gripped the dog more firmly.

'Michael, no,' Ashul said as he stepped to block Michael's passage. 'The danger lies in their shadows. Listen to the guardian. Fall back!'

Michael had fallen back once before and his mother had paid the price: her body had been invaded, her soul lost to him.

He lifted his sword. The blade that Malcarielle had previously inscribed with protective runes now glowed. He walked towards the doll, allowing the soft glow to radiate out in front of him. This light from his sword was coloured by the energy of the bonded and by the strength of his family. The mud solidified under his feet, crackling sparks of energy turning liquid into glass. Rather than calling him back, Ashul ignited his own sword.

Ashul stepped beside Michael, and the two were bathed in the radiance of Ashul's blade. Sharp angry shadows were created from the sword's glow, but they fell away from the light.

It was then that Trevlor appeared.

The mage strode towards the doll as if he feared nothing. Twists of red light shimmered from the body he wore with such disregard and snaked around him as if posed ready to attack.

* * *

The light display did not deter the Nachzehrer. Light only created shadow, the Nachzehrer's strongest weapon. Anarcus had promised the zombie king the greatest of prizes – a bonded warrior, and the fool boy – who had stepped forward, offering himself up once again. But It had no intention of allowing the Nachzehrer to claim the boy. The boy was dangerous enough. It could never allow another to control him. But he was predictable in his arrogance, placing himself in the front line. The pet bonded, would also destroy themself in an effort to protect this stripling idiot. And as if proving all of Its assumptions correct, the brat's mother shimmered into existence. Waves of energy baked off her, and a feverous rage accompanied her first attack.

It had to admit It was impressed. She had grown in power since It had last seen her, when she'd been broken and left to die in a hole in the ground. Her hatred was palpable. This was more than just fear for her young. This was so much more.

It threw the Nachzehrer towards her, forcing Its 'allies' to take the full brunt of the attack. Circles of energy danced from her fingertips, flickering light running through the air that surrounded her. She wore a nimbus of pulsating colours underlined with a powerful red. Shadows were breaking around her in every direction. Was she unaware of the Nachzehrer's power, or just too consumed by her rage to understand the danger she posed to her own offspring?

'Anarcus, this ends HERE!' The words held power, and they reverberated through Its limbs, stiffening joints that had just starting to regain mobility after centuries of bondage.

When she spoke again, her voice contained the hatred of a hundred souls. 'You destroyed all I held dear! Now I shall destroy YOU!'

Power lashed out from her. The Nachzehrer closest to her were shredded into pieces of desiccated flesh, bone pulverised and blown into a maelstrom of torn fragments and floating ash. All moisture was being sucked from the air. It felt Its own black skin split and tear. How was she doing this? Where was she getting this power? It risked a glance towards this witch's offspring. The boy had fallen to his knees, his lips cracked and bleeding, patches of dried skin flaking from his face. His bonded surrounded him, trying to protect him from the shadows that threatened. The light of their swords dimming as their power was consumed. It would not win this fight and It could not risk the boy being infected. The Nachzehrer could not be allowed to have him. Never would It grant them access to powers that only It had a right to.

It drew on Its own reserves, savagely reaching for the connections It had been cultivating since it had awakened. The ground beneath Its feet became liquid again and the mud surged upwards in a wave, engulfing the Nachzehrer that remained.

* * *

'Why are we scrying through this dark muck?' Nicola asked impatiently. 'I can barely see a thing.'

'We scry through whatever surfaces we can,' said Hazel-eyes. 'Reflective surfaces, glass, crystal and water work best, but mirrors, even beaten steel, will serve the same purpose. This mud has a fatty residue floating across the surface, giving us the reflective quality we need to establish a connection.' Hazel-eyes patiently explained all this to Nicola. 'And Kitty has confirmed the doll's presence, so there is a good chance that your son will turn up in the same area.'

They soon realised that Michael had been in the area all along.

It became clear to them that the occasional movement they'd been unable to interpret was the horse's hooves as they shifted their weight, trying to find better purchase on the ground. The image was being viewed through the conduit of mud, the surface disturbed infrequently, so the image was monotone but relatively clear.

But then things changed. The mud became more fluid, and before Nicola had time to interpret what was happening, Smoke had sunk into the pool of mud. Nicola recognised her instantly. She looked to have been caught by something under the surface and she was struggling to break free. Michael's face appeared in the mud moments later. Desperate to get to Smoke, he dove beneath the surface. He came up once to grab a breath and then they were both under again and the images became too distorted as they struggled to get free.

'Can we reach them from here?' Nicola asked.

'We can feed him your strength, as you did before,' said Hazel-eyes. 'But be wary, there is another evil here. We do not want our presence to be known until we ascertain the nature of this new foe.'

A corpse-like hand wrapped itself around Michael's shoulder, pulling him under and out of their field of vision. Smoke remained visible, but she was also being dragged deeper, the number of withered bodies clinging to her saddle weighing her down.

With the rotting limbs crowded out all else, the surface becoming too agitated to maintain the clarity required to scry. Nicola watched on in disbelief as one by one each mirror's view faded and was replaced with the faces of the memory fragments until only one faltering image of Smoke's head remained.

'Quickly!' said Hazel-eyes. 'Step forward, any who can place a warding. Who is strongest in runecraft? Now, before I lose the link.' Hazel-eyes was flickering in and out of view, the strain of maintaining a connection placing some stress on him. Nicola placed her hand on his shoulder and to her relief the flickering slowed then stopped altogether. He felt more solid beneath her fingers. She knew all of it was fabrication, a mental construct, nothing more than a perverse insistence on her own remembered body image as much as his.

A squat old man stepped out from one of the mirrors, wearing brown robes, his head shaved in a monk's tonsure. *Great! My son's life is in the hands of Friar Tuck himself*, Nicola thought to herself. Tears of frustration welled up in her eyes. The monk drew a piece of chalk from the pocket of his robe and with deft sweeps of his hand sketched an intricate symbol in the air in front of him. With a flick of his free hand, the rune spun in mid-air. Still, his hand kept adding exquisite detail to the symbol.

The knowledge of the masters buried inside Nicola recognised some of the symbols being merged in the complicated sigil in front of her. Without conscious thought, she stepped closer and added a curl here and a slash there. Her finger traced the swirls of the rune and it throbbed with purpose. 'Friar Tuck' nodded at her and they both stepped back. The completed cypher glowed, waiting to be released.

Hazel-eyes had managed to maintain the image of the mud in the mirrored surface in front of him. Sweat from the effort beaded on his forehead. Each mirror fragment raised their right hand and pushed the rune towards the open portal, giving their own energy to the protective spell. The sigil hung in mid-air, suspended, waiting.

When the only mirror that retained a connection to the bonded cleared and Michael's face appeared streaked with filth, the spell flew through the portal and his body was encased briefly in the intricate tracery before it was absorbed into his skin.

The monk bent down and extended his hand to help Nicola up from the ground. She had no recollection of how she came to be kneeling next to the portal that until a moment ago had held the image of her son.

'We have done what we can,' the monk said, and he faded back into the mirrors with the rest of the fragments.

* * *

Michael had fallen to the ground as Trevlor drew power from his body. There was a coppery taste of blood in his mouth. *What was Trevlor playing at?* Shadows stabbed in his direction, barely repelled by the light from the bonded's swords. They had little energy left – it was being drained mercilessly by Trevlor. Michael had tried to block the connection and prevent Trevlor from feeding off of him, but it was still his mother's body and he needed to protect her.

This moment of conflicted thought was all the leverage Trevlor needed: once the trickle started, it soon became a flood. Michael had become a kind of conduit. The bonded tried to protect him. They guarded him with their bodies. They attempted to shield his mind and gave him all the energy they could.

But Trevlor took all they had to give and drew more still.

Along with the energy, Trevlor somehow took all moisture from the air. Michael blinked repeatedly, needing to get some tears flowing into his eyes. He was unable to focus, could neither see the shadows stabbing towards him nor make any effort to dodge them even if he could. Titan had been whining at his side, but he was no longer there.

Michael felt the absence of his sister's thoughts, like a light had gone out. He felt alone in the dark. He missed her presence more than he missed the energy she sent his way. *She is still with you, as am I,* Smoke's gentle voice spoke in his mind. She lowered her head and blew gently into his face. Michael found himself able to finally blink and his vision slowly cleared.

You need to lock yourself off. That is not your mother. Smoke too was trying to shield him, but both the shadows and Trevlor's powers were slippery. They seemed to have a mind of their own. Neither were easy to predict.

Titan had given up on trying to remove Michael from the battle. Defensive tactics were no longer part of the guardian's plan. With the doll swallowed by a geyser of mud and the Nachzehrer retreating to whatever stinking hole they came from, Titan was running towards the greatest threat to Michael – Trevlor.

Hunched low, a grumbling growl deep in his throat, Michael saw Titan's back legs bunch just before he launched at Trevlor's chest.

Trevlor might possess unimaginable power, but he was currently inhabiting the body of a middle-aged mum that topped five foot three in heels. When Titan hit Trevlor, the mage went flying and the light surrounding him flickered and died.

The arm of a Nachzehrer reached up through layers of mud, blindly searching for something to drag down into the pit, grasping towards whatever it could reach.

The bonded reacting instantly to the Nachzehrer's presence, dimming the light flowing through their weapons. With their powers so badly depleted, what little light they were able to create threw shadows around them in unpredictable patterns. Rather than protecting Michael, they were endangering him.

Whether out of fear or outrage, or a little of both, Trevlor jumped to his feet, screaming. The head of the Nachzehrer broke through the mud, its emaciated features cracking into a lopsided smile. Its fingers managed to grab the sleeve of Trevlor's clothing , curling almost possessively around the fabric and drawing back towards the mud in a slow, purposeful manner.

The tower of flowing sludge was now little more than a puddle, all trace of the doll swallowed within its depths. Trevlor's feet scrambled to find purchase. When the ground under his feet gave way, he lost what little composure remained to him.

Blinding white light blazed out of every pore of Trevlor's being and obliterated the arm of the Nachzehrer that held him, turning the mud surrounding the mage into nothing more than a fine dust.

Michael was uncertain if in his madness Trevlor was unaware that the doll was no longer present or whether he raged because he'd missed his opportunity to make the doll pay for its crimes against him.

Michael raised his arm to shield his face as the scorching-hot powder blew into his eyes, blistering skin that was already cracked and torn. When he felt the wind die down, Michael dropped his arm and tried to blink the grit from his eyes. But an orange-white impression of clasping fingers remained in the centre of his vision, as if Michael had looked into a light for too long – the imprint of the Nachzehrer's raised hand remained burnt into the back of his eyes.

Aftermath

A concussive boom rocked the house. Dana heard the screech of tyres and seconds later, the bang as a car collided with something in the street. The shimmering network above them flared with brilliant white light and then faded and was gone.

Dana blinked repeatedly – the afterimage of the network had been burned into her eyes. Each branch was like the dark green fingers of a reaching hand.

Sheba trembled against Dana's leg.

'I'll go check what that was,' Brent said as he ran towards the front door.

'Dana, do you have any insight into what just happened?' Azuradien said as he stepped towards Dana. His hand was held in front of him, not wanting to scare the dog standing at Dana's side when it was so obviously distressed.

'Trevlor just lost his shit!' said Dana. 'That's what happened! He nearly killed Michael, drained him so he couldn't protect himself anymore. They're on their way back. I think everyone is okay. Titan isn't so sure. There's been some arguing…' Dana trailed off.

The thoughts she was receiving from Titan were confusing. Titan wanted to rip Trevlor apart, but Michael's pack was preventing it. The dog didn't see the body as having anything to do with the woman he loved. He smelt a being that he didn't recognise and that being had almost killed Michael. It was so simple from the dog's perspective. Dana understood completely. She respected the simplicity of Titan's reasoning and wished that she could view things in the same uncomplicated way.

* * *

Joseph wasn't certain what he'd just seen. He was trying to replay the last few seconds before the energy surge blew apart Sarah's network. He'd seen some flash, some energy flare. But it had appeared in multiple locations, not in the second realm, but in the house. He closed his eyes, visualising those last few moments. There had been at least five flares, he was sure. He oriented himself, remembering the positioning of each energy spike, quickly checked over his right shoulder and ran towards the bathroom.

'Joseph, are you alright?' Sarah asked, completely misinterpreting why he was running towards the toilet.

'Sars, I saw her, in your network of the second realm,' said Joseph. 'I saw Nicola. I saw her protecting Michael, and I saw something else here too.' He was standing in the middle of the bathroom looking around, trying to find something out of place.

Joseph pushed past Sarah in the doorway and ran upstairs, moving from one bathroom to the next. *Why did they have so many damn bathrooms?* All of them looked normal. Joseph was running towards the front of the house when the door opened and he ran straight into the edge.

'What the hell…?' Joseph yelled as he grabbed his forehead where he could feel a bump already forming. The sticky feel of blood on his fingertips confirmed that he'd sustained some actual damage. He turned towards the mirror hanging above the front table, inspecting his reflection. His forehead had been scraped raw, with a large egg forming right above his left eye. He barely recognised himself.

In the week since his wife had been missing, he'd aged dramatically. He'd lost weight. His skin looked sallow rather than a healthy olive. He hadn't shaved recently, which seemed to emphasise his hollow cheeks rather than disguise them. While looking at his reflection, he noticed a thin crack running down the mirror. He reached one finger forward and traced the line that ran from his forehead through his chin. He couldn't remember the mirror having recently been cracked. Nicola would have had it replaced immediately. There was no way she would allow a cracked mirror to remain on the wall.

Joseph looked back over his shoulder as Brent stepped tentatively over the threshold behind him.

'Sorry Joe… I was just… what the hell?' Brent's eyes went first to Joseph's forehead, then moved towards the mirror. 'How did you manage to hit the mirror?' Brent had also noticed the crack running through the glass.

Joseph shifted slightly to the left, not liking way the mirror dissected his face; he remembered some superstition about cracked mirrors and reflections.

The bleeding on his forehead had already stopped, the skin was only lightly grazed down the centre of an ugly rectangular bump over his left eye. Joseph shook his head in a 'don't even ask' gesture. With the motion, his perspective changed and the crack in the mirror shifted so that it now lay over Brent's features. Joseph could see one of Brent's pale blue eyes through the broken view of the crack, and for just a second, the colour shifted to a dark blue denim.

* * *

'They are back!' Azuradien's commanding tone rang through the rooms of the house.

Trevlor strode towards Dana. 'Your interference nearly cost us all our lives! I had the doll! I could almost taste it!' Spittle flew from Trevlor's lips, emphasising each word.

'My interference! You were the one who drew energy and nearly killed my brother. If it wasn't for me, Titan would have ripped you to shreds for what you did!' To add weight to Dana's words, Sheba gave a warning bark, her own spit flying.

'Tame your pets, or I will tame them for you!' Trevlor shook with rage.

'Enough!' Malcarielle yelled. Her normal soft-spoken demeanour was gone – now more like the fairy queen she would someday become. 'The bonded – what news of the bonded?' Her voice almost cracked on the last word, but her gaze pinned Trevlor, demanding of him an answer.

'Your *warriors* did nothing!' Trevlor said. 'They stood by and let the doll escape. Maybe they have outlived their usefulness.' Although his words held menace, his bearing did not. Trevlor's hands trembled, and he staggered as he walked from the room.

Tears ran down Dana's face. 'I would destroy him if he wasn't wearing Mum's body!'

'So would we all, sis,' Michael replied as he walked up behind Dana. He wrapped his arms around his big sister. 'Believe me, so would we all.'

* * *

Ashul spent the next hour filling everybody in on what had happened in the second realm.

'Are you certain they were Nachzehrer?' asked Azuradien. 'Absolutely certain?' Azuradien kept coming back to the question and Ashul replied in the exact same manner each time.

'No, I am not certain, but they behaved as such,' said Ashul. 'They rose from a pool of their own putrefying remains, they wore the decaying fragments of their own death shrouds, and they shied away from the touch of iron.'

'Did the boy get touched?'

'The boy is in the room,' Michael replied. 'And yes. It's pretty hard to fight off a pack of zombies and not get touched.' Michael looked at Ashul with a reproachful tilt of his head. 'And you could have told me that was "a pool of their own putrefying remains" before I jumped in. I got that stuff in my mouth.'

Smoke and Ashul replied in unison, 'You should ask before you jump!' Michael appreciated the fact that they both kept this communication to their mental link, but he still felt like responding *It's look before you leap,* but he'd still end up looking the idiot, so he kept quiet.

'Do we have to worry about infection?' asked Dana. They'd all watched *World War Z* and a bunch of other zombie movies.

'If they were Nachzehrer,' Azuradien looked towards Ashul, 'their physical touch cannot cause infection.'

'So, what are you worried about?' asked Brent.

Dana, who'd been on her phone, already had the answer. 'They're worried about their shadows. If their shadows touched any of Michael's exposed skin, then he'll be infected. Correct me if Google is wrong, but Nachzehrer are a zombie-vampire hybrid. They raise from the dead and consume their own family. They don't pass their infection on by their bite, but by shadow. I'm redacting the bits that don't make any sense at all, like lying in their graves with their thumbs in their mouths and being a product of suicide, et cetera.'

'This Google is very wise,' said Azuradien. 'It *is* their shadow that we fear. Can we be certain he did not get touched?' Azuradien directed this last question to Ashul, but it could not, with any certainty, be answered.

'Okay, okay,' said Brent. 'Let's just handle this as if he is infected.' Brent raised this to stop the conversation from going around in useless circles. 'What can we do to cure him?'

* * *

Ashley, who'd been standing off to the side, quietly listening to the conversation, was learning more from the emotions each person emanated than from anything they said. The dizzying range of feelings, coupled with the sheer intensity, was sometimes disorientating, but always illuminating. At this particular moment, she wished she didn't have the abilities of an empath.

Tears ran down her checks as she answered for Azuradien. 'I don't think there's anything we can do. Am I right, Azuradien? We cannot cure him!' The harsh reality of this was coming off Azuradien in waves. It was as plain to Ashley as the elegant nose on the faerie's face.

'No, there is little we can do.'

'Little?' said Michael. 'Or nothing?'

'Nothing!'

'Okay! Then let's move on. The point, as Mum would say, is well and truly moot! Tell me what to look out for. Tell me how quickly any of the symptoms will be likely to occur, and tell me when we can be certain I'm in the clear. Then can we move on, because I have something I need to share and it's more important to me than any of this!' Michael waved his hand around dismissively.

'But I won't speak with Trevlor in the house. So Azuradien, Malcarielle, tell us if that atrocity has left the building. Place some wardings around this space and let's talk about the things that we can do something about, the things that matter.'

Michael spoke with such calm conviction. His every gesture, his every word was resolute. Ashley was certain if she could pick up his heart rate it would be running at a slow and steady sixty beats a minute. he'd been placed in unspeakable danger in the second realm, fought creatures that belonged in a B-grade horror movie, yet his demeanour was calm and determined.

His words rang with loathing when he spoke of Trevlor, knowing how easily the mage had drained the bonded, with no qualms for the lives he might extinguish. Ashley alone could sense Michael's fear, thumping like a bass beat, underscoring the steady thrum of his emotions. But if his fear was the bass, then hope, joy was the melody.

He had experienced something that overrode all the other emotions, trumped them even. Some of that was just how Michael worked. He put others first, but he'd experienced something joyous in the second realm, and he wanted to share it with them.

Ashley was more than happy to oblige. Her empath abilities gave her access to his emotion. Her projection abilities allowed her to let others feel what she felt.

So she shared the love.

Who Knows?

Michael paced the room as he waited for Aunt Sarah to recreate her energy network. His mind was racing. He'd hoped having a hot shower would calm him down some, but it only gave him time to replay what had happened in the second realm.

He was trying to not get ahead of himself. So much had transpired in such a short period of time, but he thought some of what he'd seen might be very important. *Could he have misinterpreted things?* He didn't think so. But he didn't want to unnecessarily give people false hope.

To keep his mind from spinning out of control and blurting something out before Trevlor was out of earshot, he asked the only questions he could think of. 'So, what am I in for? How do these Nachzehrer work?'

Malcarielle threw a nervous glance in Azuradien's direction, but ultimately it was Ashul who provided the answers.

'All that Dana has found out about the Nachzehrer is correct, apart from the fact that they do indeed rest with their thumb in their mouths.' Ashul paused, uncertain how to continue. Almost apologetically, he said, 'It is a useful method of identification. They are a carrier of disease and pestilence. Their contagion is transferred not by bite, scratch or even contact with their bodily fluids, but through exposure to their shadows.'

'Legend states that the first Nachzehrer was the result of a suicide that did not rest easy, but this has never been confirmed, and as Dana pointed out does not make any logical sense. We do not know how the Nachzehrer came into existence. But after exposure to their shadow, infection will follow, without exception.'

Michael was listening to Ashul's words. He knew on some level that what Ashul was saying should concern him, and it did, but his mind was racing in other directions. He couldn't change whether the shadow had touched him, but what he'd felt in the second realm could change everything. So he kept his face neutral and listened while his thoughts spun.

'Once infected, those left to roam will bring plague, disease, madness to those they are in contact with, while slowly succumbing to the same symptoms themselves. The plague does not impact all those who have contact with the host. The infection rate seems to be entirely arbitrary, with no apparent way to limit exposure. Those infected will become a carrier. So, you see how this can spread quickly.'

'But only Michael may have been exposed?' said Brent. 'You are immune?'

'No, not immune. Protected by our magical shields.'

'And Michael has no magical shield?'

'No, he does not. He was not born a sleeping warrior. He was not created by magic. Michael is something that has never been before.'

'And so he's vulnerable to things that you are not,' said Dana. 'But am I missing something? The Nachzehrer are vampiric, but they also experience body decomposition to a degree, so they are technically zombies? They also have enhanced strength, right?'

Ashul nodded. 'Yes, Dana that is all correct.'

'So, when do those exposed change from being plague carrier to zombie-vampire?'

'When they die. Then they will eventually rise as a true Nachzehrer.'

'How long before they die?' asked Dana.

'I cannot say.'

'Don't hold back information now, Ashul. We need to know the details. In the creatures that you have encountered, how long before they died from the disease?'

'They fall when I kill them, then I burn the remains.' Ashul spoke in an automatic, unaffected way as if he were just reporting information, with no emotional connection whatsoever. 'Those infected via shadow have a link to the undead Nachzehrer and control over all those they infect. I suspect this link is the thing that drives them mad.'

'Okay thanks,' said Michael. 'So, is there any good news here?' Michael had gotten the gist. Ashul was going to kill him as soon as he started to go mad, then burn his remains before he could rise from the dead and start drinking his family's blood.

'Once the schattensklave – the shadow slave – is killed, those infected who are still alive will return to normal, with no knowledge of any exposure.'

'Well, okay. How can we tell if I'm infected?'

'The shadow will have burnt your skin. Are you in any way burnt, Michael?' Azuradien said, leaning forward in his eagerness for a response. Michael wondered if he would have answered Azuradien honestly if he had been burnt. Luckily, he'd seen no burns when he showered. He'd noticed scratches, bruising, patches of flaking skin the size of a hand – the result of the massive fluid loss that Trevlor had caused but all the bonded had the same patches of dead skin.

'I didn't notice anything. And believe me, I was making sure I got rid of every trace of that mud, but I'd like to get Azuradien to check me over, just in case. And Uncle Brent, can you mix something for this.' Michael lifted his arm to show the patch of skin that resembled a case of extreme eczema on the inside of his elbow, rubbing at it absently. 'It itches like a bitch.'

Brent slapped at Michael's hand, inspected the area, then rolled up his sleeves and pant legs, running his fingers over the skin with a featherlight touch, finding similar patches on his neck, legs, even on his scalp.

'On it!' Brent had already moved into the kitchen and was opening cupboards and grabbing various bottles. 'I'm listening, go on.'

'Aunt Sars, is your network ready? I need to know where Trevlor is.' Michael was ready to move onto the important matters.

With the shimmering network now illuminating the room, it was easy to confirm Trevlor's absence. The network was unmarred by his telltale red stain. Thin red threads still twisted visibly around Ashul but they represented Trevlor's ability to control him, not his actual presence.

'Okay… so, I didn't want to talk with that prick anywhere near us.' Michael double-checked the network to make sure the red was still nowhere to be seen.

Azuradien registered his concern and prompted Michael to continue. 'I have placed a warding,' said Azuradien. 'I cannot prevent his return, but I will know when it occurs.'

Michael took in a deep breath and slowly exhaled, allowing some of the tension that had built up over the last couple of hours to flow out of him.

'I don't think any of you realise how mad Trevlor is. He may have been a great guy back in the day, although I'm finding that harder and harder to believe. But now he's insane, a nut-job of the highest order. I don't know if any of you are aware how close he came to destroying the bonded?'

Azuradien nodded. 'We saw the amount of power he drew through your aunt's network.'

'Then you know than no sane individual would do that. I tried to cut him off.' Michael looked down at his hands. He forced himself to unclench his fists, and he quickly found Dana's eyes. 'But it's still Mum and I can't cut Mum off. What if she's holding on somehow? And that me cutting her off was the reason she... let go.'

Dana moved to the couch where Michael was sitting, and he automatically shifted so she could move in close to him. Out of everyone present, she was the only one who really understood. Michael was exhausted; he didn't want his emotions to get the better of him.

'So, what I'm saying is we just cannot trust him. He's so focused on the doll that he cannot see that other forces are waking up. He sent us there to draw out the doll, using us as nothing more than bait. He lay in wait until the doll showed itself, and only then did he engage.'

Ashul was nodding in agreement. 'Any true member of the blood would have tried to hinder the birth of the Bezenhart. Those creatures cannot be allowed to roam free.'

'I would have to disagree here, I see the logic behind this strategy.' Azuradien was stroking his long beard. 'The doll is the one releasing these creatures. If you stop the doll, you stop the Bezenhart as well as the other forces ready to do the doll's bidding. Trevlor is correct to focus on the doll. You would be wise to remember that Anarcus is at the heart of all this.'

Through the mental link they shared, the bonded were monitoring every word spoken. Michael heard their combined snorts of derision. *Easy to say when you fight none of the battles.* Darmead expressed what all the bonded were thinking, even if only the bonded could hear them.

'I am not certain that the doll has the level of control over the forces it has unleashed as it believes,' Ashul said. 'Just as Trevlor used us to draw out the doll. I believe Michael is correct, Anarcus was using its forces to draw us out. We have fought before, and it is not like Anarcus to engage in an attack of this kind. And now it has tried twice.' Ashul shook his head. 'The doll fights from the shadows. That is its way: weakening its prey, using its power over the mind to undermine resolve. What we fought today was no match for the bonded, yet Anarcus would have expended an enormous amount of energy in the release of the Bezenhart alone. So we must ask, what did it hope to achieve?'

'Isn't it obvious?' Dana had moved from the couch and was pacing behind Brent as he mixed his ointment. 'Michael here is a bit of a wild card. The doll struggled to break Michael before and now he's one of the *bonded*. Do *we* even know what Michael's capable of?'

Malcarielle, who'd been standing silently since her earlier outburst, chose then to join the discussion. 'He has broken through the magical defences of my father,' she said. 'The strongest faerie of his time. And he broke through the defences of one of the bonded, their leader no less. Let us not forget these facts.'

Ashul acknowledged the blow Michael had scored when they'd sparred in the faerie realm with a slight smile but made no comment.

'Both feats believed to be impossible. He warded his mind before any knew it required warding. Anarcus is right to be wary. But what if Michael has been infected? If he becomes Nachzehrer...' Malcarielle's green eyes held Michael's gaze. 'Well, steps will have to be taken. The risk is just too great.'

Sarah all but lunged at Malcarielle. 'What the hell are you suggesting?'

* * *

Joseph had been watching Sarah's network while the discussion of the doll's tactics went around in circles. Joe didn't care about saving the world. He would put his family on a plane and move to Europe if that's what it took to keep them safe. But that genie was well and truly out of the bottle. At the moment, all of his family were in harm's way and there just didn't seem to be a way around it.

He watched the grid, looking for a sign of the denim blue that was his wife's energy signature – there had been hints of it before, but it had been elusive.

When Michael had walked into the room, Joseph noticed some residue clinging to his skin. A thin blue fog shimmered around him, something that peripheral vision picked up better than direct eye contact. He'd seen Nicola in the mirror; he was sure of it. It might have been only for a second but he knew his wife when he saw her. Joseph had then watched as his son appeared on the grid. A dark blue, vibrant in his own way. It took only a few seconds for Michael to shine brighter with this new iridescent glow. Joseph reached forward and touched the shimmer on the web and he was surprised when the same shimmer appeared elsewhere on the grid.

Could Nicola have been the one to crack the mirror? Could Nicola be in the house somewhere?

He made a mental note to track this source of energy down. These energy spikes had to have a source. And if he could find that source, if he could locate where the energy was being drawn from… this could lead him right to Nicola. But at that moment the network flared with activity close by to them, possibly even next door.

Joseph looked through the kitchen window and his fears were confirmed.

Marcus' family were back. This meant the doll had most likely returned too. And it was probably in much need of replenishing its depleted energy stores. While having the doll close by might give some heads up before an attack, having it back made him feel uneasy. He thought he should tell everyone the 'good' news about their neighbours when the tone of their monotonous discussion suddenly thrummed with anger.

'What the hell are you suggesting?' yelled Sarah.

'I simply suggest,' Malcarielle spoke in a calm measured way that irritated Joseph in less than an instant, 'that Michael accompanies me and my father into the faerie realm. Time runs slower there. If he is infected, this time differential will inhibit the disease's progress. And, as the faerie are immune like the bonded, there will be no risk of the pestilence spreading. It is the safest way to proceed.'

'So, Malcarielle,' Sarah said in a low tone, 'you would lock him away and, if infected, eventually kill him?'

'We have no ulterior motives here. We need to protect Michael. In doing so we will save all those that he may infect.'

Joseph stepped away from the window. The sink he'd been leaning against sparked as his hand lost contact with the metal.

'No ulterior motives, maybe, but you also seem to be the only ones with no skin in the game. So we'll take what you have said under advisement. But you will not be taking my son anywhere. I have more faith in Brent's potions and ointments than I have in your ability to help. You have examined him, Azuradien. Could you find any burns?'

When Azuradien failed to respond, Joseph realised he'd just about had enough of the faeries.

'No, so I suggest you leave,' said Joseph. 'Read some books and try to find a cure. You can come back tomorrow morning to check on him again and if you still cannot find any sign that he is infected, I expect no more talk about my son's health. You believe the doll should be our primary focus. Well, it looks to be back next door. So why don't you go monitor it. From a safe distance, *I'm sure.*'

Joseph turned away from the faeries, rudely dismissing them. He'd had enough of their academic approach to every situation. Living for so long, they forgot how precious life was and being so invulnerable they didn't understand that families would do anything to save one of their own. Anything at all.

* * *

The dark entity arrived just as the sun dropped below the horizon, the sky orange with remembered warmth. The sheer number of supernatural beings hovering in the shadows around the house surprised him.

Paranormal beings would always be drawn to sites where magic was strongest. Had the breach in the source lured them all here, like moths to a flame? And this small area was not just a site of magic but a place where the source of all magic was seeping back into the first and second realms. So then, a beacon it had become. But still, there were so many creatures!

Sprites, brownies, gargoyles – many fled upon the dark entity's arrival. Some hid in the branches overhanging the house, hoping not to be noticed; others just dissolved into the ether. A primitive warding flared when his foot touched the ceramic tiles on the roof. He paused, still as the shadows themselves, but no-one noticed this trespass.

He blew against the magic curling around his feet and it dissipated like morning fog touched by the heat of the sun. He let his senses flow through the area and confirmed his suspicions that nothing here posed any real threat to him.

He lay down on the tiles and let the heat from the roof warm his muscles. Crossing his ankles, he listened to the conversation going on below him. He had extraordinary hearing, so he had no trouble picking up their words. With his long fingers laced across his chest, he looked almost to be sleeping. But this entity did not sleep. He listened. He waited. He was patient.

When the young female with the intriguing cadence to her voice spoke about the boy Michael, the dark entity raised himself up onto his elbows to focus on her words.

'Michael here is a bit of a wild card. The doll struggled to break Michael before and now he's one of the *bonded*. Do *we* even know what Michael's capable of?'

His instincts had been right once again. When the first slow trickle of magic had started to flow back into the world, he'd sensed it from the other side of the globe, and had been monitoring the rift ever since. He'd felt the ancient warriors stir in their sleep and decided that it was prudent he investigate what had caused their awakening.

Anarcus was a concern. *It* always found some weak-minded beings to bolster its dreams of domination, but the boy was the one the doll was most interested in. The sleeping warriors were a force like no other. Directly linked to the source, their potential was near limitless. And now to find the boy had somehow become one with the bonded? The implications were concerning, to say the least. This boy needed to be monitored. And the girl, well, he had to look upon the face of the girl that spoke with the voice of the animals.

He was happy in the short term to imagine what this creature would look like: petite, fast, with eyes that brimmed with an animal's sophisticated and unrestrained intelligence was his guess. He was enjoying this game when the screeching voice of a faerie cut through his reverie.

Whereas the girl seemed to whisper softly to him, those damn faeries spoke with a self-righteous tone that grated against his delicate hearing.

'He has broken through the magical defences of my father. The strongest faerie of his time. And he broke through the defences of one of the bonded, their leader no less. Let us not forget these facts. Both feats believed to be impossible. He warded his mind before any knew it required warding. Anarcus is right to be wary. But what if Michael has been infected? If he becomes Nachzehrer… Well, steps will have to be taken. The risk is just too great.'

So, nothing had changed. The faeries still believed they were the only ones fit to rule. Easy when none of the wars impacted them. Well, this time he intended to change all that. He sat back and laughed when the father asked the faeries to leave the family home. *Good for him.*

He had made his decision. He would monitor the boy, protect him if need be. The opportunity the boy presented was just too great. If the boy was about to turn into a Nachzehrer, he would know hours before anyone else. He might still have to kill the boy, but he was intrigued, and it had been a while since anything had piqued his interest, so he would let things run their course.

A couple of goblins – realising the warding was now broken – crawled closer and tried to lick his feet. With the faeries' unexpected rebuff, Lorcan was in a good mood for the first time in decades. He let the goblins come forward and he reached down and scratched one behind the leathery flap of skin that served as its ear.

Laying back down, he stretched and placed his hands behind his head and looked up as the first stars appeared in the darkening velvet of the sky above. At the edges of his perception now, the otherworldly creatures in the vicinity were crowding closer. They had come to soak in the ambient energy that was slowly being released from the rift. Like an African watering hole where predators and prey came together to share the life-preserving water, the magical creatures were drawn to this place.

A water sprite, overcome by temptation, fluttered closer. Lorcan dimmed his presence, waited until the creature was inches from his face then hissed in her direction, his lips curled back, his teeth exposed. The sprite dissolved in a spray of water.

Lorcan chuckled to himself. The girl would understand: the apex predator drinks alone.

Mirror, Mirror

After quite a bit of discussion, the faeries left, agreeing to return to check on Michael's condition in the morning. Ashul was not pleased with how the conversation had degenerated.

Many of the bonded believed the faeries needed to be reminded that they did not, in fact, rule the sleeping warriors, nor the blood.

The bonded had asked Michael to pass on their respect at Joseph's handling of the situation. Michael made a mental note to pass their congratulations on at a later time.

After the way they'd reacted, Michael was glad the faeries were not present for the next part of the discussion. For the first time that night, his heart was racing. Ashley sent him a wave of encouragement. He didn't want to give false hope; he wasn't certain what he'd felt, but he needed to share everything he'd experienced because so much was at stake now.

With his carefully picked words ready, Michael took in a deep breath and blurted out, 'I felt Mum in the second realm.'

Dana, never far from his side, reached out and grabbed his hand with both of hers. 'Dana, I swear she helped me over there. Mum's still in the game.'

Michael could hear Aunty Sarah sobbing. Ashley wrapped her arms around Michael and Dana, squeezing them in an uncomfortable but welcome bear hug. Dana's eyes bored into Michael's. Her voice barely above a whisper, 'Micky, tell me everything.'

'When you've finished telling your story,' said Joseph, 'I've got one of my own.' Joseph waited until both of his children were looking at him before speaking again. 'I saw her too, but not just in the second realm. It was only for a moment, but I saw her in this house, reflected in the mirror at the front door.'

* * *

Michael went to bed that night awash in such a range of emotions his head was spinning. He kept checking his heart rate, looking for the first signs of infection.

His pulse was elevated. His dad hadn't only seen his mum, but believed she might be somewhere in the house.

There was a strange energy spike that kept coming and going from the network so Joseph was waiting downstairs to monitor for it to appear again. He'd even unplugged every electrical device in the house, hoping that would make it easier for him to pinpoint Nicola's location.

Brent and Ashley had gone home to mix up another batch of ointment and to get some much-needed rest. Everybody had been exhausted.

Michael was running through another series of checks – monitoring his temperature, his heart rate (still high, but dropping), all in an effort to confirm that he was not turning zombie – when Dana popped her head into his room.

'Buddy, how are you feeling?'

'Pretty good actually, like I'm nervous. But I think Dad is going to try to find Mum, and whatever else happens, well… I think we might be alright!'

'Do you want me to stay with you? Make sure you sleep, okay?'

'Would you believe I'd completely forgotten about the doll? I've been so concerned about whether I'm running a fever, or checking my heart rate, that I never stopped to consider that the doll might still be lurking around in my dreams. Shit, Dana. Lurking in yours.' Michael was sitting up, unsure what to do.

'Relax,' said Dana. 'My connection with Titan is getting more reliable. He'll watch over my sleep and alert Sheba if I'm in any danger. So before we go off to bed, can you tell me again about Mum?' Dana pushed Michael to the side of the bed and lay down next to him.

After the third run through of events, they both drifted off to sleep.

* * *

Michael woke gasping and unable to catch his breath. He'd been drowning in mud, with hands grasping his shoulders, pulling him under the surface. Smoke's eyes rolled as she too was drawn below, her head swallowed by sludge. He'd been unable to reach her, unable to get back to the surface.

His fist held a rope attached to nothing but air.

His feet were held in a vice-like grip. *Unable to move.* His head swam with the need for air, and he knew he needed to get to the surface. He clenched his jaw, forced his body to resist the impulse to take a breath, thrashed to shake free from the hands restraining him.

Disorientated, Michael woke to a set of glowing red eyes looking down on him, his body held immobile by some creature that hovered above him.

* * *

Lorcan had to be careful. The bonded warriors were ever present. He'd dimmed his presence to such an extent that he was almost not breathing, but still he risked discovery.

The boy was showing signs of distress. His heart rate was elevated and his breathing was ragged. Lorcan wasn't certain, but he thought he heard a rattle in the boy's lungs. He needed to get closer; he needed to smell the boy.

Lorcan had been able to drop in under the mother's fading protections on the house. Being this close to the source also enhanced his abilities. One moment he was on the roof, the next he was hovering above the boy, using the force of his will to paralyse the boy's mind and body.

But this boy's mind was strong and he struggled against the mental restraints, recognising them for what they were – an attack.

Lorcan was an ancient creature and he'd danced this dance many times before. It took only a few seconds longer to place the boy in a hypnotic state that brought him into a sympathetic rhythm with Lorcan's own body. The boy's heart slowed to a rate of a single beat per minute. It would take triple that time before his chest rose to take a breath.

More importantly, the boy's thoughts had slowed, so if Lorcan worked fast the boy might not even remember the intrusion.

Lorcan sniffed the room. The boy reeked of the antiseptic cream the uncle had applied. The acrid stench made Lorcan's sensitive sinuses burn, but the smell of burnt flesh, the cloying fragrance of lymphatic fluid, was not present. If the boy had been exposed to the shadow, he should have been burnt in some way. Lorcan ducked his head, he held his mouth over the boy's, waiting for his exhalation.

There was a faint odour. The sweet scent of corruption.

Lorcan had never seen a Nachzehrer infection work in this fashion. Was the boy strong enough to fight the conversion alone? Lorcan couldn't risk this boy becoming a schattensklave. A shadow slave with the power this boy wielded could elevate the Nachzehrer far beyond their station.

Lorcan had never tried to prevent a conversion before; he'd always been happy to rip the throat out of any fool who became infected.

Lowering his mouth, he bared his teeth, waiting for the next beat of the boy's heart. His intention was to bite the inside of the boy's wrist, to draw out the poison in-between beats so as not to endanger the boy at all. He raised the boy's hand to his mouth. Lorcan felt the icy sting of a warding just as a flash of blue light covered the boy's body.

An intricate tapestry of runes now covered the boy's skin from head to toe, only raising to the surface when Lorcan attempted to bite his wrist. When Lorcan pulled back, the runes faded back into dormancy. At the moment the runes had flared, the boy's eyes had popped open.

Lorcan nodded at the simplicity of the situation.

The boy's brown eyes had not been covered by the magic protection when the Nachzehrer's shadow fell upon him.

Looking closer at the boy, Lorcan detected a small scar marring the surface of each cornea.

This boy should never gamble – his luck was atrocious.

What were the chances that a ward could protect every inch of his skin and leave such a small area unprotected? And then to have the shadow fall upon this same unprotected space. The odds were extraordinary. Yet, the slim nature of the event offered no protection against the infection.

Lorcan placed his mouth over the boy's left eye and took in a slow, steady breath. A thin black vapour swirled up from the surface of the eye. He breathed in more deeply and the vapour began to fill Lorcan's lungs.

He repeated the process for as long as he dared, marking the passage of time by the boy's irregular breaths. When Lorcan had counted to six, he knew he had to leave. The bonded could monitor the boy's thoughts. A couple of minutes of unfocused thought and it might be considered nothing but the boy dreaming, anything more would trigger their alarm.

The stink of corruption now rested deep within Lorcan's chest, and his body fought the disease as it entered his bloodstream. He had not been able to remove all of the poison from the boy's body, the capillaries in the eyes were just too delicate. If he only had more time. But he did not. Not yet.

Lorcan needed to hurry, but he took one moment to place a calming charm on the boy's thoughts before he lifted the paralysis. The boy needed to rest: the next couple of days were going to be tough on him.

* * *

The water sprite felt the boy's pain. His distress ran through her like an unpleasant vibration that disrupted her core.

But she endured. There was something important going on here and for the moment she was more puzzled by the ancient one's behaviour. She'd heard the legend of his kind's bloodthirsty nature, so she was curious when the ancient one spared her life and merely lay back, amused by his own charity.

She watched patiently as he deftly moved aside the warding surrounding the house. She followed in his footsteps and watched as he crouched over the young boy's face, then drew back in horror as the young boy struggled against the ancient one's magic. His fear – a higher note than his pain – washed over her. The young boy lay motionless as the ancient one bent down and raised the boy's wrist to his mouth. His eyes glowed a crimson red when his teeth lowered on the exposed flesh, only to be repelled when the runes flared with dark blue light.

The sprite hid in the shadows, not wanting to see the extent of his rage at being thwarted so. When she finally had the courage to turn her eyes back towards the boy, she was further perplexed when wispy tendrils of inky darkness flowed from the boy's eyes into the ancient one's mouth.

Being a creature of water, the unnatural way the mist flowed repulsed her: moving of its own accord, as if fighting the ancient one's efforts to extract it.

Then the boy lay still, his body badly depleted.

The poor boy's system cried for some form of moisture, for relief. The vapour had taken with it life-sustaining moisture. The sprite, being a creature so intrinsically linked to water's life-giving properties could sense all this.

The sprite's anguish was almost enough to make her flee. But her natural curiosity and her desire to rectify the imbalance kept her in her place amongst the shadows.

As the dark one placed his hand on the boy's forehead, she felt the boy's discomfort ease. The dark one had placed a charm on the boy. With a sigh, he turned and vanished from the room, but the sprite was certain his eyes had found her within the darkness. She'd felt the chill of his gaze. So, she waited a hundred heartbeats before she was certain he wasn't going to step from the shadows again, hissing as he drew the last drop of moisture from her body.

The water sprite sang quietly as she approached the boy, drawing water from her surroundings and carefully directing a stream of humidified air to flow into the boy's lungs. His breathing eased as parched lungs took in the relief she offered.

She had to be careful. If too much fluid entered his system in one sitting, his cells would split under the strain. So, she worked at a slow pace and allowed his body to absorb as much as it could. When she'd replenished as much moisture as she dared, she remained at his side and continued to sing, for she found the boy's presence soothing, calming.

She'd lost herself to the steady susurration of his breathing and jumped when she noticed his eyes were open and watching her.

'Are you real, little sprite?' The boy's voice cracked. She could tell the words pained him. Agitated, she flew around in a tight circle, not knowing whether she should depart or stay.

'I have been seeing some strange things tonight. I thought I saw a gargoyle looking in through the window while you were singing. He hid his head under his wings when he knew I had spotted him.' The boy swallowed; his face showed the pain this caused him.

'And I saw something else. It hovered above me and sucked at my eyes. The things I come up with.' The boy shook his head and laughed harshly at himself, but stopped himself short with a pained expression. His hand rubbed at his throat. His small bark of laughter had caused him discomfort – she could feel it vibrating through her.

The sprite drew more moisture from the air and hovered above his head, ready to fly away if he moved. She cupped her hands, and they instantly filled with cool, fresh water. Getting as close to his mouth as she dared, she sprinkled water down on the boy's face. Her voice sounded to humans like the music of soft piping. She knew the boy wouldn't understand her, but she hoped he understood her intention was to soothe some of his discomfort. She encouraged him to drink.

The first stream of water fell on his cheek, but he was soon drinking the water offered. She infused the precious liquid with as much of her healing energies as she could. Even though he did not understand her, she continued to sing to him. He even thanked her for the gift and she marvelled at this small thing. She had never had a human show her appreciation before.

She continued her song until finally he returned to sleep. Afterwards, she went in search of her fellows to tell them all of what she had seen.

* * *

Dana woke, thinking she'd heard trickling water somewhere in the house; it was a wonderful, relaxing sound, and she tried to use it to lull her back to sleep. When she'd woken in the early hours of the morning and wandered to her room, to drop into her own bed, Michael had been sleeping soundly. Although she'd been half asleep herself, she remembered to check both his breathing and his temperature. All had seemed fine. But her concern for Michael wouldn't allow her to get back to sleep easily, her mind wouldn't shut up. *What if Michael was infected? Would the faeries really remove him to the faerie realm for eventual disposal?* She needed her mum. Nicola had a way of working through things methodically that always made the situation seem more manageable. She'd know how to handle the situation and if she didn't, Nicola would go about finding out how to. She wouldn't be running with a 'let's wait and see' approach to Michael's life.

Maybe Dana had no choice. Maybe she needed to seek answers in the book.

Trevlor had escaped from the book– the greatest danger the book possessed was in their very home. Surely it would be easier to deal with now that the mind that nearly put Nicola in a coma had been released. It must be safer. The book might even have a way to deal with Trevlor.

Why hadn't she thought of it before?

Throwing back the blankets, she quietly tiptoed to Michael's room to see if he was still awake. She wouldn't risk the gypsy book alone.

She was both disappointed and relieved to see Michael sleeping soundly. He was smiling in his sleep, his hands crossed casually on his chest.

She walked closer and placed the back of her hand on his forehead. His skin was cool to the touch. She turned her head and dropped closer so she could listen to his breathing. It was remarkably slow and steady.

Nothing fazed this kid.

She wished for the thousandth time that she could be more like her little brother. She turned and opened the window. The room felt remarkably dry. Standing with her eyes closed, she enjoyed the breeze as it caressed her skin. Turning away from the windows, she reached down and pushed the hair back from Michael's face, then went to the bathroom to get herself a glass of water. Her throat was dry.

The water poured from the tap in a harsh torrent. She reduced the flow, hoping to mimic the gentle tinkling she'd heard earlier. That sound had been so soothing.

Yet she couldn't regain the feeling of peace that she'd felt. Everything about the bathroom was harsh – the lighting, the sound of her feet on the tiles. The sterile light amplified everything, forgave nothing.

She looked at herself in the mirror: her hair was a mess, her skin looked pale, and there were dark circles under her eyes. She turned the tap on again and splashed her face with water. She was so tired that, for just a second, her brown eyes seemed to flare blue, then settled to a hazel colour more like her brother's. She slid to the bathroom floor and let the tears that she'd been steadfastly holding back flow. With one hand, she reached forward and gently shut the bathroom door, not wanting to disturb Michael's sleep. He needed his rest.

She didn't know what she would do if anything happened to Michael. She couldn't even conceive of a way to move forward without him. Allowing herself another moment to cry, she straightened her shoulders and pushed her hair back from her face. She stood up and boldly faced the mirror. Her decision had been made – she would consult the gypsy book in the morning after she'd rested.

Savagely running her fingers through her hair, she pulled out the worst of the tangles, splashed her face with water once more, ensuring that none of the sticky residue of her tears remained.

The face that looked back at her was red and splotchy but the uncertainty that had shone from her eyes had been replaced with purpose. She held the edge of the sink, letting out a slow steady breath as she did so. Feeling a little less adrift, she paused for just a moment to think through her plan for tomorrow. First, she would have to find the damn book. She had no idea if Trevlor had placed it in some fifth dimension to stop others from accessing it.

Still holding the edge of the sink to steady herself, Dana took in another deep breath and locked eyes with her own reflection. *Control the controllable.* On her third exhalation, feeling no calmer than the first, she noticed a small crack in the corner of the mirror, on the outside edge. She ran her finger along its edge to make sure it wasn't sharp enough for someone to nick a finger.

She could feel no flaw in the mirror. Maybe there was a small hairline crack running just under the surface of the glass? Dana brought her face closer and tried to look at the damage from a side angle. It looked more like a hair laying over the surface than any real crack.

As she was pulling away, the thin line began to spread across the mirror, fine cracks radiating out from the corner with an almost tinkling sound. She hadn't touched a thing; she'd barely even breathed on the glass.

Dana took a step back, fearful that the mirror was about to shatter at any moment. Her reflection blurred with the vibrations running across the mirror's surface. The web of cracking stopped sharply, but she could still feel a low hum of vibrations.

She reached forward with her right hand, placing her four fingers tentatively onto the surface with the lightest of touches. The buzz ran up her fingers, all the way to her knuckles.

The image in front of her was still wavering. It appeared as if her fingers weren't quite touching the mirror's surface at all, as if the shimmer in the mirror prevented contact. She found the image unsettling – it reminded her a little too closely of the time her hand had slipped through the mirror in Marcus' room when realities had merged.

Grasping her hands in front of her, she tried to rub away the hum that she could still feel in her fingertips. Her hand appeared normal, but the buzzing sensation persisted. She looked up – her own face peered back at her with uncertainty. Thankfully, the surface had stopped vibrating, so she no longer looked like her face was about to crack or slide off the mirror's surface.

She raised her hand towards the mirror again, to confirm that things were working as they should, forcing herself to confront her fears. The reflected image moved of its own volition, mimicking her movements but not mirroring them.

The hand inside the mirror reached up and cupped her cheek. Dana's head followed her reflection's lead and tilted towards the hand, accepting the embrace. Thinking she must be in a dream, she closed her eyes and accepted the comfort offered. She felt the warmth of the hand on her face as the room filled with the fragrance of her mother's perfume.

Dana opened her eyes and knew it was no dream. She knew with all her heart that her mother had found her.

* * *

Sarah had gone home twenty minutes previous to check on Ashley, confident that the network would continue functioning in her absence. Joseph had been given clear instructions to call her if he needed anything, anything at all.

What Joseph needed was some No-Doz washed down with a double espresso. He settled for a chocolate bar and a Coke.

He savoured the sweetness of the chocolate as he interpreted what he was seeing on the network. If he focused, the colours and lines resolved themselves into images and shapes. Some for the people that surrounded him, others for the animals and insects. Even the trees radiated a soft glow of their own. Under all of this, a base energy field hummed.

The more Joseph examined the network, the more this base energy became apparent – not by what he saw, but by what he did not. Like knowing strings were attached without actually being able to see them.

Joseph had been fearful that Marcus and his family might have a technique for hiding themselves from the network, but it appeared they did not. The parents shone with a hazy burnt orange colour, Marcus a deep aquamarine.

Marcus had a strange aspect to his signature that Joseph wanted to discuss with Sarah when he saw her next. Striations of orange riddled his base print of aquamarine. The orange occasionally swelled until it blotted out all signs of Marcus completely.

It was like watching a virus slowly infiltrate the host cell.

The signatures of Dana and Michael were interconnected to an amazing extent, but their colours flowed around and through each other. They never fought for dominance. Where there was one signature, always the other was close by. But you never lost one signature completely.

Joseph had noticed some small anomalies on the system, tiny blips of light that fluttered around the network. Most of these lights stayed off to the edges, but occasionally they came closer. Joseph suspected they might be sprites or something similar. Having seen them only in the faerie realm, he didn't know what they'd look like through the lens of Sarah's network. The more he tried to focus on them, the more they skipped around and faded from view.

They didn't look to pose a threat, but Joseph was concerned about the state of Nicola's wardings on the house if strange entities were flittering around undetected. Surely Trevlor would have the sense to maintain the protection. Not in any effort to safeguard Joseph's family, but for Trevlor's own self-serving purposes.

As Joseph tried to follow the lights flickering on and off the network, he noticed an area of inactivity that bordered on absence. He'd seen nothing quite like it when he'd been studying the energy fields of the first plane previously. It was similar to the vortices that had swirled around the Bezenhart in the second realm, but it didn't have the parasitic urgency of those fields. There was energy being absorbed here, of this he was sure, but it was so subtle that he couldn't imagine any living creature able to manage the task in such a measured way.

Was this the drain he'd been searching for?

He tried to pinpoint the location, but it shifted subtly, fading from view when he focused on it directly. But by watching the drain, looking for where the baseline energy seemed depleted, he was slowly able to narrow down the field.

His gut told him it was coming from upstairs near his bedroom. Neither Michael nor Dana seemed impacted by the slow siphoning of energy. *Good. Leave them to rest for a while. They'd both been through so much.*

He nearly dropped his Coke when the network flickered red. Sharp spikes of energy arcing across the network made it hard to see anything else. Now that Michael had pointed out Trevlor's madness, the mage's signature screamed with the discordant patterns of his insanity. Recent events must have unhinged him further. His energy stabbing at the ether that surrounded him, points of deep red expanding and contracting at extraordinary speed. When the lightshow settled, Joseph pinpointed his location.

Trevlor had reappeared upstairs. The network showed him standing right in Michael's room.

Joseph turned and bolted for the stairs, but not before he saw the denim blue haze appear in the network, wafting like sea spray suspended over a wave, forming and reforming around Dana. *Could the timing have been worse? He gets a fix on Nicola just as Trevlor returns. And then Trevlor makes a beeline straight for Michael!*

He heard Michael's door close.

'Damn!' He took the stairs two steps at a time.

'Michael!'

No response.

'Michael!' yelled Joseph. 'Call the bonded!' Joseph ran up the stairs and glanced over his shoulder to confirm the blue haze was not in his imagination. It was still glowing with a fierce intensity.

He cursed their luck, and ran towards Michael.

* * *

Michael woke to the cool touch of his mother's hand on his forehead. *Why not? He'd dreamt of stranger things tonight.* She didn't smooth his hair back from his eyes or stroke his cheek. She merely sat with her hand resting on his skin. The touch slowly warmed in a way that Michael knew well.

Sudden shock coursed through Michael. He remembered his mother no longer wore her own skin. His eyes flew open, and he threw himself away from the hand resting against his cheek. Michael put as much distance between himself and the madman that inhabited his mother's body as he could.

'I am not the monster you think I am. I seek to heal you.' Trevlor moved away from the bed, steadying himself as he rose.

'You do not have the right,' said Michael. 'You are a coward and a monster.' He made a mental summons to the bonded. 'Save your healing energy for yourself. You look a bit shaky.' Ashul was already in a place between planes, ready to intervene if needed.

'The doll needs to be stopped at all costs. You have not seen what it can do. I have known the pain of losing all.' Trevlor's hands were shaking. 'What is wrong with this body?' Trevlor yelled in frustration. 'It is weak, I need to be strong if I am to succeed.' He held his hand up for Michael's inspection as if he expected sympathy and understanding.

Ashul stepped out from the shadows.

'The lady Nicola showed unheard of strength with that body as her tool. She was able to draw on the wild magic with that body.' Ashul reached towards Trevlor. 'Perhaps it is time for you to allow her to return. I promise this on the lives of the blood and the bonded, we will not rest until the doll is bound once more.'

'It needs to be DESTROYED!' Spittle flew from Trevlor's lips, his madness returning. 'Bondage will not do. Ashul, you were there at the doll's binding, you witnessed the carnage. The masters stabbed! Men and women I held dear butchered before my very eyes. There was nothing left. All was lost!' Trevlor's fists balled against his temples, acting as though his head was about to explode. He searched Ashul's face for some sign that he remembered the atrocities the doll had forced him to endure.

Michael had watched his mother deal with debilitating migraines before. Trevlor appeared to be experiencing a doozy. He was grasping his head, pounding his right hand against his forehead.

'You were there.' Trevlor's voice shook with the pain of his memories.

'YOU were THERE!' He now spun towards Ashul.

'You were there – how could I have not seen it before?' cried Trevlor. 'This is all your FAULT! It was your task to destroy the doll. Your task, not MINE! I command YOU. I command you to give me all the energy you have. *I will have the wild magic.'*

* * *

The bathroom door flew open as Joseph reached Michael's door. Dana came barrelling out with tears pouring down her cheeks. 'The book, Dad,' she said. 'Where's the gypsy book?'

'Later, Dana,' said Joseph. 'Michael needs us. Trevlor is with him.' Joseph started pounding on the door. His mind replayed the turmoil of Trevlor's energy signature. The crimson red had flared on the network in a fierce and erratic manner. Joseph's mind flew in a hundred directions. The interconnectivity of the bonded. Michael's cobalt blue twisted through with red striations. So similar to the way orange cords twisted through Marcus' aquamarine, until the aquamarine no longer existed. Each thought added an additional layer to the terror building in his mind.

'Michael, call the bonded!' he yelled. 'Call them now!'

But could the bonded help him? He'd seen Ashul fall to his knees when the red twist of Trevlor's energy forced him to comply.

Dana placed her hands on Joseph's face and spoke calmly even though her entire body shook. 'The book, Dad. You *need* to tell me where Mum put the book.'

Joseph nearly slapped her hands away. He needed to get to Michael. But as he grabbed Dana's hand, he smelt Nicola's perfume clinging to his daughter's skin. The image of the denim blue hue appearing on the network filled his vision – and the strange iridescent shimmer that always appeared at the same time.

Everything clicked into place. Dana placed her index finger over his lips when she saw him make the connection.

'Where, Dad?'

Joseph closed his eyes and replayed the movements of the blue denim energy in his mind's eye, trying to pinpoint the drain he'd recently identified. 'It's in the back of the cupboard in our bedroom. Try the top shelf.'

Joseph stepped towards Michael's room, leaving Dana to find the book. The door was closed, but he could hear Ashul speaking calmly to Trevlor. Maybe this would turn out okay. Maybe Ashul would be able to reason with Trevlor.

These hopes were blown to dust when Joseph heard Trevlor demand Ashul's power. Joseph didn't need to hear anything further. He slammed his shoulder into the door and sparks flew out from Joseph, but the lock still held tight.

Greedy Tome

Michael could feel the pull of Trevlor's command. The bonded had been created by those of the blood to serve and obey. Trevlor had tested Ashul's resolve only yesterday, and the brutal efforts he was willing to go to appalled Michael.

Ashul stood up at Trevlor's command, his every muscle tense, bands of red light pulsing under his skin.

'I will not comply, not in this.' Ashul's hands balled into fists at his sides. The veins running up the back of his arms flared crimson red. Michael felt the heat running through his own veins and knew the Trevlor was attempting to draw from all the bonded.

'You will not defy me! I am of the blood. You will obey!' Trevlor reached out, his hands drawing the red ribbons to the surface of Ashul's skin. The warrior's jaw clenched with the strain of refusal.

'I will not comply!' said Ashul. His voice rang with the strength of his brothers. Michael's lips moved as he too spoke the words. Beads of sweat ran down Ashul's face, but he would not relent.

Michael stepped to Ashul's side to offer support. He could hear the pounding on the door as his father tried to force his way inside. He hoped Joseph had a way to incapacitate Trevlor.

'Will you feel the same way when I force this boy to his knees?' said Trevlor.

Trevlor turned his focus to Michael. The veins in Michael's body burnt like a thousand fire ants crawling under his skin – red-hot pain shot along every nerve ending.

Michael gritted his teeth and repeated, 'I will not comply!'

Ashul nodded, and a few seconds later Michael's pain disappeared. Ashul's skin was almost translucent with the red veins of energy burning their way to the surface.

'In this you must go through me,' said Ashul. 'I am the bonded's leader.' Ashul's body shook, his tendons standing out from the skin, but he held his head defiantly, his back ramrod straight. 'I… will… not comply!'

Trevlor clenched his hand and Michael experienced a shadow of the pain that was twisting its way through Ashul's intestines.

Ashul's knees buckled, but he pushed himself back to his feet.

Michael had decided that the time had come to fight Trevlor head on. He couldn't see his mother in this twisted creature any longer. Whoever Trevlor had been, he was now just some deranged atrocity willing to torture others to get its way. Michael was walking towards Trevlor with clenched fists when the door of his bedroom burst open. The hinges and doorhandle sparked with electrical current.

Joseph stumbled into the room, followed closely by Dana. Her eyes took in all that was happening. Michael could see the outrage burning in her eyes but her demeanour puzzled him.

She stepped towards Trevlor, all excitement and euphoria. As if she hadn't noticed Trevlor's hold over Ashul, forcing the red-hot veins of energy to burn to the surface of his skin.

Dana virtually skipped forward with the gypsy book clutched to her chest.

'I've found the secret to the wild magic. It's so simple!' She raised the book so all could see the telltale emblem on the front cover, then she dropped her arms back down and clutched the book possessively to her chest.

Her hair was standing on end, and the air felt charged.

'YOU are not to touch the tome, it is SACRED!' Trevlor grabbed for the book. Dana dodged to the left, moving quickly to stand beside Michael. Joseph went with her, his left hand remained touching the small of her back at all times.

'But you don't understand!' Dana exclaimed. 'The answer is in the book!' A fiery ball of energy grew above her.

Michael watched his father's hand move and the energy above Dana pulsed with life. She made to open the book – her hand was covered in sparks of electricity as her fingers touched the cover.

Trevlor, faster than expected, grabbed the book from her and wrenched the pages open.

'The wild magic will be mine!' Trevlor gazed down at the pages as he spoke. The book flared up with an intense blue light.

'Something will be yours, you bastard,' said Dana. 'But it won't be the wild magic.'

Dana's features lost the ditzy, exhilarated expression and a cold self-satisfied hatred replaced all the wild enthusiasm. 'You'll be getting exactly what you deserve.'

* * *

The book sent serpentine coils of power through the emblem adorning the book, then up and over Trevlor's hands where they touched the pages. Hungry energy rippled outwards towards the mage, up and under fingernails the energy ran, greedy for the lost soul's return. Never before had one of the fragments escaped the confines of its pages.

The tome was eager for this anomaly to be rectified.

The book worked on a simple transactional basis: if one asked for aid, you provided information in payment, a memory, a shard of your own identity. The tome stored this shard for when others had need of it. Somehow this arrangement had been breached. But the arrangement was binding, and the book did not take kindly to any breach of its laws.

The fragment of identity would return to the tome. Using a mere fraction of the energy stored within its pages, it started the process of detaching the shard from its current receptacle. The book sent sinuous ropes of energy down through the nerves, through the neural pathways of the body the fragment inhabited, prying connections loose with steady, determined slithers of purpose. It filled the receptacle with its own energy until the fragment only remained in the brain.

'You will return!'

The pages of the book rustled, and the inevitability underpinning the words reverberated through the host's body. But this fragment refused to relinquish control and return to the pages; it had defied the book's command and placed hooks in the host's brain – barbed, wickedly twisted ropes of insanity.

* * *

Nicola spoke to the book directly for the first time. 'I can extract him from my body. Help expel his fragment.'

'You have caused us some concern,' the book answered, in both words and images. Its communication had a strange reverberating quality that hurt to listen to. 'You are a fragment, but you are also a complete soul. It was never the intention that we host souls. Eventually, your presence here, in this way, would place the pages' existence in jeopardy. You are free to go but your fragment must remain. You did turn to us for aid.'

Nicola waited for the last echo of the tome's words to fade, and she listened instead to the counsel of a hundred minds, each drawing on their experiences to guide her.

Nicola poured herself back into her body. She flowed like water through her own veins, becoming one with her muscles, pushing through the porous holes in bones, seeping into marrow.

The book had done a lot of her work for her, so she ran freely up through nerves and arteries into the spinal column; wasting no time, becoming stronger as she flowed. Up the neck and towards the brain, she flowed, but then stopped. Trevlor sat in her skull like a malignant tumour, hunkering down with sharp bards of energy twisted into the delicate flesh of her brain.

Nicola flooded upwards through her cerebral cortex with everything that made her her.

She knew this body, knew its strengths and its weaknesses. With brutal determination, she flicked against the damaged spirals of her inner ear, moved relentlessly to the pressure points in her neck and skull that triggered her migraines. Her body responded as she knew it would.

She was prepared: she'd had years of training on how to respond.

Trevlor had not.

As the first shoots of pain lanced through her skull, Trevlor instinctively pulled away. When dizzying loops of vertigo swept through their system to create false impressions of falling, Nicola braced and stayed centred in herself, all the time pressing forward.

When spasms ran through their consciousness, she surged into the gaps, slowly detaching each and every hook. Trevlor was only a shard of a person, and this was her body. The fight was over before it had even begun. The deafening rush of pages turning beat against the inside of her skull... then her mind was clear.

Nicola stretched out her arms, arched her back until she heard a couple of satisfying pops. She wiggled her toes, enjoying the comforting restriction of flesh.

The book was still glowing with intense light. Trevlor's fragment did not want to return to the pages, but he was nothing compared with the compulsion of the tome. His shard had always been unstable, but his time outside the protection of the pages had driven his fragment mad.

The book was not cruel.

Balance had been restored. The book would ensure the fragment's placement deep within its core, where it could be soothed by the oldest of memories.

The tome drew its power back within itself and the cover snapped shut. Coils of energy wrapped around the spine and the emblem flared with light once more. The book glowed with soft light, but that too faded until it looked merely old and well used.

* * *

Now, at one with her body again, Nicola felt a certain detachment, she'd lost the ability to run through her own nerves so she was left with a severe bout of dizziness and a headache that could kill a horse.

Nicola threw her arms wide and drew her children towards her. Her body felt weak, but having her daughter's head buried against her shoulder and her son's chin resting on top of her head made up for any of the discomfort she was experiencing. Breathing in the smell of their hair, she counted each of her blessings.

Nicola waved her hands, drawing first Joseph, then Ashul into the group hug. The five of them stood there, taking a moment in time together, that moment only broken when her stomach rumbled. No-one moved until the grumbling came again, more insistent this time.

Michael was the first to laugh and, surprisingly, Ashul the second.

Nicola spoke through her laughter. 'What the hell has Trevlor been feeding me?'

'Not much by the sounds of it, Lady Nicola,' said Ashul.

'Ashul, did you just make a joke?' Nicola said, pushing him away so she could look him in the eyes. 'What on earth has been going on in my absence?

'Well, quite a lot actually!' Joseph's tone held no humour.

'I saw some of it from within the book,' said Nicola. She didn't know what else to say. She just wanted to enjoy the moment and not be thrust back into the drama of things so soon. 'Seriously, I'm starving and my head is killing me. Fill me in while I get a cold pack and some food. Michael how are you? It looked like quite the battle from the little I was able to see. But you are obviously still in one piece so...' Nicola didn't get a chance to finish as Joseph wrapped his arms around her.

'Let's get you that cold pack and we can fill you in on the details,' Joseph said. 'We're just so happy to have you back safe. Give us a moment to enjoy that.'

Nicola picked up on the tension in his voice but fully understood the need to just chill for a moment. The kids looked exhausted. She couldn't imagine the strain they must have been under not knowing if she were dead or alive.

'Well, If I don't eat soon, I'm going to pass out,' Nicola said as she walked towards the kitchen, more in an effort to ease some of the tension. 'You're all aware that we have water sprites, gargoyles and a couple of pixies floating around the house? Can someone call on the faeries to enhance my wardings – they've been breached.'

* * *

Dana made Nicola a sandwich while Michael grabbed her a Coke. She busily filled Nicola in on all that had been going on during her mother's time in the book. After hearing that Michael might have been infected by the Nachzehrer, Nicola jumped up to check his temperature and run her hands under his neck to see if his glands were swollen.

'Michael, how do you feel?'

'It's been a rough couple of days, Mum,' said Michael. 'So, no, I'm not the best. But do I *feel* like I'm about to turn into a zombie? Can't say that I do.'

Before he could say more, the front door burst open and Sarah rushed to Nicola's side, wrapping her arms around her sister protectively.

'Sweetie, you look awful.'

'I'd like to disagree with her,' said Brent and he shrugged his shoulders, 'but… can't. Here, I thought you both might need this.' Brent handed them each a water bottle filled with a faint pink mixture. 'It's a multipurpose pick-me-up. But before we get into anything too deeply: your street seems to be riddled with police and paramedics. They look to be doing a door-knock.'

Michael's heart literally skipped a beat. He'd watched his fair share of contagion movies. First thing, the Centre for Disease Control showed up, knocking on doors, quarantining the area. Next, any person who might have been exposed to the virus would be taken away. No question asked.

'But it's… only five o'clock in the morning.' Joseph looked at his watch to confirm.

'Uncle Brent, are you sure they're paramedics? Are they wearing breathing apparatus?' Michael ran to the front of the house and was peering through the front window.

'Michael, get back here!' his uncle yelled after him. 'They're not here for you.'

Michael could hear him talking about Mr Sanderson as he walked back into the kitchen.

'I think it must have something to do with yesterday. Remember when I ran out the front because it sounded like a car had crashed in the street.' Brent waited for someone to respond. 'When I hit you in the head?' Joseph touched his forehead, indicating he'd completely forgotten the bump.

'Anyway, there *was* a car accident,' Brent continued. 'Mr Sanderson? Used to drive the Blue Falcon?'

'Yep, that's him,' Joseph confirmed.

'I checked the news last night,' said Brent. 'Looks like he crashed his car yesterday. They think he had a massive stroke while he was driving. I'm sorry, but he didn't survive.'

'But he was my age,' said Joseph. 'Healthy guy, played golf every week.' Joseph shook his head and walked to the fridge to get himself a glass of water.

'I know, I'm sorry. He seemed like a nice guy. But Joe, there must be more too it. You don't send out the police to do a door-knock when someone suffers a stroke.'

'I think you will have your answers shortly,' said Ashul. 'There are some men at your door.'

Ashul faded back into the world between worlds once he'd delivered this message. While he might have disappeared from view, Michael knew he was still watching and listening.

The doorbell rang and everyone without exception jumped.

* * *

Rather than police or paramedics, two large men were at the door. Identification showed them to be from the metropolitan fire brigade. Dana, who had a knack for faces, recognised them both as being part of the team that attended the fire in the street less than a week ago.

'Sorry to disturb you all so early in the morning,' the larger of the two men said. 'But events have transpired that requires that we speak with you and your wife, if we may.'

'It's not really a good time,' said Joseph. 'My wife has been unwell. We'll have to do this another time.' Joseph moved to close the door on them.

'Sir, I'm sorry to hear of your wife's illness, but this street has been getting a lot of attention lately and I've uncharacteristically failed to lodge my reports from last week. I was hoping you could answer some questions.'

He was obviously in a sticky situation. Dana respected the guy for not including the words 'before I turn this over to the police'. He'd come in plain clothes and was trying to appear as casual as possible under the circumstances.

Dana noticed that he'd looked over his shoulder twice since he'd started speaking.

Nicola yelled out from the kitchen to let them in.

* * *

Michael breathed a sigh of relief. At least the CDC wasn't here for him. Yet. He helped his mum get up so she could greet the visitors. As their guests walked into the kitchen, their eyes swept the room, taking in the large amount of people present. Michael wondered how suspicious they must look. It was five o'clock in the morning, and there were seven people in their kitchen.

'Let me introduce myself,' the larger man said. 'I'm Captain David Munro, and this is Lieutenant Tony Rodriguez. We attended the fire in your street last week. I'm glad to see you on your feet – I'm surprised they didn't take you to hospital.'

'I'm tougher than I look,' said Nicola noncommittally.

After a brief round of introductions, Nicola continued, 'We appreciate your help the other day. I think we all owe you a debt of gratitude. Can I offer you a drink?'

'With respect, I don't think we have time for a drink,' said David. 'The police will be at your door within the next twenty minutes. But I also believe that it is *we* who are in *your* debt. We owe you our lives. We need to understand what happened. I have a report to complete, and I think as crazy as it sounds, that you may know more about what happened that day than any of us.'

'I took a bit of a knock to my head the other day,' said Nicola. 'My memories are a tad foggy. What exactly is it you need my help on?' Nicola seemed to be trying to find out exactly what they knew or what they thought they knew.

'Okay, so I'll put my credibility on the line here. I've been a firefighter for the last twenty years, Tony here for almost fifteen. And believe me, we've seen fire act in ways that defy belief but… nothing like what happened last week. We need to understand how you were able to hold a fifteen-tonne engine at full capacity suspended above your head. And if that explanation also includes details of how your husband seemed to absorb the flames... well, that would be greatly appreciated.'

Before Nicola had time to speak, David raised his hand to stop her. 'And Nicola... can I call you Nicola? You didn't just receive a knock to your head, you were clinically dead for at least five minutes. It was Tony who resuscitated you. So, you may not believe that you owe me the truth, but you do owe it to him.'

Michael had never seen his mother get so completely destroyed in an argument in such a short period of time. He had to suppress a chuckle. Dana's eyes were as wide as saucers.

Knowing he had the upper hand, David continued, with a slight smile curling up the corner of his mouth. 'I saw a car explode in a fashion that only happens in the most over-the-top action film. This same car then exploded a second time in dazzling blue flame, I might add. A colour of which I have never witnessed even during the most extreme chemical fire. The resulting concussion couldn't have been generated from a ruptured fuel tank. And it certainly couldn't blow a fully loaded fire engine over as if it were made of papier mâché.' David paused to take a breath. No-one in the room looked game enough to interrupt him.

'A female person, namely yourself, appeared beside me out of what I can only call thin air. Somehow, we survived what should have been the crushing fall of the aforementioned engine by relocating underground. Oh, and did I forget to include that during this completely impossible series of explosions, we were all protected from the heat and flames by nothing more than your husband's upraised hands. Have I missed anything?'

Michael stood in stunned silence. None of his family had any idea what to say. They were all looking around at each other, trying to gauge how they were going to play this. They'd been dealing with this craziness in a completely isolated environment. To have someone outside their family discussing things in such an open way was the opposite of liberating. Spoken aloud, it all sounded rather insane and the truth of their situation felt like a crushing weight that he would have preferred they could have just kept to themselves.

Michael was about to protest the captain's claims when Tony jumped in. 'Captain, if I may?' Tony spoke in a calm manner that had Michael thinking of hostage negotiators, or psychologists wanting to keep a lid on the situation. 'You missed that Sarah cast a net of some material that looked like nothing more that light. This net was then able to contain the cloud of smoke. Said cloud had also defied the laws of nature by travelling against the wind.' David raised his eyebrows at Tony. 'This must have been out of your line of sight, sir, or I assure you, you couldn't have missed it.'

They were both openly smiling now. 'We don't want to intrude, we really don't, but Tony and I are the only two who saw these things. Everyone else seems to have witnessed nothing more than a gas explosion. We were both willing to write it off as some kind of joint hysteria, but there have been calls to this area all night. Completely unrelated events. Car accidents, strokes, heart attacks. Two people have fallen into comas overnight, and a woman beat her husband with a meat tenderiser when she was preparing dinner. He's in a critical condition.'

'Before I go any further,' Nicola raised her hands. 'I promise you I will tell you the truth, but I need to know, did you hear anything in your heads just before the explosions hit?'

Neither of them had mentioned this, and Michael was interested in their response. They all held their breaths. You could have heard a pin drop.

Captain David turned to Tony, seemingly seeking approval to continue.

Tony was the one who answered, 'Yes, ma'am, we both did,' he said. 'I thought it was just my imagination at the time but yes, I heard a voice. More like a chuckle, really. Even the recollection makes my skin crawl. And now that we're well and truly in the Twilight Zone, I also experienced a blast of cold air that travelled from the south-west, coinciding with the voice in my head. If you could explain these things to me, I would be forever grateful.'

'Please, take a seat,' said Nicola. 'This is going to take a while.' She gestured to offer them both a place on the couch.

'Under the circumstances,' David said as he pulled up a chair at the bench, 'I think you should call me Dave.'

* * *

Anarcus looked down at the creatures cowering before It, loathing the fact that It needed these lesser beings even if only for a short period of time. There was too much happening with the damned blood, and It did not have eyes or ears in the house to monitor exactly what they were up too. It had only realised the mother's body was being occupied by another when she showed some of her true potential by draining energy from the bonded like a greedy piglet suckling at the teat.

And would she have been able to destroy the bonded, suck them dry? Using the boy as the conduit, It believed she would have been able to do exactly that. It admired her resourcefulness allowing another being to possess her body to gain access to additional power.

Her own son readily forfeited. Maybe her potential could be used, turned even? With her aid, It could acquire the power of the bonded without the risk of battle. But It needed to know exactly who or what was running the show. The stakes were just too high to start making unnecessary assumptions. It needed the facts.

It knew the wardings on the house were useless.

A handful of eel swarms sent in corporal and incorporeal states had slowly eroded these primitive defences. This current crop of the blood was too reliant on symbols and chalk drawings to ward themselves from attack. A smudge here, the incinerated remains of an eel there, anything to mar a line and the wardings were void, nothing more than useless, half-forgotten decorations. The eels hadn't liked being used as fodder but what had they truly expected; they were barely a step above worms. If they continued their incessant whispering into Its mind, it would feed them to the Bezenhart.

It could block out their murderous thoughts any time It chose, but it allowed their presence to remain for a time because they were its best source of information. At the first sign of manipulation or misdirection, they would be consumed. Strength might lie in numbers, but strength also came from food. There was life force flowing through all living creatures. It would make use of Its allies either way.

It was pleased with the number of creatures drawn to Its cause. Each greedy for power, each wanting access to the rift. Scaled creatures with writhing tentacles and beaked mouths. Other creatures that lacked form, dark nebulous ribbons of constantly reforming matter. But not all of Its allies looked like they had swarmed out of some nightmare. One of the most powerful was a golden being, a creature of such radiant beauty that it caused despair in all those who looked upon it.

All of these creatures craved the source, hungered for power.

But the sneering face of the Nachzehrer loomed above them all.

It possessed a mocking confidence that Anarcus could not allow. Would not allow.

It had warned the creature not to lay its shadow upon the boy. Anarcus had only wanted to test how much the boy had weakened the bonded. Its instructions had been very clear. And although the boy had shown no signs of infection, the arrogant assurance exuding from the animated corpse standing before it contradicted all assumptions of health.

Without hesitation, the doll drew on Its network, reaching out to the humans now acting as Its fuel. Umbilicals that had been painstakingly constructed when manipulating their dreams allowed It to feed at will.

It felt some of the weaker humans falter, their bodies buckling, their hearts struggling to pump as arteries swelled and veins burst. Still, It called forth more energy, growing in size until Its eyes looked directly into those of the Nachzehrer. It drew Its arm backwards and in a move similar to that of the girl next door, Anarcus backhanded the Nachzehrer king, relishing the feel of flesh splitting under the force of Its blow.

The Nachzehrer's head rolled towards Anarcus' feet, the smirking visage now nothing more than a forgotten expression, dissolving under the effect of hastened decomposition.

Black ichor dripped from the barbed claw that It retracted back into the bones of Its wrist. It savoured the sweet corruption as Nachzehrer blood mixed with Its own.

It heard the Nachzehrer's words in Its own mind, defiant even in death.

'He is more than you know. You have destroyed nothing – the boy is ours.'

The link to the hive mind of the Nachzehrer faded as the small trickle of blood in Its veins turned to ash. It vented Its rage on the body that lay before it, rending and tearing at flesh already soft from decomposition, cursing when these remains finally dissolved into a pile of dust.

Another Nachzehrer stepped forward. Dust from the previous Nachzehrer circled around its feet. Anarcus watched as the face melted and warped until its features settled into the sneer of their king.

Confidence shone from the weeping white eyes.

Anarcus vowed that It would rip that confidence from the hive even if it had to forfeit the opportunity to access the boy's powers. It would kill the boy rather than give the Nachzehrer that kind of control over him.

There were other bonded that It could use. There were others of the blood. Ashul was ultimately the nexus around which all things spun. The boy had just been the easiest route to Ashul, but It had a feeling that all was not lost.

Not yet.

Connections

Dave and Tony had connections amongst the police and the ambulance services. They were both walking around the kitchen on their phones, trying to get information about any other incidents that had occurred in the neighbourhood recently. A couple of phone calls later, they had all the details they needed. Incidents of assault, verbal confrontation, domestic violence, vandalism were all being investigated by the police at a much higher rate than usual. The paramedics were just as heavily affected: strokes, heart attacks, burst aneurysms, as well as the fallout from the increased level of violent crime. Interestingly, there was an alarming number of reports of people falling into comas overnight.

'We seem to be running on two different timelines,' said Michael. 'The violence has been building over the last couple of weeks, whereas the medical-related incidences spiked at around five pm last night. Dad, when did the bonded and I get back last night?'

'At about five-thirty.'

'So five pm would be about the time of the fight with the Nachzehrer.'

Michael mentally called for Ashul to join them.

Even though Dave and Tony had been told about the bonded, they both jumped back a step when Ashul appeared at Michael's side. 'This make any sense to you?'

'More sense than the Bezenhart and Nachzehrer,' said Ashul. He nodded to both firefighters, but he didn't waste time with an introduction. 'This is the way Anarcus usually works. It plagues the dreams of all those within its reach: planting thoughts, amplifying grievances, desires, hatred. It works from the shadows, playing with the minds of those who do not have the will to oppose it. Thoughts that under normal circumstances would be kept hidden in the dark recesses of one's mind become all the dreamer can think about. Impulse control is lost.' Ashul paused to look around the room.

When he continued, Ashul's face was grave. 'But I fear it has gone further than this already. Michael, remember the injuries we sustained when Trevlor drew too heavily on our energy reserves. We survived because of our training, because we have access to stores of energy that others do not, and because we were being fed energy through Dana's link to the guardian. Anarcus may have connected himself to his dreamers and was drawing on them during the confrontation with Trevlor. It could destroy a mind if restraint was not used during the drawing. The bodies would most likely show signs of sudden onset dehydration, maybe other symptoms.'

The room was silent when Ashul finished. Dave and Tony were already on their phones texting.

Tony was the one to break the silence, indicating that they had to go. 'We're being asked to work double shifts. We'll speak to the guys on the street, keep them off your back. They'll just be looking for witnesses and information anyway. Keep us in the loop, let us know what we can do to help these people.'

* * *

When Azuradien arrived, his demeanour had changed. He was overjoyed at Michael's condition. 'We feared for you. You have no fever, no burns, no difficulty in breathing? Do you have any symptoms at all?'

'Slight blurring of my vision that comes and goes, but my eyes are really dry. Maybe some muscle soreness.' Michael's response was cool. 'So does that mean you're going to let me live?'

'Michael, that's enough,' Nicola said as she returned with Sarah after taking a quick walk around the house. 'The wardings have definitely been broken. I couldn't find a noticeable breach, but there were many places where the protection has eroded completely. Azuradien, you should have reinforced them in my absence.'

Azuradien was lost for words. His wings, usually hidden when he was in the human realm, beat furiously against his back. 'Lady Nicola?' He was bobbing up and down, his feet centimetres above the floor.

'Ashul, did you not tell him I was back?' asked Nicola, eyebrow raised.

'It may have slipped my mind,' Ashul replied. His face was as stoic as ever. Michael knew that was as close to a rebuke to the faerie king as Ashul was ever going to get.

'How?' Azuradien's feet were back on the ground but his wings continued to flutter at his back. 'Where have you been?'

'I was in the book. With some quick-thinking trickery from my daughter and some theatrical misdirection from my husband, I was able to get out.' Nicola opened the freezer to swap out her cold pack. Holding the fresh pack against the back of her neck, she drew in a deep breath and released it slowly.

'And Trevlor?'

'Yes, thank you,' said Nicola. 'I'm fine.' Nicola had answered the question Azuradien had been too thoughtless to ask.

She looked up at Azuradien, a frown creasing her forehead, angered by his disregard but not enough to ignore his question out of hand. 'Trevlor is safely back in the confines of the book, deep within the pages. The book was quite piqued by his escape. A fragment will never be allowed to escape again. That I can guarantee.'

The room stayed quiet. Nicola was the first to show her impatience, huffing before she prompted Azuradien. 'Azuradien, the wardings?'

Before Azuradien had a chance to get into a lengthy discussion about wardings and energy flows, Michael interrupted. 'You guys can fix the wardings while we're gone. Dana, Ashley and I are going out for a walk with Sheba.' Michael realised he was speaking quickly but he just didn't want to sit around while Azuradien and Nicola got into an argument about wardings that had already failed. 'We're worried about our friends. Dana can check in on the neighbourhood pets and Ashley can do what Ashley does.' Michael didn't really know how else to describe Ashley's powers, so he quickly moved on. 'After that, we'll go off to school if nobody has any objections.'

Dana already had Sheba's leash in her hand.

'Azuradien, I will have to trust your judgement on this,' said Nicola. 'My head's still a little scrambled.' Nicola had dropped into the nearest chair, obviously exhausted by the short walk around the house.

'He is showing no signs of infection,' said Azuradien, 'but I would still err on the side of caution and keep him in the confines of the house.' Azuradien's shoulders straightened and his wings had finally disappeared. 'There is nothing to be lost in being cautious.'

* * *

Lorcan was resting inside the roof. He'd made himself comfortable in amongst the Christmas and Halloween decorations stored in this space and was slightly offended by the misrepresentation of the ghouls, witches and vampires amongst the collection. He casually knocked the head off a red-eyed beast and used the stuffed torso as a pillow to rest upon. The conversation below was monotonous, the participants droning on about irrelevancies.

When the faerie king arrived, Lorcan sat up on one elbow; he was amused by the king's fawning tone. The tension between Azuradien and the humans was escalating because of his blatant disregard for the woman's wellbeing, highlighting their differing objectives. The humans were a simple lot: they hid behind small courtesies, but in reality were fiercely protective of each other.

The faeries had been isolated for too long, they no longer knew how to communicate with the humans effectively. Although, he begrudgingly had to admit he agreed with Azuradien: the boy should remain contained.

Just as he thought the parents would agree, Azuradien had to open his mouth again. *'There is nothing to be lost in being cautious.'*

Lorcan hissed his disapproval.

Fool! Humans are being consumed. That would mean everything to them.

Echoing his thoughts, the mother reacted exactly as predicted. 'There is much to be lost, Azuradien. People are dying.'

So the boy would be leaving the house. Lorcan did not think he'd completely removed the infection but he had no way to ascertain whether he was infectious. The sister had been in the boy's presence half the night and she showed no signs of illness.

He gazed at the beams of sunlight peeking through the cracks in the roof, sighed and stood up. Dusting off the few cobwebs clinging to his jacket, he pulled sunglasses out of his pocket and covered his eyes. He could walk in the light but it pained him, so he usually avoided the irritation. But the day was going to be mild with light cloud cover, so he counted his blessings and stepped out into the biting kiss of the sun.

* * *

Ashul met Michael outside and took him aside. 'Any sign of illness and you remove yourself to the second realm. The bonded and I will track your movements. Communicate your findings and we will see if there are any signs of the doll's tampering detectable from the second realm.' Ashul grabbed Michael by the shoulders and slapped his upper arm in farewell. 'Be safe.' He then nodded to Ashley and Dana and faded until he was no longer visible.

'Way to make an exit,' Michael said through the mental link. A couple of the bonded laughed in response. Their leader's ways often amused them.

'Come on, girls. Quit your drooling,' said Michael. 'Any ideas where we head first?'

'I think we should follow the flashing lights,' Ashley suggested as they moved past the temporary barricades that had been set up around the hole in the road outside the Sanderson's house.

Emergency lights could be seen in a driveway three doors down. Police were restricting traffic to local vehicles only. They walked farther up the street and politely nodded to the police as they went, before they saw another ambulance parked in another driveway. The lights on the ambulance were off and the house looked quiet. Usually that would be a good sign, but today Michael wasn't so sure. They crossed to the other side of the street, avoiding the dark house.

The morning was unusually free of traffic, human, vehicle or otherwise.

There was nobody out walking their dogs, which in itself was unusual. This was a neighbourhood where three out of every four homes owned a pet, making it almost impossible to walk your dog without bumping into another pet owner. They passed an old lady that they'd spoken to in the past. She was always out in her garden come rain or shine – pruning, raking or watering.

She stood in her garden with a broom held absently in her hands. Michael moved in her direction, preparing to stop and ask if she knew what was going on down the street. She looked down, avoiding his eyes, and started sweeping. She brushed at the ground with savage, sharp movements, cursing under her breath.

Michael couldn't be sure, but he was fairly certain he heard language coming from the old lady's mouth that he wouldn't be comfortable saying himself.

Ashley grabbed his elbow and pulled him away from her. 'Don't go near her, Micky. She's rancid.' Michael looked first at Ashley, then back at the old woman. She held her broom in her hands, peering up at him through a veil of lank white hair. Small chunks of what appeared to be breakfast cereal were stuck to the front of her jumper. Her hands twisted at the broom handle. Arthritic knuckles whitened from the strain. Her lips were in constant motion as she spat out guttural words interspersed with the foulest of language.

'She hates you, Michael,' Ashley said quietly, but the old lady heard nonetheless. The elderly lady's lips pulled back and she snapped in their direction. Wet smacking sounds accompanied the snapping of her toothless gums as she attempted to grind teeth she'd forgotten to put in.

When they moved away, she smiled sweetly and continued to sweep the garden bed, brooming dirt and pine mulch out onto the sidewalk.

* * *

'Okay, that is just a little too freaky.' Dana had been a little farther down the street when the women literally snapped at Michael. Sheba had pulled her away as soon as she caught wind of her. Ashley had been right: the woman was rancid – both in mind and body. Sheba could smell curdled milk as well as human waste. The woman had been neglecting her own personal hygiene for at least a couple of days.

'Can we walk down to Mr Stevens' house? I want to check on Madison. This is all getting a little too real.' Dana was anxious. She was trying to remember when she'd last seen Madison. It had been a couple of days ago, she was certain.

When they got to Mr Stevens' place, everything looked fine and well-tended: no stray leaves in the garden to broom, no junk mail in the letterbox. Madison wasn't in the back garden but that was alright – she often slept inside. She liked to sleep under Mr Stevens' bed when she was allowed to, which was almost always.

Dana sent out a mental call, but she received no reply from Madison. Sheba barked sharply twice at her side and they both stood quietly waiting for the Rottweiler to respond. After a few tense minutes, Dana made the decision to go inside and check on them both. She felt exposed standing in the street. The old lady had scared her, further straining nerves already twisted tight.

No matter which way she turned, Dana got the impression there were eyes boring into her back. She nervously shifted her weight from foot to foot. She reached down to retrieve the key, feeling like something was about to jump out and grab at her hand, moving quickly, anxious to get inside where they would be less visible.

'Guys, I've got the spare key. I'm just going to open the front door and give a yell. Mr Stevens' won't mind. We're just checking in on him after all. What with everything that's been going on, he'll appreciate it.' Dana had already turned over the rock in the flowerpot next to the front door and was peeling off the sticky tape that held the key in place.

'Just hurry up, Dana. That old lady has given me the willies.' Ashley kept looking back over her shoulder.

Dana was the first to step over the threshold, noting that nothing looked out of place in the house. They walked through to the kitchen; a cup and saucer lay drying on the draining board. Everything looked clean and tidy. Yet Sheba's tail was curled protectively down between her legs. Her head dropped and she let out a low whimper.

It was only at that point that Dana heard Madison. A soft whine was coming from the back lounge room. The three of them walked down the hall, the faint sound of the TV playing almost drowning out Madison's distress. The man in the infomercial was selling a vacuum cleaner that *you had to see to believe*, all perfectly normal if you ignored the soft whine of the dog sitting protectively at her master's side.

* * *

Mr Stevens was sitting in a leather chair with his back to them. As they moved closer, they could see his hand resting absently on Madison's large square head. Madison's eyes rolled in Dana's direction but her tail lay quivering at her side. Michael stretched out his arm, keeping the girls behind him and stepped cautiously around the chair.

From the angle of the body, it was clear Mr Stevens was either asleep or unconscious. Michael refused to contemplate the third alternative. He tapped the remote and turned the TV off and peered around past the high leather back. Mr Stevens was slumped with his head resting on the wing back side of the chair – his body had slid down so that his legs were sprawled out in front of him. His left leg curled under the bottom of the chair at an awkward angle. His right leg was stretched out in front of him, slipper kicked clear and sitting over a foot away. He was wearing a pair of Spider-man socks.

'Is he dead?' Dana asked from behind Michael.

'You getting anything, Ashley?' said Michael. 'Is he playing possum?' Michael wanted to be certain of what he was dealing with before he got within *snapping* range.

'I can't read anything from him, but I wouldn't be able to if he were sleeping. I can only tell you he's not conscious.'

'Is he dead?' asked Michael.

'How the hell am I supposed to know that?' Ashley snapped back.

Michael reached forward to turn on the side light, keeping as much distance between himself and Mr Stevens as possible. When the light snapped on, Michael's vision suddenly blurred. Mr Stevens' face swam in front of him. There was something covering his face, like a plastic bag, drawn tight under his top jaw.

'Aw no.' Michael dropped his head. He'd liked Mr Stevens. It shouldn't have come to this.

Dana pushed past him and placed a calming hand on Madison's shoulder and with her other hand she lifted Mr Stevens' left wrist as she felt for a pulse.

'He's alive,' said Dana. 'Mr Stevens, can you hear me? It's Dana.'

'He's alive?' Michael reached down to remove the bag. 'Get that shit off his face, he'll suffocate.' He tried to hook his fingers under the edges of the plastic, but he couldn't find the edge at all. Running his hands over the old man's face and hair, Michael searched for a loose piece of plastic that he could grip. *It was so thin; how could it be so thin?*

'Michael, what are you doing? Just calm down for a second, there's nothing on him.' Dana placed her hand on Michael's arm, gently grabbing each hand and removing them from Mr Stevens' head.

Michael blinked a couple of times and his vision cleared. Dana was right. There was no plastic covering Mr Stevens' face – he could see the old man's lips moving slightly as he exhaled.

'Michael, are you okay?' Dana was looking up at him, concern written across her features.

'My vision blurred a bit and I thought I saw a bag on his head. I thought he'd committed suicide. Can we get out of here? We can call the police from outside, geez, we could even just walk down the street and let them know.' Michael ran his fingers back through his hair then clasped the back of his head.

'I thought I'd just seen my first dead body. Not a dead creature, but a dead friend. I need some air.'

As Michael paced, Ashul's voice broke into his mind, speaking through the link. *Michael, get the girls out of the house. There has been a shift around you I do not understand. Get the girls out.*

Nobody argued when Michael suggested they leave. Without a word said Dana changed direction and ran back towards the kitchen to refill Madison's food bowl. She was placing the water bowl she'd topped up down on the kitchen floor when the door slammed shut behind her.

'Dana, go out through the kitchen. Do you hear me? Get out of the house now!' Michael yelled towards the closed door, as he marshalled Ashley back down the hallway.

* * *

Lorcan had the ability to make himself dim. Not invisible. Few creatures could achieve true invisibility, but he could bend light to the extent that even if someone looked in his direction they would be unable to detect his presence. They might perceive a small distortion, but most people brushed this off as fatigue or something as innocuous as a heat shimmer.

Lorcan had been using this ability to track the boy, shifting from shadow to shadow, keeping out of the dog's scenting range. When he moved past the fetid old woman, he momentarily lost his composure. Her stench was ripe, but it was her madness that made the hairs on the back of his neck prickle.

She was unpredictable. Lorcan had survived for centuries due to his ability to predict outcomes. He loathed insanity more than any other condition. Marking her presence, Lorcan refracted the light around him so he once again became nothing more than a shimmer.

The woman bore some grudge: Lorcan understood that her hatred had been twisted and, in all likelihood, had nothing to do with the boy in particular, but now that she had a focus for her fixation, the boy would need to be watchful. Lorcan would not let her interfere with his plans for the boy. The world would be a cleaner place without the contamination of her insanity.

Following the children inside the home of the old man and his dog required a little more skill and an element of risk that he was not prepared to take at this delicate juncture. A simple bending of the light would not be enough to hide his presence. If the dog didn't pick up his scent, one of the two girls – each with their own unique abilities – would detect something.

Moving ahead, he searched the house and found only two occupants. An old man who appeared to be in something of an enforced sleep, and his dog. Lorcan found no evidence of medication or alcohol. Without tasting the man's blood, he couldn't be sure. But he was willing to bet that nothing stronger than aspirin was flowing through his veins.

Lorcan placed a reassuring hand on the neck of the dog sitting at his owner's side and sent a small measure of his charm through the link. The animal's trembling subsided and her quiet whines of distress softened to a whimper. She lifted her snout and licked at the inside of Lorcan's wrist. He allowed the animal the small comfort – it was a fine, loyal companion. He would ensure she was kept from harm. The whine dropped to a small growl when Lorcan's eyes flared

red, his fangs lowering as he scented the air with his full arsenal of senses.

Like the bonded, Lorcan walked in both worlds – the first and second planes – but Lorcan was able to view them simultaneously if he chose. A pulsing membrane covered the man's face: a thin layer of transparent film wrapped around his features like a second skin, terminating under the top lip. Lorcan leant forward and placed his index finger on the man's chin, easing his mouth open. The thin film ran over the man's palette and down his throat. Lorcan closed the mouth with the tip of his nail.

As he continued this examination, his apprehension grew. This change in mood was tangible in more than just a tensing of his shoulders. With each notch of tension, Lorcan became more supernatural creature, and less human. He lost the carefully manicured fingernails and the long supple fingers of a pianist. His hands became strong and muscular, tipped with claws designed for the careful, precise separation of muscle from sinew.

Lorcan was an apex predator that sensed the presence of another hunter nearby. He turned the man's head left, then right. The thin membrane ran into the man's ears and under his hairline. If he were to cut the flesh away, Lorcan was certain the membrane would penetrate the skull.

'Just hurry up, Dana. That old lady has given me the willies.'

The time for examination was over. This man posed no threat, and the children were moments away. Lorcan moved quickly. The human eye would see only a blur. The dog tracked his movement and looked through the window where Lorcan now stood. One second standing over the man, the next outside, and his presence again dimmed to nothing more than a shimmer. He lifted his finger to his lips and when the girl walked into the room, the dog's eyes rolled in her direction. She whimpered her plea for aid, and the girl dropped to her knees to comfort the animal.

The animal would not betray Lorcan: it had eyes only for the girl. And until the boy interrupted his thoughts, Lorcan shared the same singular focus.

'Get that shit off his face, he'll suffocate.'

It was impossible. There was no way that the boy could see the membrane wrapped over the man's head, yet his words and actions suggested otherwise. Lorcan stepped once again into the other world. The boy looked as he normally did: the taint of the bonded affected his aura but his eyes glowed with a faint white light that was not part of the bonded's strength. Lorcan perceived danger, a threat that the boy did not pose, not yet. The Nachzehrer did not yet have control. But it was evident from the milky glow of the boy's eyes that the Nachzehrer had its hooks deeper in the boy than Lorcan had realised.

Standing behind the boy, almost impossible to perceive, was the shrouded outline of a walking corpse. Its lopsided smile slid across its face as it tilted its head from side to side. It was watching the boy's movements and seeing through the boy's eyes.

When the boy blinked, the glow in his eyes faded, but Lorcan saw the Nachzehrer turn its head just before it blinked from sight – it had seen the girl.

Lorcan could destroy a Nachzehrer, could almost feel the corrupted flesh dissolving under his claws as he imagined doing so. But in doing this he would expose himself, and the time was not yet right for that commitment. Lorcan would not have a piece of walking pestilence force his hand in this way.

Somehow recognising the threat, the boy ushered the girls towards the front of the house. Lorcan eased his grip; his claws had ripped into the wood under his hands. When the sister changed direction, running back towards the open doorway, the boy's eyes again flashed white. The image of the corpse blinked back into existence, following the girl as she ran from the room.

Lorcan moved with such speed that his feet dug holes in the ground as he ran. Clods of soil flew upwards, and the plant he'd been standing next to snapped like a twig as it was sucked into the slipstream he created. The kitchen door slammed shut when he flew past. The girl's hair blew into her face, and by the time she reached up to push it back behind her ears, Lorcan was gone.

Dark Net

Michael wasn't taking any chances. He was furious with Dana; she always went off and did her own thing.

Michael had been given no idea as to what kind of danger they were in. A 'shift around them' could have meant anything. So, he made an executive decision and asked Ashul to get Dana to safety. Ashul wasn't impressed to hear that they had gotten separated. Even through the mindlink, Michael could feel his annoyance. But with there being no-one in the house to question Ashul's sudden appearance, Ashul wasn't taking any chances. It was Dana's safety they were talking about here.

Less than thirty seconds later, he heard through the link that Ashul had her and they would meet back at home.

'*And how did that go?*' Michael asked through the link.

'*Surprisingly well,*' was Ashul's unexpected response.

Ashley and Michael had come running through the door, just moments before Ashul materialised with his arm around Dana's waist.

'Is everyone okay?' asked Sarah. 'The net went crazy about five minutes ago. Did you come into contact with the doll in any way?'

'No, the crazy garden lady almost attacked us. Then we went to check on Mr Stevens, which didn't go so well. He's in a coma.' There were gasps from both Sarah and Nicola. Everybody loved Mr Stevens, but no-one seemed surprised, they had all known things were escalating.

'Ashul warned us that there was unusual activity, a shift around us of some kind that happened just after we found Mr Stevens, so we got out fast.' Michael's brief rundown of events didn't seem to have eased any minds. Everyone looked both shocked and puzzled.

'What has your net detected, Lady Sarah?'

'Can we quit with the "Lady Sarah", Ashul? I think we're a bit beyond that.'

When Ashul nodded at her, Sarah continued, 'With Joe's help I've made some refinements to the net. We basically have the first plane with a radius out to about ten kilometres showing every person currently within that perimeter.' Michael still couldn't read the network in the same way that Sarah and his father could. Where Sarah saw various patterns that represented different people and their connections to one another, Michael saw only an intricate tapestry of interconnecting lines of energy too twisted together to make any sense of. So, he sat back and listened while Sarah gave them her rundown. 'The second plane, as you know, does not run with fixed dimensions, but what we do have is a way to track when the people on the first net cross over into the second plane.'

'Basically, once they go to sleep, they pop up on the second grid. We could track Dana when she left the first plane with Ashul and transitioned to the second. Only the bonded and the faerie seem to leave the first plane completely when they move over into the second.'

'You mean, they take their bodies with them, don't you? That's the difference, right?' Dana was looking intently at the grid, trying to understand all the connections.

'Yes, exactly,' said Sarah. 'The rest of us retain the link to our bodies in the first realm. This link is critical. Without it you wouldn't be able to find your way back. Both body and soul would eventually die. But when the bonded take you through to the second realm, you make the full transition. Which is exactly what we saw happen with Dana just now. Although... I believe the rest of us will soon have the same ability as the bonded.'

'Anyway, when you went to see Mr Stevens, the net went haywire. On the first network, Mr Stevens is virtually dormant. You see how his aura is static and faint?' Sarah reached forward and pointed to a splodge of unremarkable colour with no texture or flow. When Sarah moved closer to the network, the threads she indicated seemed to clarify, not brighten exactly, but they gained focus. Michael was able to recognise Mr Stevens, so he shifted a little closer. 'And this is Mr Stevens in the second plane.' To Michael, the points on the network representing the first and second planes looked identical, which probably made sense if he was truly asleep or in a coma. 'Yes, but this is not how he looked when you were in there with him. Joe, can you run it back for me?'

'You can do that now?' Dana asked. 'Run the network backwards?' She wasn't the only one impressed with how quickly their dad was learning to use his powers. Michael was grateful that he was adapting the knowledge into something useful. They needed all the advantages they could get.

'I can only replay the whole thing if I've been there to witness it, but individual strands I can replay at any time. Your current energy signature is directly made up of what you've absorbed and expended. All of this detail is held within your profile. And because all interaction causes a small level of energy transfer, those interactions are captured. Basically, your energy signature contains details of all of your experiences. Here, I'll give you an example. I'll use Dana. She's the amber signature standing next to the blue of Ashul. I'll leave it to your mother to correctly name all the different hues, because all the bonded just happen to be various shades of blue. Once you get the knack of it, you can actually see the person, not just the colours. I feel like I'm learning to decode *The Matrix*, but anyway...' Nobody laughed at Joseph's attempt at humour, so he moved on.

'Dana is here in the first plane, her amber signature shimmers with cobalt blue. That's coming from Michael. This is virtually always the case with these two – they're quite literally joined at the hip. Their interconnectivity is amazing. You can see Ashul has wrapped a few protective ice blue threads around her also. I'm betting he uses these to sense when she's in danger.'

'I have a duty to protect her,' said Ashul. 'I would know if she required aid.' Ashul looked slightly embarrassed at this.

'Okay, so let's play it backwards. See how she disappears from the first plane and appears in the second. In the second plane, her interaction with Ashul increases since he's the one enabling her to cross over. Let's go back further to when you were with Mr Stevens. You must have touched him, I'm guessing?'

'I was checking for his pulse,' answered Dana in a distracted manner. Her attention was completely absorbed by the network in front of her. Michael understood, the implications of what their dad and aunty had created was mind-blowing. They were literally looking into the past.

'Well, check out what happens in the second plane. Watch Mr Stevens.' In both planes, Mr Stevens was a fairly drab olive-green lump with a couple of silver ribbons running around and through his aura. When Dana touched his wrist, the olive-green erupted and thick ropes of energy reached out towards her.' Dana jumped back in response. Michael had to admit the whole scene had a disturbing quality to it. Joseph was pointing at the network like a lecturer explaining some fundamental truth; all he needed was a laser pointer. Michael was a little uncomfortable with how dispassionate he had become.

'It didn't exactly look predatory,' said Joseph. 'More… desperate. Basically, Mr Stevens knows he's drowning, and he saw Dana as a piece of driftwood.'

'What the hell is that?' Michael couldn't interpret the data the same way his father obviously could, but what he was seeing repulsed him nevertheless.

Before the olive-green feelers had been given a chance to grab onto the lifeline – which in this particular example was his sister – the silver consumed them.

'I know, it's horrifying,' Joseph said, finally allowing his own revulsion to show. 'Can you see how these silver ribbons pulsate and thicken, wrapping themselves around the olive-green host until the feelers wither and withdraw. I don't know if you guys can see this in the same way I do, but in a matter of seconds, Mr Stevens had been completely covered by a thin transparent membrane.'

All this was happening to a kindly old man in Spider-man socks, who just wanted to watch some TV with his best friend.

'Dana, Ashley, I told you I saw something. He had a bag or something wrapped over his head.' Michael turned to

Ashul to explain. 'When I tried to remove it, I couldn't see or feel anything.' Michael shrugged. 'The girls couldn't see it so I thought I must have imagined it.'

'Well, let's look at what happened when you touched Mr Stevens, Michael,' said Joseph. 'Everything goes haywire, see how the silver ball reacts.' The pulsating ball, throbbed once, twice, then threw out feelers of its own. It whipped around Mr Stevens in a kind of aggressive defence. 'I think it knows you wanted to remove it. It might be a good thing that you couldn't feel it.'

Not for Mr Stevens, Michael thought, but he kept that to himself.

'Watch the doll during the same time frame. Its activity goes from near zero to a hundred in both the first and the second plane.' Joseph looked at all of their faces 'Have a look at it the second Michael touches Mr Stevens' head.' Joseph held the image still, occasionally running it forward and back like super slow-mo. The doll's image in the second plane had a mass of what looked to be pulsing umbilical cords running up what Michael perceived as its head. They twisted and looped in a confusing knot of sliding, twisting coils.

'We've been able to track three of the umbilicals to the point of contact. One of them is Mr Stevens. The other two are also coma victims. It's feeding off people. We're sure. We have no way of knowing whether its activity around Michael was annoyance at losing another potential source of fuel or anger at Michael's attempt to remove the bag.'

'Forget that for a moment,' said Michael. 'Have you worked out why there are so many people in the second plane at nine o'clock on a Monday morning?' It didn't make sense to Michael. If people entered the second plane only when they were sleeping or in a deep mediative state, either he was suddenly surrounded by Zen masters or he'd missed something. 'I'm reading this right, aren't I? All of these different colours are different people?'

'We suspect the doll has various ways to feed off people,' said Joseph. He rubbed the stubble on his cheek as he spoke. 'We know it tried feeding off you in your dreams, Michael. And we know it feeds off of blood. The doll has little concern for the wellbeing of those it feeds upon, except maybe for the fact that you can't get energy from a dead battery.' Joseph paused for a moment; speaking about people dying was never easy. Taking in a deep breath, he continued. 'When extreme circumstances force its hand, like last night's little performance, it drains people to an extent that endangers their lives. We think the strokes and heart attacks are caused when the doll suddenly drains them of all energy. The weakest point in the host's body is the first thing to fail. If someone has a weak heart, they most likely won't survive the encounter. Healthy individuals will eventually have something blow in their brains, the strain on the body is just too great.' Michael didn't need that part explained to him. Trevlor had attempted to drain him of all of his energy and he'd felt his heart stutter in his chest – and he had the bonded's strength to draw on. Michael understood fully why Joseph was so sickened by what he'd discovered. *Something needed to be done. The doll couldn't be allowed to drain people like they were its personal Red Bull supply.*

'Ashul, is this the disturbance you warned me about?' asked Michael. 'The doll getting all territorial? Because, although it doesn't look great for Mr Stevens, I'm not sure that we were in that much danger.'

Ashul had been watching the network closely when Joseph replayed the moment the doll's activity increased. He measured his words before he spoke. 'I was not watching the network. I was monitoring the three of you as a precaution. There was a shift around you. The distinction between the first and second realms became muddied. I cannot explain it better than that. It happened for the briefest of moments. But I thought it best to get you all out of there.' Ashul didn't seem satisfied with his own words.

'The doll caused this shift?' Michael asked.

'It would appear so…' Ashul replied. Michael did not hear the certainty he was used to when speaking to Ashul.

Before Michael had a chance to put another question to Ashul, Dana jumped into the discussion. 'So tonight, we have to go into the second realm and track down every person connected via these umbilicals,' said Dana. They may or may not be joined at the hip – Michael couldn't comment on that, but there was no doubt that on the important issues they thought the same way. Dana was pacing as she spoke. Michael understood her reaction completely: what the doll was doing was abhorrent. And if it were somehow creating 'shifts', well, that had to be addressed.

'And we find a way to sever the link. Mr Stevens reached out to me for help. I didn't even feel his attempt…' Dana brushed away a tear that ran down her face. 'What the doll is doing is disgusting! I thought feeding off Marcus' blood was bad, but this, this is worse.' When Dana finished speaking, she went outside to get some fresh air. Sheba followed at her side.

Ashley was watching Dana from the window. Michael could feel concern baking off her. 'We also need to track down the crazy garden lady,' said Ashley. 'See if there's a way to identify people like her. I've got a feeling there are more of them out there than there are people being used as human batteries.' Ashley turned to look at Michael as if he were the one that needed convincing. 'They'll be killing each other soon.' Her gaze didn't waver. Michael could feel the depth of her concern. 'Michael, that woman today was wishing she had a rake!'

Ashley wasn't looking at Michael anymore. Her eyes were unfocused, staring off into the room. She probably didn't even realise she was still speaking: 'She was imagining the feel of the swing, the dull thud as rake buried its teeth into Michael's head.'

It was the detached tone in Ashley's voice that made Michael's skin crawl. Ashley still had that crazy woman's thoughts running through her head. She blinked as if startled and came out of her daze.

'She needs to be watched,' said Ashley. No detachment this time. Ashley was dead serious. 'That's what I'm trying to tell you. She needs to be watched.'

Nobody knew how to respond. Sometimes there are just no words.

Sarah wrapped her arms around Ashley, trying to provide some comfort. Michael just stood wondering how bad things were going to get.

* * *

Michael met Dana at the car. Nicola had agreed to drive them to school if they still wanted to go. They were going to be very late, but the point wasn't about which classes they attended but how many people they could interact with. They needed to get some kind of idea of the scope of what they were dealing with. The network that Sarah had created gave them an idea of the numbers of people already impacted by the doll, but no detail as to whether they were a potential coma victim or a broom-wielding mad woman.

'You up for this? Michael asked.

'We have no choice, Michael. I just wish Ashley went to our school. She can perceive personality shifts much more accurately than either of us.'

'Well, the dried-up cereal, extreme body odour and excessively foul language sort of gave her away.' Michael paused, making sure Dana was following his joke, then dropped into the back seat of the car. 'Shit, that's not going to thin the herd at school much is it?' Michael nudged his sister in the ribs, knowing she hated it.

'Not amongst your friends, anyway.' Dana flicked her hair over her shoulder and walked around the other side of the car. Looking back at Michael, a small smile lifted at the corners of her mouth.

During the drive, no-one said much of anything. Nicola was particularly quiet. Michael knew that she hadn't liked the idea of everybody separating for the day but had understood the importance of gathering information. Until they had some kind of idea of how many people had been affected, they had no ability to formulate a plan.

Nicola stopped them as they were getting out of the car. 'Guys, be careful today. Watch out for each other. If there's any sign of danger, grab each other and leave. Trust your instincts on this.' She went to say more then stopped herself and just gave them both a quick hug, before driving off.

'Good luck!' Dana said as she shrugged her shoulders not knowing what else to say.

'Any trouble, we'll call each other,' Michael said. 'Then go straight to the common area. We'll met there and then decide what to do. Okay?' Dana nodded her agreement and then walked off towards her locker.

Michael wasn't certain what he was expecting, maybe speak to one or two people that had been affected, put a couple of names on the list to give to Aunt Sarah. What he wasn't expecting was the outright aggression people were showing towards each other.

He saw a teacher wielding a red crayon, marking paper after paper with a giant red F. One student, used to getting straight *A*s decided to ask if there had been some kind of mistake. The teacher snatched the paper back from her and bent over the essay. His arm curled protectively so she could not see what he was writing. His crayon broke twice. With the second snap he glared up at the girl as if to say *'See what you made me do.'* She was oblivious to the teacher's scowl and was probably too busy imagining another *A*-graded paper pinned to the fridge at home.

What he handed her back was a paper covered in red scrawl. The words *THIS is Fucked* and *F is for you Fucked this up* were repeated over and over again. In his determination to convey this simple message to the girl, he'd written the words all over his desk as well. The girl didn't seem able to process what was happening in front of her.

'Mr Gordon, surely you're joking?' the girl replied in outrage. She leant forward, waving the paper in Mr Gordon's face.

Michael chose this moment to try to intervene, stepping forward just as Mr Gordon – or Gordo as he liked to be called – stood up, knocking his chair over as he did. Mr Gordon reached his hand up around behind the girl's head, like he was about to whisper something important into her ear.

Michael spun the girl out of his grip, certain Mr Gordon had intended to whisper something, perhaps more insight about how f'd up everything had become, illustrating this simple truth by ramming her head into his desk. Repeatedly. Maybe then the words would stick. The image was clear in Michael's head. He could imagine the thud where her head first struck, then again and again, the sound getting wetter and softer as more red ran across the desk.

Michael pulled the girl away, trying to clear the ugly imagery from his mind. She kept protesting that she'd never received anything lower than an A− in her life.

As they walked past a teacher in the hallway, Michael took a moment to suggest that Mr Gordon might need a mental health day.

'What he needs to do is change this to the A+ I deserve,' the girl said.

Michael thought Gordo might be mad, but that didn't mean the man didn't have a point. Everything was f'd up.

This became Michael's mantra as his day progressed. He was waiting in line to grab himself a sandwich and really not sure what to pick. His mum usually made their lunches, but she hadn't had time given all that was going on. None of the canteen sandwiches looked appealing, to be honest. Just the thought of eating one of those soggy salad sandwiches made him want to gag. He had just decided that maybe an apple was the safest bet when he was forcibly pushed out of the line.

'We don't have time to wait, you feeb! Come back when you have a clue,' someone yelled as Michael was pushed forward roughly.

He turned back, looking for his attacker, intending to teach someone some manners. Michael was repeating under his breath, 'This is f'd up! This is f'd up!'

Not one set of angry eyes glared at him, but a dozen. His vision swam for about the third time that day. Of the angry faces that stared at him, three were covered in the wet sheen of the doll's influence. Exactly like Mr Stevens, their faces had a transparent coating that ran over their heads and under the top jaw. The bottom of each of their faces was unaffected. Michael stepped forward. Something needed to be done. The doll's connection offended him.

Some of his schoolmates still waiting patiently in line were looking around, throwing glances in every direction as if sensing something was brewing but unable to identify the danger. Most just stood with blank faces, the expression of people waiting in queues the world over.

He pushed his anger back down, not because confronting the angry stares fazed him, more because it had occurred to him that he was the one causing the frightened glances.

Besides, he didn't feel like the apple anymore, and if he caused a fight, he would be held back after school and then miss soccer training, and it was the thought of training that was getting him through this bitch of a day.

When he bumped someone in the hallway, making them drop their things, he apologised immediately, and dropped to his knees to help them gather their books. Although truth be told it was as much their fault as it was his – and he didn't see them rushing to apologise – still, he reached for the maths textbook that had flown halfway across the corridor.

The boy he was helping decided not to thank him, but instead chose to spit at him. Or to be more accurate, spit at his hand. Michael jerked away. The spit hadn't come close to hitting Michael but that was hardly the point.

'Are you right?' Michael almost yelled but he could see that the boy on the ground was not paying any attention to him. As soon as Michael had moved away from the boy's possessions, he had ceased to exist in the boy's world.

There was no doubt about it. The doll was making people fixate on things. Like OCD on steroids. He was no psychology student, but it was easy to see the more the doll forced the fixation, the more protective people got. The need to protect quickly became aggression when they were threatened. The girl needed to maintain her straight A record. The kids in line wanted to protect their position in the queue. The spitter didn't want his books touched by another. And Mr Gordon, well Michael didn't really care what Gordo was trying to protect. He probably saw himself as a struggling author that was selling himself short by sitting in school grading papers.

Glad that it was the end of the day, Michael wasn't sure how much more he could take. His head ached but what did he expect: his vision was constantly in and out of focus. He'd barely been able to read the board in half of his classes and had stopped even trying to take notes. But he didn't have a temperature. He placed his fingers on the inside of his wrist. His pulse was slightly elevated but still strong and regular. So, apart from the occasional blurred vision he was golden.

He grabbed his stuff and turned away from his locker, looking for a clear path so he didn't accidentally set somebody off. He barely had time to note that a small girl stood in front of him, barring his way, before her palm connected with the right side of his face.

He'd just been slapped by a twelve-year old girl in pigtails. His vision swam but for a second, he could see the doll's umbilical running up from the back of her neck into the ether. He blinked a couple of times, and his vision was clear once more. All impression of the sac covering the girl's face faded. Her lips were drawn back from her teeth, no sign of any film running into her mouth. Noting these facts, he only just reacted in time when she drew her arm back ready to hit him again.

He caught her hand before she completed her swing, his own hand twitching, eager to hit her back. As his anger grew, hers seemed to dissipate. Her eyes became round and startled, with tears running down her cheeks. Pushing past her, Michael walked through the corridors not caring who he bumped. His heart rate climbed as he stalked through the school.

Michael didn't stop at the common area. He kept walking until he was well outside of the school grounds. Being surrounded by people running on a hair trigger had wound his nerves so tight, he couldn't be bothered with the rundown he would need to give his sister and parents.

He gave himself a once over. Again, no fever, no swelling of any glands. Heart rate still slightly elevated, but that seemed reasonable since he was still smarting from the slap the girl in pigtails had given him. His head throbbed deep behind his eyes but his vision was focused and clear.

He sent his family a text that he would catch a ride to soccer training. He included the list of the fifteen people that he believed had been affected by the doll's influence, plus another five who managed to be arseholes all by themselves.

He took the time to note down that on four separate occasions he'd seen people walking around with an umbilical cord attached to the back of their neck. Puzzled by the fact that he'd seen nothing on Mr Gordon, Michael was unsure if he was just overly tired or if his ability to perceive the umbilicals was transient. He would let everyone else puzzle over that.

He turned his phone off – he didn't want to think about it anymore. He would jump over to the second realm and ride to soccer. Ashul would want a proper debrief anyway and there was no avoiding him. Flipping to the second realm just to get to soccer seemed like a misuse of his powers, but what was the point if you couldn't cut a couple of corners?

* * *

Lorcan had been shadowing the boy throughout the day. He barely had to use any powers to conceal himself. The students at this school walked around with earbuds in and spent the majority of their time staring at their phones. Their two most acute senses were nullified by technology.

A young girl brimming with self-confidence stepped into his way and placed her hand on his chest, boldly stopping him from walking down the corridor.

'Are you a new teacher? I would love to take one of your classes.' Lorcan glanced at her eyes. The pupils were fully dilated. She was either high, or a natural donor. He had met humans before who willingly gave of their blood. He didn't bother sniffing her skin to see which one this one was. He didn't have time to be distracted by food.

She persisted. 'What do you teach?' As Lorcan pushed past her, he responded, 'Food Tech. I take paleo to a whole new level.'

He was following Michael down the corridor when the child approached Michael. Lorcan didn't need to step between worlds to know the doll's touch had already corrupted her.

Hatred pulled her lips back from her teeth in a snarl of loathing, and her arm rocked backwards as she swung towards the boy's face. Lorcan could stop the impact, but not without damaging the child, and there would be no way to manipulate Michael's mind when he was fully conscious of Lorcan.

He let her hand swing through its arc, heard the sharp snap as her palm left a vivid red brand across Michael's cheek. His head barely moved as he absorbed the shock of the impact. The girl was small, but she'd placed all of her anger behind the blow. Her urge to harm had not been satisfied. Her fingers curled into claws as she raked her fingers towards the boy's eyes. In Michael's startled expression, the light brown of his eyes shifted and started glowing with a white light.

Michael grabbed her hand out of the air and his fingers easily encircled her slim wrist. He twisted her hand back ever so slightly.

There was a war going on behind that strange white glow in the boy's eyes. Part of him wanted to hurt the girl, the twisting of the wrist said as much, but his shoulders were pulled back. Not the body language of a person about to inflict harm. Lorcan could read every twitch of the conflict. Michael's expression remained neutral, which was what concerned Lorcan the most. Behind the boy rose the shadow of the ghoul – it reached its hand to place it upon the boy's left shoulder. The boy blinked once, twice, brown, white, brown. There was no way the boy could possibly control the poison that was coursing through his system, but somehow, he did just that. He released his grip and lowered the hand that had been ready to strike the retaliatory blow. The ghoul blew to dust behind him.

* * *

Dana had spent the day writing names down on a list. Everywhere she turned, there was anger and aggression. Teachers, students, even the school groundskeeper seemed to have grievances that were suddenly spilling to the surface. She was reading the text from Michael as she walked towards the bus stop. The crossing beeped its warning and the green walking man was replaced by the red flashing man.

Leaning against the signpost, she waited for the lights to change. Her thumbs moved rapidly as she texted Michael back a curt reply. She modified his list to include seven extra names, six to the column labelled 'doll's puppet'. Next to Marcus' name, she placed an asterisk. Nobody had heard from Marcus in days, which should make her feel relieved, but instead left her a little concerned. The seventh name made her chuckle. Michael's name was now the latest addition to the natural born arsehole section of the list. She hit send and looked up to see what was holding up the traffic.

The small, polite, Japanese lady that manned the school crossing stood in the middle of the road holding her stop sign. Dana would have said she was around forty years of age but then Dana had thought the same when she started school over a decade ago. She never seemed to change: she was always smiling, always courteous. The light went green and a white van rolled forward an inch. The polite, little Japanese lady ran over and kicked his bumper. Without pausing, she swung the stop sign, wielding it like a baseball bat. The front headlight popped, followed by the tinkle of falling glass. She stood back satisfied, raising the stop side, now twisted and damaged, and ushered the preschool children across the street. She smiled sweetly, waving the children through until the police came to relieve her of her hi-vis vest and red STOP sign.

Contagion

Michael decided to keep himself to himself for a little while. He was nervous as to whether any of his soccer mates had been caught within the doll's reach, and he was anxiously counting down the minutes until training started. They had no idea yet whether it was possible to decontaminate someone impacted by the doll's malicious interference.

Michael thought the doll might be using some form of hypnotic suggestion that it imposed on people while it walked through their dreams. But if the doll could mess with a twelve-year-old girl enough to make her slap him in the face, what would be the extent of the impact on a sixteen-year-old boy used to throwing his weight around?

They played a sport where muscling someone off the ball was a required part of the game. During the normal course of a game of soccer, people often took offence at how certain players used their strength. How easily could that offence turn to outrage? It wouldn't take much of a push, a slight shift in perception before punches were thrown.

These thoughts and more were circling around Michael's head. Having arrived more than half an hour early at the ground, Michael got changed into his soccer gear, and went for a light run. The steady rhythm usually soothed his nerves, but today his gait felt awkward and forced. The ground had recently been mowed and the grass clippings had blown together to form wet clumps. Why they'd decided to water the grass just before training was incomprehensible to him. The day had been mild and now they had a wet ground to contend with? His boots were already covered in a layer of green that he would have to clean off before he put his boots back in his bag. He hated cleaning wet grass off his boots, the smell always reminded him of cat's piss.

He took a note as a few of his teammates arrive and watched as they ran, trying to gauge whether players were going through their normal routines.

After the warmth of the day, a fine mist was rising off the pitch. Michael slowed his pace and walked over to where his teammates were sitting, putting on shin guards and boots, talking absently about school. His breath plumed around his mouth as his breathing slowed.

The smell of wet grass, deep heat and deodorant hung around the group like a fog. The smell that he associated with the game was usually comforting. Today, he found it slightly nauseating. To limit his exposure to his teammate's stench, he continued to breathe through his mouth, his breath fogging in front of his face with each exhale. As distracted as he was, he missed his opportunity to chat with the boys. Their coach had arrived and started dropping balls at their feet, issuing commands to the group as he went. They needed to get warmed up: the other team would be arriving in ten minutes.

The other team? Michael hadn't been aware that a game had been scheduled, but the coach was in no mood to be questioned on the subject. He wasn't the only player looking around confused, but their coach wasn't the most approachable person on game day so everyone just went about the task of warming up. Two minutes in and the coach was already warning the players to lift their work rate.

* * *

Lorcan needed to find the boy. He'd vanished into the second realm too quickly for Lorcan to follow. Although Lorcan had the ability to walk in both worlds, he did not possess the ability to track someone through the second realm. That place didn't run by the same laws as the first plane, so a scent was a tricky thing to follow. His best option at finding Michael lay in following the sister, Dana. She had a connection to the boy that rivalled his link to the bonded, and she would soon sense that he was in peril. The Nachzehrer poison had been building in Michael throughout the course of the day. Through some means that Lorcan was yet to understand, the boy had neutralised its effects.

But Michael had been infected in the second realm, and the virulence of the infection might well increase on his return to that realm. The boy wasn't aware that he needed to conserve his power in order to keep the infection from flooding his system. Lorcan was confident that if he found the boy again soon, he could stabilise the condition. And then, once it was nightfall again, Lorcan would be able to draw out more of the poison.

A couple of infected humans were none of his concern. He needed to protect the boy and if he couldn't protect him, then he would have no choice but to kill him.

* * *

Fifteen minutes after the other team arrived, the whistle had been blown for the start of the first half of the game.

Michael was playing defensive midfield. He liked to get his first touch under his belt as quickly as possible. Rushing the opposition, he intercepted a late pass and pushed forward. He felt a pull on his jumper. Michael twisted his shoulder to the left and flicked the ball off to his right.

Not waiting to see whether his pass made it through, he turned to the player that had been holding him, intending to give him some counsel on player etiquette. The guy clipped him on his shoulder as he muscled past.

Michael's vision momentarily blurred. Somehow their feet tangled, and they both went down. Michael rolled, coming up onto his feet and the other player pushed up from the ground calling for a foul.

No foul was given and play resumed. Michael blinked, trying to clear the fog from his eyes. The ball came back through midfield. He stepped to the left to push the attack back and fell forward as he was hit from behind. The air left his lungs in a painful whoosh. His muscles locked and his chest felt like he was being squeezed in a vice. He waited for the whistle to blow as he struggled to his feet.

Again, no foul was given. Michael was left to struggle for breath. He lifted his arms over his head, trying to get some air into his lungs. He spat on the ground, a wad of phlegm dislodged from his throat, and he could now suck in small shallow sips of air. He jogged over to the sideline, somewhat dazed, calling for a water bottle. He caught the one that was thrown to him and took a long pull. He swirled the cool water around in his mouth, then spat a mouthful onto the ground, trying to wash out the foul taste that had suddenly built up.

He gulped down clean cool liquid to soothe his parched throat. Finally, the whistle blew, a foul had finally been awarded. His teammates erupted when the foul was called against Michael for taking a drink on the sideline.

This was a friendly, what was up with this ref? He was taking things a little too seriously. Michael jogged back onto the field, each breath aching as the cold air burned in his lungs. His vision distorted, doubling up, and he squinted as he tried to focus.

It was like looking through lenses smeared with grease. The image of the referee in front of him swam in and out of focus.

The referee reached into his pocket to extract a yellow card. His face was blurred and his features seemed to merge into one another, partly because Michael's vision was playing up, but also because the referee's face was covered in a thin transparent membrane that enclosed the top half of his face. The lip under the second skin curled up almost in a snarl. The referee pushed one of Michael's protesting teammates away and strode towards Michael with the card raised in his hand like he was brandishing a flaming sword.

Michael chuckled to himself. He had a flaming sword too.

He tried to shake his head clear as his instincts warned him to back away. He rubbed at his eyes, desperate to clear his vision. He could see his teammates holding the opposition back. A half-dozen faces leered at him from behind cauls of pulsating skin. Michael called out to the bonded as he turned and vomited onto the ground. The last thing he saw before he passed out was his sister's face as she ran onto the ground. His deteriorating vision made her features swim.

Something else appeared beside her, something huge, but he was unable to keep the images separate. In the shifting blur as darkness wrapped around him, his sister's teeth took on a canine aspect and her eyes seemed to glow a fierce red.

* * *

The girl was like a beacon, easy to follow even when she was inside a vehicle. Lorcan couldn't remember ever encountering someone with such a complicated scent. He followed her to the ground where her brother was playing sport. From a distance of more than a kilometre away, Lorcan could smell the corruption of the Nachzehrer.

He no longer needed to track the girl, and the stench of the boy was easy to follow. Keeping his presence dim, using his gift to keep a foot in both worlds, he raced towards where he found the boy running around the perimeter of the ground, occasionally spitting into the grass. Michael's feet caught the ground and he stumbled. The boy was naturally trying to conserve energy but his rhythm was off and he would eventually fall.

Lorcan allowed Michael to run past him. Plumes of steam rising from the boy's overheated body. The boy would not be able to continue much longer but Lorcan was still hesitant to intervene and make his presence known.

He moved forward and found where Michael's spittle lay burning into the ground. Pinching a piece of grass in his fingers, Lorcan brought the smoking blades up to his nose. His nostrils flared as he delicately sampled the fumes twisting up from his fingertips. The acrid stench held a sweet cloying note that reminded him of every disease-filled human he'd ever had the misfortune of crossing paths with. It surprised Lorcan that the boy could even run with the amount of fluid that had accumulated in his lungs. But run on he did, back towards his teammates.

Lorcan was hoping for an opportunity to remove the boy from the field. The boy was using all of his focus to fight a battle he didn't even realise he was waging. His sister was doing everything in her power to draw the boy's attention, but he was currently jumping at shadows. Or more accurately, he was seeing into the shadowland.

That the boy could see the doll's puppets was obvious, in every twitch and tensing of his muscles. Lorcan understood now that the boy's link to the Nachzehrer was giving him a new kind of sight, and the Nachzehrer were exploiting the link. Each time the boy's eyes shifted colour, the ground behind him would shimmer and a ghoul would rise. Not visible to the humans but easily detected by Lorcan. The Nachzehrer stayed always behind the boy, reaching out to players as they ran past, their insubstantial hands unable to close on the flesh so close to their reaching fingers. The Nachzehrer's flesh dissolved as it passed through the player's exposed limbs – their link to this plane tenuous.

But those touched felt the Nachzehrer's presence on some deeper level. Despite their exertion, their skin betrayed them. Goosepimples broke out on arms as they felt the Nachzehrer's caress.

Only one Nachzehrer was not tempted by the warm bodies. The Nachzehrer king watched the boy from behind him. With each second that the boy's eyes glowed white, the Nachzehrer took one step closer, gaining more substance as he neared the boy. Closer each time with a firmer footing in this world.

Lorcan could not allow the ghoul to reach the boy. He was not certain how the conversion took place, but on an instinctive level understood that proximity to the Nachzehrer precipitated the boy's corruption.

Lorcan placed a foot in each realm, neither fully in either.

In the first plane, his eyes burned a fiery red and his fangs extended to their full length; his body lengthened until he took on an almost lupine form. In the second realm, he became his true self. In that place, he unfurled his wings and flew towards the boy.

The sister had run out onto the pitch, making a beeline for her brother.

In the sister's efforts to get to her sibling, she was going to run through the Nachzehrer king – it had almost reached the boy's shoulder. Lorcan wasn't certain how the boy's infection spread but he was beginning to suspect that the Nachzehrer was using the boy's essence – his sweat, his spit, his blood – to enter this world, and then infect whatever it could.

The girl was in real danger. Lorcan wasn't certain he was going to be able to reach them both in time. With a split second to decide, he rolled to his left and grabbed the girl around her waist. The bonded warrior, Ashul, flickered into existence behind the Nachzehrer, his sword drawn and flaring. The ghoul's arm reached towards the boy, inches away from his flesh and the sword swung, severing decomposing flesh with a wet crunch. The creature's flesh charred at the touch of the sword; the arm lying at the boy's feet smouldered and disintegrated, leaving a greasy dust to blow across the ground. The Nachzehrer turned to face Ashul, but the ghoul was too slow. The warrior had already disappeared back into the ether. The warrior could move at speed when he wanted to. He blinked back into existence next to Lorcan and managed to remove the girl from Lorcan's arms before Lorcan had time to protest. Placing his free hand on the boy's shoulder, Ashul vanished, taking a moment to nod to Lorcan before he stepped back into the second realm, taking his charges with him.

So, Lorcan's presence had been noted.

No more hiding in the shadows. Lorcan was not certain how the bonded would react when they next stood face to face. Either way Lorcan was slightly annoyed that he'd been the one left to clean up the mess. Once the touch of iron had tainted the Nachzehrer's flesh, the process of decomposition was swift – the flesh peeling back from scorched bone, until all was consumed… and there was nothing more than dust in the wind.

Ashul left the children at the mother's feet. Still weak from her time spent dispossessed in the book, the mother knelt beside her son. The girl bent down next to her brother, occasionally glancing up to search the shadows, clearly not understanding what had just happened. Lorcan could feel the boy's fever baking from him even from a distance, but he had to trust that the mother, weakened though she may be, would be able to protect her children from here on out.

Lorcan then removed himself from the first plane. He'd exposed himself enough for one day.

* * *

Lorcan remained at the soccer-ground after the mother had taken her children away. As suspected, when her children required her aid, she found the strength to provide it. With the mere touch of her hand, she was able to reduce the boy's fever. His skin still burned, but no longer was he in immediate danger.

Lorcan stayed, hoping to better understand the Nachzehrer's method of contagion. The boy hadn't succumbed to the poison, yet the ghouls had still managed to gain a foothold into this realm.

Staying hidden, Lorcan walked the field and found the patches of grass where the boy had spat on the ground. Where the grass still smouldered, Lorcan could detect the presence of the ghouls. He smelled their corruption intermingled with the 'clean' aroma of the boy. Their stink seeped up through the ground where they'd mired themselves as they waited for warm flesh to pass overhead. It seemed they'd absorbed the essence of the boy and that this gave them some purchase in the physical realm.

To amuse himself, he drew his knife and stabbed down, driving his blade into the hidden heads of the beasts. A puff of dust blew up through the ground, signifying the ghoul's demise.

The brawl that had erupted between the teams continued long after Ashul had removed the boy from the ground. Lorcan had to agree, the referee throwing a yellow card into an unconscious boy's face had been a bit over the top.

He noted several boys stumbling as they ran past the tainted ground. Insubstantial hands rose from below, attempted to grip ankles. Although they were little more than smoke, the nails marked the flesh, allowing the ghoul's poison to seep in. Lorcan noted that only those that the boy had touched were targeted. Somehow this was part of the contagion process.

It pleased him when he saw the one who'd gripped the boy's shirt stumble and fall. The nails of the Nachzehrer scored a path down his exposed thigh. A poetic kind of justice that Lorcan appreciated. He would wait a while longer to see whether the referee was likewise targeted. If not, Lorcan would take matters into his own hands, whether his inequity was born of the doll's touch mattered little. He'd ruined what looked to be a fine match with his bias and Lorcan had wanted to see the boy play.

Lorcan walked around to the sideline of the pitch. There, he found the water bottle that the boy had fouled with his spit. Not just fouled, but infected with the Nachzehrer's essence. The water had been consumed by others during the game: there was no telling how many people had drunk from the polluted source. Lorcan considered the Nachzehrer grabbing each boy's wrist as they raised the bottle, the boys only feeling an icy touch as they drank.

There was nothing more to be seen here. He stepped into the second realm and flew towards the family's home, certain he would arrive before the mother had the time to tuck her son into bed.

Ascension

ana was frantic. Michael's head lay in her lap and her hand rested on his forehead. Despite holding a wet towel to cool him down, heat was baking off of him.

She considered pouring a bottle of water over his body to bring his temperature down, but she was trying to keep her composure and that act felt a little too desperate.

And she refused to be desperate. Michael needed them to fix things, and they couldn't do that if they succumbed to desperation. So she wet the towel, placed it on his forehead and whispered just to him, 'I'm here, Micky. Just hold on, Micky. We'll think of something.' Soothing words she hoped he would be able to hear.

* * *

Michael could hear his sister's words and he wanted to assure her that everything would be fine. But she felt so far away that she wouldn't be able to hear his reply.

His conscious 'self' lay submerged in a cocoon of water.

Part of his mind had visited this place before – it had been created as a containment zone, a mental construct, as soon as the Nachzehrer poison had activated in his bloodstream. He'd known on some deep level that the contamination had been lying in wait, poised to strike when his defences were down, and his subconscious – his own CDC – had supplied a way to keep the contagion contained.

Once the water around him had been cool, but now it was scolding hot. The liquid that filled his ears deadened all sound. He still breathed while in the water, but the water burned as it entered his body, lungs aching with the unnatural heaviness of the fluid he was forced to inhale. But he had to remain submerged, because it was protecting him from the decomposing corpse standing, watching him from the water's edge.

The Nachzehrer was wary of the liquid cocoon around Michael. It had tried to reach down and grab his wrist but hissed in pain as the skin folded away from its fingertips. The Nachzehrer was forced to pull away before its flesh fell from the bone. It now paced back and forth on the shore of his consciousness, uncertain. Its leering lopsided smile soon returning as it drew back to what it must deem to be a safe distance.

Radiating cool patience, the Nachzehrer stared with its white, glowing eyes down into the water's depths. It was undead – it could wait forever if need be to claim him.

Michael let more water pour out from him and the cocoon soon became a lake. Still, the white eyes stared down into the depths, always able to find Michael no matter how much distance he endeavoured to place between them. He heard the distant rumble of hooves beating against the ground, felt the slow, heavy vibrations moving through his chest. He wished he could call out to Smoke, but the deeper the waters became, the farther away he drew from his connections.

In this place, he felt isolated and alone. But he allowed the sound of the hoofbeats to calm him; he focused on the deep rhythmic nature of the sound, hoping that at some point he would be able to hear his sister's words flow through to him, to have her words once again reach his ears.

* * *

'Nicola, we no longer have a choice,' said Azuradien. 'We must take Michael to the faerie realm.'

Azuradien was waiting for them when they returned home. Nicola pushed past him, holding her son's hand as Joseph carried him from the car. Ashul emerged from the shadows, helping Dana as she stumbled out of the back seat as she shook with fear.

'You will shut up or I will banish you from this place!' Nicola yelled. 'If you cannot help us, then get the hell out!' She couldn't deal with the faerie king right now, she was struggling as it was.

'You do not understand the risk he puts us all in. The Nachzehrer…'

'Puts us all in. Puts *us* all in! Once again, you are not at risk, yet you stand here and preach about the danger. My son fought those ghouls and you… you did nothing. Now he fights them again. What will you do this time, Azuradien? What?'

'There is nothing to be done. Once infected, he cannot be cured. Ashul, tell her there is no other option.'

'There was no way to get those damned eels out from under your skin,' said Nicola. 'But somehow Michael did it. So while you tell me what is impossible, my family and I will find a way to do exactly that. My son will not be lost to some damn infection.' Nicola advanced towards Azuradien, needing some outlet for her rage. Ashul stopped her with a hand gently placed on her shoulder as she tried to push past him.

'We will not abandon him. He has our aid,' said Ashul. The words were spoken for her alone – he understood Nicola's fear.

A soft clapping came from the corner of the room where an incredibly handsome stranger stood leaning casually against the wall.

'Once again you let the mortals fight the wars while you stand protected by your covenants. How very noble.'

'You!' Azuradien snaped. 'Get out of this place, you foul creature.' Azuradien's iridescent wings spread out behind him, beating furiously against his back. Although shaped like butterfly wings, they were as thin and translucent as dragonfly wings. Rather than looking fragile the blue veins of energy that laced through the wings radiated nothing but strength. His hair flew about his head as he hovered erratically above the ground.

'Am I supposed to be frightened? I do believe mine are larger than yours.' And as the stranger spoke, the brief impression of black, leathery wings unfolded from behind his shoulders, brushing the ceiling before fading, leaving Nicola unsure of what she'd seen.

'Ashul, kill this abomination,' Azuradien commanded. 'He cannot be allowed to live.'

'First, I would see why he is here,' replied Ashul. 'He has done us a great service today. For that alone I owe him the courtesy.'

'What great service has he performed?' Nicola asked.

'He protected both Dana and Michael from the Nachzehrer

when I could not get to them in time.' Ashul nodded to the stranger, acknowledging his indebtedness.

'Then I thank you from the bottom of my heart.' Nicola reached out to shake his hand, almost choking on the words. She hadn't realised the danger her children had been in and still her son burned with fever.

'Do not touch him! He is damned! Damned for what he is.' Azuradien attempted to push Nicola's hand away.

'My name is Lorcan,' the stranger said. 'I am not infectious, nor am I damned. But of more import, I think I may be able to help your son.'

'How?' Nicola's voice betrayed her willingness to believe. 'How can you help?'

'Last night I leached the poison from the boy. Unfortunately, I couldn't get all of it out of his system because the boy has some protection.'

'You knew he was infected last night, and you didn't tell us,' Joseph said. The anger at this information being withheld from him was evident from the aggression in his voice.

'I am rarely welcomed into a home. I believed my efforts would hold throughout the day. My plan was to leach the poison once more tonight, and each night for as long as was necessary.' Lorcan looked back at Joseph as if daring him to prickle at his words.

'Ashul, do you know anything about this man. Can we trust him?' Nicola wasn't interested in any male show of strength. She needed to help her son, and she asked Ashul this question, hoping against hope that the answer would be yes.

'I cannot say that I trust him. His kind are a savage breed, not often befriended. But he has conducted himself honourably. So I would hear him out.'

'Will this leaching cure him, Ashul?' said Nicola, starting to sound frantic. 'Azuradien, will this leaching stop the Nachzehrer poison?'

'I do not know,' said Ashul. He locked eyes with Nicola. 'I am sorry, but I have never seen someone be cured once infected.'

'There is no revoking the Nachzehrer curse,' said Azuradien. 'We must take the boy to the safety of the faerie realm.' Azuradien seemed a little too impatient for Nicola's frayed nerves.

Before Nicola had a chance to respond, Lorcan interjected, 'You've never tried to prevent an infection, always happy to order the murder of those exposed, under the guise of the greater good. We have no time for this discussion. I can smell the boy from here. The poison needs to be removed from his body immediately. But you will need to remove your wardings if I have any chance of getting enough of the infection out of him to give him a fighting chance. I must extract the poison from his blood.'

'This is the kind of beast you are dealing with,' spat Azuradien. 'A common vampire!'

Lorcan looked offended. 'I am many things, but common has never been one of them. I am one of the ancients. Vampires are as ants compared to me.'

Lorcan turned towards Nicola, seemingly understanding she was the one who needed to be swayed here. 'I can give you a full accounting of my history, but in the time it takes for me to recount a little more than my birth, your son will be beyond any hope of aid. Let me draw as much of the poison as possible, in the same way I did yesterday. Then you can decide whether I help you further.'

'Mum, I think you should let him,' said Dana. Nicola trusted her daughter's instincts above all others. Nicola indicated for Dana to continue. 'He has saved us both today.

Although I'm not certain he's telling the complete truth, I don't believe he's lying.' Nicola glanced towards Joseph. He raised his palms to her, feeling as inadequate as she did. 'Lorcan, show me.'

'I will not take any part in this,' Azuradien advised them.

Ashul looked at him coolly and walked with Dana to Michael's room.

Nicola followed the stranger into her son's room.

* * *

When they entered Michael's bedroom, Malcarielle was already seated at Michael's side. She held in her hand a piece of the most radiant crystal Nicola had ever seen.

'Peace,' she said. 'I do not agree with my father. We need to work together to help Michael. I give you this as a gift. Its healing properties have never been fully explored. I pray that together we will be able to help Michael.'

'Malcarielle, the crystals are sacred to your people,' said Ashul. 'Is it not forbidden to remove even a small chip?' He understood the risk she'd taken for Michael. She could be excommunicated for this sacrilege.

'He is worth it,' Malcarielle said softly, but all could hear the conviction in her voice.

'Okay, so do what you did to him yesterday and then we can decide on the bloodsucking,' said Nicola. Lorcan rolled his eyes at Nicola's choice of words.

'You may not want to be present, it is slightly off-putting, even for me.'

'I'm staying, so just get to it,' Nicola snapped. 'And Lorcan.' Her patience was about ready to break but she realised her son was in this man's hands and she needed to express how grateful she was that he was even attempting to help. It had been a long drive home and she needed some shred of hope to cling to. 'Thank you for trying.'

Lorcan lightly bit at Michael's wrist. Nicola jumped forward protectively, reacting instinctively, feeling her body pulling in energy to defend her child if the need arose.

Michael's eyes popped open as an intricate set of runes glowed softly on the surface of his skin. The wardings covered every inch of Michael's body, including his eyelids.

But no blue runework covered the surface of his eyes.

It only took a few moments for Nicola to process this information. His exposure to the infection had been her fault – she'd left Michael with an Achilles heel.

Lorcan lowered his face so that his lips rested just above Michael's left eye, then he inhaled the longest breath that Nicola had ever witnessed. And as he inhaled, inky tendrils coiled out of Michael's eyes like smoke drifting up from a lit cigar. Although the coils fought to turn back into the eye – twisting like a nest of vipers as they did – Lorcan did not let any of them escape.

He repeated the process on the right eye. Once he was done, he held up his finger to the group and faded into the shadows and was no longer present amongst them.

'What is he, Ashul? Can you tell me before I decide to place my son at his mercy?' Nicola was trembling. Watching the inky, black shadows being sucked from her son's eyes had shaken her. She ran her hands over Michael's forehead, trying to draw some heat from his body.

And then she was suddenly feeling too pressed in, the room too close, with too many people standing around watching Michael. Watching him being consumed by an infection she couldn't protect him from.

She was about to scream for Ashul to answer her when the dark-haired stranger returned, slipping out of the shadows like he was shrugging off a cloak.

'I should explain,' said Lorcan. 'We have bought ourselves some time.'

* * *

'Firstly, let me explain my hasty departure. My body functions at a higher rate in another realm. I needed to destroy the poison I extracted from your son from my bloodstream as quickly as possible. By removing myself from this realm, I both sped up the process and eliminated the risk of breathing the contagion onto those susceptible.' Lorcan was somewhat annoyed at the lack of response from the family. He understood they were all under a certain amount of strain but he'd just processed a deadly poison into his own blood, making himself a huge sterilisation devise. That warranted a little respect, surely.

'If you allow me to proceed, I will remove the liquid from his lungs,' said Lorcan. 'Much of the toxin resides there. Ashul will help me destroy this poison once I have safely extracted it. I will then draw the remaining poison from his body by taking a quantity of his blood. I have ways of forcing the infection into a confined area of his bloodstream. This blood will then be processed within my own body and returned to the boy.'

Azuradien stepped into the doorway and interjected, 'Why do you need to take his blood at all? This sounds like some kind of fabrication so you can open the boy's veins.'

Lorcan felt his eyes flare. He kept his gaze fixed on the boy until he could regain his composure.

'The small tissues of his lungs cannot process the amount of toxin that we have to deal with here, nor can the blood vessels of his eyes.' Lorcan looked down on the upturned face of the mother only when his eyes had returned to their normal colour.

'With your skills you can surely feel that what I am saying is true.'

The mother had the sense to nod her head.

'What are you? Before I let you proceed, please tell me what exactly it is that you are.'

'Did I ask you what you were before I offered *you* my aid? Did you ask the bonded of their origins before you drew them into this world? Were the faeries asked the same question before you let them into your home? No. Don't answer, there's no need.' Lorcan raised his hand, allowing his fingers to lengthen and talons to creep from his fingertips.

Lorcan's eyes blazed. 'My kind does not label itself. Your folklore links us to vampires, aufhockers, dhampyr, even the strigoi. Label me what you will. I'm none of these and more than all of them combined. I do not harbour the soul of a demon. I am not the product of sorcery or the union of human and wolf. I am the result, of shall we say, natural selection and nothing more. We can discuss my family tree at another time, but know this, I am the most evolved of my species, and therefore the most powerful.'

'But you do feed off humans?' Dana asked from the corner of the room, curious more that fearful. '

'I eat what I like, but I get more sustenance from humans, yes.' Lorcan returned to the form he used when walking amongst the human, all his predatory aspects dulled.

'He is a monster,' Azuradien said calmly. 'Would you allow him to feed off your son?' Azuradien's belief that the debate was over showed in every arrogant line on his face.

'No-one has spoken about feeding,' said Ashul, speaking in a measured tone. 'Lorcan has offered to purify Michael's blood, and he has shown that he has skills in this regard. A decision must be made. I can feel Michael's struggle. Remove him to the faerie realm or allow Lorcan to make the attempt.

Time is not our friend.' Lorcan could detect the urgency in his tone – Ashul obviously feared for the boy.

'Would you take the words of an animal? He feeds off your kind!' Azuradien no longer sounded so self-assured. Lorcan knew the battle was over.

Azuradien, with his lack of understanding of the humans had tripped up because the girl, and therefore her family would indeed take the word of an animal – they'd been doing so for some time.

* * *

Lorcan turned again to look down at Nicola. 'Do I have your permission to proceed?'

'I don't have any choice?' Nicola whispered under her breath. She reached forward and removed the wardings from Michael's body.

'Warrior, can you reach the boy? This will not be pleasant,' said Lorcan.

'I will when I must,' Ashul replied cryptically. Nicola barely registered his comment because Michael's eyes had opened and she could see him present behind the gaze.

'Ah… the man with the red eyes. We meet again! Mum, my lungs are full of shit and my throat is dry as. What are the chances I could get some chicken soup?'

Nicola's heart nearly broke. She turned to Lorcan. 'Do what you need to do,' she said. 'If Michael allows it.' Joseph and Dana had moved to her side to show their support and to get closer to Michael as he grew more alert.

'Michael, do you give me permission to take some of your blood?' asked Lorcan. 'I will purify it within my body then return it.'

'What are you, some kind of vampire?'

Dana suppressed a small burst of laughter. Nicola understood her reaction. The situation was becoming almost farcical.

'No! I'm one of the last "ancient ones".' Lorcan spoke in a controlled manner, but Nicola thought she saw his eyes flash.

'*Vampires* are to you, as the stupidest monkeys flinging their own excrement are to, say, me.' Michael's voice was nothing more than a rasp but they still conveyed the amusement he felt at the situation. Nicola loved him more in that moment than she thought possible – he was always trying to make others feel better even in the worst situation. And this situation couldn't get much worse. She knew she would agree to anything to save her boy.

Michael placed his hand on his chest in a mocking way. 'I know. I heard most of it, but seriously will I turn into a vampire?' Michael's words dissolved into a coughing fit. His chest rattled.

It surprised Nicola that he could even talk with the amount of fluid she could detect in his chest.

'I think the bonded would kick me out of the club if that happened. Mum would understand and Dana would probably be kind of jealous, but I just don't think Ashul would approve.'

Ashul flinched. Michael's attempt at humour had either hit too close to home, or completely missed the mark. She hoped it was the latter. The bonded warrior stepped forward regardless and placed his hand firmly on Michael's shoulder.

'No. You will not be turned in any way.' Lorcan seemed genuine to Nicola, but she knew this was a kind of "all-in" situation.

Michael obviously agreed. 'Then let's do this.'

Lorcan nodded and began issuing instructions. 'I need a stainless-steel bowl,' he said. 'And Ashul, you will need to have your sword ready.'

Dana left the room and a minute later ran back in and handed Lorcan a stainless-steel mixing bowl. Lorcan thanked her with a nod of his head and looked at Joseph, then at Nicola, for confirmation. He paused for a moment to ensure their acceptance, then proceeded with no further hesitation. He ducked his head and exhaled a long sharp breath of frosty air directly into Michael's mouth. Michael's lips turned blue and ice crystals formed on his skin. A faint cracking sound accompanied the frost as it spread across his face. His body bucked and his eyes glazed over with pain.

'I need you to hold that within your body for as long as you can. It will burn, but the longer you retain the breath, the more of the pestilence we can freeze out of you.' Lorcan's face hovered inches away from Michael's mouth, ready to accept any expelled vapour that escaped.

Ashul leaned forward, needing both hands to restrain Michael as he thrashed and bucked on the bed.

Nicola watched on horrified as the frost continued to spread out in a crackling pattern, running down Michael's neck and through his hair. His hands clenched around fists of fabric; the blankets pulled taught under his body.

She dropped to her knees and grabbed one of Michael's hands – it was incredibly cold – and he gripped back with fierce strength.

'Give him no aid,' Lorcan warned Nicola. 'Feed him and you feed the infection – they are still one.'

Nicola felt helpless. There was nothing she could do but watch as the skin around his eyes turned blue and frost formed on his eyelashes. Michael closed his eyes as the ice crept across the wet surface of his corneas.

'How much longer? Lorcan, how much longer must he endure this?'

'He will endure as long as he must,' Ashul said, his face neutral. His clenched jaw was the only sign that the sight in front of him impacted him at all.

Then Ashul too closed his eyes, and the frost raced up his arms. In seconds his face too was a mask of white ice.

* * *

Michael closed his eyes and submerged himself back in the waters of his subconscious. He had created the lake as a means to protect himself from the Nachzehrer poison. Now, he used it as a way to escape the pain of the vampire's breath as it burnt deep within his lungs.

The water was no longer scalding hot; a thin layer of ice now covered the water's surface and he could see a network of crystals slowly turning the liquid into a solid. He wished the frigid water would numb his skin against the bite of the cold but it did not. The sting as needles of pain lanced through his body drove deeper as the seconds passed. He knew these sensations were in his control – that by simply exhaling Lorcan's breath he could rid himself of the freezing cold – it made it that little bit harder to resist the impulse to expel the arctic breath from his lungs.

Brother, give me your pain through the link we share. Let me take this burden.

Even though his muscles were frozen solid, Michael felt the weight of Ashul's fingers digging into his shoulders. He resisted the urge to let the pain run out of him and into Ashul. He couldn't just allow another to experience his agony. He wouldn't inflict his pain upon Ashul.

Brother, the pain of not sharing this burden is too much to ask. Do not force that upon me.

It was the suffering in Ashul's thoughts that allowed Michael to let some of the ice flow from him into his friend. His lungs still burned with the vampire's breath, but the needles of cold withdrew from his flesh and his bones no longer felt like they would shatter. He lay in the frigid waters, cold fire coursing through him. He focused on the fingers gripping his shoulder and imagined that warmth flowed between them.

Out of the depths, red eyes appeared, burning in front of Michael's face. 'It is enough. Expel the breath. You have done enough.'

The ice around Michael shattered as he blew the air from his lungs.

* * *

'Lorcan, this cannot go on any longer,' Nicola pleaded with the vampire. 'It has been minutes. He needs to breathe.' Nicola was frantic. Michael's skin was blue and coated in a thin layer of ice. Ashul stood immobile, his hands digging into Michael's shoulders.

'He can endure a little longer,' said Lorcan. 'This boy is strong.' Lorcan hovered over Michael's mouth, watching the pulse in the boy's neck slow. 'A little longer.' When the heart stuttered in the boy's chest, Lorcan called him back. 'Expel the breath. You have done enough.'

Lorcan pushed the mother to the side as Michael vomited out a stream of foul yellow liquid. The thick sludge fountained up from Michael's mouth. Lorcan held the stainless-steel bowl steady to catch the flow. The thick liquid hissed as it hit the inside of the bowl, swirling up the sides, condensation beading the steel's surface. With deft movements, Lorcan kept the contents from spilling over.

Lorcan hissed at Ashul, 'Warrior, defrost later, we have need of your sword now.' The boy was strong but with every second that ticked by his heartbeat grew more erratic. They had no time for the warrior to reacclimatise.

Ashul flicked his wrist. Ice cracked from his skin, and his sword appeared in his hand. Without needing instruction, Ashul placed the tip of his sword into the thickening liquid. The effect was almost immediate: the liquid solidified around the steel then carbonised and within seconds flakes of ash were all that remained at the bottom of the bowl. With its purpose served, Lorcan threw the bowl and its contents to the side.

Lorcan lifted Michael's wrist to his mouth, fangs lowered, and bit down on the exposed flesh. Lorcan allowed the boy's blood to run into his mouth, but his heart was barely beating so the flow was thin and weak. Lorcan sucked against the skin, forcing the liquid to course into his mouth, resisting the urge to tear at the flesh under his fangs. His body was awash with bloodlust.

The boy's blood contained an intoxicating cocktail of flavours, the likes of which Lorcan had never experienced. Lorcan sensed the faerie king rush into the room screaming some senseless banalities, but Lorcan's ears were ringing from the heady mixture he had consumed.

He turned and hissed at the king, claws raised, ready to slash through the faerie's defences. The boy's memories had given him the means to destroy the faerie king if he threatened to interfere again.

* * *

The vampire stood before Nicola, his face twisted in a mask of rage, her son's blood staining his lips. His eyes burned a demonic red and the impression of leathery wings beat against his back. Azuradien jumped back as Lorcan's claws swept in front of his face.

Ashul's words cut through the chaos. 'Complete what was promised or you will not leave this room!' Ashul's sword flared in his hand and the vampire shrunk from the light. The appearance of wings dissolved, and the fire dimmed in his eyes. Lorcan nodded towards the warrior and dropped his mouth to his own wrist, breaking the skin with the daintiest of nicks. Ashul stepped forward, raising his sword above his head.

'His heart is about to stop,' said Lorcan. 'He needs blood returned and only mine will suffice.' Lorcan no longer looked like a threatening creature. Nothing but an arrogant young man stood at her son's side.

Nicola nodded her assent. Michael's skin remained blue and ice crystals hung on his eyelashes.

Lorcan crossed his wrist over Michael's, placing the open wounds on top of each other. Lorcan wrapped his free hand around both of their wrists, pushing them closer together. Blood ran down from their bare arms and dripped onto the sheets.

Nicola waited. One second passed, then two, then Michael leapt up from the bed. It was like he had taken an adrenaline shot straight to the heart. Water ran from his skin as the remaining ice warmed and melted.

Lorcan pulled his arm away and stepped back from the bed. His face appeared a shade paler than it had previously. 'I have done what I can, I must process this poison.' He dissolved into the shadows before the last word was spoken. Nicola knelt by Michael's side and grabbed his hand. His skin was warm to her touch.

She waited by Michael's side, wishing his eyes would open, fearing what she would see when they did.

* * *

The faeries had brought the crystal into play.

It could feel the incessant buzz running through Its bones. It was like being shaken apart from within. The constant, unrelenting nature of the vibration was maddening. How dare they? The crystal had never left the confines of the faeries' little realm in all the time It had been in existence. The faeries were conspiring to make It act before It had time to gain the strength required to merge the realms. But the faeries had never used the crystal against It before. It was the key to their realm. Why would they risk such a thing?

It had something to do with the boy. He was a manipulative little whelp, but It had no idea what could be achieved by this play.

It could not stay exposed to the crystal for any length of time. It could not focus Its thoughts while It remained nearby. And without focus It could not control the minds of others.

It did not have the energy to move again. It had expended too much of its resources cultivating the current crop of connections. Every good farmer knows that you don't leave your land until it's been harvested. It needed to stay to continue to feed. And if it moved, it would not be as close to the breach. And that was just not acceptable.

The disciples were not yet ready to intervene. But It had enough of them at Its disposal to force the lamb's hand. It would spare Marcus no longer.

There would be no more delays. It needed life's blood, not the pitiful trickling it had received so far. If they did not comply, It had enough fingers in enough minds to force submission.

This family might have been able to hinder Its rise to power, draining the ether of energy like fire consuming oxygen. But they were also feeding off the warrior. Clinging to his back, sucking at him like leeches, corrupting his purpose, weakening his resolve.

It had to act now. It might not be able to merge the realms without the warrior's life, but with the drawing of life's blood, It could punch a hole through the barrier that separated the realms for long enough to make things interesting.

Control

Ashul watched over Michael's sleep. The warrior did not move from his side and he refused to rest. Nicola tried to reach out to Michael, but he was insulated from her. She could sense his presence but couldn't get close enough to make contact with him.

'Can you speak to him, Ashul?' asked Nicola. 'Can you reach him?'

'He has taken his mind to a place of protection,' said Ashul. 'It shields him from the Nachzehrer influence.'

'But you found him before.' Nicola was almost pleading with him.

'He needed me then,' Ashul replied. 'He rests now.'

'How can you be sure he doesn't need you now?'

'I would know, as would you.' He looked at her sideways as if to say 'don't ask me questions you already know the answers to'. 'Reaching out to him now may endanger his recovery,' he said.

Nicola sighed. She knew Ashul was right, but she feared for Michael. His body had responded quickly to the release of the poison from his system, but she had no way of knowing whether he still held infection within his body. When she washed the briny residue from his face and arms, the puncture wounds on his wrist had already healed over. Two pale patches on his skin were the only sign that the 'ancient one' had bitten him. She had only Lorcan's word that his bite would not impact Michael. Azuradien loathed the creature, and Nicola had nothing apart from her daughter's instincts saying that she should trust Lorcan and even that had been given with caveats.

'You had no other option,' Ashul said from behind her shoulder.

'It was my fault he got infected. My warding was flawed. I didn't protect him.' Nicola barely kept the tears from her eyes.

'All wardings are flawed. If they were not, the battle would be over before it began.'

'My son isn't a battle to be won or lost,' said Nicola. She turned towards Ashul – sometimes she hated his twisted view on the world.

'I disagree. And if you did not agree, you would not have risked the "ancient one's" bite. I did not understand that before. I do now.' Ashul looked down upon Michael. Nicola had once again misjudged his stoicism. His fear was as great as hers.

'You have changed,' said Nicola, acknowledging the pain in his eyes.

'I cannot change.' Ashul looked like he would turn away, but he only straightened his shoulders. 'They did not create us with the ability to change. Adapt to circumstances, yes. But to actually change, no.'

'Were you created with a mortal boy as one of your number, one of the twenty-eight?' Nicola reached up and grasped his hand.

She waited for his response. When none came, she used his strength to pull herself to her feet.

'I'm going to grab us some food.' Bending down, Nicola kissed Michael's cheek and whispered into his ear, 'Twenty-eight and always, my love.' When she raised herself to her feet, she saw the Ashul had mouthed the same words. Where she professed the infinite nature of her love for her children, Ashul spoke of duty and obligation.

Nicola walked from the room, wishing on some level that she could hate the warrior that stood at her son's side. He had drawn her son into this battle and would command him to fight many more. But the words Ashul spoke for no-one but himself left no room for hate: 'He cannot be lost.'

Nicola paused in the hallway, one hand resting on the wall, and she let her tears fall.

* * *

Dana had fallen asleep surrounded by multicolour Post-it Notes. She'd started sticking them to the side of her computer, then decided she needed a larger area. She was looking into the people that were suspected to be under the doll's influence, trying to find a pattern. She'd spent half the night searching Facebook profiles and stalking social media accounts, looking for some connection. There was an obvious cluster that lived in the immediate vicinity but there were some outliers. She'd also identified a second smaller more scattered group. After clearing some pictures off her wall, she had created her own map, pinning strings of connection where there seemed to be an obvious link between individuals. Currently things seemed to be mostly geographical.

She suspected she'd found the general area that Marcus and his family had taken refuge in after the explosion in the street, somewhere further out from the city, in farming land. It confirmed that the doll's taint had not spread like an infection: the doll needed proximity to work its special brand of magic.

The radius of influence was definitely growing, so they could also assume the doll's strength was increasing. If the doll's strength waned, would the people impacted just revert back to normal? They had no real idea of what the doll did to a person's mind. She would have to contact Captain Dave to compare notes, see if his sources were coming up with the same kind of data. What did puzzle Dana was why there was a proximity base at all.

The doll was attacking people in the second realm and the second realm did not have the same geographical boundaries as the first realm, so why the expanding field of influence? Why not a random scattering of violence? It was better for them that there was some kind of limitation to the doll's influence. It would be easier to monitor, but Dana was uncertain how monitoring the spread actually helped them.

They knew already that the doll was the cause. And where they found Marcus, they would find the doll. But Dana was not so certain. She made a mental note to ask her dad if he'd actually seen Marcus recently. He hadn't been at school, and when she'd asked around, nobody had seen him in the last week at least. Why this should concern her, she wasn't entirely certain.

In her sea of multicoloured notes, she fell asleep, and dreamt of her brother. His features kept blurring. At first, he looked unconcerned, carefree. Michael's normal expression.

Then his face would grow stern, light brown eyes fading until they were a cool ice blue. Ashul's features merged with Michael's: the jaw strengthened, the hair became streaked through with ash highlights. Just as the face settled, Michael appeared again only for his hair to darken all the way to black, a sneer turning up the corner of his mouth. Michael's olive skin grew sickly and pale. Marcus' image stayed true for only a moment.

Like a cheap B-grade movie, the image changed again. Red eyes glowed, canine teeth extended and although the skin stayed pale, it now shone with inner health. Lorcan stepped forward, his handsome features in no way diminished by the white teeth displayed confidently. The lips remained turned up at one corner, but where Marcus sneered, Lorcan smirked with his amusement palpable. He closed the gap to her dream self, inching closer. His head tilted to the side as if he were trying to understand what stood in front of him. As sometimes happens in dreams, when he reached his hand towards her, she moved closer to him without making any attempt to do so. She tilted her head, trying to understand him in return.

She couldn't read Lorcan, although she felt that in time this would change. He seemed more animal than human, so if she just studied him more carefully, she'd be able to gather more truth from his body language than she would ever gain from listening to his words.

Lorcan's face blurred. Dana was intrigued: whose face would be the next to appear?

The smile grew warm, the features less angular: an amalgamation of both Lorcan and Michael. The face before her seemed to notice Dana for the first time, and with this recognition the smile finally reached the eyes. Dana closed the gap between them and the smile broadened, then broadened further. As it did, it started to slide and the skin split and slid from the bone. Hair twisted into matted ropes while the gums receded and the exposed teeth turned yellow. Mouldered flesh barely held the eyes in place as they rolled in the sockets. When the eyes finally returned to stare at her, thick cataracts had formed and the pupils were a milky white.

The moment held. The image stood unnaturally still. The head tilted ever so slightly in mockery. The mouth opened as a snarl ripped from its throat and diseased teeth snapped at her face. The Nachzehrer struck fast as a snake. It gripped Dana behind her head and pulled her closer.

* * *

Michael lay submerged in the cool, still waters of his protective lake. He did not know how he'd created this place, but knew it insulated him from outside influences.

He had not been aware of the Nachzehrer's slow creep into the recesses of his consciousness until it tried to take full control. So focused on monitoring his body for signs of infection, he didn't feel the insidious presence infecting and overwhelming his thoughts. When the urge for violence blossomed in his mind, he first thought of the doll. It had played with him before, and he'd witnessed just how strong the doll's parasitic attachments were becoming. Throughout the course of the day, the doll's slaves had attacked Michael on two separate occasions. So when the referee's features blurred behind the doll's amniotic membrane, he recoiled, knowing a third attack was imminent. But far too quickly for him to control, his anger had risen. The need to destroy the man in front of him had become overwhelming.

He imagined his fingers curling under flesh, tearing the second skin from his face. He had wanted to pry the man's jaws open, force him to eat the caul that he'd allowed by his own weakness to envelop him like a second malignant skin, infecting his thoughts, polluting his mind. The doll was trying to mess with business that was no longer within its dominion. The boy had been marked. The boy would be claimed. And the doll would pay for the temerity of endeavouring to subvert the normal, natural course of things.

As fingers curled and muscles bunched ready to tear at the doll's minion, Michael threw himself out of his own body, knowing that the Nachzehrer had risen to the fore of his mind and was trying to take control. Michael did the only thing he could: he removed not only his consciousness, but also something more.

In the embrace of the protective waters, Michael floated, holding a small, curved device in his hands. It looked and felt like a standard video-game controller but it represented much more in this mental construct of his. The controller represented power, the power of movement. Michael had thought the Nachzehrer wanted to feed off his energy, parasitic like so many other creatures he'd come in contact with. But the Nachzehrer was more like a virus, and some viruses protected the host so they could reproduce and infect others. It was not his mind that the Nachzehrer wanted, just control of his body. But the Nachzehrer, in that moment standing in front of the referee, had given too much away. With its blatant desire to destroy the doll's puppet, it had let its true purpose be known. The Nachzehrer was a hive mind that wanted to control Michael. Once subverted by it, he would be used to create more of its kind, to create a legion.

Michael watched as the thin tendrils of Lorcan's blood circled around him, threading through the water but never dispersing. Michael knew that there was great strength to be gained if he allowed the blood to mix with the liquid that protected him, but it was a choice he didn't have to make, not yet.

The Nachzehrer waited at the shores of the lake, but it no longer looked down hungrily.

It sniffed the air, wandering around confused, searching for Michael. He knew it would pick up his scent again eventually. The poison in his system had been greatly reduced, and although the vampire's blood had sent it into a form of remission, it still sat in his bloodstream dormant, biding its time.

Michael breathed in deeply as the water filled his lungs, the energy the liquid contained thrummed through his system, bolstering his reserves but as a consequence the distance between himself and the shore diminished.

Everything was a trade-off. It was just a simple fact, so he welcomed the energy, knowing the cost. Thankfully, the zombie continued to stride around without immediate purpose. But it would not stay that way. Michael knew that he would not be able to maintain the size of the lake indefinitely. The distances between the shore and himself would diminish to the point that the zombie would be able to reach him, and when it did – controller or no controller – his body would belong to the Nachzehrer.

Michael knew all of this but he focused his resolve regardless and made the flip back into his own body.

* * *

Nicola sat with the gypsy book in her lap, the weight heavy against her legs. Her fingers trembled slightly as she traced the emblem on the cover. Dragon's wings, tree of life, the sword held by the dragon's tail, raised ready to defend but also precariously balanced above the dragon's head.

The book had clearly warned of all that was at stake. She'd thought the dragon only represented the bonded, she now realised it was a symbol of all of those of the blood. Balancing the need to defend the source of life against their own wellbeing. Her own son was such a crystalline example of the war that they'd been driven to fight. It almost broke Nicola's heart to think of the sacrifices he'd made already.

She would not let some trumped-up infection be the thing that caused the sword to drop. If she needed to lose another piece of herself searching for a solution to his predicament, then so be it. She'd always intended to enter the book and help release the trapped memories, but hoped she could find a way back that did not require a fragment of herself to be left behind.

But the book required payment.

If you required the answer to a specific question, then you had to pay for that knowledge. Nothing came without a price.

Nicola took a deep breath and curled her fingers around the book's edge. The smell of dry paper assaulted her nostrils. The sound of pages turning whispered to her.

'Mum, we don't need that just yet,' said Michael. His long fingers gently closed the cover of the book and removed it from her hands.

'We may later on, but not right now,' he said. 'So, call in the troops, all of them. And can we get some eggs and bacon cooking because I am starving?'

Nicola jumped up and wrapped her arms around his neck, having to stand on tiptoes to reach his face. His skin was cool to the touch and his eyes were clear of any colour but his own. She patted his hair down, brushing at the errant strands around his ears.

'Mum, settle! I'm fine. But I really do need those eggs.'

* * *

Michael sat back and shovelled the last scoopful of scrambled eggs into his mouth. Ashul had eaten almost as much as him. The two of them fought over the last hash brown but Michael let Ashul have it. They were only out of a packet. Now if they'd been homemade, then that would have definitely been a different story.

Michael stretched and looked around at the crowded room. The kitchen area was full. Ashley and her parents had arrived within minutes of receiving the call. Captain Dave and Tony had arrived too, and they were now fascinated by the two faeries standing at the kitchen table.

'Okay, does anybody know how to get in touch with the vampire?' Michael turned to Nicola, then Azuradien. 'He needs to be included in this discussion.'

'He is an atrocity and should be destroyed,' Azuradien said from the corner of the room.

'Technically, he's not a vampire,' said Dana. 'And he saved my brother's life. So if anybody deserves to be part of the conversation, then he does.' Dana was already bristling at Azuradien's attitude.

Ashul nodded his agreement. 'So how do we get in contact with him? Any ideas?'

'You have but to speak my name and there I shall be.' Lorcan walked around the kitchen bench, casually running his fingertip through the bacon fat left on the plate. He lifted the finger to his mouth to savour the flavours.

'You respond to no summons,' Azuradien said, stepping towards Lorcan. 'You answer only to your thirst.'

'True, and somewhat partially true,' hissed Lorcan. 'But what exactly is your point, old one? Is the boy any less alive because I am not to your delicate taste?' The points of his teeth were clearly visible. Dave and Tony jumped from their chairs when they realised who and what had entered the room with them.

'Okay guys, we get it, you hate each other,' said Michael. 'Lorcan, I'm sure you had some ulterior motive for intervening, but to be quite frank, I don't really care. I am just grateful to be alive. Wasn't quite ready to be the harbinger of death. So, thank you.' Michael nodded this thanks to Lorcan. 'But we have to refocus. The doll is the enemy here; the Nachzehrer are just a nasty distraction—'

Azuradien interrupted, 'The Nachzehrer will release a plague on the world and you will be their instrument.'

'I was very nearly their instrument – it was a close call. But with Lorcan's aid, the infection has been contained.'

'I notice you say contained but not eradicated,' countered Azuradien.

'I could have lied.' Michael was fast losing patience. 'Would you have known? You had already written me off—'

Ashul placed his body between that of the faerie and Michael and his family. 'This conversation is beneath us,' he said. 'The infection is contained. All can see the proof of that. Do you believe you can keep it that way?'

'I have a means of evaluating my level of exposure,' said Michael, barely above a whisper.

'You will exhaust yourself keeping the balance.' Ashul said this so all could hear. The words spoken into Michael's mind showed the depth of his concern. *The bonded will share this burden. You cannot maintain the level of your 'lake' without us. We can keep the shore at a safe distance.* Michael almost broke down at his friend's willingness to share the load and his understanding of the lake's purpose. *I was there with you, brother. I have seen the depth of your spirit.*

'I will maintain the balance for as long as I must. Then I'm hoping Lorcan will cure me completely.'

'Hang on, hang on,' said Dana. '*If* Lorcan can cure you. Let's get that done first. We can focus on the doll when you're better. I promise Michael I have been working on some theories. I think with Ashley's gifts, we can track down the doll's unwitting allies. Maybe then we can…'

'… cut off the supply line,' Michael finished.

'I would have said food source, but essentially, yes. Michael, if you can be cured, the rest can wait,' Dana said, almost pleading with Michael.

'The vampire can cure no-one…' the faerie king said.

Nicola turned on Azuradien. 'I asked you here as an advisor. We respect your knowledge. But if you keep making statements purely on personal bias, then you give us no choice but to ignore everything you say, because we have no way to discern truth from fiction. Please, Azuradien, we take none of this lightly, but you disrespect us when you try to manipulate us in this way.'

Without waiting for any further rebukes, Nicola turned to Lorcan. 'Can he be cured?'

'I believe he can. It will be a painful process. I would need to transfuse a larger quantity of my blood into his system. At higher levels, my blood will hunt down and eradicate the poison.'

'Will your blood then become a new infection my son needs to fight?' Nicola asked the question that all of them were concerned with 'Will the cure become worse than the disease?'

'Only if I choose it to be so.'

'And will you so choose it? Please speak plainly, we talk of my son's life.' Nicola was obviously getting exhausted by the constant talking in circles. Michael had to agree with her. Lorcan and Azuradien spent more time scoring points than they did actually providing insight.

'No, I will not turn your son into one of my own. But I do believe in keeping my options open, so at a later date your son and I may have a little chat about conversion.' Lorcan spoke about the conversion of Michael into a blood sucking beast with such disregard that Michael thought he could actually see the blood rushing to his mother's head. Nicola's jaw clenched, but Ashley intervened before she lost all of her composure.

'So why don't we cure him now?' said Ashley. Michael didn't envy Ashley's ability to pick up on all the emotion in the room. She must be well and truly over the bullshit.

So Michael answered as plainly as he could: 'Because I need to be able to see with Nachzehrer eyes. The Nachzehrer poison gives me the ability to see the things that they see.'

'Nicola, you cannot listen to this talk,' Malcarielle said, adding her voice to the discussion. 'Michael's safety should be our primary concern here.'

Joseph agreed. 'I'm with Malcarielle on this. Everything else be damned. I want Michael safe.'

Michael ignored the arguments. He spoke only to his family, and his brothers. 'I can see the doll's embryotic sac hanging over the faces of its victims,' he said. 'It's connected to victims by a sort of umbilical, but I reckon it might be more like a mosquito's proboscis. It's sucking away the energy created by the mayhem it is forcing the puppets to cause. I can't see these cauls all the time, but I can see them when the Nachzehrer poison has reached certain levels in me. I'll be reliant on Lorcan to help to maintain those levels.'

'If I could interject,' said Lorcan. 'You are not seeing through Nachzehrer eyes per se, I think it's the scars on your eyes that give you the ability to see what you do. And what you're seeing is actually called the shadowland!'

Malcarielle's and Azuradien's reactions mirrored each other. Their wings beat against the air, causing the curtains to bang against the window frames.

Malcarielle was the first to speak. 'Nicola, Michael you cannot believe this! The shadowland is a story made to frighten young children. It does not exist.' Her gaze jumped from one face to another, begging for someone to hear the madness in Lorcan's words.

Lorcan said, 'Ah faeries, you never believe in what you cannot control.' Lorcan turned away from the group.

'I know what I saw,' said Michael. He was growing impatient. They just didn't have the time to fight over every remark. 'Explain how it is that I can see the doll's connections to these people.'

'You have been ill, delirious most of the time. You have vampire venom circulating in your bloodstream. Are you sure you actually saw these cauls?' Azuradien made this remark in a patronising way that made Michael grit his teeth.

'Step lightly, Azuradien,' said Ashul.

'The shadowland does not exist.' – Azuradien was adamant in his stance – 'The second sight of the boy's is either delusion or something else altogether.'

Michael was trying to find a way to move the conversation forward. It was like arguing with flat-earthers. Some people believed what they wanted to, not always where the facts led. Truth be told, he didn't really care if there was a shadowland. It made no difference to him. He just wanted to exploit any advantage they had, while they had it.

'This is getting us nowhere.' Lorcan had turned back to the group. He locked his gaze with Michael. 'I believe it is the burn they inflicted, the point of contagion that gives you the sight. We can test this theory rather easily.' Lorcan stepped closer to Michael as he spoke. 'We can activate the scars by revealing the shadowland without the risk of the

Nachzehrer poison, or their proximity.' Lorcan was studying Michael's eyes carefully. Michael was sure that with his superior eyesight he could make out the hand-shaped scar on each eye. Michael had seen them himself in the mirror when the lighting was just right.

Lorcan placed a foot into the second plane. He did not call forward any of his powers, yet Michael was able to see him in his other form.

Michael felt it when his eyes flared white. He took in a long calming breath. No-one else in the room reacted. 'Okay, so you can be pretty scary when you want to be.'

Lorcan slowly cast his gaze around the room, first at Dana, then eventually back to Michael. 'Would you like me to show you my other, older form? Now that we've proved that you see what others do not. Proved that you, indeed, see into this fictional shadowland.'

Lorcan's hugely powerful, leathery black wings sprouted from his back and his eyes burned with internal fire. His ears were sharply pointed like a bat's, constantly twitching in different directions. His body elongated with legs that somehow made him look like a wolf. Lorcan needed to crouch because the roof was too low for his body in this form. Yet Michael couldn't call the creature that stood in front of him repulsive. It was scary because if he chose to, he could kill him in any number of interesting ways. Michael doubted he would have time to even register an attack. But Lorcan was still somehow majestic. Like all apex predators, they had their own deadly beauty that could not be denied.

'No, I think I'm good.' Michael was relieved when Lorcan placed both feet in the first plane and the shadowland disappeared. The room stayed quiet; they all knew Michael had seen something, but no-one was willing to ask what it was.

'Okay, so Lorcan just sort of… placed a foot in the second plane…' Michael said. He thought an explanation was warranted.

'No creature resides in both realms simultaneously. Their soul must be in one realm or the other. You cannot split your life force,' Malcarielle said with some hesitation.

'Malcarielle, I just witnessed it!' Michael didn't know what else he could say to make the faeries believe him.

Lorcan was pacing back and forth. 'The Nachzehrer are both dead and alive. They have a place in both worlds.' Lorcan said this directly to Ashul. It appeared that he was done trying to convince the faeries.

'Yes, but they inhabit only one realm at a time,' said Ashul. 'Much like we all do.' Ashul indicated with his hands and a nod of his head that Lorcan was possibly an exception.

'Agreed. But we have an active outbreak on our hands. As Michael's infection increases, it may give the Nachzehrer the ability to access both realms, exposing the shadowland to them.'

'Do we care?' Joseph asked what everyone else had been wondering. 'If this shadowland is just another realm like the second plane, then who cares?' Joseph shrugged without apology.

'The shadowland is not just another realm. It is like a reflection of the first plane, but distorted. Darker, but intrinsically linked to this world and the second plane' Lorcan studiously ignored the faeries' protests. 'How these worlds interact has never been explored. Which is a good thing because the first plane and the shadowland are polar opposites.'

'The shadowland has not been explored because it does not exist,' said Malcarielle. She tried to take the sting out of her words with an explanation. 'Many have searched but no proof of its existence has ever been found. There are stories, yes. Tales of darkfields, underworlds, otherworlds, afterworlds. All cultures have such dark places, a land filled with horrors used to reinforce a belief that this world is special. The shadowland is a setting for cautionary tales used to scare children!'

Malcarielle's words were having no impact on the group. No-one was convinced. They had been forced to believe in things recently that months before would have been laughed away as nothing more than nonsense. The faeries' existence ironically being one of those very things.

Malcarielle gave it one more shot. 'The faerie have ever been connected to the earth. If another realm existed, connected to this one, then it would have been discovered. Believe me, we have tried to find proof.'

'And there was a time that humans believed the moon to be made of cheese,' Lorcan said dismissively. 'Believing something to be true does not make it so.'

'Dogs have been proven to hear things outside of our range,' said Dana, jumping into the discussion. 'Maybe we just don't have the senses required to perceive the shadowland.'

'But those sounds are measurable, Dana,' Azuradien countered.

'Michael just measured it. He saw something that we did not.' Dana had already dismissed Azuradien and posed her next question to Lorcan. 'If we assume that the shadowland exists for just one moment,' Dana held up her hand to forestall any protests, 'you believe it is this touching on both realms simultaneously that, what, opens a portal? That because the Nachzehrer are accessing both, that Michael can too through his scars.'

Lorcan seemed to be thinking out loud more than trying to debate the issue. 'Well, not a portal no, more like a viewing platform. What I have seen recently would indicate that this is indeed what is happening. The problem we have is that we cannot be certain that Michael's scars – his lens into this other world – will remain after the poison in his system has been destroyed.'

'Does the shadowland pose any risk to Michael?' Nicola asked.

'Not the seeing itself,' replied Lorcan. 'But I would not go around broadcasting the ability. There are creatures in the shadowland that may take great offence at their privacy being breached.' Azuradien scoffed loudly at Lorcan's remarks.

'You think you know more than I do, Faerie King? I was old and jaded before the first whiskers sprouted from your chin. You would be advised to treat me with respect. The Nachzehrer have unknowingly given you a very powerful tool. Use the bonded to help maintain the control you require to keep the infection dormant, and use this gift to hunt down the doll's puppets.'

'I think the doll knows of my infection,' said Michael, wishing he had something positive to say. 'The doll's human troops have attacked me on three separate occasions. The Nachzehrer within me believed the doll was trying to subvert their attempt at full ascension.'

'So, even the doll fears the Nachzehrer,' Azuradien said. 'The Nachzehrer alone is a significant threat. I believe none of these tales about the shadowland. Nor do I believe this creature and his claims of a cure. Nicola, let me take Michael to safety. Many lives depend on it.' Azuradien was almost begging Nicola.

'The Nachzehrer is little more than the common cold with delusions of grandeur,' Lorcan countered. 'The bonded have already destroyed countless of their kind. We can extinguish them when the boy is cured. I will even join you. It has been a few hours since my last zombie hunt.'

'And why do you care?' said Ashul. 'Lorcan, you have stayed out of our battles for millennia. Why now do you offer us aid?' Ashul didn't ask this in an accusatory tone, he was purely after information.

Lorcan noticeably paused before he answered, 'Would you believe I've had a change of heart?'

Ashul folded his arms across his chest. 'I would believe no such thing.' His sword had appeared on his back, summoned forth from the second realm.

'Lorcan, I have access to the memories of some of the strongest mages to have ever lived,' said Nicola. 'Inside me is the knowledge of a master combined with the ruthless determination of a woman whose son is being threatened. My husband could call down a lightning bolt that would send millions of volts of electricity coursing through your body. and if you still stood, he would burn you with fire that raged so hot it would make your bones melt.' There was no anger in Nicola's tone, yet her words rang with the promise of what she was willing to do to protect her son. 'Do you really think it is wise to play games with people whose children are in danger?'

'Well, if only you had asked so nicely in the first place.' Lorcan smiled. Michael didn't think he felt threatened in any way. 'Your son has a potential that has never before been seen. He is mortal, but he has access to the bonded and all of their considerable powers. Yet he has no magical protection, so any creature with the ability to capture, control or possess him will endeavour to do so. Because in controlling him, you control the bonded. And the bonded without their oaths would cause a considerable shift in the current power structure.'

'So you want to control my son?' said Nicola. 'Not to help us, just to further your cause.'

'My dear lady, you misunderstand me. I am the most powerful creature you will ever have the misfortune of meeting. I will not allow the rise of one whose power might rival my own. So I will ensure he stays mortal and bonded, but no more.'

'So we cannot trust you.'

'I never asked for your trust. I have been honest with you in all my dealings. I have great admiration for the boy's strength. So I will continue to keep him safe. That you do not appreciate my motives is for your own conscience to dwell upon. But you can be sure that my motivation will always be my own, not the product of a compulsion written into my DNA. Nor will my actions be limited by a covenant that is tantamount to hiding behind your mother's skirts.' Lorcan turned abruptly. 'Michael, Dana always a pleasure.' With a quick twist that was almost a twirl, he vanished into the shadows.

Finding the Dreamer

Michael thought that the impromptu war council had gone pretty well, all things considered. Nobody had killed each other. The faeries hadn't imprisoned Michael, pending disposal – because for all of his pretty words, that was the king's intention.

'Are we going to discuss the ramification of the vampire's motivations?' asked Azuradien. *Had Michael actually thought that Azuradien could move on?*

'What exactly is there to discuss?' said Michael. 'I think he was pretty candid about his "motivations". He's going to help me keep the infection dormant, which, based on the prognosis yesterday, is a pretty big win.' Michael began to turn to speak to Ashley.

'His soul is corrupt! He will betray…'

'Azuradien, you do not have the right to judge the ancient one,' said Ashul, his voice commanding. 'You were not part of the cleansing. He put himself in grave danger to take the infection into his own body and Michael is safe because of his actions.'

'The boy is not safe. The inevitable has just been postponed. I speak these words not to harm, but to prepare you all for what is to come.'

'But you harm, nevertheless. The boy's name is Michael, and you will refer to him by name and with respect. He had the strength to endure last night where most would have succumbed.' Ashul was showing signs of genuine anger for the first time in Michael's memory.

'I had a little help,' Michael interjected, not liking the direction the conversation was taking.

Azuradien countered, 'The vampire does not help you, he is looking out for his own best interests.'

'I wasn't talking about the bloody vampire. You need to get over yourself. I was talking about Ashul. He helped me get through the cleansing.'

'I shared the burden. Nothing more,' said Ashul.

'How exactly did you share this burden?' asked Azuradien. 'Did you absorb his pain?'

'Michael would not allow me to do so. So I travelled with him – we endured together.'

'Travelled where?'

'Where we travelled is not your concern,' said Ashul. 'I would not leave Michael to stand alone. We are bonded, we stand together.' Ashul placed his hand upon Michael's shoulder.

'Tell me you have not endangered the bonded.' Azuradien was looking more agitated.

'The bonded are here to serve the blood,' said Ashul as he drew himself up tall. 'The very nature of the call has always placed us in danger. You seem to have forgotten the bonded's place in things, but we have not. We sleep until there is peril and then we rise to fight.'

Michael could sense that all the bonded, on both the first and the second planes, were listening to Ashul's words, and their thoughts mirrored their leader's resolve.

Michael wasn't sure exactly what Azuradien was asking, but he'd offended Ashul by the inference that the bonded would do anything less than everything in their power.

Nicola had picked up on something Michael had not. She reached forward to grasp Ashul's hand and asked, 'Ashul, have you been exposed to the same infection? Are the bonded at risk of getting sick?'

'The bonded were exposed to the same infection the moment the Nachzehrer burned its image onto Michael's eyes.'

'I'm not talking about Michael right now. Were *you* exposed?' Nicola asked gently. The warrior was getting irritated by the questioning.

'If you understood the nature of our bond, you would not ask such irrelevant questions. There is only the bonded. We are one.'

Nicola was about to ask it another way, but Captain Dave stopped her.

'Leave him be.' Dave spoke quietly. He gained volume as he continued, 'Maybe only those who have served together would understand. Don't push him further. He *has* answered your question.' Nicola looked ready to argue, but nobody seemed to support that decision, so she nodded and moved back to her place by the bench.

Everybody in the room seemed hesitant, but they had no time for that kind of shit.

'Dana, your list, have you given it to the captain?' Michael said, trying to move the conversation along. 'We need to get some idea of scope on this thing.' Michael knew Dana would be the first to snap out of the mood Azuradien had placed on the group. Dana needed to be active – she couldn't stand around having inane discussions for hours on end. She would want to be working towards some goal. And as Michael predicted, she ran up to her room and quickly returned with pages of notes relating to the people they had suspected of being under the doll's influence.

Dave pulled a map of the area out of his jacket pocket and marked the addresses Dana provided. She texted Dave a set of notes with names, ages, addresses and even the school or place of work of the people identified. Michael made eye contact with Dana and raised his eyebrows in an 'are you kidding me?' expression.

'Give me a break, Michael,' said Dana. 'I was worried sick about you. It was getting a bit awkward with the three of us standing over your bed watching you sleep.' Dana returned to the map laid out on the table. Dave and Tony produced lists of their own. Ashley shrugged and pulled out her phone, adding four names to their list. Soon Dana was giving everyone a crash course in social media stalking. In less time than seemed decent, lists of personal information for almost all the doll's suspected puppets had been compiled.

Michael reviewed the map. Referencing Dana's notes, he grabbed a yellow highlighter and circled the people he'd seen with the doll's embryotic connection. 'Dave, can you mark those who are in a coma?' A couple of names were circled in blue.

'Damn, I was hoping for more,' said Michael.

'Michael, there are over thirty people marked on that map. We have got to assume the number could be double that.' Nicola's voice shook on the last word.

'No, Mum,' said Michael. 'I was hoping for more coma victims. We're going to be able to see them on both of Aunt Sarah's networks, present in one form in both the first and second realms. Body in one, soul or whatever you choose to call it in another, right?'

'They're in a deep sleep,' said Azuradien. 'Their soul will be present in the second realm, unless it's only their body that remains. A body can't survive in the first plane long after its life force has moved on. It may continue to breathe for a time but this is more from a sense of habit. Eventually, this too will cease.'

'We definitely have to work on your bedside manner, Azuradien. A simple yes would have sufficed.' The faerie had the decency to look apologetic at Michael's rebuke.

Michael gave a quick shake of his head. He was constantly surprised by the faeries' lack of empathy.

'So why were you hoping for more coma victims? Nicola asked.

'My thoughts are that we go over to the second realm now, check out the coma victims, see if we can sever the doll's connection. Malcarielle and Azuradien could work with Dave and Aunty Sarah. We need to see if we can get the energy net to show all the people connected to the doll, starting with the people on this map.' Michael felt like the instructions should be coming from Ashul or his mother but Azuradien could go all 'end of the world' on them again at any moment so he thought it best to rush on through.

Maybe Ashul heard his thoughts because he started issuing instructions to the group.

'The bonded will split up,' said Ashul. 'Sarah has us marked on her network, no?' At Sarah's nod, Ashul continued, 'So half the bonded in Sarah's group go with Dave and Azuradien to find those linked to the doll.' Ashul turned to Sarah.' Am I correct in saying that when direct contact is made, the energy signature should appear on the network?' Sarah nodded that he was correct. 'Then Malcarielle, Joseph, Sarah and Tony will monitor the network from here. The bonded that remain can share messages back and forth between them, and us.' Ashul continued when he received nods from all of Sarah's team. Though they were already starting to break off into separate groups, they were still listening to Ashul – just eager to get to it.

'Nicola, Dana, Brent and Ashley, you ride with us.' Ashul turned all of his focus onto those that would be accompanying him. 'We follow the network to each comatose individual. Ashley and Brent, we will be relying on your perceptions to keep us appraised of the health and wellbeing of each individual. You can sense this more deeply than the rest of us.' Ashul looked at each person in turn, a leader waiting for acknowledgment that his instructions had been understood. Ashley was the only one to look back hesitantly.

'Ashley, you were the first person to know that something was up with the crazy garden lady,' said Michael, understanding her hesitation. They were all new to their powers. 'I don't know if coma victims still give off emotions, but I *do* know that you would be the first to sense it if they did.' Michael looked directly into Ashley's eyes, bending his knees slightly so he was at her level. 'Are we good?'

'We're good,' said Ashley. 'But how are we going to locate people in the second realm? It doesn't have the same geographical properties as the first. It's not as if we can just head "north".'

'Michael, how did you get to the soccer match yesterday?' Nicola asked.

'I rode through the second realm.'

'But how did you know *where* to ride?' said Nicola.

'I had the location fixed in my mind, so I just rode.'

'We shape the second realm? Am I right, Ashul?' Dana asked. And when Ashul nodded she continued, 'It has no geographical correlation, but when we have a location in our minds we can travel towards it.' Dana seemed lost in thought, more talking to herself rather than the group. When she lifted her head, her words were directed at the room. 'So we start with Mr Stevens – that one should be easy. The bonded on the first plane will be able to use Sarah's network to guide us if we go astray.

* * *

Michael helped Ashley make the flip over into the second realm. Dana was so closely connected to both Michael and Titan that she found the shift easy to accomplish.

The grey void surrounded them. Michael no longer found the damp air or the oppressive atmosphere threatening. Ashley sat behind Michael on Smoke and gripped his waist tighter than was actually necessary. She was taking small shallow breaths as if the smell of the place offended her.

'Ash, try to breathe normally,' Michael said over his shoulder. 'Remember, this place is like modelling clay, it can become whatever you imagine. If you fear it, it will give you something to fear. We're just travelling through, so it won't pay us much mind unless you draw its attention.' He had to raise his voice to be heard over the wind generated as Smoke galloped through the void.

'Michael, just saying… your bedside manner could use a little polish too,' Ashley replied.

Michael noted her breathing had steadied even if her grip remained firm.

Ashul and Dana rode together, leading the group. Nicola rode with Darmead on Ember, tracking just behind Ashul's right shoulder, with Uncle Brent in the rear riding with Bellisan on Flint. Michael had to shake his head. A beaming grin split his uncle's face; he was almost hooting as the wind flew past his face.

Michael marvelled at the strange nature of the void. Mr Stevens lived in the same street as Michael's family, yet they galloped – perceiving no change in their surroundings – for what seemed like an hour. In almost imperceptible increments, the grey thickened around them, darkening with the speed of a storm front forming on a summer's afternoon. Soon, the void's dark mists enveloped them. A scattering of purple sparks that occasionally lit the darkness reinforced the impressions of thunderclouds.

Ashul called out over the wind, 'We travel to the dream quarter. It is removed from the part of the void we normally travel through in a way that is difficult to explain. The sleepers themselves know how vulnerable they are in this place and create their own protections. Each dream is a separate bubble suspended in the substance of the void. Sometimes the bubbles merge harmoniously, other times the overlap causes strange and frightening results. When we enter this honeycomb environment, we must stay neutral. Try not to show emotion. Remember, all that you see is of the dreamer's creation.'

Ashul had pulled to a stop as he spoke. He looked serious. 'We have not the right to intervene, nor to judge.' He dropped from Lightning's back in a smooth fluid movement. 'It is better we walk from here; the horses can oftentimes be perceived where we are not.' He waited with patience while everybody dismounted. Smoke nuzzled against Michael's neck before she kicked off and disappeared up into the swirling clouds. She was the first to be consumed by the grey mist, the colouring of the clouds perfectly matched to her silvery coat.

'Ashley, you must be our guide,' said Ashul.

Ashley's eyes were wide open. Whether she felt the burden of responsibility or was just remembering her last visit to the second realm, Michael wasn't certain. What he did know was that fear was baking off of Ashley in waves. So he gave her shoulder a quick squeeze.

She reached up and grabbed his hand, linked her fingers with his and squeezed hard. 'The dreamer is not always easy to identify in their own dream, and it will be your instincts that will help us understand what we are truly seeing. We must walk and wander. We shouldn't have to trespass into too many imaginings before we find your Mr Stevens.'

Ashul moved over to speak with Nicola and Brent. 'Be wary, we know not what we might find. Be ready to defend, but only if no other option is available. We are the intruders here.' Ashul nodded when Brent patted the canisters and small bottles that hung from the bandoliers that crisscrossed his chest.

'Well, it looks like you came prepared,' said Nicola. She had also noticed the weapons belts, but it was the X-Men style clothing Brent wore that made her lips twitch into a smirk.

'It felt right,' said Brent as he smiled back.

Michael took Ashul's cue to move on and stepped into the thickest concentration of swirling mist. He experienced a moment of resistance and his ears throbbed with the increase in pressure. Like walking through a thin plastic membrane, Michael felt the torn, pliable sheets drag against his face, clinging to his skin. With an audible pop, his ears readjusted, and the membrane re-knitted behind him.

He stepped through into a place where the sky above him was of the clearest azure. His feet lifted, and he felt a moment of dizzying vertigo when he realised there was no longer any ground beneath his feet.

The six of them hovered, suspended in the freedom of open air. With only the suggestion of movement, Michael was able to propel himself through the sky. The intoxicating thrill of the air blowing past his ears was so much like the first time he rode Smoke it made his heart race.

He indulged in a quick somersault, then after a mental reprimand from Ashul he refocused on the task at hand. An old woman dressed all in white appeared in the sky in front of them. She banked sharply to the right when she saw them, her eyes wide in fright. The white hair flowing behind her twisted in a maelstrom of crosscurrents. Michael tried to stay calm, but his hand reached across his shoulder to where his sword lay.

'Relax, Michael. You scared her. She's just an old lady dreaming of flight.' Ashley smiled as she spoke. 'Can you not sense the freedom she feels? Waking, she is alone and in a wheelchair. She is content with her own company but wishes again for the freedom of movement. Tomorrow she may run with the horses or swim with the dolphins. Today, she flies with the eagles.' And as if Ashley's words had summoned the birds, the wind beat with the sound of a hundred wings.

A great flock of eagles split apart, half banking left, half banking right. The wind buffeted Michael as the eagles flew past. The old woman slowed, allowed the birds to surround her, then they all dove towards a ground that Michael had not been aware existed until he watched them swoop amongst the treetops.

'They are all part of her, part of her subconscious,' said Dana as she watched the birds fly before her.

'Can you sense it too?' said Ashley as she turned to Dana for the briefest of seconds. 'I can see her connection to them. The trees and the sky are all part of the void, but the birds are aspects of her own spirit.' Ashley spoke. In awe of the beauty in front of her.

'No, I can't see the connection,' said Dana. 'But I would know if I flew amongst a convocation of eagles. There are no thermals in this place, the birds would struggle to fly so close.'

Where Ashley saw the connection of spirit, Dana recognised the errors in the bird's flight pattern. Michael marvelled at the strange paths each of their powers were taking, powers so linked to each of their personalities.

As Michael moved forward, he once again found resistance. Gravity seemed to reassert itself and a fine dusting of sand blew across his feet.

In the distance, a young woman walked hand in hand with a young man. Eyes only for each other. Crystal blue waters lapped at their ankles. The couple stopped to look out at the sun setting on the horizon. Yellow fire danced over the tips of the waves.

'Tell me it isn't the guy,' said Michael. 'This dream is a tad too rom-com.' Michael hoped Ashley would confirm his analysis.

'It's neither of them. Open your eyes, Michael. It's that girl there looking over her book and watching that couple.' Ashley pointed to the pair on the beach, then to the young girl reading her book.

'She hasn't turned a page. I can see a connection linking them. She's the source, all the others feed out from her.' For a moment Michael saw a network of thin cables running from the girl towards the couple and the other people laying on the beach. Ashley was transfixed by what only she could perceive.

* * *

Nicola had been standing back, taking in the details, trying to see a little of what Ashley did. The construct of the void was clear to her. Behind the sand and sky, a faint grey veil shimmered, ready to consume the details of the dream's fabrication as soon as the mind generating the specifics returned to consciousness. She felt a level of unease in this dream that she didn't perceive in the previous dream. One was about freedom, the lifting of constraints, this one was about something altogether different.

Nicola didn't need Ashley's gift to feel the edge of uncertainty simmering below the surface of the dream. The sun shone a little too bright, and the water on the horizon looked ready to ignite. The sun did not simply reflect off the ocean peaks but threatened to catch like a match held to gasoline. When the girl pretending to read dropped her book to the sand, Nicola felt a cold gust of wind brush against her face. Sand blew into her eyes and a dark shadow fell over the young woman's face.

As the cloud moved in front of the sun, the girl's shadow lengthened and distorted. Arms grew longer, legs bowed. In the few seconds that it took for the cloud to travel across the horizon, the girl's persona had changed dramatically.

Gone was the timid young girl. A vengeful siren now stood in her place.

Hair that had been pushed neatly behind her ears now blew about her face, lashing out around her in a twisted mane lit by a fire that came from within.

Ashley confirmed what Nicola had suspected. 'The doll is here. I can see him. He's stuck to her like a second skin, a distorted shadow.'

The girl on the beach threw her arms around the boy's neck. She laughed as she pulled the boy down into a passionate embrace, yet her eyes also seemed to mock the dreamer. And as can only happen in dreams, the girl was able to simultaneously kiss the boy while remaining facing the dreamer, laughing too. The image flickered and the distance between the two women halved.

'Do not intervene,' said Ashul in a commanding tone. 'This is but a dream. We do not want to draw the doll's attention.'

The landscape was changing with the dreamer's mood. Smooth sand was now polluted with rocks and debris. Calm water held the threat of a tsunamic change. Winds whipped around, creating small dust devils. The dreamer flickered again. She knelt and picked a rock up from amongst the rubble strewn amongst the sand. Another sudden leap and the rock was raised high, ready to strike. The force of the dreamer's hatred was palpable. She would destroy the woman that was taking what was hers. She held the rock high, preparing to bring it down, again and again until nothing of the mocking face remained.

Nicola looked around the group, uncertain what to do. Brent held a small blue bottle in his hand, poised to throw it. Dana turned away, understanding the inevitability of the next few seconds. Ashley's face showed the horror she felt at the doll's manipulation, and Michael's sudden glowing eyes were a faint milky white…

* * *

On another shore, in another place, a zombie stopped its aimless pacing and turned towards the water. Under the rippling surface, the faint outline of a young boy could be seen. The water swirled. Where before there had been darkness, now the water shone as the boy's eyes opened, glowing with an eerie, white light. A dark shape walked in the shadows, seeing the glow, and knowing what it represented.

* * *

Michael knew the precise moment the doll entered the dream. He heard its snide snickering as it walked up behind the girl with the book. Its lank coils of hair brushed against her face as it bent to whisper in her ear. He didn't need to hear the words to know the poison that dripped from its tongue. Even without hearing the enticements of the doll, Michael felt the sway himself, nearly heeding their call to violence. Michael had experienced this before. He knew how difficult it was to resist when the words spoke with your own voice and came disguised as your own thoughts.

When the doll wrapped its hands around the girl's head, caressing the line of her jaw, a trail of sticky residue wept from the doll's fingers, leaving a shining trail to mark each stroke. As it pulled away, a thread of mucus stretched from the girl's face back to the doll's fingertips. The girl shook her head as if disturbed by something, and the string of mucus snapped.

The doll hissed its disappointment. Again, it reached for her face. She was already moving towards the couple, but the doll could match her step by step, following behind like a corrupted shadow.

Michael watched on, revolted as a patchwork of secretion slid across her cheeks, merging with darkened spots already there, attempting to form a second skin. Some patches were liquid, fresh; others had solidified so that they resembled a thin layer of congealed jelly.

Michael understood that the doll had been visiting the girl in previous dreams, laying groundwork with each manipulation. Once the secretion formed a solid film across the girl's face, it would attach the umbilical and the girl would be under the doll's control.

Michael heard Ashul through their link. They couldn't risk drawing the doll's attention. Michael agreed, knew that Ashul was correct, but he vowed he would return when the doll was not present and attempt to remove the film stuck to the girl's face. He could not allow the doll to visit her dream after dream until its umbilical was complete.

When the girl raised the rock high above her head, Michael tried not to judge. He couldn't hold her accountable for what she did in a dream. When the rock reached the zenith of its arc, Michael hoped that she might reconsider. As the rock dropped towards the couple's upturned faces, they flickered out of existence a fraction of a second before the rock impacted. The girl remained for a heartbeat more and looked around dazed. The rock dropped from her fingers and she too flickered and faded.

'The poor girl… she couldn't, she just couldn't,' said Ashley, tears pooling in her eyes. 'Even with the doll's words egging her on, she still couldn't bring herself to do it.'

'Then she still has some time. The doll has not corrupted her yet,' said Ashul. He appeared concerned as he looked around the dream environment. 'Ashley, can you sense the new dreamer? This place should be fading, but the beach remains.'

Michael looked around. A dog ran down the shore, occasionally snapping at the water, barrelling in their direction. Michael didn't need Ashley's help with this one. Madison was easy to recognise.

'Guys, we've found Mr Stevens.'

Supply Lines

While Michael was correct that the dog was Madison, it wasn't the actual animal herself, more Mr Stevens' dream representation of his chosen companion. Dana picked this up easily enough. Ashley confirming the details only moments later.

'I can see the link connecting Madison with Mr Stevens, though the doll's involvement has corrupted even that link. The connection usually pulses with the dreamer's aura, making it easy to discern the dreamer among their creations. This one's striated with greens and greys, flowing along the connection like scum on top of a pond.'

'Ash, where is Mr Stevens?' Dana asked. 'Shouldn't he be here?' Dana and Michael had both been scanning around trying to find the old man.

'He should come through those palm trees at any moment,' said Ashley.

Ashley's prediction was spot on. In less than a second, Mr Stevens stumbled through the tree line, pausing to lean his shoulder against a palm tree. His face pressed against the sharp bark, unaware of the discomfort. He held onto the tree with a death-grip, struggling to remain upright. It was obvious that he was exhausted, mumbling words under his breath. He seemed like a man pushed past the limits of emotional and physical endurance.

'Okay, so what do we do now?' asked Dana.

'Dana, you know him the best, see if you can get close enough to hear what he's saying. I can tell how terrified he is. It's something to do with Madison but his thoughts are so confused. So desperate. I can't be sure of the detail.' Ashley motioned for Dana to move forwards.

Dana took careful steps in his direction, trying to look casual, worried that any sudden movement might startle him. She didn't need to get close: Mr Stevens was mumbling the same two words over and over.

'Not again! Not again! Not again!'

And as if the words were some kind of trigger, Madison ran towards the water.

Pushing off from the palm with what little strength he had left, Mr Stevens stumbled down the beach towards his dog, calling out to Madison. *'Stop, come back! Please, Maddy! No, I can't lose you again.'*

The dog ignored her master's plea and swam out into the surf. Within just a few steps, Madison was already paddling and there was no doubt that she was having some difficulty.

Seaweed lay draped across her back; strands of it were curling up and over her muzzle, twisting around her shoulders. She snapped at the red leaves that were threatening to drag her under. Mr Stevens found some hidden reserve of strength and struggled forward, forcing his way through water already clogged with a thickening mat of weed.

Tears were pouring down the old man's cheeks, his features were contorted with the pain of a dog already lost. He looked to have tried this a hundred times and lost the battle just as many times.

Mr Stevens eventually reached her. Madison's eyes were rolling wildly in her head. Terror had caused her to froth at the mouth and her jaws snapped madly, ripping at anything she could get a grip on, including Mr Stevens' wrist.

It only took moments for them both to be dragged under the water.

Madison whining through the blood that dripped from her muzzle, Mr Stevens with his arms wrapped around her waist, trying to keep her body above water. His arm and face were red from the wounds made by Madison's teeth and claws. They both barely bobbed above the surface.

'Be calm, he will not die here,' said Ashul, in a soothing voice. 'This is his dream and although he suffers, he is safe.' What they were witnessing was unnerving everybody. When the water stopped churning, the dream flickered. The sand beneath their feet ran together then hardened into dark concrete. The palm trees multiplied, straightened as the trunks merged, becoming a solid wall. Their colour deepened until they too were made of concrete.

The scene around them reformed until they were standing in a train station. It appeared late at night and there were a handful of other people milling around aimlessly. A couple of young boys pulled spray cans from their backpacks and started to tag the walls.

* * *

'Here he comes,' said Ashley as she pointed towards Mr Stevens walking down the platform towards them. There was no evidence of the bites and scratches Madison had inflicted upon him in the ocean. He was dragging his feet, barely able to put one foot in front of the other. His body might be whole, but his spirit was broken. He shuffled along only a couple of paces behind Madison. His hand kept reaching towards her collar, but he could never quite reach her. His attempts became more desperate. He almost tripped when he made a frantic lunge for her neck.

'He knows she's about to be pushed under a train,' said Ashley. 'This is his ongoing nightmare. The details vary, but he loses her every time. He is never able to save her.' Ashley suppressed a sob. 'We've got to stop this. We've got to help him.'

'We have to be careful,' said Nicola. 'The void will fight us if we interfere with the dream. And we might draw out the doll. I'm trying to think of a way to help. Ashul, any ideas?' Nicola was searching for anything that might be of some assistance.

'I can't look at that bag pulsating on his head much longer.' Michael stepped tentatively towards Mr Stevens. 'Ashul, do you think I could remove it?' The bags offended him – they were a repulsive device used to subvert someone's will. Nicola had to agree, but they seemed to affect Michael in a more primal way that she could hardly explain.

'Are you seeing the embryotic connection?' When Nicola turned to look at Michael, she saw his eyes had changed. 'Michael, your eyes. They're glowing.' More specifically, the scars on his eyes were glowing. Nicola approached him in concern. She turned towards Ashul to ask for an explanation and was shocked that his eyes held a very faint glow of their own.

'I cannot see it as clearly as you, but I think we have no choice but to try,' said Ashul. 'I will warn the bonded in the first plane so Sarah can alert us if we cause him any harm.' Ashul tried to ignore Nicola's scrutiny, obviously annoyed by her concern over details that he did not value. Regardless, she kept looking back and forwards between Michael and Ashul, staring at the glow emanating from their eyes.

Ashul asked, 'Ashley, can you monitor Mr Stevens' emotions, tell us if we're causing him any further distress?' When Ashley nodded, Ashul and Michael walked up beside Mr Stevens, trying to keep a pace that would not disturb him.

Michael was concentrating with his eyes screwed shut. When he opened them again he was holding a small fish knife in his left hand, not sharp, just a regular piece of kitchen cutlery.

* * *

'I know we can take these "bags" off. The Nachzehrer tried to make me remove the bag on the referee just before I passed out.' Michael slipped his right hand onto Mr Stevens' shoulder and Ashul had placed a hand on Madison's neck. Both dog and owner stopped moving along the platform. Mr Stevens turned to Michael in a puzzled fashion but showed no signs of distress. He looked more confused by this change in routine.

Michael felt a low hum rumbling under his ribs. It was yet to become audible, but Michael suspected the void's defences had already been triggered, and the dull drone was a warning to cease and desist.

'I don't think we have much time.' Michael ran his hand across Mr Stevens' shoulder and up his neck until his fingers were almost touching the membranous sheath covering his head.

Taking a breath, Michael allowed his fingers to brush against the outside edge where it ran across the base of the skull. He felt the membrane pull away from his fingers, but within seconds it pushed back, returning to its original position.

Nicola stepped to Michael's side. 'Can you place my fingers on the edge of the membrane, so they're just touching it.' Michael gently placed his mother's hand where his own had been a moment earlier. Again, the membrane recoiled, but this time it was slower to return.

'I can feel it. Did it pull away?' Nicola gently explored the membrane with her fingertips and watched Michael's face for input.

'Yes, it recoiled from you. Try using both hands.'

Michael showed her where the edge of the membrane was and guided his mother's hands into position. The membrane pulsed. The silver-grey surface now rippled with olive-green undertones. Before Michael had a chance to voice a warning, thin green strands of glistening fibre ran up Nicola's fingers and wrapped around her hands.

'Aunty Nic, don't pull back,' said Ashley. She spoke quietly as if she had a wild animal in front of her and she didn't want to startle it. 'That's not the doll. That's Mr Stevens trying to reach out to you. He senses your presence. He is very scared. On some level he's well aware of his situation.'

Ashley had moved forward as she spoke, her fingers reaching towards Mr Stevens' face. Michael grabbed her hand and placed them just above his ears. Michael had noticed the olive-green swirling near the edges of the caul. As soon as Ashley's fingers got close enough, the green tendrils raced up her hands, wrapping thick cords around her wrists.

'Easy, Michael,' said Ashul. 'The doll is becoming active in the second plane again. At this point, it does not appear to be connected to what we are doing here, but it is difficult to tell.' Ashul had his eyes almost screwed shut. He couldn't see the membrane as clearly as Michael did, which Michael was quietly relieved about because using this 'gift of seeing' brought him closer to the Nachzehrer hovering on the shores of his lake and Ashul's use of the power might tip the balance.

The small part of Michael that resided in in his subconscious refuge was maintaining the distance between himself and the shore. But with his focus already so dangerously split, he couldn't allow any further distractions. If he did, all of the balls he was trying to keep in the air would come tumbling down.

He needed to focus. Mr Stevens needed his help. He could see the silver threads, the doll's energy becoming active, becoming agitated. They swarmed over and around the green coils. Thicker, faster, more aggressive. But old Mr Stevens had a glimpse of freedom and he intended to take his chance. Ropes of green flew towards Dana. She let out a bark of fear as the tendrils of olive raced up her arms like strange, animated strings of mucus.

The hum they had all felt deep in their chests finally became audible. Michael's eardrums pounded painfully as the structure of the dream quivered around him. The train station shuddered like a tuning fork struck near a crystal glass. The movement made the concrete appear to shimmer and blur as everything around them vibrated at some unbelievably high speed. Michael's teeth were buzzing in his head and he felt that his own integrity might be in jeopardy as his bones sang with the force of the soundwaves.

* * *

On the shore of a crystal-clear lake of near infinite depth, the guardian turned his head and whined. He heard the distant call of his master. Titan knew she needed his help but he couldn't respond; he'd alerted his littermate to the danger, but she was in another place and wouldn't be able to reach her either.

Whining softly, he sat looking across the water's surface, watching as the rotten piece of meat that walked like a human turned its head and peered into the depths. The enemy was searching for his other master, the one he hoped to protect. The dog batted his paw tentatively towards the shimmering liquid. The cool water accepted his paw readily and the dog's distress quietened, soothed by his master's essence.

Titan would watch and wait, hoping that the boy beneath the surface would remain protected within the embrace of his own unbreakable spirit. But if a time came when the water was no longer deep enough – if it dissipated – the dog would be here to buy his master whatever time he could.

* * *

Sarah stood in the centre of her web, trying to track the many threads that had suddenly sprung up on her network. Azuradien was by her side, but it was Malcarielle who had a knack for separating the interconnected energy signatures that had suddenly appeared before her. Malcarielle had easily tracked Nicola's passage through the second realm. An intangible shift in the texture of the whole signalled her entry into the realm of dreams.

A light representing a young woman sparked onto the grid, near the group yet separate. Michael came closest to connecting to her but her energy flared and dropped off the grid, appearing back on the network that represented the first plane. Sarah made a note of the woman's position, then shifted her focus back to the second realm.

'You can see the doll's influence speckling her aura, but it's still peripheral. We should approach her and see if we can find if there's a reason she has been able to resist. It could be nothing more than timing, but you see those spikes around the edge of her signature…' Joseph monitored what Sarah was capturing on the network.

For Sarah, this process was like a tapestry, where threads intertwined to make complex patterns. Her task was to grasp the threads before they could slip away. Once she'd captured one, she could mark its place and link it to her network so she could easily find it again at a future point in time.

She had to be delicate, her touch had to be feather light because each thread had the capacity to recognise her presence and she felt that she could influence the overall pattern if she was not extremely careful. This had not been her intention when creating the network, it was just something that had happened when they'd started to use it.

So she left Joseph to analyse each thread. She couldn't perceive the differences that he could, and she felt that if she tried, she might alter the thread's integrity, becoming something worse than the doll. When Joseph pointed out some small identifying characteristic, she nodded and left him to discuss the details with Malcarielle.

* * *

Lorcan observed the network from the shadows. An inquisitive little water sprite hid amongst the plates lying discarded in the kitchen sink, surreptitiously watching his every move. Normally, he would scare the sprite until it was nothing but a puddle of water, but he was currently focused on the brutally inept yet incredibly powerful display going on in front of him.

The network alone amazed him. How had it been created? And more importantly, could it be destroyed? He didn't possess the powers to use the network, but he recognised it as the weapon it could become in the hands of the weaver. This woman, Sarah, twisted and bound the strands with a lightness of touch that allowed her to mark someone's location without impacting the thread's integrity. But if her touch had some other purpose, she might alter the threads' makeup, change its course, with nothing more than a brush from her fingertip.

Sudden activity bloomed on the network representing the second plane.

The second the Michael's eyes flared white, Lorcan felt the Nachzehrer in him stir. In this other place, this other world Michael had created in himself, the boy had drawn their attention. The Nachzehrer would soon resume their attack upon his defences. Another cleansing so soon after the last would kill the boy. Lorcan needed to get Michael out of the second realm and turn off this connection.

Michael had a crude understanding of the delicate war being fought within him. If it was purely a physical problem, Lorcan knew the boy had the strength to maintain the upper hand, but there was a mental aspect to the battle. The bonded warrior's involvement complicated things further, making the boy's task almost impossible.

Lorcan was still contemplating options when Dana came under attack from the dreamer's consciousness. Olive-green coils were running up and over her face. She was trying to hold her nerve, but the dreamer had been almost driven insane by the doll's manipulations and she was in real danger of possession.

They still viewed the dreamer as a kindly old man. Lorcan saw only a trapped animal desperately seeking a way out.

In the first plane, the girl's dog sensed her danger and clawed at the screen door trying to get inside. With only a moment to assess his options, Lorcan swept through the room and out the door. He wrapped the animal in his arms, soothing her distress with mumbled words and calming tones. When he drew away from the animal's home and her connection to Dana, the dog grew agitated, twisting and snapping, trying to break his grip.

The animal knew her master needed her and Lorcan was pulling her away from where Dana had last been seen. Almost driven into a frenzy, the animal sunk her teeth into Lorcan's arm, but instinct stopped the dog from breaking skin. Her eyes rolled as she searched for any way to escape. Lorcan growled into the animal's ear, and finally she calmed. If her teeth had pierced his skin, she would have been dead in seconds. With his limited options, it came as no surprise to him that using the animals was going to be his best one. Humans will argue and debate and then do whatever suited them, whereas animals just needed to be placed in a position where they could help and they would.

It took Lorcan no time to get to the old man's house. He found the proud Rottweiler curled in a shaking ball. He gently placed the girl's Doberman beside her. He allowed them a moment to calm each other.

Lorcan cursed the doll and the impact it had on these proud creatures. He would tear layers of flesh from its scorched and blistering back in punishment for the distress it had caused this day.

Even in his fury, neither dog turned to bite Lorcan again. Once their initial distress had passed, they crouched at Lorcan's feet and licked the hand he offered them. He whispered into their ears and each animal's breathing slowed.

Lorcan's eyes glowed with a faint red light and both dogs dropped off into a peaceful sleep. Lorcan had no need to compel them to find their masters. Even though he possessed the power to do so, it would be a wasted instruction. The animals would always seek their masters in their dreams.

He would let the animals find them and clean up the mess that had been made with their master's inept efforts to 'save the day'.

Lorcan was not yet ready to intervene directly, but the time was coming when he would have to decide what he was going to do about the boy. In the interim, the animals could teach the doll some manners.

* * *

'Hold steady, Dana,' said Ashul. 'Sheba approaches!' Ashul spoke with some wonder in his voice. 'The bonded have spoken to us over the link. Two dogs approach.'

Dana needed no-one to tell her that Sheba was coming. She felt her energy level rising with each step Sheba took in her direction.

She had been trying to extricate herself from the coils wrapping around her body without damaging Mr Stevens' essence. It was difficult to fight an enemy she could only feel.

There were thick coils running up and over her arms, becoming bands of pressure as they wrapped around her chest. More distressing was that each touch against her skin imparted a thought, conveyed a memory. She was being bombarded with Mr Stevens' most precious recollections, his brightest dreams, his darkest fears.

Dana was terrified by the impact this contact must be having on Ashley. She wished she could protect Ashley somehow but was having to use every ounce of her energy to keep herself whole. The dream was breaking apart around them and the void would be pressing against the boundaries, ready to clean up any residual 'material' left behind.

The final scene from the movie *The Langoliers* kept popping into Dana's mind. She had found the idea of what happened to reality when the present moved on fascinating. Bouncing balls full of teeth, that literally ate the sky, the ground, everything, was not what she'd expected. A cosmic cleaning crew of demented Pac-Man was hard to accept. The movie sucked, but the concept didn't. It made her realise that the void worked in much the same way: it cleaned up what was left behind and in this particular instant that would be them.

Sheba's arrival mercifully blocked the onslaught of emotion she was receiving from Mr Stevens. As soon as Sheba's body brushed against hers, it acted as some kind of insulation. When Madison reached Mr Stevens, the coils wrapping around Dana unlocked.

She sighed in relief. 'Michael, what's happening?' Dana called out. 'What can you see?' Her relief seemed short-lived.

Something felt wrong. She could sense that Madison was in pain.

* * *

Michael was using the Nachzehrer-vision to work out what exactly was going on. It put him in jeopardy – he knew that – but it gave him the insight to interpret what was happening in front of him. Without the sight, he would not be able to see the doll's connections, nor Mr Stevens' efforts to just hold on. The more Mr Stevens searched for something to hold onto, the more separation there was between his essence and the caul of the doll.

When Mr Stevens recognised Dana, he reached out with almost every fibre of his being. The silver membrane had previously contained striations of olive-green, the two intricately intermingled, impossible to separate. The more purchase Mr Stevens found, the more the green and silver tendrils became two distinct forces, each opposed to each other. It now looked as though Mr Stevens wore a strange silver hat with a mass of green animated hair flowing out from beneath it.

With Madison's arrival, the separation became complete. Michael dug his fingers under the flap of skin wrapped under Mr Stevens' top row of teeth. Ashul helped with the line of membrane running across the base of Mr Stevens' skull.

'Mum, protect him!' screamed Michael, even though Nicola was beside him. 'You need to run a protective layer over the surface of his skull. The doll is going to realise we're intervening in about three seconds…'

The background hum was rising in pitch, and it sounded like air was rushing past his ears even though the air vibrated more than gusted. It was a disorientating feeling, and it made Michael impatient to get this job done.

Michael ensured Nicola's hands were placed exactly where he wanted them. He looked into Ashul's eyes and counted down, *three, two, one* – they then he nodded.

Michael and Ashul pulled upwards in perfect unison, gripping what looked like a cross between a swimming cap and a jellyfish. A mass of silver tentacles thrashed around, trying to bore back inside the exposed skull. Mr Stevens' hair – scant as it was – had been reduced to nothing more than a string of threads plastered to his head, the skin pink and vulnerable.

Despite the squirming feelers digging at his skin, Nicola's protection held up. A dark blue light began to shimmer over the surface of Mr Stevens' exposed pate. The silver feelers danced over his head, searching for a way around the barrier.

'I can't hold this for long,' Nicola hissed through her teeth. 'What's the plan?'

Michael had freed one hand and raised the knife he'd made appear in the second realm, but he didn't need it. Sheba jumped forward and gripped the mass of tentacles in her teeth. With a shake of her head, she tore them from the base of the silver cap with a couple of vicious snaps left and right. The tentacles became nothing more than a mass of shredded jelly. Sheba opened her jaws and let the remains fall to the ground as though their presence in her mouth revolted her.

The umbilical hung in mid-air pulsing.

After a moment's hesitation, Ashul spun around, sword in hand and severed the throbbing cord. What remained of it dissolved and a splattering of liquid rained down to the ground.

Cutting Ties

Joseph watched the network flare. The bonded had passed on the details of the encounter with the girl on the beach and Joseph could see the doll's signature hovering around her, waiting for her to go to sleep again, like a spider poised watching for the fly. As she drifted off to sleep, the doll became active. Joseph couldn't read the specifics of what the girl was dreaming about. He had no notion of whether she dreamed of a beach or a movie theatre, but he needed no aid to read the ebb and flow of the energy surrounding her. The doll was expending huge amounts of stored reserves, trying to convert the girl into its very own emotional Eveready battery.

'Malcarielle, pass the word through the bonded,' said Joseph. 'We need to get Dave over there and wake that girl up.' Joseph looked around frustrated as he waited for a response.

He spotted Tony in the corner with his finger raised in the air in a 'wait just a second' gesture, his mobile phone held in his other hand. A few seconds later, Tony dropped his phone into his jacket pocket and smiled up at Joseph.

'Now, I know I don't have your "magic", but Dave's banging on that girl's door as we speak. If she isn't awake already, she will be soon.' He pulled his phone back out of his pocket and waved it from side to side. 'We don't have to rely on pigeons, you know, Joe.'

Not for a second had Joseph considered picking up his own phone and calling Dave. Joseph's own stupidity stunned him.

His thoughts were broken as a mass of energy points converged on the area surrounding the girl.

'Sarah, I'm looking at the first realm over here, aren't I?' Joseph motioned towards the mass of energy signatures around the newly marked thread of the beach girl.

'Absolutely.'

'Then why have I got so many new threads popping onto the grid.' Joseph was busy trying to sort his way through the signatures that he recognised and those that he did not, but it wasn't easy. The section of the network surrounding the girl was very congested.

'Dave, Azuradien and eight of the bonded are in that area,' said Sarah as she glanced to where Joseph had pointed. Malcarielle was tapping threads so that they remained on the grid, but as a dimmed down version, making it easier to isolate and examine the new arrivals.

'It looks like a goddamn Christmas tree.' Joseph's eyes darted in every direction, not wanting to miss some crucial detail that could put his family in jeopardy. He pointed to one thread after another in rapid succession, so that Malcarielle knew which ones she should be keeping an eye on. 'The doll's pulling in reinforcements. It either suspects that we're on to it or it likes an audience.'

Joseph turned to Darmead, who had returned from the second realm to assist with the relaying of communications. 'Let Ashul know we have a mass of activity on our hands. All these new signatures are already puppets of the doll. I can see the links clearly. Michael was right about there being more than we suspected.' Joseph placed a hand to his mouth when the number of threads suddenly doubled. 'Tony, get back on the phone. First, warn Dave there might be some interference. Second, get some ambulances on the scene. Two more signatures just dropped into a coma. I got it wrong, it's not the reinforcements it wants, it's just their energy.'

* * *

The dream was shattering around them, but Mr Stevens refused to move on. The gusting wind that had been threatening for a while had picked up, screaming around them, making Dana's hair fly in all directions.

Madison lay in Mr Stevens' arms panting. As the dog's eyes rolled towards Dana, she saw such pain in her eyes, and so much confusion. Sheba's howl joined the cacophony of sounds that assaulted her ears.

At first, Dana suspected the dogs feared the disintegration of the dream as much as she did, but Sheba was snarling at Mr Stevens.

Why was Madison in pain?

'Ashley, is Mr Stevens okay?' Dana called out, trying to be heard over the screeching of the squalling wind. 'Something's wrong.' She grabbed Ashley to force her to listen. 'Ashley, what's happening in the dream?'

Ashley looked back at her, confused. She was having some trouble interpreting what was going on. 'He has her. He finally has her. He'll keep her safe. He loves her, Dana. Don't worry, he'll do anything to protect her.' But none of that information helped Dana.

It was Mr Stevens' love for his dog that the doll had been feeding from. Dana stroked the dog's neck, desperate to provide some comfort. There was no doubt this was not a product of Mr Stevens dream – this was the real Madison laying in front of her. The pain flowing from the dog through her touch was nauseating. Dana tried to look past the dog's agony, to piece together what was happening but the pain was all-consuming; she couldn't move past it.

'Michael, what do you see?' Dana yelled, desperation seeping into her voice. The dog's neck seemed to ripple under her hands.

When Michael turned towards Dana, his eyes were tired and red-rimmed, but they no longer shone with the pale white haze. He looked around but his expression showed that he couldn't understand what Dana was asking him. Nicola was the first to recognise Dana's distress.

'What is it, honey?' said Nicola. 'Tell me.' Hair blew around her face. She held Dana's hair in place so she could look her in the eyes, trying to calm her with her words. 'What do you see?'

What did she see? She heard Madison's cries and Sheba's erratic barking – but what did she actually see? Dana looked at Sheba; she saw her hackles raised and the spit as it flew from her mouth as she barked, snapping at Mr Stevens. Sheba lunging forward then pulling back, hesitating, her actions confused. She could have bitten him, torn at the old man's flesh as he lay mumbling, holding his dog. Dana reached down and grabbed Sheba by the scruff of her neck, worried about what she might do next. And as Dana's hand touched the neck of her own dog, things became clear. Waves of fear washed over her. Sheba's fear.

For a moment, Dana saw her own aura dancing around Sheba. An amber haze that swirled and combined with the kaleidoscope of the dog's own colours.

When Dana turned to Madison, she wondered why she hadn't understood earlier. She'd felt the tight bands of Mr Stevens' consciousness grasping desperately for something to hold on to. Something to stop the dreadful dreams from repeating.

When Madison and Sheba entered the dream, the grasping tendrils had loosened almost instantly. Looking through Sheba's eyes now, Dana could see the mass of olive-green coils wrapped so tightly around Madison that from the dog's viewpoint Madison was perceived more than seen.

'Ashley, you need to get Mr Stevens to loosen his grip.' Dana screamed as the horror of what was happening became clear. 'You need to make him feel safe. Make him understand Madison is safe as well. Quickly! the dream is collapsing. He won't leave without her. Ashley, please get him to understand. He has to loosen his grip.' The words came out of Dana in a rush. She feared for a moment that Ashley hadn't heard her; she could barely hear her own voice.

But then she felt waves of reassurance wash over her. Dana felt her own hand relax its grip on Sheba as the tension left her own body and she wondered for a moment at the power her cousin could wield. The coils of Mr Stevens' consciousness withdrew and Madison could be seen clearly again.

Madison's tail gave a brief wag, and then she flickered and was gone from the dream. Sheba made a quick grab for Dana's hand, teeth briefly locking painfully around her wrist, but then Sheba dissolved too. The grip on Dana's wrist remained for few seconds after Sheba's presence had left.

'The dogs have the right idea,' said Nicola. 'We have to get out of here.' Nicola nodded towards Ashul, who stepped forward and grabbed Dana. 'Michael, go. Brent and I have got Mr Stevens.'

Dana saw that Michael was ready to protest. But when Brent lent forward with a bright bottle of liquid in his hand and dribbled some into Mr Stevens' mouth the effects were almost immediate. Mr Stevens smiled serenely, then he too faded and disappeared completely from view.

This departure triggered the final breakdown of the dream. The world around her was being sucked into the void that marked the place that Mr Stevens had inhabited. With his presence no longer there to give the construct form, the world was collapsing in upon itself with a finality like the closing of a tomb.

Dana was left standing in the heavy grey void, her teeth chattering with the waves of energy forcing all that remained of the dream to be broken apart and absorbed. She had a moment to think, *'So this is what remains when the dreamer wakes,'* then Ashul's fingers dug into the welts already ringing her wrist and he dragged her back into the first realm.

* * *

It hovered above the girl with her stupid dreams of beaches and revenge, dreams that if allowed to run their normal course would have amounted to nothing, forever destined to remain just violent imaginings. It could be said that It was freeing these people, removing their inhibitions, the shackles that kept them civil, compliant to their society's doctrines.

It fed off them as their need to make these dreams a reality grew. It fed when they exacted their revenge or allowed the hate that coloured their thoughts to finally shape their actions. And It would control them to make the feeding that much more powerful.

But this girl was resisting, brushing It away like It was merely an annoyance to her. It would not stand for such. Would not allow these humans to believe themselves to be anything other than the food source that they were.

So It looked down on her through the smallest of portals, all that It could create with the power It had left.

The Nachzehrer may have been a mistake, but how could It have anticipated just how stupid that boy was? The bonded had warned him, the guardian had warned him, but still the impudent brat had thought he'd known better, hadn't he? Through his own arrogance and idiocy, he let himself get exposed to the Nachzehrer. It had been forced to waste valuable energy trying to prevent his infection.

Anarcus needed energy. The time was coming for the disciples to re-enter the game. They had been playing in the shadows but must soon shed their cloaks and disguises and return to the fore.

With the blood that It had consumed, It should be able to step from plane to plane, but the damn barriers still held.

The divide had lessened, but not enough for It to be able to step through at will, so It was forced to wait like a spider. This girl would eventually sleep, and then the final connection could be made. And while It waited, It could turn over in Its mind every reason It hated the boy, so that when the time came, It could savour his destruction.

Oh, the energy It would have received If the damn boy had allowed his anger free rein.

All that energy, lost now.

The dreams, the manipulations had been for naught.

The boy had needed only to revel in his skills. He held a talent for destruction that only required the right circumstance to bloom: it came so naturally to the boy. He'd shown that he had no compunctions around killing; the Bezenhart and Nachzehrer had both fallen to his blade. But the lamb, Marcus... after a single blow, the boy had walked away from the fight.

The mother also shared the blame. She had feigned regard for a child not even her own, a child that had drawn blood from her offspring. And what could this performance possibly achieve? The boy and his mewling sister sympathised now with what should have been their enemy.

Now they had given the detestable lamb, not hope, no, but an unacceptable amount of entitlement. The child Marcus had been pliable, submissive, broken. But now he believed he deserved something other than his fate. As if any of these creatures had a right to decide how their lives were to be lived.

They walked around under the misguided belief that they were something more than fodder. The sun had gone down on their time and now they needed to be reminded of their place. With their ill-informed, superior attitudes, they were not the top of anything, least of all the food chain.

It still watched the dreamer. It waited for her transition to the second realm. When the girl's eyes drooped closed, It followed her to the dreaming place. The first wisps of sand floated around her heals, beginning to whip up into a beach. While this was happening, It crouched behind her, sticking to the back of her legs like a badly fitted second skin.

It brought Its mouth down closer to her ear and whispered about infidelity, immorality, and lack of appreciation – all the things the girl wanted to hear because they so echoed the emotions floating around at the bottom of her deepest, darkest thoughts.

It was bringing Its fingers up, moist with the connective membrane, when Its head was pierced with a sickening stab of agony. It was like a hook had been buried in the soft tissue of Its brain. Then the hook twisted. Like a rabid animal, It shook, biting at the imagined source of pain as strings of saliva flew from Its mouth.

The girl in front of It wavered in and out of existence. Its focus was split by suffering so intense that It would have bitten Its own hand off if that had been the source. It had expended too much energy already trying to create a connection with this girl. It dug Its fingers into her flickering skull. Despite Its agony, It gripped with a force that would either enslave her or destroy her. Dragging on Its other connections, It felt them drop into unconsciousness.

Weak, unreliable creatures!

Agony once again lanced through Anarcus' skull and this time It felt the hook move, It was being ripped from deep within. Neural connections were being pulled from Its system like knots being yanked from a ball of wool.

The girl before It wavered, flickering in and out of its vision. It was being pulled away from her, like a fish caught on a line. It struggled but could not break free. Anarcus had time to see an old man at a train station below It. Then teeth flashed in Its direction; the pain soared to new heights and before It could make out anymore, Anarcus, Reaper of Minds, retreated into the wooden construct that still restricted Its movements in the first realm, fleeing the pain of the second, wondering what new beast dared oppose It.

* * *

Lorcan pulled both animals out of the dream as soon as the danger became too great. The dream was collapsing, and the void was beginning to remove anything that remained. The bodies of the living would not be spared. After all, they had no right to be in the dreaming plane in the first place. The void would eradicate them with an efficiency that was beautiful in its brutality.

The large Rottweiler was taking longer to recover. She'd been traumatised in the dream and had returned to a life without a master. She had no understanding that her master lay in a hospital bed and could not return and be with her.

Lorcan understood her pain. He lifted the animal into his arms. Dana would be able to get through to the dog in a way that Lorcan could not. Lorcan could compel the animal to a course of action, could force it to feel something other than pain, but that was the limit of his influence. And he would not use his powers on this creature. As he walked, the girl's dog followed closely at his heels, lifting her head to lick the back of his hands.

Standing with a foot in both worlds, he was back in the kitchen before the others had time to materialise. He chose to stand in the light. He would not be a bystander in the conversation that was to follow. Action needed to be taken. The doll was gaining too much power, and these humans were being forced into situations that gave them no choice but to unlock more powers of their own. This family did not covet power, but they would not leave any stones unturned when faced with one bad deal after another. He didn't want them to further develop their abilities. Lorcan would prefer that balance be restored before abilities that would forever alter the power structure were acquired.

Lorcan liked things the way they were. So, he stood in the light, yet still draped in darkness, and he waited. Waited until his presence was noticed, aggravated that with so much power these people saw so little.

It didn't surprise him that Michael registered his presence before his body had completely formed. Lorcan suspected that even before the boy had been touched by the Nachzehrer he saw what was truly in front of him. It was part of what made him so dangerous. He reacted before he allowed doubts and questions to cloud his judgement.

The girl materialised seconds later. Pale, ghost-like impressions of fingers gripped her wrist and soon solidified and expanded into the form of the warrior.

So much could be read by the first thing a person saw when they entered a room.

The girl brushed her fingertips down her brother's arm. She scanned the room, eyes flicking to Lorcan, then to her own dog, then falling to the dog held in his arms. Her head tilted slightly as she processed everything she was seeing. Her size suggested prey, but her mannerisms were all predator.

She had assessed the risks within the room in a matter of seconds. All this, while removing any doubts as to the wellbeing of her brother after their experiences in the dreams. The girl's powers were growing too. It intrigued Lorcan to imagine where this blossoming strength would take her.

'This animal is severely distressed,' said Lorcan as he carefully placed the dog on the couch where the girl indicated. She didn't question his actions, appearing to have almost dismissed him. But he noticed she'd turned her body in a way that enabled her to watch him out of the corner of her eye.

Lorcan stepped back into the shadows purely to vex her.

* * *

'Tony, can you check the hospital?' Brent asked almost before he had time to form out of spiralling motes of thin air. The kitchen was quickly filling up as everyone returned from the second plane. 'I need an update of Mr Stevens' condition.' Brent then turned to Nicola. 'He got out of the dream, didn't he, Nic? I didn't just watch a man die, did I?'

'I'm not sure. Joe?' Nicola moved over to lean against her husband, peering at the network over his shoulder. Joseph had anticipated her question and nodded his head and showed them the olive-green thread on the network.

Joseph gave her a quick kiss on the cheek before he responded, 'Yep, he got out of the dream. He got out of his coma too by the looks of things – see, he only appears on the one network.'

'And he looks clear too, no silver striations. The doll's connection has been severed.' Nicola smiled up at her son. 'Michael, it just may have worked.' She circled the grid to examine it and noticed a large knot of activity in one area.

'What's going on here? That's Dave and Azuradien, isn't it?'

'I've just gotten word than Dave has had the girl taken by ambulance to the hospital,' said Tony. 'On Azuradien's suggestion, they've taken her outside of the area. She seems fine and doesn't understand why she needs to go to the hospital after a bad dream. But David spoke with the paramedics and suggested there might be a connection to the recent spate of comas in the area. They've had no other issues and no-one's been acting irrationally. Some nosey neighbours, a couple of concerned citizens and a local reporter. Nothing else to report. He's going to stay with the girl in the hospital for a while.' Tony put his phone back in his pocket. 'Also, Mr Stevens is conscious. If you don't need me here, I'd like to go check on him, maybe see what he remembers.'

'Tell him Madison is fine,' said Dana. 'I'll keep her here until he gets out of hospital.' Dana was stroking the dog's neck. Madison was no longer shaking but her eyelids were heavy. She lifted her expressive eyebrows at Dana's words but didn't appear agitated. A few moments later, the Rottweiler was asleep.

The room was quiet. Everybody seemed to be processing all that had occurred in the last couple of hours. Nicola was watching the collection of dots that were still hovering on the periphery of the network.

'Sarah, can we pin these?' Nicola asked. 'There's something about them I don't like. Joseph, are these people under the doll's control. Its puppets?'

'I'm not sure,' said Joseph reaching up to rub his cheek. 'They feel different. It's so subtle. They have the doll's influence all over them, but I can't see the same connection.'

'I think we need to track them and look at them in the second realm.' Nicola had barely spoken the words when the strange dots flickered and disappeared.

'Malcarielle, did you get any of them?' Sarah asked, alarmed. She stepped to the section of the network where the cluster had been.

'No, I'm sorry. I couldn't isolate them. I agree with Nicola, there was something different but I can't say what that difference was.'

* * *

Lorcan stepped out of the shadows as if the light streaming through the window had suddenly found him. He squinted but endured the discomfort the sunlight caused. He walked through Sarah's grid as if its existence was beneath his notice. With a casual sweep of his hand, the network sparked, some sections flaring while others dissolved as if the colour were being slowly drained away.

He made it clear that he could disrupt Sarah's creation if he chose to, but his manner suggested that he would allow the children their playthings. He continued to walk through the network until he stood silhouetted by the sun's rays shining through the kitchen window. He held this position for only a moment before he turned his back on the light.

'So, you saved the girl and have awoken the dreamer,' said Lorcan. 'Oh, and of course sent the poor doggy off into the land of nod where it can dream of the master that almost killed her. You must be so proud.' His voice was full of anger barely held in check. 'But can I ask what exactly you have achieved? More importantly, do you have any idea of what this little enterprise has cost you?' Lorcan's eyes glowed red as he searched the room for answers. Azuradien appeared behind his daughter, but said nothing. 'Well, from where I'm standing, you spent the afternoon saving an old man who would have ceased being an asset to the doll within the week.'

'We learned that the doll's connection can be severed,' Michael responded.

'I could have provided that knowledge, and the service,' said Lorcan. 'Free of charge.' Lorcan said this as if he were offering to pick up some takeaway for dinner.

'And you would have too, wouldn't you?' said Azuradien. 'Fed your own greedy appetites while expecting our appreciation as the blood dried in your mouth.' He seemed almost like the powerful king Nicola had first encountered in the faerie realm, able to command attention without raising his voice, authority evident in the set of his shoulders.

'Your appreciation should already be secured, should it not?' said Lorcan. 'Or have my recent efforts already been discounted.' He looked down at the faeries. The suggestion of dark wings hovered around his shoulders.

Malcarielle placed a hand on her father's shoulder and stepped past him until she stood between the faerie king and the vampire. She held her back straight and raised her green eyes until they held Lorcan's red stare. 'I acknowledge the debt on behalf of the faerie realm. I am the next in line to the throne, so you know the power my words hold.'

Nicola was watching the exchange closely. She racked her mind for details as she searched through the memories of the masters in her head and understood the magnitude of the words. Lorcan paused for a moment – for just one moment, almost theatrically – before he resumed speaking with his usual arrogance.

'So the faerie will not raise a hand against me. How very comforting. All this time, I thought the covenant protected me.'

Azuradien rose off the ground at this outrageous slur. His daughter had made a solemn vow of protection, one that all of their people would have to honour. Azuradien's hair flew up from his shoulders. A wind started blowing around the room, causing the blinds to bang against the windows.

Nicola clasped the pendant hanging around her neck. She saw the faces of the masters staring out from every reflective surface around the room. Hazel-eyes himself stared at her from the face of the watch wrapped around her husband's wrist.

'We all acknowledge the debt owed to you.' Nicola's voice echoed with the power of the masters. The wind ceased blowing and the room became a place where the air now seemed frozen. Nicola felt the first stirs of the wild magic surge within her.

The power that was building inside Nicola was not something she understood. She could feel the cells in her own body responding to the call of the wild magic, yet she was still surprised when her drawing of power became evident by the twisting of the energy within the room, subtly pulling Sarah's network out of skew.

'You speak of costs,' said Nicola. 'And I know you speak of my son. I will not have you hold back on information. Don't test me.' Nicola's words reverberated with the strength of perfectly controlled chaos. 'You don't understand what I'm willing to do to protect my family, to protect my son. I speak to you, ancient one.' She turned her gaze on Lorcan and Nicola saw through his flesh to the virulence that coursed through his every cell.

'And to you, Faerie King.' Her cold stare bored inside the old man to the once young magic-wielder who'd broken the covenant and paid for his vanity by hosting a parasite within his own flesh. 'To the water sprite hiding amongst the dishes and to the gargoyles perched on the roof, I speak to you all. Do not test me. Do not test what I will do to protect them.' Nicola finally looked towards her son, with the power coursing through her, she could see his face submerged below a lake of the purest water. A monster stood at the shore, patiently biding its time. As the vision faded, she marvelled at the almost infinite depths, the sheer immensity of what he had created. The futility of it almost crushed her.

Nicola forced the wild magic down, balanced her rage upon an edge of empathy. Her emotions swirled through a maelstrom of pure undeniable logic, lined up and accountable.

This was not the time for its release; these few before her were not the cause. She would allow the magic to seep out of her soul in a flood of uncontrollable purpose. She must balance the contradiction because it was the only way the wild magic could be made to consume itself and revert to its static state.

The wild magic would fight her. It wanted to burn unchecked, but she stubbornly refused to be manipulated by a power that wanted her to unleash its almost unlimited potential for destruction.

With the control that allowed her to walk in a straight line when her vertigo told her the room was spinning, and with the focus that gave her the ability to distance herself from pain that could soar so high it blotted out all else, she used her years of inadvertent training to control the uncontrollable. Nicola banked the fire but kept the coals glowing, because the small sliver of insanity that allowed her to remain sane, understood the flexible nature of things, knew that only a crazy woman would play with wildfire but she was willing to roll the dice on that, anyway.

The room stayed quiet for a while after her outburst. Nobody really knew what to say. And they didn't want to risk upsetting her, fearful of her going nuclear.

'Madam,' said Lorcan. 'In the interest of maintaining our current position of honesty, I am concerned. But I'm also somewhat intrigued – by the sheer scope of the powers that this family is slowly building up. It is quite an extensive arsenal you have here. I cannot stand by without talking about the long-term implications. You must understand strength calls to strength. I will support you as long as it doesn't interfere with my own agenda,' Lorcan did not seem cowered by her display. He stepped closer to Nicola almost to show his lack of concern.

'As you are aware, the boy has a kind of second sight because of the scarring on his eyes,' Lorcan continued. This has proven to be a very useful tool when endeavouring to identify and destroy the doll's connections. What you are all forgetting is that the Nachzehrer poison in him is highly contagious. When it was just the boy, I felt confident that I could maintain the level of infection in his blood and eventually cure him. But others have already been infected, and they do not have the ability to resist the disease the way Michael does.'

Nicola's heart was racing but she chose not to interrupt. It might just cause Lorcan to clam up and she needed every bit of information she could get. Michael dropped his head and placed his hand over his face obviously struggling with the piece of news that he had infected others.

'I can guarantee that every time he uses the second sight, the infection becomes active, not just in his body but in others who have become infected. Now, I have little regard for his teammates, who even now are suffering from flu-like symptoms.' Lorcan glanced around as if he wanted his detachment to be noted. 'Soon, they'll become aggressive and irrational. We cannot really predict how this outbreak will progress; nobody has ever been able to stave off the Nachzehrer infection. But Michael has some ability to control the infection's progress and the others seem to be directly linked to his level of contagion.' Lorcan seemed to have shifted gears, now speaking quite reasonably. Maybe some of his usual arrogance had been taken down by Nicola's outburst.

'As I said, I care nothing for these others. I do, however, care if Michael or the bonded succumb to the disease. These others weaken the boy, this aspect of the contagion is beyond my ability to control. But it can be neutralised,' Lorcan held himself calmly in front of his audience with no suggestion of wings and glowing eyes he somehow felt more lethal, 'which is the course of action that I would take.'

His face held nothing but the absolute certainty that he could kill everything in the room without raising a sweat. Nicola wondered at the extent of his powers.

She didn't respond at first and merely sighed. The room was otherwise quiet while everyone processed the information. 'How many boys are infected?' asked Nicola.

'Seven.'

'And you have no ability to control the infection's progress?'

'Now who speaks in half-truths? We can control the infection's progress by limiting the boy's use of the second sight. We can eradicate the risk posed by his teammate's infection… by eliminating *them*.' Lorcan was losing patience with the discussion, and it showed.

'But if Michael is cured,' said Nicola, ignoring Lorcan's more extreme remarks. She had to remember that it was not just Lorcan who was willing to kill the infected. Ashul had admitted to taking the same course of action in the past, without question.

The bonded were warriors first and foremost.

'Assuming you can achieve that miracle. We'll lose the ability to see the doll's minions, but the threat from the Nachzehrer goes away. It's not really the hardest choice.' Nicola was pacing. She knew Michael didn't have the strength to go through another cleansing so soon, but it was the next logical step. She'd seen the corpse prowling on the shore of his consciousness. It must be a drain on his strength, protecting himself in such a way. Time was actively working against them.

Lorcan looked around the room expectantly and the corner of his mouth twisted in scorn. 'Will no-one remind her of the Nachzehrer legacy? Or are you happy to let the wicked "vampire" be the bearer of all the bad tidings?'

'What?' Nicola asked. 'What am I missing?'

'His teammates may remain infected,' said Ashul with his usual controlled indifference. 'We have no way to be sure, this concept of a cure has never occurred before. Therefore, we must proceed on the assumption that Michael's cure will not automatically transfer to his friends. The most likely outcome would be that the protection that Michael is providing will be removed and the infection will progress at its standard rate.'

'So my friends will be dead, in what, days?' Michael asked. His voice was barely above a whisper, shaken by the reality of the situation. The blood had drained from his face.

'They would have to be killed prior to that time. We cannot allow the disease to spread.' Ashul spoke the frightening truth they didn't want to hear.

The room broke down into a series of overlapping curses and denials. Nicola's head spun.

'Lady Nicola, may I remind you that the crystal cave in the faerie realm offers protection,' said Azuradien. 'It can slow the infection's spread to such a degree that the disease is almost halted.' Azuradien looked almost diminished by the conversation. 'I speak now, not of Michael, I speak of his friends. I offer them the protection of our realm.'

Malcarielle gasped at her father's words. 'Father?'

Only magic-wielders had been allowed inside the faerie realm since the faerie had suffered at the hands of mortals previously. This separation was their only defence. Nicola understood the magnitude of the offer.

'Mum, I can keep the infection at bay,' Michael said, now sounding desperate. 'We don't need to make any hasty decisions.' He looked to Ashul for confirmation.

'The Nachzehrer wants you, Michael,' It hurt Nicola to say the words. 'They will continue to create situations that force you to use your second sight.' So many thoughts flew through Nicola's mind then, images of crystals and lakes, dolls and mirrors, books and blood. 'What do you think the doll will do to stop your infection? We know that this curse was not its intention. Would it protect you in this? Would it defend you?'

'Anarcus would kill the boy, as would I.' Lorcan's face showed his lack of understanding of the question. Nicola was happy that he remained uncertain of the direction her thoughts were taking. She could hardly believe what she was contemplating herself.

'Yes, I don't doubt in its arrogance it would choose the same course of action. But it would have to get past a lot,' Nicola said, surveying the room, 'to achieve that goal.' Her family stood defiantly, ready to defend Michael to the death. She wanted Lorcan to acknowledge the strength that surrounded him.

Nicola locked eyes with the ancient one, nailing him with her unspoken question, and then asked the question anyway. 'Would the doll really risk it all? Would you?'

Motivations

'Some would consider it unwise to threaten the one that holds your son's life in his hands.' Lorcan's tone was light though his demeanour was anything but. Wisps of black vapour rose from his shoulders and his eyes glowed with smouldering fire.

'You speak of ending my son's life a little too easily,' said Nicola. 'I understand we are entirely in your hands, but I know also that you came here of your own accord. I'm not sure why you chose to help him, but you did. I'm going to push my luck a little further and assume that you will continue to do so, in the short term at least.'

Nicola had no intention of pushing anybody's luck.

She needed to plan, and plan quickly, and if she made Lorcan feel a little uncertain about the power at her disposal, well, that couldn't hurt. The doll had to be stopped before any more people died, and her son and his friends needed to be cured.

'Brent, I need to introduce you to a friend of mine,' said Nicola. 'I think he may help you create a tonic that can hold back the progression of the infection.' Everybody looked around the room expecting a visitor. When no-one walked in the room, they looked at Nicola with almost matching puzzled expressions.

'Hazel-eyes, I would like you to meet my family.' Nicola smiled as the familiar face of her hazel-eyed saviour appeared in the shine reflecting off the glass splashback that ran along one wall of their kitchen.

'Dana, can you bring Dad's shaving mirror down from our bathroom, please,' said Nicola. She noticed Dana hesitate, not because she was stunned by the arrival of the new visitor, but more because she was focused on their old one. Dana seemed to have eyes only for Lorcan. She was watching him with a puzzled frown. Nicola made a mental note to ask her about it later.

* * *

Lorcan was starting to think he should just cut his losses and leave these people to the faeries. They didn't seem to grasp the simple fact that they were at war. Anything that did not harm the enemy was a waste of time.

Risking themselves to try to save the old man was idiocy. With his failing health, he would have been dead in days. One should never put oneself at risk to halt a supply line that had already been drained dry. The doll would have to be neutralised at some point, but Lorcan was not certain how this was even done.

The boy and his sister might have been onto something: sever the connection to the feeder puppets and the power stopped flowing. But there was a much easier way to accomplish that end. He did not relish killing people in their sleep, but the doll was gaining too much power.

The boundary between the worlds was thinning. Soon, others would master the ability to walk in both worlds. And then the carnage would begin.

He had been enjoying this long period of rest, the first time that the power structure of the world was in its proper order. Magic had been effectively neutralised, and the magical creatures had been relegated to a kind of half-life.

If the doll kept gaining power, and the defenders of the land kept making soft choices, the distance between the realms would reduce to such an extent that any fool creature with a bit of patience and some luck could stumble onto the knack of walking in both worlds, and have access to powers that were rightfully the province of Lorcan alone.

He had no intention of allowing lesser beings to gain this power.

These humans needed to be given the impetus to move quickly against the doll. The faerie were weak, diminished creatures without the stomach for the task at hand, and it was not within the warriors' capacity to make their own decisions.

But Lorcan had sensed something different in Ashul. He'd broken a basic tenet when he allowed his own defences to be breached, putting himself and the rest of the bonded at risk. Lorcan could smell the poison running through his veins. Was it purely the fact that the boy was bonded that allowed him to share the Nachzehrer curse? Or was there more to it than that? Had the boy's initiation into the group allowed a shift in the restrictions imposed on the bonded? Had it given them the capacity to break the governing tenets?

The bonded unfettered was a frightening concept.

The last couple of minutes of conversation had left Lorcan with much to ponder. Firstly, Malcarielle, future queen of the faeries, had acknowledged 'blood debt'. To have this debt freely voiced by a member of the royal house allowed Lorcan to ask a boon from any of the faerie at any time.

No restrictions.

If the faerie refused his request, the queen's own life would be forfeit. He would make the king suffer for his self-important superiority. Let him stew for a couple of centuries before Lorcan put forward his demands. Maybe he should even sit on the faerie throne.

But then the *witch* had dared to reprimand him, her voice ringing with the strength of a hundred masters. Lorcan knew she spoke the truth; each word sang with the promise that she would do anything to protect the boy. Nicola might not have fangs, but she would rip his throat out if Lorcan threatened her children.

He had not known she had the ability to draw on wild magic. It was a power that he'd never seen tamed in his very, very long life. Many had tried, but all had died as a result. Most in excruciating pain. By its very nature, it was a force uncontrollable, but she'd shown him only the first glowing embers of her rage and then banked the coals, with no noticeable cost to herself. It was as Lorcan was wondering whether he would be able to tear her throat out before the wildfire could be unleased that he noticed Dana staring at him.

For a moment, he feared she could read his thoughts. But she shook her head as their eyes met then left the room to retrieve the mirror. There was no hostility in her eyes, just puzzlement.

He would need to educate this family. They were treating him with a decided lack of respect. When Lorcan heard

Dana's footfalls upstairs, he placed a foot in each realm and stepped in front of the girl as she reached for the mirror, travelling the distance to the upstairs bathroom in less than a second.

* * *

Dana refused to flinch when the vampire materialised out of a cloud of black vapour. She took a slow, steady breath and hoped her heartbeat did not give her away.

'Why are you so puzzled by my behaviour?' said Lorcan with a quiet calm. 'Have I not been honest with your family from the start? My motivation is and always will be self-preservation.' Lorcan's left eyebrow raised as if he were honestly baffled by her confusion.

'Lorcan,' said Dana. 'You have been unfailingly honest in all of your actions…' Dana paused when he looked down at her. His face now beamed with fainted sufferance. Dana was watching his every move, hoping to read the truth. 'All except one. You brought the dogs to help us. Michael wasn't in danger. You weren't protecting him. What motivated you then? I was the one in danger, but I'm not conceited enough to think you were actually protecting me. So please explain the need for self-preservation at that particular moment.'

Lorcan closed the gap between them. 'Ahh, but you are very fetching. You intrigue me – there are depths to your eyes that I have rarely encountered.'

'Okay, we'll put aside my ability to enchant.' Dana's words dripped with cynicism. 'But why save the dog? Why bring Madison here?' Dana watched as his demeanour shifted from playful mocking to indignant. The twinkle left his eyes. His shoulders lifted as the muscles tensed across his back.

'The animal is blameless. If you don't understand that, then I have greatly misjudged you.' Dana was unsure how much to give away, but she felt the pressure of time ticking away from her. She was also wary of how much she should push him now that his back was up.

'Madison was safe at home, but you risked both her and Sheba by bringing them into the dream. If your motivation was purely my "fetching smile",' Dana lifted her fingers in mocking air quotes and continued, 'you could have gone to the hospital and killed Mr Stevens and neither dog would have been endangered.'

'Please. You seem to have this all figured out, enlighten me. What was my motivation?' said Lorcan, attempting to keep his tone light, though Dana noticed the clenching of his jaw. The tips of his teeth poked out from under his top lip, just slightly raised in anger.

'I have absolutely no idea. But I know Sheba looks at you like a pack elder. She fears your displeasure, but she doesn't exactly fear you.'

'I do not feed off her kind,' said Lorcan. 'She has no reason to fear me.' Lorcan had quit trying to hide his anger – his eyes started to glow a faint red.

'No, but you do feed off my kind and Sheba would defend me to the death if she sensed I was in danger. So, we come around full circle. Why did you bring the dogs into the dream?' Dana wasn't expecting a response: she had pushed him as far as she dared. She hoped she'd read his mood correctly. He reacted more like a wild animal than a human being, but the telltale signs were there if you watched and listened. She turned and walked out of the room, and she felt his eyes smouldering like red coals at her back.

The room was deathly silent. She resisted the need to turn around, her back prickling in anticipation of a strike. All that followed her were his words. 'Because you are indeed fetching!'

A lightness had returned to his voice as he called after her, but she suspected a hint of canine tooth was still visible. She hurried down the stairs. When she handed the mirror to her mother, Dana noticed her fingers had left foggy crescents on the surface. She wiped her sweaty palms down the legs of her jeans.

Dana sat on the couch next to the sleeping dog. Lorcan was already standing in the shadows smiling at her, a fine trace of smoke rising from his shoulders.

* * *

Nicola had no time to lose. She felt the weight of time dragging at her, slowing her movements, her thoughts, like a tangible burden that she would be forced to carry around until this whole thing reached its conclusion. When Michael had become a bonded warrior, she'd feared the danger it posed, the strength that he would wield. How ironic that it was his very humanity that had put the bullseye on his back.

But it was also the depth of his spirit, his own special gift that gave him the protection that would hopefully keep him whole.

Nicola pulled Ashul aside and asked him a question that she already knew the answer to. 'How much can you protect Michael from this?'

'As much as we need to,' Ashul responded, just as Lorcan had predicted.

'Can you protect him from the infection?' Nicola asked the question more forcefully – she needed the truth.

'We can,' Ashul said.

Nicola waited, knowing there was more, knowing Ashul didn't have it in him to dissemble. 'Up to a point.' Nothing about Ashul's body language changed, it was his words that showed he carried a burden similar to her own. Each syllable dropped from his mouth like stones hefted into a well. This time he did not force her to drag more information out of him with a constant string of questions, driving him to the full disclosure like a cattle dog rounding up errant sheep. This time he answered fully, holding nothing back. On some level she wished he had, but deep down she'd known the truth. 'We can protect him until the point where the bonded themselves have been drained of resistance.'

'Is that possible, for the bonded to be drained?' Nicola asked, shocked by his statement, although she'd suspected as much. In this, she wished he could have lied to her.

'It is now. I am sorry that this is not what you need to hear but believe me, to the bonded it is a great gift. Forever we have lived to give our all – or as much as we were able – to protect the blood, to serve the source, to safeguard the land. It is a curse having to watch others die because we could not quite give everything. This restriction has been lifted. We still retain our magical shields, but for Michael we can channel our strength, share his burden.'

Ashul reached out and grabbed Nicola's hand, emphasising and needing her to understand the importance of what he was saying. 'And we do so with grateful hearts. Our enemies would rejoice if they found out, wrongly perceiving that we have been weakened. But I assure you the opposite is true. I believe this change will become our greatest strength.' Nicola suspected that this may have been the first time she'd heard Ashul speak with genuine passion.

'Can you share the full extent of your plan with me?' asked Ashul. She had wondered how long he would take to ask her this question.

'Not at this point. I don't even want to say the words out loud. What I'm planning would probably sound crazy. And I cannot afford to be anything less than fully committed. Hesitation, even a moment's worth, could cost us dearly.'

'I will obey your commands without hesitation, I give you this promise.' Ashul spoke this like a solemn vow.

Nicola doubted that he would, if the command was to not give his all.

Interference

Nicola had sent the warrior off to escort the empath and the spider-witch home. She'd sent everybody else to bed. Lorcan was asked if he had any knowledge of healing.

'I know how to kill, infect and influence through the use of pheromones and subtle enchantments. Healing is just doing the opposite. So yes, I think I have more than a working knowledge of the process. Have I not proven this by my continued efforts with your son?' Lorcan's answer didn't help the already strained relations with Azuradien.

'I was more asking if you knew anything about potions that could interfere with the progress of the infection,' Nicola said, sounding frustrated by Lorcan's attitude. But it was the pair of hazel eyes staring into the room from every reflected surface that rolled dramatically. 'You agree that Michael, with your help, is able to keep the infection in his blood stable.' Nicola pushed on when Lorcan only raised an eyebrow at her. 'You have also suggested that it is the connection to his friends, the ones infected that puts this balance in jeopardy. His friends react when he uses the second sight. Well, this information has to be transmitted somehow. If we can create something to interrupt this signal's transmission or maybe mimic a stable baseline, Michael might be able to use the second sight without impacting his friends.' Nicola let out a sigh as she waited for Lorcan's response, but it was Azuradien who spoke first.

'Nicola, you waste time here,' said Azuradien. 'Helping Michael's friends is not a priority for the ancient one.'

Lorcan suppressed the desire for theatrical sweeps of clothing and produced a water bottle from deep within the folds of his cloak. 'I may not have your knowledge of the healing arts but I was the only one who thought to pick up this.'

He waved the bottle around, just keeping it out of Nicola's reach.

'I would wear gloves if I were you. The bottle is the source of the contagion for the seven boys. Each of them will have this strain flowing through their veins.'

Finally, the faces of the family showed some grudging respect. Lorcan 'the deceiver' had delivered once again.

Malcarielle leaned forward and took the bottle from his hands. 'If we had a way to isolate the infection, we would have a much better chance of creating a suppressant with the right frequency to interfere with the infection's non-physical aspects.' Malcarielle was peering into the bottle as if she could see the disease crawling over its surface.

'Can anyone think of a safe way to remove all contaminates without degrading the sample?' Brent asked the room. Azuradien's brows furrowed. He stroked his beard as if trying to extract some wisdom from the hairs that sprouted from his face, but eventually he responded with the usual amount of usefulness. A shake of the head. He had nothing to add.

Lorcan waved his hand impatiently. He demanded the bottle's return. Malcarielle looked puzzled, but handed the bottle back to him.

Walking over to the sink, Lorcan politely asked the water sprite hiding amongst the cups to fill the bottle with a couple of centimetres of water. She was happy to oblige, so she flew over to his hand. She sang in her little piping voice and filled the water bottle as requested. The water sprite flew back to the sink with little pips of excitement as it nestled back amongst the plates.

Brent asked, 'Are there any special properties of the sprite's water that we should be made aware of?'

'What, the water?' Lorcan responded, raising the bottle in his hand. 'No, there are no special properties, but you haven't really tasted water until you've had it given to you by a water sprite! You must try it sometime.' Lorcan smiled at the group, daring them to criticise him.

When they all stood mute, he gave the bottle a shake and lifted it to his lips and drank the contents. He grimaced slightly when the black sediment from the bottom of bottle ran down his throat, but he made sure he'd drained the bottle dry before he tossed it into the trash.

'Shouldn't we dispose of that safely?' Nicola asked.

'All the infection is now in me.'

'Some may remain on the bottle,' said Azuradien. 'Your flippancy puts others in danger. This is just a distraction for you. We are trying to save lives.' Azuradien made his displeasure at Lorcan's attitude known. Lorcan found his impotence quite amusing.

'I am the king of disease,' said Lorcan. 'I can assure you that no trace of infection remains on that bottle, but by all means, do go take it to the safety of the faerie realm. Off now, shoo.' Lorcan twiddled his fingers in the king's direction but kept his gaze on Brent. 'What form would you prefer this pure infection to be expressed in?'

When Brent didn't immediately reply, Lorcan elaborated, 'I can force the infection out through my skin. It will have a tar-like consistency. I can bleed it out through my tear ducts. Neither are an overly pleasant experience. Or I can just spit it out. Your call.'

'Spit, yep…' Brent stammered his reply. 'Spit will do just fine.'

'Just spit it out, Lorcan,' said Nicola, her words short and clipped.

He'd gotten under her skin. He gave her a curt nod, ducking his head so she could not see him smiling. 'And tone down the theatrics just a bit.' Nicola stepped forward with one of Brent's small crystal decanters. 'We're all a little stressed, so please don't antagonise things further.'

'I must admit I find him highly amusing,' Hazel-eyes interjected from his place in the mirror. 'The faeries have a tendency to make even the most stimulating tasks arduous.' Both of the faeries ignored the face speaking from the mirror.

'This infection has the ability to link those who are contaminated,' said Brent. 'To do this, it has to transmit on some kind of frequency. We just need to find out what could interrupt this transmission, or maybe even to mimic it to a certain degree. Keeping things stable while Michael uses his abilities.'

* * *

Nicola had something in mind: she was hoping Malcarielle would think along the same lines because it was big ask. But to her surprise it was Azuradien who suggested the use of the crystal cave before she even had to mention it.

'If we brought a small piece of crystal here, we could use its resonance to imbue water with the correct frequency to negate the infection's ability to link. Those drinking the tonic would have the progress of the infection halted for the time-being. It might be almost as effective as placing those infected in the cave themselves.'

Hazel-eyes added from the mirror, 'If we use the sprite's water, we would have the benefit of her uplifting energies, which could even help ease the symptoms of madness and aggression.'

'Azuradien, Malcarielle, would it be possible to have some of those flower cups you serve tea in?' asked Brent. 'And some of the honey cakes? The flowers had some awfully strong healing properties and I think they'll help the tonic's effect stay in the system of those infected for a longer period of time.' Brent was slowly reaching Hazel-eyes' level of enthusiasm.

Lorcan said. 'I will donate my body to science and become your test subject. I've left a small portion of the infection inside my body. I can feel its need to be near Michael, to be in harmony with him. This infection will react to Michael's use of his second sight in the same way the infection does in his teammates.'

Azuradien whispered something to Malcarielle and then blinked out of the room, off to get supplies from the faerie realm. Nicola barely noticed, more concerned with what Lorcan had been saying.

'Are you sure?' asked Nicola.

'Of course, I am not sure!' Lorcan snapped back. 'I have never allowed the Nachzehrer poison into my body until I met your son,' he said. 'But I can feel the link to Michael, and it would make sense that it is this link that causes the disease to progress or hold steady based on Michael's own infection levels.' Lorcan was talking directly at Nicola. Almost as if he wanted her to be completely aware of the exact nature of the situation. Defining the terms so that later no-one could accuse him of not being clear.

Nicola didn't need the extra attention, she was already hanging on his every word, trying to hear if anything sounded off, or calculated. 'It is but a guess, but I can assure you my guess is another person's measured certainty. It will be easy to test. I am indeed curious as to the effect this crystal will have upon my body. Maybe it could cure me of my ungodly thirst.' Lorcan's last words dripped with sarcasm.

A sudden gust of wind blew around the room as Azuradien returned from the faerie realm. He had flowers and honey cakes with him and a small satchel that contained a variety of mosses and seed packets. 'Brent, I have brought these just in case they have any properties that may help.'

Brent opened the jar containing one of the mosses, pinched a piece and rolled it between his fingers. He screwed his nose up as an acrid green mist rose from his fingertips. He moved to the sink and washed the green stain from his hands.

'It's too strong. It will destroy the flower's restorative effects.' He moved to the packet of seeds and sniffed, warier this time. He placed one on his finger and tentatively licked the seed. 'Perfect!' A wide grin on his face. 'Nicola, this may increase the longevity of the tonic immeasurably.'

After about fifteen minutes of pounding and mixing, Brent placed a mortar full of a mustard green paste before the mirror on the kitchen bench. 'Azuradien, can I have the crystal now, please?'

'Daughter, I believe you can help here?' Azuradien said as he raised his bushy eyebrows, keeping the rest of his expression neutral.

* * *

'You knew,' Malcarielle said, her head held high. She had no intention of apologising for the theft. Nor was she interested in explaining her actions. She had broken the law of her kind to bring the piece of crystal to Michael, but she did not believe, there had been any alternative. The doll threatened all realms. Her people could hide behind their defences but eventually if the doll was left unchecked, they too would be at its mercy.

Regardless, she believed Michael was worth the risk. She'd initially had her doubts about the new brood of the blood that Ashul had brought their way. Ignorant and arrogant was her first assessment, and she'd not been wrong, but there was more to them. More to *him*. She left the room with her back straight, unfazed by whatever her father might think of her actions.

* * *

'Dana, how long do you think they'll take?' asked Michael, agitated. 'I know Mum wants us to rest but there are people being forced to do terrible things while we wait.'

'I understand, Michael,' said Dana, almost too casually for Michael's liking. 'But your friends are relying on you to maintain balance and you can't do that when you're exhausted.'

'This is not just about my friends.' Michael swung his legs around and over the side of the bed. 'Dana, I remember what it felt like to have the doll in my head. It speaks with your own voice. I was so exhausted from the nightmares: I didn't know the thoughts weren't my own. Not until it was almost too late.' Michael leant forward, wanting Dana to understand what he was saying. 'I almost smashed Marcus' head in. It was a close thing because on a not too deep level I wanted to hurt him, still do. Only at the last minute did I realise the doll was in my head. To have that thing rummaging around in your thoughts, having access to damn near everything, it's wrong Dana. We can't let that continue.' Michael lay back down, twisting the bed sheets in his hands.

'Have you been wondering at all about Marcus? With everything that has been going on, I haven't had a chance to talk to you about him. Like where the hell is he?' Dana asked. Michael had not expected the conversation to turn to Marcus.

'Who cares? In case you have forgotten he was happy to be the doll's little assistant in their nightly torture Michael sessions.'

'No, but that's my point,' said Dana. Some enthusiasm entering her speech. She turned towards Michael. 'Previously he was in every dream the doll entered, now he isn't in any. Dad says he's next door but have you seen him? I know I haven't. Was he there when the doll attacked with the Nachzehrer? He wasn't, was he?' Dana didn't pause to allow Michael to answer any of these questions. Michael didn't need to. It was clear that Dana had a point. 'So where is he? He was the doll's first source of fuel; I can't believe it has stopped using him just because it cares for his health.' Dana shifted to lie diagonally next to Michael. She rolled over as she was speaking to look him in the eyes. 'I think we need to check on him.'

'Dana, what exactly do you mean by "check on him"?'

'We find him and Ashley checks on his… I don't know, his wellbeing?'

'And we do this exactly how?'

'Um, by breaking into their house.' Dana paused as if feeling the irony. 'Again'

Malcarielle's polite knock interrupted the conversation. 'We need the crystal now.' She looked around Michael's room with curious eyes. Michael wished he'd put some of his clothing away rather than leaving it piled high on every available surface.

Michael reached into the top drawer where he'd lain the crystal wrapped in a t-shirt. He jumped out of bed and handed the crystal to Malcarielle, casually kicking clothing underneath the bed as he got up and handed her the gem. The crystal hummed like a struck tuning fork, the tone just on the edge of comfort. A touch higher and he didn't think he would be able to listen to it.

'How long has the crystal been vibrating at that pitch?' asked Malcarielle.

'Since you gave it to me. I thought it always sounded like that.'

'It does when it is working.' Malcarielle smiled as she walked out of the room.

* * *

Malcarielle returned with a faint smile playing across her features. The crystal was quietly singing. She placed the crystal in Brent's hands, but not before locking eyes with her father. She raised her chin, her head held at a haughty angle. There was something that Malcarielle wanted Azuradien to acknowledge. Nicola was sure that it had something to do with the delicate song that filled the room. There was no doubt that Malcarielle felt vindicated in her decision to bring the crystal to Michael. She almost glowed with satisfaction.

Azuradien pulled at the hairs of his beard and nodded curtly then looked away. Nicola marvelled at his dismissive nature.

Completely oblivious to the exchange between the faeries, Brent brought the crystal close to the side of glass jar that held the purified poison. He ran the crystal around the rim of the jar, the hum of the crystal dropped in pitch, and then died away. Brent ran the crystal around the lip for a second time, and Hazel-eyes' low humming joined in with the sound of the crystal. He brought his voice down a notch to try to match that of the crystal. The hum from the crystal lasted for a good five seconds longer, but still faded and died.

Nicola looked towards Lorcan for help. 'The depths of my charms are indeed near endless,' said Lorcan. 'But I do not sing, and for future reference. I do *not* dance. Look elsewhere for help on this one.'

A tiny sound pipped from Lorcan's left shoulder. With her wings shaking, the water sprite appeared. Her large blue eyes darted back and forth between Lorcan and Nicola. 'Why will you not leave me alone?' Lorcan hissed at the sprite. The sprite flickered but remained standing on his shoulder and pipped in reply.

'You are no help to us anyway, your voice is too high.' Lorcan moved to brush the sprite from his shoulder. The sprite dodged his hand and sang defiantly at Lorcan's words. Her voice rang at a pitch so close to that of the crystal that the gem vibrated in harmony with the sprite.

Her song rang for a few minutes, and then a low note joined her from elsewhere in the room. A deep baritone rumbled from within the cupboard above the fridge.

Nicola opened the door, moving slowly as she did. A large grey gargoyle, hiding its head behind a fleshy arm was not what she'd expected. Although he shrunk away from her, hiding himself behind some cookbooks, he continued to sing. The deeper sounds of his voice wrapped around the sprite's high notes, their songs combining until the liquid inside the jar almost seemed to join them. It started to vibrate. The three tones merged together seamlessly.

The two 'singers' adjusted their pitches effortlessly until together they reached the perfect note. When their song stopped, both the crystal and the liquid continued to hum.

'I need some water,' said Brent, turning towards the kitchen sink. 'This needs to be diluted. It will be easier to maintain the pitch if the liquid is loosened.'

Lorcan brushed the water sprite off his shoulder and flicked her towards the bowl Brent held in his hands. She hovered above the liquid, shaking, looking around the room nervously. Lorcan bared his teeth at her and issued a low growl. The sprite dissolved into a stream of clear water that poured into the bottom of the bowl. Lorcan smiled and nodded for Brent to continue.

Brent worked quickly and poured the humming potion into the water-filled bowl, careful not to allow any of the mixture to spill. The liquid shimmered as if the tiny vibrations were being created from under the surface and were therefore somehow organic in nature. Michael didn't like the thought.

Brent gripped the crystal above the bowl with a pair of stainless-steel tongs. 'Malcarielle, will I damage the crystal in any way if it touches the liquid?' he asked.

'No, Brent. The crystal is safe, but I do appreciate your concern.' It was hard not to notice the faeries' anxiety over the crystal's care – they were watching Brent like a hawk, as if one wrong move and the crystal would shatter. Nicola had to remember to speak to Ashul about the importance of the crystals. The master's memories weren't helping much. She knew that the crystals, and the crystal cave especially, were central to faerie culture, almost the bedrock of their people, which was why they were not allowed to leave the faerie realm. There were some theories around the crystals being linked to the covenant in some way. But the more she searched through the memories, the more hazy the details became. No real mention had been made of the significance of their visit to the faerie realm for training. Nicola had a sneaking suspicion that Azuradien wouldn't be forthcoming with details if he were asked.

Brent must have picked up on the faeries' concern because he hesitated before immersing the crystal in the liquid, letting out a deep breath when the crystal did not react as it was submersed. More confident now, Brent stirred the mixture, allowing the crystal's energies to infuse into the liquid.

From the mirror, Hazel-eyes began to chant again and Brent joined in. When they stopped a little later, the crystal ceased its humming. Brent gently removed it from the liquid and held the crystal in front of him. 'It may need to be cleansed,' said Brent. 'But to be honest I'm not sure that boiling water will do the trick.'

Lorcan held his hands out in front of him and said, 'If you would allow me?' He posed the question to Malcarielle and Malcarielle alone. Nicola had to give Malcarielle credit, she barely paused before nodding her head in assent.

Brent gently dropped the crystal in Lorcan's outstretched hands. He closed his long fingers around the gem. A soft hiss came from within his clasped hand, a small amount of steam.

Lorcan opened his hands where the crystal gleamed in his palm and it radiated a green warmth throughout the room. Lorcan handed the crystal to Malcarielle with a polite bow. Nicola watched the whole exchange, even more intrigued than she had been before.

Blowing out another sigh, Brent reached for the small packet that Azuradien had given him, the one that held a single seed. He held the packet above the shimmering liquid, gave one quick shake, and the seed dropped into the liquid with barely a sound. There was no puff of smoke, no hiss or sudden colour change, but Nicola could feel the shift in energy as soon as the seed disappeared under the surface.

There was no doubt that the seed had added great strength to the brew.

'Before I put any of that into my body, I would know the origins of the seed,' Lorcan said, a note of concern in his voice.

Azuradien seemed only too pleased to provide an answer. 'It is from an acorn that fell from an oak that imprisoned a very great mage. The tree has long been lost to us, but the seeds hold a little of his vitality.'

'Well, that changes things now, doesn't it?' said Lorcan, his handsome face showing signs of his anger.

He was controlling his anger well, but Nicola could see the tightening of the skin around his eyes. 'This great mage had no love for my kind: his *vitality* might still contain some of his bias.'

'Is the fearsome beast finally afraid of something?' asked Azuradien from the corner of the room.

'I would say this is beneath you, but to be honest it is exactly the kind of trickery I expect from you, Faerie King,' Lorcan said, words dripping with loathing.

'Get the boy down here,' said Lorcan. 'If this seed of yours harms me, I will visit ten times the pain upon you and your kind, *King*.' Lorcan spat this final word.

'I can see that you would love to, and I am sure that you would do exactly that if you could,' said Azuradien. 'But I am protected by my magical shield. You can talk of pain, but if you try to harm me, you will be the one who suffers.'

'Continue to think that, faerie. Your disbelief will make my enjoyment all the more sweeter when I finally taste your blood upon my tongue.' Lorcan's fury began to smoke up from his shoulders. Black claws grew from his fingertips. 'Now, get the boy before my forbearance of this diminutive king is exhausted.'

Growth

Malcarielle walked back into Michael's room with her wings flickering in and out of view. 'Lorcan needs you downstairs. I would say it is urgent.'

Seeing her agitation Michael asked, 'Didn't the potion making go as planned?' Michael tried to keep his tone light but wasn't sure he succeeded. Something had obviously upset Malcarielle. When she just gestured for him to hurry up, Michael turned to Dana.

'Dana, we'll talk about this later. The ancient one has summoned us and I'm not going down unless you come too. He seems to like you.'

The corner of Malcarielle's mouth twitched into a smile. Dana, always quick, had a pair of socks in her hand. Michael dodged them when they flew in his direction. Malcarielle, however, did not.

Michael held back his laughter. The faerie queen was no longer amused.

All levity left Michael as he sauntered into the kitchen and saw the expression on his mother's face. Without saying a word she'd made it clear that now was not the time for his humour. 'Michael, I'd be quick about this if I were you,' Nicola said.

'Boy, I hope you appreciate all that I am risking for you,' said Lorcan through gritted teeth. He held up a small glass of a translucent bright yellow solution.

'Hang on, what are you risking?' said Michael. 'I thought you were immune to the Nachzehrer poison?' Michael was confused by what was going on.

'I am, but the king here upped the stakes. I am now about to drink a concoction that may contain the essence of a being who tried to eradicate my kind.'

Azuradien went to speak but Malcarielle placed a restraining hand on her father's arm and he stayed silent.

'Let the old man come, he needs to learn his place.' Lorcan's eyes glowed. He grew in height but still retained the shape of a man.

Michael felt Ashul's presence a moment before he heard him speak. 'You act like children! Every time I leave you unattended, you fall to bickering. What has transpired in my absence?' said Ashul, angry words barely held in check.

'The vampire has agreed to test the potion that Brent and his friend in the mirror have created,' said Azuradien. His tone was sounding self-righteous even to Michael's ears.

'And?'

'And I offered all the resources the faerie realm had at its disposal.'

'So, we still play games!' Ashul turned his back on the king. 'Brent, the specifics, please.'

'I added a seed that had enormous potency. It appears to have come from an acorn that—'

Ashul interrupted to address the faerie king. 'You ask much of a man you demanded to be removed from your presence.'

Ashul reached for the bottle of the yellow liquid. 'Lorcan, you need not do this. I can test the potion. The mage's life force will not endanger me.'

Azuradien, always quick, had realised the importance of Ashul's words, understanding exactly what had been confirmed with Ashul's offer to drink the potion – that Ashul had the Nachzehrer poison in his system too.

'So, you are infected,' Azuradien whispered. The confirmation of this fear had visibly shaken him. 'You have risked the lives of the bonded?'

Michael was having trouble following the conversation, but he could feel the anger among the bonded. He heard the rumble of hooves somewhere above his head. Smoke filled Michael in on the seed's history and the implications it might have for Lorcan's safety. Before he had time to fully understand what was occurring, there was a shatter of glass at Michael's feet.

A dark haze hung around Lorcan's body and his wings beat at the air. 'View me through your second sight, and monitor your shore,' Lorcan growled from beside him. 'We will know soon enough whether your uncle's potion lives up to its promise.' Michael could tell the moment Lorcan had placed a foot in the second realm. The world shimmered around him and Michael could see the suggestion of the void eating at the corners of his vision.

Lorcan rose before him, his black leathery wings brushing against the ceiling, and smoke rose from his shoulders. A hand tipped in hooked talons reached towards Michael's face. Before he'd a chance to react, Lorcan had wrapped his hand around Michael's arm, his nails digging into the flesh of his bicep.

'Tell me what you see!' With a casual beat of Lorcan's wings, Michael was transported into the shadowland.

* * *

The faerie king had enraged Lorcan. He'd offered his assistance in good faith. This underhanded treachery against one who offered aid was lower than low. And they deemed *him* the animal! The only thing keeping the family alive was the knowledge that they were unaware of the magnitude of what the king had done.

The seed has been imbued with the great mage's essence – the great mage, a powerful magic-wielder who had once revelled in the termination of his kind. There was no way to know the damage the mage's essence would have on Lorcan's body, what it would do to his mind. But once again, they underestimated him. If they thought he would cower before the memory of a tyrant, they knew nothing of his nature.

Lorcan lifted the bottle to his lips, waiting for the mage's dark presence to gnaw at his mind. It did not take long for the first flashes of pain to rip through his body. It was as if his cells were rupturing, one at a time. His body burned.

Lorcan turned towards Michael; they boy's eyes went wide as he viewed Lorcan in all his otherworldly glory. Lorcan regretted that he had to use the boy in such a brutal way. No human had ever walked in the shadowland, but there was no alternative. Lessons needed to be taught and he didn't have the time to worry about how his methods might be viewed.

'Tell me what you see!' He gripped the Michael's arm and propelled himself into the shadowland, dragging the boy with him. Let the faerie explain to the mother where her precious Michael had gone.

* * *

'Where… where have they gone?' said Nicola, spinning around.

Ashul focused on a point somewhere above her left shoulder and his eyes glowed a faint blue. 'He has taken Michael into the shadowland.'

'Well, go get him back,' she said. 'Get him out of there.'

'I cannot travel there.'

'Has he been harmed?' asked Nicola. She couldn't catch her breath; she was finding it harder and harder to breathe.

'He is… distanced from us.' Ashul's words were hollow, as if he himself had somehow been taken between worlds. 'But I can track him.'

* * *

Titan had been crouching in the shadows on the lake's shore when he saw the zombie become active. He was his master's guardian, so he assessed the danger, sniffing the air. The scent of rotting flesh assailed his nostrils. This creature smelled of unnatural things.

Titan circled the edge of the lake, careful to remain behind the creature. A faint glow rose across the surface of the lake, bathing the shore in an incandescent light. The guardian knew that Michael was the source, and the dog felt his chest fill with pride. Titan would not let this creature pollute the shore any longer. The muscles in his hind legs tensed. He was ready to launch and peeled his lips back in eagerness, growling deep in his throat.

He paused when the surface of the water rippled as if some leviathan moved just under the surface. A faint vibration grew around him, coming from all directions at once. The sound reverberated at a frequency that caused his teeth to hum. He lowered his ears, fearful that the pitch would change. The sound held the potential to cause great harm, but it was currently at a range that the dog could tolerate.

The bag of sticking flesh stalking the shore cringed as the volume increased. The guardian eased back as the creature stumbled around confused.

The dog stepped backwards, into the shadows until he was sure the current danger had passed, returning to his former position. A silent sentinel on the shore of his master's consciousness.

* * *

The shadowland was a place of smoke and mirrors. Everywhere Michael looked hurt his eyes. Shapes in front of him bent, twisted, distorting his focus.

Lorcan's wings beat at the air and their rhythmic nature reminded Michael of Smoke. 'Call not to your bonded, they cannot follow you here,' Lorcan said from behind his shoulder.

Like a gothic interpretation of hell, Michael could see the shape of his neighbourhood hiding under the surface of this twisted reality.

The two of them flew over the trees that grew in the park near his home, and Michael sensed something in the branches reaching up to grasp at his feet. Lorcan's powerful wings pushed against the air and they rose higher.

The beat of Lorcan's wings started to lose rhythm. The motion stuttered and they dropped a couple of metres, once again close to the trees. Lorcan let out a strangled moan.

'Is it the potion, or the poison?' said Michael.

'And you care, why?' Lorcan muttered so low that Michael barely heard the words. 'I will not drop you.' He felt the unseen hands pushing up through the trees reaching for his feet.

Michael called forth the sword that lay forever within his reach.

'You would slay me with faerie steel?' Lorcan hissed at him through his pain.

Michael didn't bother to respond. He swung the blade around and its light shone through the darkness; the world solidified around him. The seeking hands pulled away from the light but dark shadows remained, dancing on the edges of Michael's vision.

'I want to help you. But you must know I cannot stay here.' Michael held the blade before him, using it to help keep the world in some kind of focus. He thought he heard the whinny of a horse over the wind tearing at his ears.

'But I could, if I must,' replied Lorcan.

'Yes, I know you're a complete bad-arse,' said Michael, and he thrust his blade at a grasping claw that flew towards him out of the twisting shadows. The blade connected with nothing but thin air.

Michael turned in Lorcan's grip and saw a dark shape – filled with throbbing flashes of light – rise up behind the vampire. To Michael, it looked like a chunk of the sky had folded in upon itself, the heavens a facade now turned back to expose the bare heart that throbbed behind the sky.

How could anything be so immense it eclipsed even the sky?

The shadowland felt like a place that the human mind could not comprehend. Michael's mind would need to break for this place to make any sense to him. Just as his vision had twisted and distorted here, so too did his perception of the things around him.

Michael raised his sword again, hoping to use it to force a more fixed structure on the entity that threatened them. The edges of the *thing* sharpened within the halo created by the sword, but the immensity of the entity continued to billow out behind them, suggesting untold depths.

The fire burning within Lorcan's eyes was the only warning of the power about to be unleashed. Michael had just enough time to shield his face.

A wave of heat baked out from Lorcan and was accompanied by a dull *whump* like the sudden release of a pent-up breath.

Moments later, Michael felt ashes rain down upon his face. When he opened his eyes, the sky no longer contained the being pulsing with inner light, only warped clouds remained forming and reforming above him.

Michael heard the rumbling of hooves drumming behind the strange acoustics of the shadowland. He yelled over the din, 'Are you sure the bonded cannot reach me here?' The surrounding shadows swirled in motion. The shape of a rider on horseback formed out of the darkness, only to be torn apart by the wind moments later.

The vampire's body shuddered again. He said, 'You think I brought you here as some kind of elaborate punishment?' Lorcan's chest heaved with troubled breathing, his words punctuated by slow, irregular gasps for air.

Lorcan coughed and silvery sand poured from his mouth.

More of the fine silvery grains trickled from Lorcan's nose and Michael realised Lorcan had stopped breathing altogether.

He could do nothing more than grab hold of the vampire as they plummeted out of the sky.

The twisted branches of a silver tree formed from the dust that had poured forth from the vampire's mouth. A brief impression of an anguished face trapped within the bark quickly dissolved as the swirling winds claimed the silver dust to become just another part of the kaleidoscope sky.

Michael wished for wings, but this was not the second plane where he could just imagine himself soaring through the sky. As he dropped to the ground with Lorcan's dead weight dragging at his arms, he heard Smoke's voice call.

I am here.

And she was.

* * *

Michael slammed into Smoke's back and the air blew from his lungs. He was not able to keep his grip on Lorcan and felt the vampire fall away from him.

'I've lost him,' Michael tried to say, but he was winded and couldn't draw in any air to speak. He yelled into Ashul's mind. *Ashul help him. He can't fly. He isn't breathing.*

I have him, brother, Ashul called back. Michael was struggling to get himself turned around in the saddle. The muscles in his chest were starting to unlock but he was only able to suck in small breaths and turning around on a horse flying through the air was no easy feat. He was struggling with his vision and the constantly shifting landscape was making him nauseous.

Can we get back? asked Michael. He tried to find Ashul is the sky around him. *Can we get home.* But even before he'd finished his second question, he noticed the sky had regained some focus, edges no longer pulling his eyes in different directions. At some point, they had ridden back into the first plane.

'We need to get him to the ground!' Michael yelled. He spotted Ashul just in front of him. He had one arm wrapped around Lorcan's chest. He hadn't been able to pull Lorcan up onto Smoke's back and his dead weight was pulling Ashul out of his saddle. Lorcan hung lifeless, his face bouncing against Ashul's leg.

Smoke banked to the left, flying over the trees that bordered the back of their property. Michael flinched as they drew near the lower hanging branches.

You are safe.

Michael sent back to Smoke his love and gratitude. His mind was awash with so many different fears. Smoke's calming thoughts were a blessing. The shadowland had shaken Michael. Its ability to twist his senses was more than disorientating, it was downright frightening. Looking through the scars on his eyes to see the doll's connections was one thing, riding through a world that literally bent your mind was something altogether different. Michael couldn't help but wonder what Lorcan's reasoning was in taking him to that place. Hopefully, he would be able to ask him soon.

He didn't look at Lorcan as a villain, he didn't want to see the vampire in that light. Michael viewed him as an ally and he didn't want that opinion to be shattered. Mostly he just didn't want to see Lorcan harmed. Michael couldn't imagine how something as innocuous as a seed could put such a powerful creature's life in jeopardy. And that is what he feared right now, that Lorcan might be dying.

These thoughts were pushed to the side when Smoke landed on the lawn of their backyard. Her hooves danced over the surface of the grass and not a blade was broken. Ashul jumped off Lightning's back and pulled Lorcan to the ground. Michael's family were already running towards them.

'Mum, Uncle Brent, he's unconscious. He coughed up all of this silver sand and now he isn't breathing.'

'How long has he been like this?' asked Nicola. She ran towards the prone form of Lorcan.

'Only a couple of minutes at the most,' said Ashul. 'We grabbed them both as soon as Lorcan's grip on the shadowland started to fade.'

Dana was already at the vampire's side. 'He's not unconscious; something's preventing his breathing.' She rolled Lorcan over and pounded against his back.

'Look at his hands,' said Dana as she looked up for help. Michael hadn't noticed that Lorcan's hands were clenched into fists. Drops of blood leaked from the creases between fingers. His talons had pierced through his own flesh. The tendons on Lorcan's arms stood out from the skin, and his arms shook from the strain.

Brent wrapped his arms around Lorcan and with Joseph's help lifted him to his feet. Brent stood behind Lorcan and gripped his fist with one hand. He gave a short, sharp upward pull, performing a standard Heimlich manoeuvre.

Nothing.

Brent pulled back harder, more sharply. Still nothing.

Dana reached around and carefully pushed her fingers between Lorcan's teeth. His eyes rolled when she did this, and his jaw clenched further still.

'There's something in his mouth,' said Dana. 'I can't open it, his teeth are too tightly locked.'

Ashul dropped to her side. 'Be careful. Remember what you are dealing with,' he said.

Nicola came forward now with a water bottle she'd grabbed when running out of the kitchen and poured a small amount of water onto Lorcan's face. The vampire shook his head violently, thrashing as if to throw the droplets from his face.

'Right idea, wrong liquid,' said Dana as she ran the tip of her finger down the sword that lay at Michael's feet. She dripped blood into Lorcan's mouth.

The response was immediate.

He lunged forward, teeth bared, snapping towards the source of blood. Dana had anticipated this and had one of Sheba's bones ready. She thrust it into his mouth.

With dexterous fingers, Michael watched as Dana reached around past the bone to grip the obstruction lodged down his throat. She had performed a similar manoeuvre many a time when Titan, the sock thief, was still alive. Often stealing things that he shouldn't have. Dana's quick hands had been the only thing stopping an emergency visit to the vets. She didn't have as much room to work with as when she had her hand down a Doberman's throat but the shape of Lorcan's jaw was changing, elongating become more canine as the seconds ticked past.

Michael could see the cords standing out on Lorcan's neck. He seemed to be somewhat aware of what was happening to him.

'She's just trying to help you.' Michael leaned forward and in a low, measured voice said, 'Please don't bite her.' Lorcan's eyes moved in his direction and Michael thought he perceived a slight nod.

'Careful, Dana,' said Brent. 'Whatever that thing is, it goes deep into his throat. Be very careful not to let it break off.' Dana turned to Brent and gave him a look that said 'tell me something I don't know' and then immediately returned to her task removing the obstruction.

Dana was moving with extreme care. Slowly, a small green shoot emerged from around the edge of the bone, with the roots still trailing into Lorcan's throat. A thick layer of saliva coated the sprout.

From over Lorcan's shoulder, Brent exclaimed, 'It's an oak sprout! Behind the seed will be a taproot. A thicker root. You need to get it all out. Those fine filaments aren't the issue, It's the taproot that will cause him concern if it breaks off.'

It was difficult to see in amongst the fine tracery of fibres that had sprouted from the base of the seed, but it did indeed have a thick white root below it. Michael had helped his Opi plant enough shrubs in his time to know what he was looking at. Two words came to mind: *pot bound.*

When a plant had been left to grow for too long in a pot that wasn't large enough to support it, one of two things happened: the plant died, or the plant did everything it could to expand its root system, often including breaking through the pot that was causing the restriction. It was always difficult getting a pot-bound plant out because the roots had often sprouted out through the drainage holes.

Michael was contemplating how this all translated to the current situation. The image of roots probing down into Lorcan's stomach ran through Michael's mind.

'Okay, so it's stopped coming out,' said Dana. 'I don't want to pull any harder. It feels about ready to snap.' Michael could hear panic creeping into her voice. Nicola had run into the house and returned carrying the first aid box. She brought out a pair of needle-point tweezers and a bottle of lubricating eyedrops.

Standing beside Dana, Nicola took in a deep breath and reached down Lorcan's throat with the tip of the tweezers. 'Don't let go just yet, Dana.' Nicola gave a slight pull on the root now that she had a secure grip. She shook her head. 'It's not budging.'

'Can someone pour the eyedrops down his throat?' asked Nicola. She held the bottle out and Ashul assisted her by unscrewing the cap. 'How much do we need?'

'All of it, but hurry.' Tremors were running through Lorcan's body and wisps of grey smoke rose from his hair. Blood was now dripping from Lorcan's palms, and from the backs of his hands. Dark patches had formed on the legs of his pants as some of the blood soaked the fabric. 'He hasn't taken a breath in almost ten minutes now.'

One talon had stabbed all the way through the back of Lorcan's hand. The tip could be seen poking through the skin like a malignant growth.

There was no way that Lorcan could maintain his self-control for much longer. Michael didn't know the extent of his reserves, but when your own body started tearing through flesh, the tipping point must be close… and then they'd all be at risk. Dana most of all because she literally had her hand down the vampire's throat.

Michael closed his eyes. When he opened them, he was looking through the Nachzehrer's scars. Ashul's eyes also turned a pale white, the glow a more subdued version than what was radiating from his own eyes. Ashul had witnessed more horror in his time than Michael ever would, yet still Michael noticed him wince when the magnitude of what was happening to Lorcan was revealed.

Lorcan's body was encased in a network of fine white roots, all sprouting from the seed. The roots ran around his face and down his neck, spreading in every direction. The vampire's legs had become rooted to the ground. Michael wanted to believe that the roots ran down and around his legs, but this second sight allowed no room for this deceit. The roots had torn through the flesh in an effort to find the ground.

'Damn!' Nicola cursed. 'I'd hoped that the lubricating drops would loosen things up. It is really stuck in there!'

Michael barely registered the words as he watched a pale, fibrous worm of oak root push against the skin on the back of Lorcan's wrist. It punched through his skin and raced down the vampire's legs and anchored itself in the soil at Lorcan's feet.

Ashul drew forth a fine silver knife from the air and used it to slice through the roots that were twisting around the vampire's neck.

'Mum, we need to kill this thing and quick – it's eating through him.' Lorcan's eyes flared again and a soft hissing sound accompanied the barely discernible small shake of his head.

An acrid stench rose up from the ground. Lorcan's blood bubbled around the roots searching for nutrients in the earth under his feet. But whatever his blood touched dissolved – including the roots. This little display made it very clear to Michael that Lorcan was more than able to kill this thing if that's what he wanted. The difficult question was, what did Lorcan want them to do?

'Okay, so don't kill it,' said Michael. 'But it's using him like a bag of fertiliser, literally. What you can see is nothing compared to what's really happening to him.' Michael's voice held all the horror of what he was able to see.

Malcarielle moved closer to Lorcan. Her translucent wings fluttered against her back, blowing her hair up around her face in a halo of burnt gold. A buzz of energy ran across her skin and she gently reached a finger behind Dana's hands and touched the taproot. A soft squeak issued from the seed and the white fronds trembled. Michael felt tremors of pain run through the ether.

Malcarielle tilted her head. The energy flowing over her skin glowed a little brighter, and again she touched the root. A high-pitched squeal – more perceived than heard – beat against Michael's mind. The burnt roots around Lorcan's feet had been replaced with a new crop of white questing feeders.

'It's going to take more than that,' said Michael. 'The roots are still growing.' Michael could feel heat baking off Lorcan.

Lorcan's body shook, his muscles quivering with the effort required to keep still. It was obvious to all that he couldn't maintain his outward calm for much longer. Wisps of black smoke were curling up from his shoulders. Michael had seen Lorcan's other form, had seen what he was capable of when under attack. Michael also had some idea of the control Lorcan needed to exercise every second of every day to rise above the thirst that plagued him. Michael knew that if Lorcan's control slipped, blood would be spilt. Even without the benefit of second sight, Michael could see Lorcan's form changing as he became more predatory, more lethal.

Lorcan lowered his head and closed his eyes, eyes now burning deep crimson.

Malcarielle drew in a long, deep breath and her whole being glowed with an incandescent light. Azuradien, who had been relatively absent until this time, placed a hand on Malcarielle's arm. 'You will not break the covenant.'

'It is not my intention, but I will not allow *this* to continue,' said Malcarielle, and she pushed her father's hand away. Through his second sight, Michael could see the magical shield around Malcarielle shifting and dissolving. Michael was about to intervene when Lorcan's arm slashed outwards to shove her backwards, a blast of heat accompanying the blow.

Azuradien appeared ready to retaliate. He glowed with an intense blue light, his skin rippling with power running under the surface of his skin. He'd always looked like a scholar to Michael, but now he looked like a gladiator ready to attack.

Malcarielle dropped against Joseph, who'd reached out to break her fall. There was a loud snap of energy as they touched, but then the electricity flickered out and died.

A sudden insight lit Joseph's face.

'Ashul, grab the other bottle of that solution,' said Joseph. His voice held a level of conviction that made Michael feel some glimmer of hope. There was no hesitancy to his actions either. 'Pour it down his throat.' Joseph took the tweezers from Nicola, careful not to lose the all too tenuous grip on the root pinched between the metal prongs. Joseph nodded to both Nicola and Dana. 'On three, step back.'

And on three they did, and a sharp jolt of electricity surged through Lorcan's body. Joseph gave a gentle tug, but the root remained lodged. Lorcan's eyes flicked open and Michael thought he detected a slight eye roll.

'Sorry, big guy, can you handle another?'

The red eyes glowed brighter. Lorcan's legs lengthened and his taloned toes dug into the grass beneath his feet. Michael's second sight allowed him to see the wings, the skin darkening to deep indigo as they broke free from the roots that bound him. The wings beat at the air in what Michael deemed to be impatience.

Michael and Ashul replied in unison: 'He can handle it!'

A blast of energy ripped out from Joseph, pouring through the seed and then through Lorcan before grounding itself in the grass.

A smoking black patch of scorched earth now ringed Lorcan. For a second, a vision of the seven-foot, winged vampire appeared in the first realm and Joseph jumped back. But Lorcan quickly regained control and his eyes dimmed from glowing red back to a darker hue. The vampire looked down at Joseph; his expression was difficult to read.

Bone cracked and splintered as Lorcan clenched his teeth. He spat the pulverised pieces of bone at Azuradien's' feet. Michael watched as his gaze then returned to Joseph.

'My thanks.' Lorcan sucked in a long-pained breath. As he exhaled, he reached forward, holding an outstretched hand in front of Joseph. 'Now I best be taking that. It is a dangerous thing.' He gestured to the small sprout pinched between tweezers held in Joseph's fingers.

'The seed will be returned to us,' Azuradien protested. 'It is the responsibility of the faerie.'

Michael looked into the shadowland and saw the thin tendrils fanning out from the taproot, searching, pushing at the skin of his father's fingers.

'Dad, I'd bag and tag that thing for now,' said Michael. 'It's too hungry just to hold in your hand like that. Uncle Brent, have you got a heavy duty jar you can put it in?' Michael was relieved when his uncle nodded. Brent ran to his car and return moments later with a green, glass screw-top jar. Michael only relaxed when the seed was dropped into the jar and the lid screwed tightly shut.

Michael blew out the breath he wasn't aware he had been holding.

In the first realm, the seed looked like nothing more than an overdeveloped bean sprout. Through the second sight, Michael could see the fibres probing at the edge of the glass, the seed moving ever so slightly as more tendrils sprung from its core.

'The seed is sacred. We will see to its growth,' said Azuradien calmly. Despite his calm, Azuradien's eyes had the glaze of a fanatic.

Brent said, 'You should have considered giving us the details prior to having me mix it into a potion we intended to use on Michael's friends.' At Brent's words, Lorcan raised his hands as if to remind everyone present that if anyone was going to be offended it would be him. Brent waved him down in an overly casual way.

Michael thought if his uncle had seen exactly what Lorcan had been put through, he would be a little less dismissive of Lorcan's attitude. 'I trusted you when you gave me the ingredients that they would not be harmful in any way,' said

Brent. 'I don't think you fully understand the ramifications of what you have done.'

'There was no way we could have predicted that the seed would sprout,' said Azuradien. 'We have been trying for centuries to achieve what you have done this day.' Azuradien seemed unaware of the disgust Michael and his family felt towards him right now. Azuradien continued on, oblivious. 'We must now ensure the seed's survival. It might provide answers to the great mage's final resting place.'

'I don't care about what you have or have not been trying to achieve,' said Brent, looking more outraged than Michael could remember ever seeing before. 'You used me, and you used Lorcan. You had absolutely no right bringing something here when you could not predict the outcome. That seed was germinating inside him, you understand that?' Brent was fuming, and the faerie king's blasé attitude towards the vampire's wellbeing was not making things easier.

'Azuradien, what you have done this day is inexcusable,' said Ashul, his voice ringing with authority. 'Your own daughter understood you crossed the line. In stepping forward to protect the vampire, she placed herself in grave danger. If you could have seen how close Malcarielle came to becoming a food source for this seed's growth, you would be on your knees thanking Lorcan for your daughter's life.'

'My daughter was never in peril, we are protected...'

'Enough!' Ashul commanded. 'I saw. I know exactly how close she came. What do you think would have occurred if the seed started feeding off her when her magical protection was down? Would she have survived?' Azuradien tried to protest but Ashul continued on. 'I saw the roots running under his skin, puncturing his flesh to get to the ground. Your daughter would have been lucky if she died quickly.'

'We stood here and saw nothing of the kind,' said Azuradien. 'The Nachzehrer poison in your system is giving you visions. This second sight – this shadowland – does not exist, if it did the faerie would know.' Azuradien moved to take the jar from Brent's hand.

'The seed is no longer yours,' said Ashul, allowing no room for argument. 'No-one asked you to offer it as an ingredient to include in the potion. You have said yourself you could not achieve its germination. It is Lorcan's by blood rite.' Ashul removed the jar from Brent's hands. 'If nobody here protests, I will place this in the ancient one's care.'

'You cannot give this sacred seed into that beast's possession,' said Azuradien. His face was starting to turn red in outrage. 'I will not allow it.'

'If I chose to take it,' Lorcan said, 'you could not prevent me.' Lorcan's signature calm had returned. He was once again his handsome self, but he still retained the air of greater size.

Michael understood Lorcan spoke the words, not as a boast, but as a statement of simple fact. He'd witnessed the ease with which that Lorcan blew away the entity in the shadowland, had watched his restraint as he allowed the roots to rip through his body.

Michael spoke through his mindlink to Ashul, *Why did he allow the seed to survive? You saw his blood burn through the roots. He could have destroyed it easily.*

Ashul's response did nothing to reassure Michael. *He has his own agenda. We know this. He also saved Malcarielle when he could have allowed the seed to eat into her exposed flesh. While he acts honourably, I will treat him so.* And spoken almost as an afterthought, Ashul said, *I believe he is truthful when he says we would not be able to prevent him. Do you wish to try?*

Ashul was looking at Michael with a slightly raised eyebrow. Before Michael had a chance to speak his mother asked the question that had been on Michael's lips.

'What do you intend to do with the seed? Will you destroy it?' Nicola asked this almost casually. Michael could see that if the answer wasn't to her liking, she might decide to cause some trouble.

'I will take it to this "fictitious" shadowland,' said Lorcan. 'It seems to like it there. If it would ease some of your concern, I am more than happy to keep Michael appraised of the seed's progress.' The vampire's eyes twinkled as he smiled guilelessly towards Nicola, his threatening aura now replaced with effortless charm. He held out his hands, and at Nicola's nod, Ashul placed the jar into his care.

The vampire turned with a flourish and nodded towards Malcarielle. 'I thank you for your efforts on my behalf, Faerie Queen. And my apologies for the rough treatment. You caught me somewhat by surprise.'

The faerie queen had the good grace to nod her head in return.

Lorcan then clasped Dana's hand. 'But you, once again have both surprised and amazed me. I thank you for your intervention but ask that you think twice before you drip your blood into a "vampire's" mouth.' He turned Dana's hand over and inspected the wound on her finger.

With a speed that was unnatural, Lorcan lifted her hand to his mouth. 'Not all would be the gentleman that I am.' He kissed the inside of her wrist, and before anyone could protest, he dissolved into a puff of black smoke.

Agendas

There was to be a couple of hours to recharge, rest and recover before the family was to get together again to discuss the situation. The faeries were asked to leave to give the family some time to refocus. There'd been no real choice given to them.

'I will consult with those within the book,' said Nicola. 'See why my wardings are letting through every creature under the sun. I would like some notice before Azuradien or Lorcan returns.' Nicola left the room, her hand clutched around the crystal at her neck.

Discussion looked to have already begun if the absent look in Nicola's eye was anything to go by.

Michael went up to his room and decided that he would wait to see who would be the first to come to talk to him. In the past he'd found this to be the best policy. If he tried to force a discussion before people had time to mull things over themselves, a lot of time would be spent talking in circles. So he sat and waited and was not surprised in the least when Dana walked through the door. She looked around to try and find a place to sit, pushed some clothes aside on the bed and dropped down to sit.

'I'm trying to work out what the story with Lorcan is,' said Dana. 'I don't know whether he can be trusted or not.'

'You have to stop thinking that he can be classified like you would a person or even an animal,' said Michael. 'He's stronger than you understand. You didn't see him in the shadowland – he batted away some creature that literally blocked out the sky as if it were nothing more than an insect. All of the while that thing was growing in his throat. You know that Lorcan allowed that seed to grow inside him. It ripped through him like he was a bag of manure, and he stood and allowed it.'

'The control that took… no human or animal for that matter, could endure that.' Michael's voice shook on the last words. He was remembering the cleansing and knew that he wouldn't have been able to endure it without the aid of Ashul, yet Lorcan had suffered far worse without aid. And Michael had been trying to save his own life. Lorcan had no reason that Michael could see to allow the seed to germinate. Lorcan motives were unclear to him.

You would have endured, said Ashul, standing in the doorway. It was only into Michael's mind that he spoke, perhaps hearing a measure of Michael's thought.

'May I enter?' asked Ashul. It was Michael's room, but it was to Dana that he posed the question. 'He underestimates his own strength. I have seen its depths; he would have endured. But I believe that Michael is correct. Lorcan's actions cannot be predicted. He is a rule unto himself. I have been observing his powers – they are greater than that of any of the ancient ones that I have ever come in contact with before. He is something different. I believe him when he says that he is greater than any of his kind. We would be wise to remember this fact in our dealings with him.' Ashul had leant against Michael's wall but there was nothing in his posture that was relaxed.

'Oh, but your mate Azuradien, he's trustworthy?' Dana lifted herself up into a sitting position.

'He has always been so,' said Ashul. Dana was about to turn away when Ashul continued, 'But I fear something in him has changed. His judgement has become tainted. Now he sees only what his prejudices allow him to, not what is actually in front of him. I believe it must be the result of having the corruption of the eels under his skin for so long. Their voices might have impacted his thought process to the point where he is making grievous errors of judgement.'

'You mean the eels may have driven him mad.' Michael could understand how that was possible. The doll's voice had been in his head for only a few weeks and it had changed his personality during that time. It had amped up his anger levels and made him paranoid. Would he be making the same kind of decisions as Azuradien if he'd been put through that torture for centuries? He hoped not, but he thought he would cut the faerie king some slack just the same. Azuradien hadn't been given any time to adjust. Maybe he just needed some time.

'So what you're saying is that we cannot trust the faeries,' said Dana. She was never one to forgive quite so easily.

'No, that is not what I am saying,' said Ashul. 'Azuradien is suspect and he must be watched. But Malcarielle has shown herself to be more than trustworthy. She risked breaking the covenant to save Lorcan. I think she has proven herself.'

Their conversation was interrupted by a familiar voice. 'As much as I would like to disagree with you, warrior. I have got to say I think you've summed everything up nicely.' Lorcan was sitting at Michael's desk, one leg draped over the arm of the chair, his other resting on the bed. 'Have a word to your mother about her wardings. They're much better, but if she wants to keep me out she needs to make crossing them a little more… difficult. A bit of burnt skin is barely going to stop me.'

Michael could hear Nicola's footsteps as she ran across the lounge room and up the stairs. She stopped at the bedroom door, her hand reached out for the doorhandle – once grasped, she gripped it tightly. She was swaying slightly despite her hold on the door. 'Okay, Lorcan, so what did I miss?'

'My lady, your wardings are secure. None but a creature that walks in two worlds such as I could break through. I congratulate you.'

'No offence, Lorcan, but it was supposed to keep you out too.'

'But it warned you of my presence,' said Lorcan. 'Truth be told, I hadn't expected that. Touché.' Lorcan lifted his hands up over his left ear and gave a silent clap. It looked more like a dance move than a sign of praise.

'How do I secure this house against those who can walk in two worlds? How do I protect it from creatures from the shadowland?' asked Nicola. Michael could tell his mum wouldn't be distracted by his antics.

'Come now, would you really expect me to answer that honestly? I like our little *visits*.' He raised his eyebrows and had a slight pout to his lips.

'I can live with you popping in, but I would like to know that others cannot come through.' Lorcan ducked his head, gratefully acknowledging Nicola's words.

'You need to increase the strength on the structural lines you created for the hex. Once you have done that, create a duplicate, invert the pattern and set it in the exact centre of your home, which in case you are unaware, is at the ceiling line above the doorway that leads into the kitchen.' Lorcan said all this as if he set hexes every day. 'If you want to make them pay for their impudence, I would add a crossline wherever a spiral touches a straight line.'

'And that would do what exactly?' asked Nicola.

'Make their bones melt and their skin burn,' Lorcan said with a smile. 'Even the incorporeal beings will feel like they have been given skin,' Lorcan paused for dramatic effect, 'that is in fact burning.' Lorcan was a little too nonchalant on the concept of burning a creature's skin off for Michael's liking.

Dana wasn't troubled – she nodded in approval.

'I'm assuming you had the foresight to add an intention exception.'

'I'm not a complete idiot,' Nicola snapped back but she couldn't quite sell the attitude.

'No, but I obviously *am* an idiot,' said Michael. 'Mind explaining to the slow kids in the room exactly what an intention exception is?'

Both Lorcan and Nicola started talking at once. Lorcan paused and waved for Nicola to continue. His manner was all subservient deferral, but the head tilt and slight smirk told another story. Lorcan was having a joke at his mother's expense.

'Stop with the charm,' Nicola admonished Lorcan. 'I'm not a teenager anymore, I don't fall for that kind of thing.' The vampire raised his hands in surrender, expression all innocence. Michael thought she might just be underestimating Lorcan's charisma because his mother was grinning even as she protested.

'An intention exception means that anyone who tries to enter will have their intent analysed by the warding,' explained Nicola. 'And if they mean no harm, they will be able to enter and they won't even know they walked through a spell.'

'I'm glad. I kind of like the gargoyle. The idea of him getting hurt didn't sit well.' Michael was relieved because a number of creatures had helped them recently and he didn't think it was a good idea to lock them all out.

'Well, that's good,' Nicola said with a tilt of her head. 'Because he's hiding in your cupboard under all your clothes.' Nicola waited for their reaction, then turned to walk out of the room. She was trying for a dramatic exit but she needed to place her hand against the wall to steady herself and to dull some of the impact.

'Is it the magic that gives you the pain, makes you unsteady on your feet?' Lorcan asked, sounding puzzled.

'Not as such,' said Nicola. 'The pain and dizziness are something that's always in the background. Part of my illness. Usually I can control it, damp it down, but when I use the magic, it drains me and my control slips a little.'

'But you could easily draw the energy required from your family, from the source,' said Lorcan. 'Why suffer when you don't have to?'

'Because then it will have won and I will have cheated. I won't let it win,' said Nicola. 'Once I start drawing on the source to cure a little dizziness then I'll start relying on it to fix a migraine, and on and on it would go. The source isn't meant to be used to cure aches and pains. It isn't right, and I won't do it.' Nicola shrugged her shoulders and left to return downstairs.

Lorcan called after Nicola as she walked away, 'In future, when you draw from the source, draw a little extra energy so that you maintain your own personal energy stores. Surely that cannot be considered cheating.' Lorcan waited for a response and when none came, he gave an impatient head shake as if not understanding her attitude.

Lorcan said, 'On to more important things.' Lorcan's body language went from slouching in the chair barely paying attention to sitting up straight with both feet resting on the bed and his hands crossed over his chest. Still semi-casual for most people, though for Lorcan it was anything but.

'Michael, I asked you what you saw in the shadowland. And Ashul, because you were able to track Michael, I will expand my question to include you. What did you see?'

'I saw you getting torn apart by a mutant bean sprout,' Michael answered.

Lorcan waved his hand in a *get on with it* motion.

'There was some entity that blotted out the sky,' said Michael. 'And you blasted it away with barely a moment's thought.'

'I did think, for just a moment. I was mindful of not obliterating *you*.' Lorcan looked around the room to make sure everyone understood the gravitas of his words. 'That kind of creature is not common. The chance of coming across one is similar to those of being hit by lightning.' Lorcan paused for effect. 'Not once, not even twice. What do you think may have brought it to this place?'

'Is it being drawn to the breach?' asked Dana. 'Does this kind of thing feed off the source?' Michael thought that Dana might be on to something.

The barrier that had been created to isolate the magical reserves, protect the source from overuse was no longer intact. Something had caused a rift to form and with every major use of power, this breach became wider allowing more energy to flow. Michael had used a lot himself recently, Trevlor even more so. He wondered how much of their power had been drawn from his family and the bonded and how much had come through the breach. *Was he inadvertently making things worse?*

Ashul replied, 'All life feeds off the source. Only supernatural creatures and magic-wielders can draw upon it at will.' Ashul turned to Michael. 'And remember, there has always been magic to draw upon. This rift is just allowing more energy to be readily available.

'Ashul is correct,' said Lorcan. 'But the breach does not extend into the shadowland. Only the first realm has a geographical connection to the breach, technically speaking. Although all realms are feeling the increase in energy flow, the breach exists only in the first realm. But we are getting side-tracked. What did you see?'

'I'm not exactly certain what you want me to say. I was a bit distracted at the time, having been kidnapped by an "ancient one".' Lorcan tilted his head in recognition of the use of his correct title. 'And I was being carried through a land that's not supposed to exist, according to faeries.'

'You saw more, you both did?'

Michael closed his eyes to try to remember the details.

'Michael, describe it for me,' Dana prompted him.

'It looks like our world if you were on a really bad trip. The colours and depths of the place bend so your eyes are constantly being pulled out of focus. The sounds are distorted in the same kind of way, but it's harder to describe. There's a constant wind howling in the background that rips at your ears, altering things somehow – it's almost like you see the sounds. I don't know how to describe it but it's like your senses have all been merged slightly, they overlap and contradict each other.'

'That is exactly what has occurred,' said Lorcan. 'A perceptive description.'

'Oh, and Dana be careful in those woods out the back of our house,' said Michael. 'There's something in them. It tried to pull me out of Lorcan's hands.' Dana nodded at his words. They had both always sensed something out there.

'When the sand poured from your mouth, it formed into the image of a tree. A man's face was buried in the bark. He looked pained. Then the wind tore the image apart and we fell from the sky.' Michael raised his hands. That was all that he could remember. 'Smoke spoke into my mind, and then she was there. Ashul was able to catch you and then we came home.'

'I will ask later how you followed us into the shadowland, warrior,' said Lorcan. 'But that can wait. We were falling over the trees…'

'I knew you weren't breathing. We turned straight for home. What other choice was there? Our house was no longer distorted. We'd managed to ride out of the shadowland. I'm guessing because you were unconscious—'

Both Dana and Lorcan interrupted, words mirroring each other's. 'He wasn't unconscious.' / 'I wasn't unconscious.'

Michael closed his eyes again. 'You may be right.' Lorcan's look indicated there was no 'may be' about it.

'Next door was barely recognisable. The walls were twisted all out of skew, more so than the houses surrounding it. There was a pulling sensation, like you were standing in front of a black hole.' Michael opened his eyes. He was starting to understand what he'd seen.

Ashul confirmed his suspicions. 'We rode into the shadowland through a *thinning*,' he said. 'I thought it was Michael's power drawing us in and I still believe that had a lot to do with it, but the resistance was less over the house next door.' Ashul turned to Lorcan. 'Have our enemies punched through into the shadowland?'

'I believe they are very close, but I also suspect they are not even aware of the fact. Only a few creatures know of the doll's existence. To most, it is a myth told within a fairytale,' Lorcan said. 'Much like myself.' A strange smile crossed Lorcan's face for the briefest of seconds then he moved on before Michael was able to interpret it. 'The doll's purpose is to draw the first and second planes together, which is what it requires to unlock all of its powers. Anarcus is going about things differently this time. Would you not agree, warrior?

Ashul answered without need for consideration. 'In the past, the doll has always been easy to predict. Working from the background. Placing as many fingers into as many minds as possible. A slow build-up of power. Nothing wasted. Now its actions are erratic, expending huge amounts of energy to release creatures that could potentially become rivals. I have said this before, its actions make no sense to me.'

'Agreed,' Lorcan said. He looked pleased that he and *the warrior* were on the same page. 'I believe it is this change in tactic that has caused this thinning, allowing the shadowland to be glimpsed. In your case warrior, ridden into. I cannot allow this to continue. I am giving you fair warning. I will be travelling next door and I will do whatever it takes to close this thinning.'

Michael and Dana, shared a look and they both spoke at the same time. 'We're coming with you.'

'Ashul, it's not my place to control your charges, so tell them they're not going.' A degree of tension showed in Lorcan's shoulders – he'd finally stopped looking relaxed.

'They will be going, as will I,' Ashul responded without hesitation.

From downstairs, Michael heard the doorbell ring. 'I think you're going to have to hold that thought.' Seconds later: 'Guys, Aunty Sars is here. Get down here for dinner.'

Lorcan clenched his fists at his sides. Before he had time to protest the delay, Ashul placed a hand on his shoulder. 'Lorcan, I believe that invitation includes us. The Lady Nicola can be very insistent.'

Dana rolled over on the bed and nudged Michael. Despite the circumstances, they both started laughing, then raced each other for the door.

'She is quite the cook,' Ashul commented to Lorcan, who was looking around the room frowning. 'And you really don't want her to come and get you.'

* * *

Ashul walked into the kitchen behind Michael. Lorcan materialised next to Dana who had the temerity to hold his arm and forestall his entry into the room. Dana stood at her full height, pulling on his arm to bring his head closer to hers and whispered, 'You do eat, don't you?'

'On occasion,' Lorcan replied. *How had he gotten himself into this position?* Not only did this family refuse to fear him, they also appeared to have accepted him as one of their own. He would play along for the moment. All their objectives were currently the same. While this remained the case, he would appear docile and compliant. And the food... did indeed smell very good.

'Save me the rare piece in the middle,' said Lorcan. He reached forward and grabbed a plate. He met the warrior's eyes as he scanned the room. Ashul shrugged at him – the irony of the situation wasn't lost on either of them.

'I hope this doesn't contain any garlic?' The mother's face dropped as she reached forward to stop Lorcan from taking the meat. Nicola actually appeared concerned.

'Despite what you call me, I am not a vampire. I can eat garlic, but I thank you for your concern. I also thank you for the kind offer to eat with your family.' Lorcan was uncertain how to continue: everyone in the room was looking in his direction.

The girl sensed his discomfort and thankfully started talking about the plans to investigate next door. Lorcan sat back watching as each person jumped in with questions, observations – each one talking over the top of the others but somehow they filled one another in on the major points in a remarkably short period of time.

* * *

'Okay, I hate to say it, but I agree,' said Nicola. 'We need to see what's going on next door.' Nicola seemed to surprise everyone with this statement, always the one to be overly cautious. 'Ashul, can you give us any indication of what may be over there?'

'Unfortunately, I cannot,' said Ashul. 'Whatever is happening over there is making it impossible for us to get close. Lorcan and I could go over and investigate and then return.'

Lorcan leant against the wall, picking roast beef out of his teeth, nodding his agreement that he and the warrior could indeed go over to investigate.

'Sarah, what can you see on your network?' asked Nicola.

Moments later, the shimmering grid appeared over the kitchen table. 'Nothing, really,' said Sarah. 'The family is all home, including Marcus. His aura doesn't look right but I don't really know how to interpret the difference.'

'But there's nothing else, nothing non-human? Michael's spooked me with his description of the sky creature from the shadowland.' The agitation could be heard in Nicola's voice.

'I don't think we can assume the network picks up all supernatural creatures yet,' Sarah said.' I can get the faeries, but they were here when I created it. Lorcan over there is nowhere to be seen. And Nicola...' Sarah paused almost apologetically. 'I think Azuradien is waiting for you to let him through. Doesn't that mean they've triggered the intention aspect of your wardings?'

Nicola had the decency to look slightly abashed. 'Well, I may have put in a little bit of extra "code". The warding will hold the faeries in a kind of suspension until I decide to release them.'

Ashul said, 'I understand your feelings, but I am not sure if it is wise to antagonise the faeries.'

'Well, maybe they need to understand the consequences of antagonising me.' All signs of abashment had been quickly put aside.

'Ashul, I'm beginning to understand your connection to this family,' said Lorcan. 'I quite like the way they think!' Lorcan crossed his arms, eager to see what happened next.

Brent said, 'Nicola, before you let them through, I've been meaning to speak to Lorcan. It feels rude after all that he went through. But…' Lorcan indicated with a casual waving of his hand to go ahead and ask the question. 'Well, do you think the potion worked? Is it safe to give to the boys?'

'The potion was only dangerous to me or any other creature persecuted by the "great mage",' said Lorcan. 'So basically, just me. Because there aren't that many of us left. This mage was many things, thorough being one of them.'

Lorcan was going to say more but he pulled himself up short. This family had shown they did not respond to information that was seen to harbour bias. So, he damped down that rage that still burnt inside him and continued. 'So, you don't need to worry, the infected will be safe to receive it. Whether it has worked, that's difficult to say. I would need to examine them. I can say I feel somewhat removed from both Michael and the others, so I suspect the potion is causing some level of interference.'

Lorcan didn't like the way the boy had looked at him. He'd seen Lorcan's hesitation and marked it, then lost himself in contemplation. Probably speaking with the warrior about what it was the 'vampire' might be hiding. He knew he was judging the boy harshly; he'd seen nothing but empathy in Michael's eyes but that only infuriated him more. So when the boy didn't respond to his next question Lorcan allowed his irritation to bleed into his words. 'Michael, can you still feel a pull towards those infected?'

'Until you mentioned it, I hadn't noticed anything,' said Michael. 'But I sense that my mates are feeling agitated, restless and a bit aggressive. Something has them riled up.'

'Michael, what is the status of your lake? Are the water's deep enough?' Ashul asked. The question seemed overly personal to Lorcan but Michael didn't seem to take offence at the inquiry.

'Currently crystal-clear and deep as an ocean but…'

Ashul grabbed Michael's shoulder. 'What are you concerned about, Michael? Do you need the bonded's aid?'

'No, it's not a Nachzehrer problem. There's something… something there… sitting in the shadows. I can't see it clearly, but I don't think it means me harm.' Michael scanned the faces in the room, hoping someone would have some insight. It surprised Lorcan that the inquiring look included him.

Michael was still in the middle of talking when the faeries appeared. They materialised out of the second realm with a lot of fluttering wings and displaced air. Lorcan chuckled to himself as everyone in the room studiously ignored them.

'This lake is of your own creation?' asked Lorcan, going with the consensus and disregarding the faeries' arrival. 'Effectively a place that represents your battle against the Nachzehrer ascension?'

Michael nodded confirmation.

'Then there should be nothing but Nachzehrer on the shore. Your consciousness forced the Nachzehrer into this place to monitor it. You allowed Ashul in because you are, on many levels, one. Are there any others that you would allow into your mind, or more correctly, would allow access to your soul?'

'My family,' said Michael. 'I wouldn't think twice. I'm sure Dana was able to reach me there – I heard her voice.'

Lorcan shook his head as he said, 'The living cannot abide in another's soul.'

Dana slapped her forehead. 'But the dead can?'

'Yes, the dead can,' said Lorcan. 'If they do not fight for dominance, then yes they can.'

'It's Titan, buddy. It has to be. He's found you, somehow. I'd been wondering why he didn't come when Mr Stevens' mind nearly swallowed me whole. Sheba and I have been able to sense him, but not communicate with him. This makes total sense now.' The girl was smiling, her joy of this discovery radiating palpably from her being.

Malcarielle raised a hand in a peaceful gesture. 'Are we welcome in your discussions, or would you prefer that we leave? I ask only out of courtesy; I fully understand if you no longer trust us.' Lorcan turned away even though Malcarielle said this sincerely.

Brent chose to speak on the family's behalf. 'We have no issue with you, Malcarielle. You have shown great courage. But your father has treated us with little respect. I speak only for myself when I say I feel manipulated. I would not have used the seed if I'd known the pain it would cause.'

'There is no time for the faerie king's pride to move aside so he can realise the extent of his transgression,' said Ashul, stronger than Lorcan had expected. 'And I have no intention of recapping everything we have discussed. So shall we continue?'

Lorcan noticed the warrior had no need to wait for assent – the family trusted him implicitly.

Lorcan interrupted the conversation, just to be contrary. 'Ashul and I are the best equipped to deal with whatever's happening next door. The rest of you will just get in our way.' Lorcan walked over to Ashul, ready to make preparations.

'If something's happening to Marcus,' said Dana, 'Ashley is the one that is best *equipped* to detect it and may be better able to advise on what exactly is going on.' The rebuke in her tone at Lorcan's assumption was plain for all to hear.

'And the three of us work better together,' Dana reminded them. 'Our first priority is Marcus, the merging of worlds secondary.' She had repositioned herself so that she stood at Michael's shoulder.

'This Marcus means nothing to me,' said Lorcan coolly. 'I will not allow some schoolgirl's crush to become a distraction.' He was growing annoyed with Dana's lack of respect. He was even considering leaving and venturing next door on his own.

He owed this family nothing. But the boy was easier to monitor when he was close, and Lorcan suspected the wilful girl would proceed with her brother in tow regardless. Lorcan allowed the discussion to continue around him as he faded into the background out of habit.

* * *

Dana flashed a look in Lorcan's direction and Michael intervened before she could respond to his remark about schoolgirl crushes.

'I can't read the network like dad but even I can see Marcus' aura isn't right,' said Michael. 'Something's obviously happening to him. I'm not exactly fond of the guy but I am concerned for him. And we don't know that the two things are not connected.'

Lorcan might be standing off in the shadows but Michael could still feel the weight of his stare. 'Going over to check on Marcus doesn't preclude us from looking into this thinning. Marcus and the doll do sort of go hand in hand, so I think one may lead us to the other.' Michael placed a calming hand on Dana's wrist before he spoke again. He hoped to keep his sister from getting into a needless debate with Lorcan just because he had offended her with one stupid comment.

'Lorcan, you obviously have you own priorities.' Michael raised his hands to show no offence was meant. Lorcan seemed completely unfazed, picking dirt from under his fingers then looked up only to give Michael a *hurry along* gesture.

'And that's perfectly reasonable,' said Michael. 'But the girls will need my second sight, as will Ashul. So it's back to our plan.' Michael knew that his logic was solid but it only took Lorcan a moment to point out the one flaw in his reasoning.

'Have you considered the impact of using your second sight before your *friends* have received the potion?' Lorcan asked.

'I have,' said Michael. 'But short of calling them over for a game of pool and slipping them a spiked drink, my hands are slightly tied.' Michael wasn't exactly sure why Lorcan was bringing up his friends at this point but he didn't like the way that Lorcan examined his face. It was as if he were searching for signs of a lie. Michael decided just to break the uncomfortable silence. 'I can keep the balance for one more night.'

You may not need to, Ashul said through their mental connection.

May not need to what? Michael almost spoke out loud but realised Ashul had kept silent for a reason.

We have been monitoring your friends. They are on their way. Ashul's voice had the same tone of calm authority when he spoke through the mindlink as when he spoke aloud. *I thought it best not to mention it when our strategy was still being formed.*

Nicola, unaware that a silent communication was going on between Michael and Ashul, moved on to what she deemed to be the next obstacle. 'Has anybody thought about how we're going to get past Marcus' family?' Nicola asked. 'We can't exactly just break and enter then top it off by assaulting his parents. Not that I care what they think anymore, but they could call the police and there'd be no way to explain any of this.'

Nicola had been quite during the course of the conversation, listening while Loran questioned Michael about his second sight. While they had been discussing what to do next, she'd been thinking about what happened tomorrow and the day after that. Her ability to play the long game constantly surprised Michael.

How long have we got? Michael asked the bonded.

Smoke was the one to answer. *We have but minutes.* She then spoke in his mind alone. *Calm, Michael, your friends are already agitated.*

Nicola continued, 'I think Lorcan and Ashul go in search for this thinning.'

Michael took in a deep breath. There was no way this conversation was going to be wrapped up in the next couple of minutes. He was trying to find a way to get the faeries to leave before his friends arrived. Michael wanted to interrupt. but Nicola held up her hand before he could protest. 'Joseph, Brent and I go in with the kids, find out what's up with Marcus. Sarah, you monitor things from here. Maybe we can get the bonded to create a ruckus of some kind?'

They all jumped when the doorbell rang. Well, all of the humans did. Ashul merely turned his head and Lorcan lifted an eyebrow as if he were mildly amused by the coming and goings of the humans, but he wasn't in the least surprised. Before Michael even had time to look up, the bell was rung again.

There was a brief pause and then the person at the front door decided to place their finger on the button and hold it there.

'Nicola, any idea? What has the warding detected?' asked Sarah, looking towards the door.

'Friends,' said Nicola. 'Not the best intentions, but not exactly bad.'

Ashul gave instruction for the bonded to remove the boys to the second realm if the faeries approached them in any way that could be considered hostile. Michael was struggling to keep track of the two separate conversations.

'We can't just wait around,' said Joseph. 'I'm going to get the door. It could be Dave and Tony.' Michael followed a couple of paces behind as his father walked down the hallway, saying softly, 'Dad, it's not Dave and Tony.'

Joseph yelled out, 'Hold your horses! I'm coming already.'

There was a loud *bang* just as Joseph reached to unlock the door. This was followed by another *bang* out in the street. Joseph held up his hand for Michael to stay back, then he turned the knob. Standing in the way so as to bar entry to any intruders, Joseph eased the door open a crack. Michael looked past his father's shoulder, not knowing what to expect. What did 'agitated' mean when you were dealing with zombie-infected individuals?

'Michael, it appears that some of your friends are here,' Joseph said as he looked back over his shoulder at Michael. It was at the mention of Michael's name, not the door opening, that brought the incessant ringing of the bell to a stop.

'Andy, can I help you?' Joseph asked, obviously at a loss as to what was going on.

Michael peered past his father. Five of his friends stood on the doorstep. There were two others who were in the front yard kicking over the rubbish bins lined up against the curb.

'I think we just got our distraction,' Michael whispered in Joe's ear as he walked past to meet his friends.

'Hey guys, what's doing?' Michael grasped Andy's arm and gave him a quick hug, pulling him into the house.

Straight away Michael could tell that Andy was burning up. His face had a greyish cast and his eyes wouldn't fix on any one point for more than a few seconds. If Michael didn't know better, he'd have assumed that Andy was high on some strange cocktail of drugs.

'Get in here, you guys,' Michael yelled across the yard. 'Stop kicking the bins.'

Almost as one they turned at Michael's voice and trouped towards the front door. Their faces were red and flushed, covered in a sheen of sweat. When they moved into the entryway, they paused calmly as if they were waiting for new instructions.

'Hey. you called us, Mikey?' said Andy. His voice has a nasty rasp to it, an almost grating quality that he didn't usually possess. 'We saw you flying high. When you dropped from the sky, we figured you needed our help. Do you need our help or not? Because those bins are really starting to piss me off.'

Andy leant forward conspiratorially and whispered to Michael, 'One just jumped out at me!' Andy's words were slurred and hard to understand. When he raised his arm to show the heights he'd seen Michael fall from, he staggered and almost fell. Anyone listening to him speak would think he was delirious. But Michael had indeed fallen from the sky, and with the infection running through their system, his friends had obviously been able to see this somehow. Michael hoped the malicious bin was just a fever-dream. He just wasn't in the mood to start worrying about inanimate objects attacking them on top of everything else.

'Do you guys want a drink? It's awful hot and my uncle's just mixed some wicked punch.'

Entrapment

Azuradien was more restrained than Michael had expected. It might have helped that the effect of the potion was almost instant. The guarantee that the boys be removed to the faerie realm if Ashul deemed the danger to be too great might also have swayed things favourably.

So it was decided. Michael would get the seven soccer players to cause some innocent trouble in the street. Since they all had some strange fixation with the rubbish bins, it wasn't hard to convince them to get up to a little hijinks. The creation of some rubbish bin sculpture in the middle of Marcus' front lawn wasn't a difficult agenda to push. The boys decided they would make the largest rubbish bin sculpture the eastern suburbs had ever seen. Michael figured this should keep them out of any real trouble, create the distraction they needed, and it pleased the boys that they were able to keep a close eye on the troublesome bins. It was a win-win situation.

Brent had agreed to monitor the boys to make sure there weren't any adverse effect from the potion. They'd all guzzled it down without question as soon as Michael suggested it.

Now, they were hanging on Michael's every word, and acted as if they felt his emotions. This made it clear to Michael that it was his panic during his freefall from the skies of the shadowland that brought them to him. Michael hoped it was just those that he had infected that were able to track his movements, that it was only his teammates linked to his mind. He knew that the Nachzehrer were in his mind somewhere but had believed them to be contained. Keeping his emotions in check became more important now that ever.

At least it should be easy to tell if the potion had worked or not. If, in the next hour or so, they weren't quite so enamoured with Michael's every suggestion, they could take that as success.

The bins were already enthusiastically being claimed from all the houses in the street and the process of repositioning them on the front lawn of their neighbours was well under way. A couple of the boys, comfortable that the bins had stopped jumping out at them, were having a race down the street, the bins turned into makeshift billycarts. Michael saw Stevo and Tom go flying down the street, pushed by Andy and Mark. Both jumped clear as the bins careened into a side fence. From the great whoops of laughter echoing around, nobody had been badly hurt.

Brent's potion had taken down their fevers and returned some of the colour to their faces but it had also made them all act as if they were slightly drunk. They now staggered around because of this inebriation.

Marcus' parents had their Lexus parked in the driveway. There was a loud discussion about whether the car should be included in the boy's 'sculpture'. There was a unanimous roar of approval. If all of this didn't distract Marcus' family, nothing would.

'Lorcan, Ashul you must lead us in,' said Nicola. 'The kids and I will break off and go straight for Marcus' room. Any problems, Ashul will let us know. Then get your butt over to us for support. Joseph, are you coming with us or are you watching over the boys?' Nicola was eager to get going.

'No, I'm coming with you. The boys are in the mood for some harmless fun, let them enjoy themselves. Brent and Sarah will make sure things don't get out of hand.'

'Michael,' said Brent. 'Can you give your friends some clear instructions now just in case the potion blocks your ability to communicate with them?'

'Sure, Uncle Brent,' said Michael. 'I'll give them some clear instructions not to include any people or their pets in the sculpture.'

* * *

Lorcan was losing patience; he didn't need any diversion. *He* was diversion enough. He understood the family had to live in this place after the issue with the thinning had been dealt with. But they didn't understand the need to act as a matter of urgency. If Lorcan could perceive the thinning, then the creatures of the shadowland would be able to as well. Once they saw that a doorway was almost in existence, they'd do everything in their power to break through. The family would then have more than just the doll to contend with.

Those infected appeared to be taking the potion well. There was no more time for distractions. Lorcan chafed at the delay and turned to the faeries both as a way to relieve some frustration and also to clear up some misconceptions once and for all.

'As you are aware,' said Lorcan, 'we travel next door where the doll has tampered with the very fabric of the first and second realms. Will you give us aid?'

'You know the covenant binds us,' said Azuradien. 'If we use our power to destroy, we will be stripped of all magical protection, left defenceless.'

'Nothing binds you,' Lorcan retorted. 'You are merely protected by the covenant.' Lorcan was angered by their refusal to see the covenant for what it truly was. An excuse. 'You have heard what we face, all life is in jeopardy if we fail.' Lorcan held nothing back.

'We are of no use to you,' said Malcarielle, the disappointment in her voice evident. 'We cannot use our powers to kill, you know this – our magical shields would fail us.'

'But you would still have your powers, you could still defend yourself. Yet you would allow the humans to go in completely unprotected,' said Lorcan, pausing for just a moment, waiting until all eyes turned to him. 'They operate under those conditions constantly, so you would be in exactly the same position as them. In no more or less danger.'

'It is different,' Azuradien objected.

But Lorcan hadn't yet finished. 'Yes, the weak humans are willing to die for what they believe in. Whereas you faeries are happy to sit always at a safe distance to watch the battle being fought.'

Azuradien tried to protest Lorcan's analysis, but Lorcan had said what he'd wanted to say. These humans needed to be under no illusions as to what made these faeries tick.

Lorcan placed a foot in both worlds and moved with a speed that bordered on teleportation. Ashul walked across the yard to join him a few moments later.

'This family is my priority,' said Ashul. 'The bonded and I will do everything we can to assist you but if my family is in danger, I will go to protect them.'

This was as Lorcan had expected from the warrior. He was encouraged by his offer of aid but the warrior was no fool: the two realms could not be allowed to merge, so Ashul's assistance had always been guaranteed.

It was Ashul's use of terminology that spoke volumes. Lorcan took much from this small bite of conversation. Ashul had referred to the blood, his masters, as his family, inadvertently including himself in the grouping. This small slip told Lorcan all he needed to know about the shifting dynamic between the bonded and the blood. There was nothing the warrior would not do to protect these few. Lorcan didn't know whether this was good or bad. Ashul would be easy to manipulate if the time came for such things, but he would also be a more formidable enemy. Lorcan would have to try to remain on Ashul's good side.

When Nicola joined them and stood next to Lorcan, he leaned down to her and asked a casually impudent question. 'Do you intend to use the wild magic?'

Nicola's lack of guile surprised Lorcan. 'I cannot control it,' she said.

'Well, you seemed to control it fairly well when threatening me!' he added, a trifle indignant.

* * *

'For a man who's so charming and charismatic, you sure do get under my skin,' said Nicola. She smiled to soften her words, noticing for the first time how traditionally good looking he was. Gorgeous dark eyes. High cheekbones balanced by a strong jaw. Body tall and lean.

His looks were just another way to beguile. Nicola had to be on her guard since he probably had the power of compulsion – he'd even suggested as much. She needed to remind herself that his looks, his way with words, were all carefully designed to put someone at ease, making it easier for him to spring the trap. *How can you trust what is designed for deception?*

'So, you find me charming,' Lorcan said with a smirk, breaking into Nicola's thoughts. 'Charismatic, even.'

'Who's charming?' Dana asked, bending down to pat Sheba who was walking less than a pace behind her.

'I am, of course,' said Lorcan, smiling at Dana sweetly. 'Is there somebody else you find charming? You have but to name him and I shall dispose of him forthwith.'

Dana chuckled. 'Well, actually, I find Ashul both terribly charming and undeniably cute. In a slightly socially awkward kind of way.'

Ashul shuffled his feet. A faint flush coloured his cheeks.

Michael joined them and rolled his eyes. He reminded them all that the fence and gate to next door were booby-trapped.

'Booby-trapped?' Ashul asked.

'It was before we pulled you through, Ashul,' said Dana. 'When we broke into this house the first time, Michael's hands got cut up when he tried to jump the fence. There was glass and barbed wire embedded along the top, just out of sight. Michael was very lucky.'

'You travel with an ancient one now.' Lorcan grabbed Nicola and Dana by their arms, 'You have no need to scramble over fences.'

Sheba grabbed for Dana's wrist but her speed was no match for that of Lorcan.

Nicola was consumed by the shadows. There was the impression of shifting darkness, the sensation of great speed and then they simply *stopped*. The journey from outside the house to inside had lasted only a second.

When her surroundings stopped churning around her, Nicola stood in the middle of a deserted kitchen with Dana at her side.

Lorcan looked around the room and sniffed the air. Obviously satisfied about something, he nodded to Nicola and wisps of black smoke ran up and over his arms. Moments after, his body was consumed by the smoke and then next he was gone. Again, Nicola could take in no details because Lorcan moved at such speed. Nicola had the time to open her mouth, intending to make some remark about travelling with this ancient one being less than pleasant, but she didn't have the time.

There was a sudden gust of wind and Lorcan once again stood in front of her, his hands now wrapped around the wrists of Ashley and Joseph.

Ashley pulled away from Lorcan's touch. Joseph just looked at Lorcan as if to say 'Was that all really necessary?'

Michael and Ashul made their way into the neighbours' house by means of the second realm. It just took them a little longer than accompanying the ancient one. There was no sudden gust of wind, Nicola noted, they just simply stepped into the room: one second nothing, the next Michael and Ashul were beside her.

Nicola barely had time to register Ashul's presence before he spoke. 'Let's look into Marcus' room. I like not the feel of this place.'

* * *

Marcus' room was immaculate. Nothing seemed out of place. Nicola whispered in Michael's ear that it would be nice if his room looked like that. *Yes*, Michael thought, *psycho-chic. It's all the rage.*

Ashley had been standing in the hallway slowly taking in the vibe, probably remembering the last time they were here. It hardly seemed possible that it was only three weeks since they'd first broken into Marcus' house. It seemed like a lifetime ago, so much had changed in that short time.

'There's no-one up here,' said Joseph. 'All of the bedrooms are deserted.' He gently closed the master bedroom door behind him. 'We need to try downstairs.'

Working methodically, they searched the house from top to bottom. They moved from room to room. Ashul was in the lead, with Lorcan always being the last to enter. 'I can tell you now, you will find nothing down here, the house is empty.'

'How can you be so sure?' Nicola asked.

Lorcan gave Nicola a sideways look and pointed to his nose. He walked past her with his nostrils flared, lifting his head now and again to sniff at the air.

'I'm sure.'

Michael could find nothing out of place. As they said in the movies: there was no sign of a struggle.

So where was everyone?

Remote controls had carefully been placed on side tables, throw pillows arranged just so – there wasn't a casually kicked-off pair of shoes anywhere to be found. Michael couldn't imagine living a life that created so little 'disturbance' to the world around him.

This house held no imprint of the family that lived within its walls. Nicola was a bit of a neat freak but anyone walking into their home could tell she loved to cook by the number of cookbooks, knife blocks, and pots and pans drying waiting to be put away. Similarly, you could tell they were a family who owned and loved their dog. At any point in time, there was bound to be a chewed tennis ball or bag of dog treats sitting out on a bench somewhere. You knew by the framed memorabilia in the lounge room that someone in the house loved all kinds of sports. *How could a house not harbour the imprint of the personalities that lived within it?* Logically it could not, which meant this house was screaming something to Michael; he just couldn't understand what it was saying.

'Dad, you sure they were all over here?' Michael asked, speaking in hushed tones even though they had just traipsed all around the house, opening and closing doors, making more noise than seemed decent under the circumstances.

Joseph nodded his confirmation, equally as conscious that they weren't being as quiet as they should be. They found themselves outside the upstairs bedroom after checking the rooms for a second time. There was no sign of the family, no sign of the thinning that had been perceived when they were in the second realm.

'We need to go up!' barked Lorcan. The vampire's sniffing of the air now resembled more of a pant.

'You smell something?' asked Ashul.

'How can you not?' Lorcan was looking up at the ceiling, searching for a way up.

'Can you elaborate?' said Ashul impatiently. Rarely did he need to play twenty questions with Lorcan – usually the difficultly lay in shutting him up.

'The stink of humans,' said Lorcan. 'Distressed humans. There's something else building, but this stench is driving all other smells away. We cannot delay.' Lorcan looked more than agitated.

'When we saw the thinning, it was above the house, so maybe it is being generated in the attic,' said Ashul.

Joseph found the pull-down stairs. Their own family had a set that led into their garage roof for extra storage space. 'We should have thought of this,' said Joseph as he grabbed the chain. He paused for a moment, took a breath, waited for Ashul's nod then pulled the chain: the stairs unfolded.

The stench that dropped from the attic hit Michael in the face like it was a physical thing.

He tried to hold his breath, then forced air through his teeth in slow snatched gasps. The smell was so strongly tainted with the stink of antiseptic and stale urine that it seemed to run down the walls and envelop them. It smelt like a hospital under the pump that just didn't have the resource to keep their patients clean anymore. It smelt like a public toilet on a hot day. It smelt like all of these things yet none of them.

The springs on the stairs squeaked as the stairs were lowered. Michael cringed at every metallic ping and looked back over his shoulder down the hallway as if expecting someone to be stealthily approaching. They were making so much noise.

Joseph went to climb up, but Ashul held his shoulder and shook his head sharply.

Lorcan's back stiffened as the full force of the stink hit his nostrils, Michael saw his eyes flare red, and he wondered how bad it must be for a creature whose senses were more acute that any animal's.

Michael tried not to think about it, but his nose had its own ideas. He tried to break the smell down, analysing each component. When he detected the iron rich hint of blood, bile rose up in the back of his throat. Michael covered his face with his arm and forced himself to breathe through the fabric of his shirt. He turned warily towards Lorcan.

'Are you going to be okay with this?' asked Michael. He didn't like the idea of Lorcan driven mad by bloodlust being trapped in confined spaces with his family.

The ancient one's nostrils still flared but he did nothing to cover his face.

'I will be fine,' Lorcan answered. His speech was clipped and Michael thought he saw the sharp point of canines when he spoke.

Ashul and Lorcan agreed that they would both climb the attic stairs first, with Ashul leading and Lorcan in the rear.

As Lorcan's feet cleared the stairs, Michael heard his sharp intake of breath. The vampire's breathing became ragged and uneven and echoed through the tight space of the attic. *What could he have seen to impact him in such a way?* Michael had seen Lorcan angry, but it was always in a measured way – the only other emotion he seemed to feel was an amused sufferance.

The strange acoustics of the place brought the sound of Lorcan's panting to his ears. Michael could almost feel the vampire's thirst. With each gasp it sounded to Michael like his hallmark control was about to slip, and Michael wondered again if it was safe to be around Lorcan in these conditions.

It was Ashul who called down the stairs. 'Joseph, I don't think you should let the girls come up here.' Ashul was talking to Joe, but to Michael he spoke simultaneously in his mind. *Michael, keep them away; they do not need to see this.* Ashul may have lived a life that spanned centuries, but he had no concept of how this family worked.

Nicola grasped the steps in front of her and looked towards both Michael and Joseph as if daring them to stop her. Understanding that Ashul did not see any signs of immediate danger, Michael did not move to stop her. His mum might not understand how things were now but if Ashul told him that it was unsafe – and he needed to hold her back – then he would try to do just that.

Michael wasn't certain that he wanted to enter the close confines of the roof and have to breathe in the stink while standing face to face with whatever was causing it. Yet he climbed the stepladder regardless, reluctantly pulling himself up into the attic.

As Michael's head cleared the last step, he saw what had been upsetting Lorcan.

Before Michael stood what could only be described as a makeshift operating theatre.

* * *

Marcus was lying on a gurney, angled so that his head was lower than his feet. Tubes had been inserted into his arms and legs, some to drain his blood, others appearing to be replacing lost fluids. A catheter had been inserted and a bag collecting urine hung from his waist. What appeared to be saline and plasma were being fed into his body. So it looked like they weren't trying to kill him, which was some small relief.

Lorcan surveyed the scene from the corner of the attic, as far away from Marcus as he could get. He pushed his face against the small ventilation grate in the wall. 'We must hurry!'

'Ash, can you get anything from him?' Nicola asked. She sounded calm but Michael could see tears running down her cheeks.

Ashley tried to speak, but her voice broke. She coughed, wiped her arm across her face. 'Aunty Nic, he's locked in a recurrent nightmare. I'm picking up something strange about his dream though. There are others in it. And they're not a projection of his own mind they're actually in his dream.'

Ashley was swaying on her feet. 'Is it the doll, Ashley?' asked Michael.

Lorcan interrupted, 'There is more than just human depravity here.' Lorcan's eyes were starting to glow a deep red. 'We must go!'

But Ashley was lost in Marcus' dreams, she continued on as if no-one had spoken.

'It's his parents,' said Ashley. 'They're in his dream… torturing him in his dream. Hold my hand, I can show you.' Ashley used one hand to grab one of Dana's and offered the other to Michael.

He held his breath. He didn't want his parents to realise he was awake. If they knew he was awake, they would beat him. But if they believed he was in a deep sleep they would start sticking pins into his body again and pour liquids down his throat so he woke coughing and sputtering unable to breathe. Either way, he would be punished.

As Michael held Ashley's hand, he was three years old, then seven, then five. No matter what his age, *they* had been visiting him at night for all of his life. There was a brief reprieve when he went on a school camp, but still they haunted his dreams. Through every nightmare they repeated the same mantra. 'You will take what is offered and you will give back to us. You will take what is offered and you will give back to us.' No anger, no love, no rage, no enjoyment. Even the pain they inflicted on him seemed to give them no pleasure.

Ashley's knees buckled and Michael made a grab for her. Ashley was no longer connected to Marcus, but she was sure still connected to Michael. He could hear the blood rushing through her veins and feel her head ringing. She was about to pass out.

Michael felt all these sensations as if they were his own: he dropped her awkwardly to the floor.

After a few deep breaths, Ashley indicated that she wasn't going to faint. She gave him a weak smile and she closed off their connection. Michael didn't want to admit how relieved he was when his mind became his own again. Dealing with so many conflicting emotions as Ashley did was no easy thing.

* * *

Sensing there was something more in the attic, Nicola reached forward and pulled back the thick curtain that had separated the room. She nearly jumped out of her skin when she heard the muffled sound of the rubbish bin tower toppling over in the front yard. Michael's teammates were screeching uproariously at their antics.

Nicola's heart beat frantically as her mind tried to process what was in front of her. Behind the curtain were Marcus' parents laying on hospital gurneys, each tilted to a forty-five-degree angle. Tubes ran from their arms and across the floor leading to the cannulas inserted into Marcus' feet. Their skin, waxy and pale, stretched too tightly across the angular bones of their faces. With dark circles that ringed their eyes, they looked a little too much like corpses. But Nicola could see the slow rise and fall of their chests, each breath pulling against the tight straps crisscrossing their bodies. The restraints were the only thing preventing them from slipping off the beds.

Nicola said, 'They've been extracting Marcus' blood in large quantities and then supplementing his dwindling supply with saline and blood of their own.' She seemed to be talking to herself more than to anybody else. 'Apart from being abhorrent, it's also very dangerous.' Nicola tasted acid as the contents of her stomach rose in the back of her throat. She forced herself to take slow, steady breaths. The stench of the place and the horror of the situation was making her head spin.

'Ashul, you need to remove Marcus now,' said Nicola. 'Take all the paraphernalia with you. Brent can call Dave and Tony and get these tubes taken out of him safely. They can organise the police. They'll hopefully go to jail for what they've done here.' Nicola pulled out her phone and took a couple of photos, just in case the evidence disappeared.

'Mum, are you certain this isn't the doll's doing?' Michael asked. 'Do we really want to put people in jail because the doll manipulated them into doing something they would never normally do.'

'Have a look around you, Michael,' Nicola almost screamed to him. 'This is no crime of passion. This isn't an emotion that the doll has manipulated and amplified. This is something altogether different.' Nicola looked at Michael; she needed him to see what she saw here. 'The doll played with your dislike for this boy, made you angry, justifiably so and you lashed out, but this…' Nicola almost sobbed out the words. 'What would you need to tap into to make this the result, make you do this to your own son?'

Michael didn't argue. He didn't look like he agreed with her either. But there was no time to ask him what he was thinking.

'Ashul, get your people out of here now,' Lorcan snarled from the corner. 'There is something coming. It is almost upon us, the scent is getting stronger.'

Ashul asked, 'What is it?'

Joseph moved towards Nicola. 'Nicola, we can get the police to handle this. I want everyone out now.'

'I can't leave him, Joe,' Nicola said as she grabbed the bags down off their hooks.

Ashul already had Marcus in his arms. Nicola placed the bags across Marcus' body and nodded to Ashul that he was good to go.

Ashul slipped away with Marcus in his arms and into the second realm.

She'd barely had the time to rub the sweat from her face before Ashul returned, still holding Marcus.

'The boy cannot be removed from this place,' said Ashul. 'They have placed a warding around the building.' He drew his sword. 'They have allowed us entry but will not allow the boy to leave. This is beginning to have the feel of a trap about it.'

'Nicola?' yelled Joseph. 'Enough, it's time to go.' Joseph grabbed her arm and pulled her towards him.

'Ashul, can you get us out?' Joseph asked calmly. A quick shake of the head was his response.

Ashul indicated that Michael should also arm himself. Seconds later, Michael's sword was in his hand.

'Lorcan, can you please confirm that you are able to leave?' said Ashul.

Lorcan's eyes were overly wide and his canines were visible. Yet he left the room with his usual style: smoke built on his shoulders, then he was consumed by darkness.

Everyone waited for a couple of moments. The quiet was so intense that Nicola could hear her own blood ringing in her ears.

The air in the room had become thick and syrupy. Nicola felt the floor shift under her feet as vertigo suddenly hit her and the room spun. Changes in the air pressure were making her ears throb painfully. Heat pulsed through her head. Working her jaw, she tried to ease the pressure building. *Was she having a panic attack? Surely not.* She reached out a hand to steady herself, tried to force calm onto her mind, counting each inhale of breath, counting each exhale.

A measure of stability returned.

Dana and Ashley were swaying on their feet and grabbing at each other to steady themselves. 'Aunty Nicola,' Ashley said, 'my head won't stop spinning. My ears feel like they're about to burst.' Both girls were rubbing their ears with their free hands.

Ashul cursed. 'Cover your ears!' He punched upwards to remove some tiles from the roof above his head. He kept working at the hole until it was large enough for a person to squeeze through.

'Ashul, I don't think we should be going up,' said Nicola through gritted teeth, trying to control the rising vertigo. 'We're all too disorientated, we can't even walk in a straight line let alone climb up onto the roof.' Nicola was holding her daughter in her arms: Dana's skin was covered in a thin sheen of sweat and she was struggling to stand. Joseph moved into support Ashley. Neither of the girls looked able to move quickly.

'We are under attack from imps,' Ashul said curtly, unused to his order being questioned. 'They are weakening us by upsetting the inner ear – we'll be unable to walk if we don't get away. Soon, you would not be able to formulate a clear thought. A sound beyond your ability to hear is destroying your balance. Executing magic will become impossible.'

Nicola found the irony of the imps' method of attack darkly amusing. They'd picked the wrong girl to try this on. She had an advantage over the others. She dealt with this kind of shit every damn day.

The shadows around them thickened, and Lorcan shifted back into the room. He had deep gashes running down his arms. 'Their warding cannot hold me,' said Lorcan. 'But I won't be able to take anyone from this place, their bodies would not survive the assault. Ashul, get your family to the roof. I will hold the imps here. The warding extends to the fence-line and only prevents magical forms of travel. If you can get them to the fence, you can walk straight through the warding.'

Then let's go back through the house,' Nicola suggested. 'Joe can carry Marcus.'

'No, that way is already swarming with the imps' presence,' said Lorcan. 'Ashul is right! Going up is safer, I will guard your retreat.' Lorcan's patience was about to break. 'Do you not understand, it is not safe here. I have detected the thinning. Other creatures are gathering. I must stay here and close this doorway before we are overwhelmed by creatures that make me look like Prince Charming.'

Ashul boosted Ashley up through the hole he'd made. The bonded warrior, Darmead, was there to reach down and pull her through.

'Dana, you are next,' said Ashul. As he readied to lift Dana up through the opening, he was hit from behind as a dark mass tumbled through the roof.

A high-pitched screech issued from a squat, leathery beast that was all hind legs and ripping talons. Its face had the characteristic of a human twisted with the features of a bat. Wide shining eyes, thin slotted nostrils, a gaping mouth looking more like a tear in a mask than part of any face.

Tiny needle-like teeth could be seen running around the edges of the mouth. It opened its maw wider than seemed possible and buried its teeth into Ashul's shoulder.

It hung off Ashul's back, flapping its wings, unable to spread them because of the limited space of the attic. The warrior's magical shield prevented the teeth from breaking his skin, but the force of the imp's bite enabled it to stay hanging from his shoulder.

Ashul's sword piercing its throat caused the imp to drop away. Nicola could hear Darmead fighting more of the creatures on the roof. *How many were there?* The high-pitched squeals as the imps fell turned her stomach.

Lorcan was standing over the hatchway, kicking and tearing at flesh as more imps tried to force their way into the small attic space. Lorcan's eyes burned a clear crimson and one of his talons pinned an imp to the floor. 'Ashul, get the humans out of here,' said Lorcan. 'I cannot use my magic with them around.'

Lorcan's body was changing, his eyes already glowed a fiery red and now his skin darkened to the deepest indigo. Wickedly sharp canine teeth hung in a mouth designed for ripping. During this transformation, he was being forced to crouch, his body too large for such a confined space. His black wings bunching up against the roof above.

For each wound inflicted on the imps, the intensity of the wail increased. Nicola shielded her daughter, ignoring the vertigo that was trying to send her to her knees. She swallowed back bile and found the place within her where control reigned in the middle of a magnificent maelstrom of chaos.

She tried to tap the wild magic – just a little – but the wild magic didn't work that way.

Thick snaking bands of power rippled out of her. The imps below her were wrapped in coils of her design. Where Nicola's energy touched the imps' skin, their molecules were broken down into atoms, atoms were broken apart into subatomic particles, and then reformed so that a light dust blew where the imps had stood moments before.

Nicola allowed the magic to dissipate rather than calling any of its force back into herself.

'To the roof, we have no room to move here.' Ashul grabbed Dana around the waist and lifted her towards the hole. Darmead had his entire upper body hanging through the gap so that he could get his hands under Dana's arms and pull her through. Dana barely moved as she was lifted through the hole. She was listless, almost in a daze.

Joseph nimbly made his way up then reached down for Nicola.

Michael grabbed Nicola's hand and dragged her towards the hole. He boosted her up, and once she was through he followed quickly onto the roof. Ashul was just behind him, but Lorcan remained below as he said he would.

'There will be more coming,' said Ashul, just as he staggered under the increased intensity of the attack. A shrill whining reverberated through Nicola's skull. 'Michael, Darmead, keep your swords drawn,' he said. 'Ensure you have at least three metres between you. Place a foot on either side of the peak. If you need to drop onto your knees, then do so. Despite this vertigo you will still be able to swing a sword.'

Ashul placed himself in the most dangerous position nearest the roof's edge.

'Nicola, Ashley, Dana, stay low,' said Ashul. 'We are as much affected by this form of attack as you.'

The subaudible screech as the imps climbed the outside walls of the house bounced off the ceramic tiles, creating a kind of feedback that set Nicola's teeth on edge.

Imps were scrambling up trees and hanging from branches. There were hundreds of them. Now that the warriors had drawn their swords, the imps were sitting back and attacking them from a distance, opening their mouths wider still in their silent screeching.

Smoke and Lightning ran through the sky towards them, but their path was twisted and erratic. They reared up at one of the trees that held the most imps and struck at it with their hooves. They hit more branches than they did imps. Michael could sense the wail of the imps also destroying the horse's equilibrium.

More of the bonded arrived, materialising out of the sky: mounted warriors, magnificent, but limited in what they were able to do. They couldn't risk firing a shot towards the roof since the vertigo severely hampered their accuracy, so instead they focused on not allowing any more of the imps to get near the roof.

Imps dropped from the trees as their leathery hide was pierced by crossbow bolts. Just as many arrows and bolts were going wide as those that struck their marks.

Michael dropped to one knee, trying to protect his ears. But he needed his hands for his sword. When he stumbled and nearly fell, Nicola reached out to grab the back of his shirt. Her steadying hand was the only thing that stopped him from falling over the edge.

'Why don't they fly?' said Michael, his voice holding no strength. He went to speak again and only managed to vomit in the roof's gutter.

'They are playing with us,' said Ashul, somehow still standing. Trickles of sweat ran down his forehead, pouring into his eyes.

As if hurt by Ashul's words, the imps launched the second phase of their attack. Unnaturally quick, they used the wickedly barbed hooks that sprouted from the tips of their wings to climb up and across surfaces where any other creature would struggle to find purchase. Two of the imps were shot down by the bonded before they were able to clear the roof's gutter.

Michael pushed himself back to his knees and glanced over his shoulder to make sure Dana and Ashley were still safely inside the protective triangle created by Darmead, Ashul and himself.

When an imp hurled itself bodily towards Dana, Ashul thrust his blade into the air just as the imp flew over his head. The body dropped less than a metre from Dana's feet, yet she didn't respond. Joseph kicked at the imp's body and watched it roll and drop off the side of the roof.

Electricity arced across the backs of Joseph's hands. When another imp drew close enough, a bolt of energy flew from his clenched fist, blowing it backwards through the air, its skin sizzling as it burned. But all too quickly the sparks sputtered and died. The imps' subaudible attack was making magic erratic and unreliable.

'Is Dana okay?' Michael asked as he kicked forward to keep an imp's claws from his face, not having the time to turn and check himself.

Darmead held the creature pinned and leaned sideways to thrust his knife into the creature's back. Any reach advantage had been cancelled by the need to fight from their knees.

There was a dull whump from inside the house that nearly knocked Nicola from her feet, followed by a ferocious growl. The tiles beneath her shook as a wash of baking heat blew out through the roof. Ceramic cracked and broke. One thump was followed by another. The tiles between Ashul and Michael disintegrated as three imps flew through the gap where part of the roof had stood moments before. The imps crawled across the tiles, the disorientating attack still issuing from the rip of their mouths.

Ashul's sword hummed through the air, blurring with the speed with which he dispatched the three imps. He turned defensively as a huge black shape burst through the roof. Sharp splinters of tile flew in all directions.

Lorcan's eyes looked like pools of molten lava. His outstretched wings beat at the air behind him. He was magnificent in his deadly simplicity. His body dripped with the black ichor of imp blood.

'The imps are swarming up from the ground under the house,' Lorcan said to Ashul. 'If I destroy them. I destroy the roof you are standing on.'

But Nicola was more than just a wild magic-wielder, she had other magic at her disposal. She was able to ignore the screech of the imps. Tinnitus had plagued her since she was five. Having a disease eating at your inner ear suddenly had some advantages. She focused on the sound of the air blowing through the trees and drew the air to her, forcing it to twist and swirl as she did so. 'Ashul, get the bonded on the ground. It's about to get a bit windy up here,' said Nicola. Fingers of air were already whipping at her hair.

'Lorcan, Ashul, grab hold of the kids.' She could hardly hear herself over the gale rushing over the tiles.

Lorcan covered the girls in his wings. Tiles were being ripped from the roof by the wind. The imps still tried to crawl closer to them, but Nicola was having none of that. A blast of magic blew out from her hands and the imps lost their hold, wickedly barbed hooks shattered by the blast's impact. Their bodies tumbled to the edges of the roof and tipped over to fall to the ground.

Nicola could feel a heat growing inside her stomach and knew that the wildfire begged for release. The heat ran up and down her nerve endings. She could hear the imps scratching their way up the stairways inside the house. The wildfire had a need of its own, and that was to destroy. There was a tingle in her fingertip that she knew meant parts of her body were being destroyed and recreated at a rate that made her shimmer. She needed all of her willpower to keep the wild magic contained. Tiles around her feet started to turn to dust. The destruction was leaking out of her.

More scratching and scraping, this time from the downpipes running up the side of the house. She stood poised, ready to call the wind back to her.

But it wasn't a hooked claw that rose above the roof's edge, it was a swishing white tail, followed by the body of a fluffy white cat.

More cats followed, jumped up onto the roof. The felines made their way across the tiles with a grace that so epitomised the species. They leapt onto the roof from the thin branches of nearby trees, and they made their way straight to Dana's side.

Dana pushed back Lorcan's wings, allowing the cats to come to her.

The imps screeched their defiance as more black claws hooked into the guttering, the cats replied with a long, drawn-out mew, from low within their throats.

Dana no longer looked pale and drained. Now, she looked energised. Nicola was beginning to understand Dana's unresponsiveness earlier. It wasn't just the effects of the imps' attack; she'd been sending out a call. That Marcus' fluffy white cat was the first to respond seemed poetically just. Dana had saved its life when it was near to death from torture and abuse and now it was trying to repay the favour.

Nicola didn't know how these small animals could match the brutal strength of the imps but she would soon find out. Nicola pushed the wildfire down and watched as the cats stalked across the roof. They kept their bodies held low, tails swishing and all the while continuing their mournful yowl. The white cat was the first to engage. It struck like a snake, claws ripping across the skin on the back of an imp's arm. A hiss of steam released from the broken skin, forcing the wound open.

When the head of one of the climbing imps cleared the guttering, the cat raked its claws across the creature's shining black eyes. The imp reacted as if its face was on fire – it dug at its own skin, trying to remove the source of pain.

'Cats are the natural enemy of the imps,' said Dana from where she rested near Michael's knees. 'Their claws burn through the imp's skin like acid.'

'How did you know that?'

'The cats told me.'

Michael laughed. 'Of course, they did.'

'Where did they all come from?'

'We live in a neighbourhood of pet owners,' said Dana. 'You should see how many budgerigars I could call.'

* * *

'I know the location of the thinning between the realms.' Lorcan ducked his head as a dark shape flew towards him out of the trees. Ashul's sword cut through the air, and another imp fell. 'It is the boy. He is the source.'

Knowing the fight was almost over, the imps flew at them en masse.

Lorcan grabbed an imp from the air and twisted its head: there was an audible pop and he tossed it aside. The sharp spurs on the tips of Lorcan's wings acted like a set of extra hands, the soft flesh of the imp's bellies yielding easily to the lightning quick strikes.

Ashul's blade lit up the night sky and another group of imps charred and fell from below.

'We have no choice,' said Nicola. 'We have to go back through the house. 'Dana, are the cats strong enough to guard our backs?'

'A couple of holes in the roof will be easy for them to cover,' Dana said with absolute certainty. 'We are actually getting in their way.'

'Okay, good. One of you grab Marcus on the way through.' Nicola could barely be heard with the screams of the imps dying blotting out almost all else. Nicola wished they would die as silently as they attacked.

Returning to the attic took only a few moments.

Dana and Ashley lifted Marcus into a sitting position.

The fight from above died down completely, and after a brief pause the cats started up an ungodly caterwauling. Sheba's howls rang out from the direction of home and Nicola had time to turn towards Dana to get some insight.

Marcus' eyes had opened. The faint outline of the doll was rising behind him. Dana was listening to the animals, a puzzled expression on her face. 'They're warning of the doll,' whispered Dana.

The ground beneath them buckled, twisted and snaked like a living thing – the thinning opened behind Marcus, a place where the first and second planes became so close to each other they almost merged. The silhouette of the doll stood in the centre of the divide, gaining clarity as the doorway between worlds was forced open.

This thinning didn't allow the shadowland to become visible – they weren't quite there yet – but it was evident. Michael could see the telltale signs. The very structure of things was being bent and twisted out of true. Michael resisted the urge to use his second sight.

The doll stepped fully into the first realm and placed one hand on Marcus' shoulder.

Michael thought he saw Marcus twitch at the doll's touch. Michael threw himself towards Dana. She was too close; she hadn't realised what was standing behind her. He cried out a warning.

Marcus wrapped his arm around Dana's neck and her eye's widened in shock.

A victorious smirk twisted Marcus' features.

Michael saw a flash of movement as Lorcan reacted. Marcus closed his eyes and the thinning folded back in upon itself, folded back towards his body like a flower blooming in reverse. The moment his eyelashes touched his cheeks, the thinning was gone. As was the doll.

Marcus and Dana had been engulfed by nothingness, disappearing as the thinning closed.

Lorcan moved fast, but even he hadn't been able to move faster than the blink of an eye.

Fallout

When Dana disappeared, the wild magic within Nicola responded in force. Her centre of calm destroyed in that blink of an eye. Lorcan sensed the danger and moved closer to Nicola to shield the others with his body, but Nicola barely noticed.

Her little girl was gone, taken from right from under her eyes. She tilted her head back and let the first snakes of power twist from her body, accompanied with a scream of purest despair. She had no way to stop the power once it started to flow and she had little desire to anyway. She needed to push away her anger, her fear, her desperation. The emotions were choking her, yet she continued to scream.

The gurney where Marcus had been bound softened and started to melt, metal dribbling and pooling on the floor. The smell of burning foam drifted towards her as cloying clouds of acrid smoke rose from the mattress as it smouldered, flames exploding from the mattresses core. Lorcan rushed towards her, knocking Nicola from her feet.

Nicola turned to him, but saw only an obstacle, something standing in the way of her rage. She felt the wild magic shift within her, revelling at finding a new target. Lorcan tilted his head as if accepting the outcome, because even he must know that nothing could stand in wildfire's way. And it was this head tilt, the resignation in her eyes that so mirrored the pain she was feeling, that allowed her a brief moment of sanity. So somewhere amongst the rage, Nicola found some reason and she turned the power skywards. What remained of the roof dissolved as the wild magic unmade all that it touched.

The molecules in the air continued to heat up as Nicola struggled to get the wild magic under control, but she was losing the battle.

The words you *cannot play with wildfire* running through her head.

Lorcan moved closer and Nicola knew that he was going to strike. He had no choice. The wild magic threatened to consume them all. But, instead of attacking her, the ancient one wrapped her in his wings. Nicola slumped against him as she struggled for breath. Whether it was the vampire's compulsion, or a lack of oxygen, Nicola could feel herself losing consciousness and rather than fighting it, she embraced the darkness. She felt the wild magic lose it focus as she allowed herself to drop to the ground.

* * *

Joseph had carried Nicola home like a fallen soldier being taken from the field. The ground was littered with dead imps. Joseph had stepped over them like they were nothing more than fallen logs. The warding that had prevented their exit from the property no longer mattered as no-one even thought of using magic. Michael was shell shocked. Smoke spoke reassurances into his mind but he barely heard them.

He snapped back to reality when he heard Lorcan speak beside him, almost surprised to find himself standing back in the middle of their kitchen.

'They are not in the shadowland,' said Lorcan. 'The doll has no awareness of its existence.' Lorcan barely moved, looking like he was carved from marble.

'But Marcus, is he aware of the shadowland, would he be able to travel there?' Joseph asked.

'Anarcus would not allow the boy to hold so much power,' said Lorcan. The vampire had returned to his normal self, but his eyes still glowed with fire.

'I don't need to know where she isn't, I need to know where she is,' said Joseph, barely keeping it together. 'I need to get my little girl back.' He was randomly picking up fruit and then slamming it back down into the fruit bowl, the skins charred and smoking.

'She is not in the first plane,' said Ashul. 'The doll does not have the power of teleportation. If it did, it would not have restricted its feeding to this area. No, there is little doubt, she is in the second plane. I suggest we look for her there. The bonded are already searching. Lady Sarah, what does your network show?'

Ashul seemed to be the calmest one in the room.

'Currently, it's a mess,' said Sarah. 'The disturbance the thinning caused when it closed was phenomenal. It basically blew the network away. Things are just starting to settle down. I'll tell you when I've reconstructed things.' Sarah was busily trying to rebuild the network. Michael watched as she tried for the fifth time to set up the base framework. It flickered and sparked like an old fashion TV picture responding to static before it fizzled out and died.

Michael removed the scorched banana from his father's hand and passed him a tea towel to clean up with. 'Dad, I'm going with the bonded to search in the second plane.'

'No,' said Joseph. 'No, you are not! You're staying right here where I can see you. *He* took you from me today.' Joseph pointed a shaking hand at Lorcan. 'I was lucky to get you back then. I will not allow you to be taken away from me again. I can't lose the both of you.' Joseph clenched his hands and looked over to Nicola where she lay unmoving on the couch. 'I can't lose *all* of you!'

* * *

Nicola was not catatonic as the others had assumed. Instead, she was scrying for her daughter. She had fled to the pages of the book when the world faded to black around her. She felt the vampire's magic wrapping her in its embrace and allowed herself to succumb. Words hovered around her. *You cannot play with wildfire. Ignore your body at your own peril.* She'd heeded their words and still her daughter had been taken. So she took Hazel-eye's hand and they walked through the pages of memory, searching for anyone who might have some knowledge that could be used to find Dana.

The minds in the book had narrowed things down in a matter of minutes. Every mirror around her showed a different face. Dana was not being held in the first realm. There would have been a trace of her energy to pick up on. Then whole segments of the second realm were disqualified due to their inability to hold anything more that an idea, or a dream.

There was no argument, no discussion needed.

When a book fragment felt they had no further guidance to offer, they looked at Nicola apologetically and faded from their mirror.

One by one they disappeared. In time, almost every panel held nothing but her own reflection.

Only one old man remained. He muttered and ticked off regions of the second realm methodically on his fingertips almost oblivious to Nicola's presence. 'The dreaming plane is much too fluid,' he said. 'The energy required to hold the void at bay would not be maintainable. The ethereal plane would not support a full state being that has transferred over.'

'The ethereal plane?' Nicola asked.

'Girl, I have not the time to educate you. Just to inform you.' The old man looked flustered to have been interrupted, but he continued: 'The ethereal plane, another of the many dimensions of what you call the second plane. It is possible to travel through it for short periods of time but anything more and dissolution would occur. Trust me on this.' The old man's eyes bored into her. Nicola nodded, nothing more was necessary. She had experienced this man's memories and knew that he had forgotten more than she would ever learn. So she bowed her head in respect and allowed him to continue.

'No, he must have taken her into the astral plane – this is the area of the second plane that you use for travel.'

'Are you sure?' Nicola risked the question. She didn't want to upset him further but her daughter's life was at stake.

'I am sure. We will continue to search. Trust that we will find her.' The old man reached forward through the mirror and touched the centre of her forehead. As the hall of mirrors faded to white around her, she heard the old man's last piece of advice.

'Speak to your son, he is your key to this. His connection to his sister is strong and he can detect the changes in the second realm better than the bonded themselves.'

* * *

Nicola opened her eyes. It was like a fog lifting. It felt as if her eyes had been covered in some obscuring white layer and now the light from the kitchen seemed far too bright.

'Michael is right,' said Nicola before anyone had the chance to realise she was back. 'He will need to go into the second plane.' Everyone started to speak at once and she silenced them with a chopping motion from her hand.

'Michael is better able to perceive changes in the second realm. The bonded have lived there too long and they're accustomed to the feel of the place. Michael is like a person stepping foot on board a boat for the first time. Every shift under his feet is detected, exaggerated. The bonded are the weather-hardened sailors so used to adjusting to the sway of the deck they no longer even feel the gentle rocking.'

'And you know this how, Nic?' Joseph had tears welling up in his eyes. He was looking to her for direction, and she was glad that she was able to provide it.

Nicola clutched Joseph's hand, offering whatever reassurance she could.

'I have consulted with the minds in the book,' said Nicola. Her voice was firm, making it clear that now was not the time for debate. 'For the doll to have created somewhere to hold a person against their will, it will have caused a great deal of disturbance. Michael, you must search for this change. I cannot tell you what to look for. It may be a sound or a smell. The hairs on the back of your arms may react. I just don't know, but the fragments say that *you will know.*'

'It's a thickening of the air,' whispered Michael. It was like a light bulb had gone off in his mind. He spoke with more purpose. 'Mum, I know where to start. I have to go back to where the Bezenhart and Nachzehrer attacked us. I knew there was something going on there. The doll's actions didn't make any sense at the time. Maybe it wasn't attacking at all, maybe it was defending something. Maybe it was trying to distract us.'

Nicola knew as soon as he said it that Michael was right. If someone was being held captive, it would require a prison of some kind. A structure of that size would surely register in the void. Nicola had previously felt the pressure the void exerted if you just stopped moving for too long. A large structure would draw the void's attention in a similar way, so a thickening of the air sounded about right.

'She will be guarded,' said Ashul. 'Likely by the Nachzehrer. Your equilibrium will be put under great stress so close to the source.' Ashul turned to speak directly to Michael, 'You may need to pass on *all* the burden and there will not be the time for discussion.'

'You have already been infected, what more do you want me to do?' Michael said through clenched teeth.

'I could speak to you of this over the mindlink, but this is too important for us to play games,' said Ashul. 'Michael, you and I both know you are still protecting the bonded. You have created your lake of consciousness, but it is not invulnerable and your reserves are not inexhaustible. If the time comes that I tell you to pass the burden on to me, fully, you will do so, not because I am your leader and I command it of you, but because I am your friend and I ask it of you.' Ashul took a step towards Michael and placed his hand on his arm. 'Will you promise me this?'

'It's not really a fair request,' Michael protested.

'Yet I make it, anyway,' said Ashul.

'I'm sorry but I don't think I can promise that,' said Michael. Ashul lowered his head at this. 'But I promise, if push comes to shove, I will *share* the burden as much as I'm able to this time.'

Michael grasped Ashul's arm. 'Let's just make sure it doesn't come to that.'

* * *

When Dana felt Marcus' arm close around her neck, she could already feel reality dissolving around her. Once before, she'd been pulled out of one plane of existence into another, transported by the power of her mother's magic. This was nothing quite so elegant. Marcus' arm locked against her windpipe, and she could not breathe. He tightened his hold, and her world went black as the blood flow to her head was pinched closed.

She came to in a cage that appeared to be made out of nothing more than thickened air. The walls had no definition, and there was resistance under her fingers but not the hard feel of stone or concrete. It didn't have any texture that she could discern. There was simply something under her.

The size of her cell was difficult to gauge. The walls could have been miles away or they could have been centimetres from her face. Only a slight, barely perceptible darkening of the air suggested there were even walls around her. She lifted first her arms, then her legs, trying to make her movements small and inconspicuous. She didn't want to draw attention to herself if she didn't have to. A little exploration proved that she hadn't been restrained. She waited for a moment, trying to decide what to do next. Nothing could be gained by lying on the floor playing possum, it was not as if they weren't aware of her presence. So, she got to her feet.

Nothing happened. *So far so good.*

Dana tentatively reached out to explore the dimensions of the place she was being kept in. She knew from the way her own breathing echoed back to her that the room had to be small. Two paces forward and her hand felt resistance. Her fingertips brushed against a cold, hard surface even though her eyes detected no change. When she pushed against it, the temperature dropped further and the wall that she couldn't see moved towards her, sliding closer.

She refused to relent, placing both hands against the frigid surface, and she pushed harder. Her heels slipped as the wall continued its relentless forward movement. In slow, unmeasurable increments she slid backwards until her heels locked against the wall at her back. She placed one hand on the wall behind her, having to peel her palm off the icy surface to do so.

Dana now stood in something the size of a coffin. Condensation formed on the panel in front of her, blowing back hot air into her face. She let her arms drop to her sides, and from her breath alone she could detect the walls receding. The message was very clear: *resistance would be punished.*

She took in one long, deep breath to steady herself and pushed against the wall at her back. The air grew frigid again. She persisted. Once again, she dug her heels into the ground, pushing back through her legs with as much force as she could muster. Her shoulder went numb where it was in contact with the wall but she continued to push. Her feet began to slide, more quickly this time she felt the walls closing in. Dana raised her right leg and braced it against the wall when it was within reach. She eased off the pressure and started to spider-climb the wall.

Her hands chafed raw after less than three metres of climbing. With each upward reach she left a little more skin behind.

She was forced to stop because her head was wedged against another cold, hard surface. She had reached the ceiling. The space available to her made any further movement impossible.

Her own exhalations coiled around her face like a hot, humid mask. She didn't suffer from claustrophobia, but she panted as if there wasn't enough oxygen available regardless. Her legs shook with the effort it took to hold her position, so she allowed herself to slide to the floor.

Dana's heart rate slowed. With forced calm, she stretched her legs out in front of her and felt no further resistance. The air seemed lighter, the room almost expansive. To ensure the doll knew exactly how she felt about this whole situation, Dana rose and walked forward until she felt the cold that indicated the wall was close. Without further consideration, she threw her right fist into the wall she couldn't see.

There was a dull *crack*. With the cold shooting up her arm, she was uncertain whether she'd broken her hand or the wall.

After a bit of exploration with her left hand, she realised with both despair and a little relief that it was neither.

* * *

Nicola paced back and forth across the kitchen, her calm at having a course of action slowly dissolving. 'Before we go to the second realm, I need to know what those people next door know,' said Nicola. 'They were over there, performing some strange blood transfusion at the behest of the doll. Now their son has taken my baby. Ashul, Azuradien I expect you to get me through whatever shielding they have in place. And if I hear one word about covenants… I will put you in a position where you have no choice but to break it. Am I understood?' Nicola was already walking towards the front door, with Ashul following her and his sword flickering into place on his back – one moment visible, the next not.

She walked past the tower of rubbish bins that had been restacked on top of the black Lexus, barely noticing the seven boys sitting listlessly by the curb. As Nicola walked up the path, she was already preparing to ask Ashul to kick the door in. The time for banal pleasantries was well and truly over. But force wasn't required.

The door swung open before Nicola could get there. The cold, detached visage of Marcus' mother, Martina, stood in the doorway. Nicola was surprised that she was able to walk, let alone open the door but she refused to allow her shock to show. She was slowly rolling her sleeve down over her arm. The edges of her mouth lifted into a smirk when she saw Nicola had noticed the gesture.

'I've been unwell,' the woman said. 'There must be something going around; the emergency rooms have been an absolute nightmare! I hope you've all been spared.' Her tone was all concerned sincerity, but her eyes looked like they were made of glass.

'Save me your bullshit,' said Nicola. 'I'm only going to ask you this once. Where is my daughter?' Nicola's voice held some of the same detachment as Marcus' mother. However, Nicola was keeping her temper finely balanced.

'I don't know what you're suggesting, but I can assure you she's not here,' said Martina. 'No disrespect intended, but your daughter isn't really Marcus' type. Now, if you will excuse me,' She fixed her eyes on Nicola, all pretence of social propriety gone, 'I have a bit of unexpected cleaning up to do.'

'Shut that door on me you black-haired bitch and I'll blow it off the hinges, just like I did your roof. My preference would be for your hand to still be resting upon it, but...' She tried to shut the door anyway. Nicola let a little of her power out and the door flew open, banging against the wall. Martina jumped back quickly and raised her stinging fingers to her mouth.

'Your daughter means nothing,' she said with her hand including them all in a sweeping gesture. 'You all mean nothing.' Her face contorted with the zeal of a fanatic. 'We have provided the gateway. We will be the ones rewarded. And when Anarcus steps through, you and your friends,' she sneered at each one of them and paused for nothing more than dramatic effect, 'will suffer pain beyond imagining.'

So consumed in her zealous rant, Marcus' mother was completely unaware of the cold wind that marked Lorcan's passage. He rose out of the shadows of the entryway. He reached forward and wrapped his fingers around the woman's neck, long talons digging into the flesh under her jaw. Nicola watched as the skin dimpled under his grip.

'If you know of the girl's whereabouts, speak now,' said Lorcan. 'I *will* ask you this only once.' Lorcan dragged her back. Blood, stained black by shadows, flowed down her neck as the door slammed shut.

* * *

Lorcan had been monitoring the altercation between the females, annoyed by the blatant waste of time. This family had power, but it did not have the sense to wield it effectively, nor the logic to understand basic strategy. The woman from next door would know nothing. The doll had been plotting for centuries. It wouldn't allow something as expendable as this woman to hold so much knowledge.

He intended to rip out her throat. Her blood was already running over his fingertips when he felt the cold pulse of power and realised that he might not be dealing with anything as simple as an expendable woman.

'So have you finally come to bend the knee?' The woman was somehow prising Lorcan's fingers away from her neck.

'I... do not... bend,' Lorcan hissed against her ear.

'No, but you do break,' she said as she bent back Lorcan's finger until it cracked.

She grasped the next finger, and the next.

She'd made her way through breaking three fingers before Lorcan had time to fade away to safety.

Imprisonment

Michael followed his mother outside. He hadn't wanted to let her out of his sight.

His soccer friends were sitting despondently at the side of the road. As he approached them they barely raised their heads.

'Something doesn't feel right, Mikey,' said Steve, his words slurred. 'I thought a bit of a muck about would make me feel better, but it hasn't.' Michael noticed Steven's movements were slow and clumsy.

Michael ran back inside to grab his uncle.

'They were fine when I checked them last,' said Brent. 'Actually, more than fine. I forgot to check on them once…' Uncle Brent stumbled on the words. 'Can't you get them inside?' Michael was trying to convince the boys to move, but they seemed unable to focus.

'I don't have time for this.' Michael cursed under his breath, trying to calm the panic that threatened to seize him.

Smoke spoke softly into Michael's mind. *Calm, Michael. They came here to aid you. They are blameless in this.*

But wasn't that just the point? They were all blameless, Dana just as much as his friends. None of them had signed up to be used as pawns in a war. Michael swung around and kicked out at the broken bin that lay discarded in the street, hating the situation they'd all been put in. At this, the seven boys lifted their heads and snarled, rising to their feet as one.

'Ah, Michael. I think you best take it down a notch.' Brent placed himself between Michael and the boys, but it was obvious that Michael was in no danger. The boys had arranged themselves in a circle, facing outwards in a defensive position with Michael and Brent at the centre.

Michael blinked in a way that activated his second sight. With this other vision, he could see a ghoul crouching beside each of the boys, reaching towards them, but drawing away before they could sink their fingers into flesh. They were being prevented from touching Michael's friends, though only by the narrowest of margins.

Now that Michael was attuned differently – his eyes glowing with the pale light of the Nachzehrer curse – he heard the soft thrumming that emanated from the boys.

'The pitch is off,' said Michael. 'Uncle Brent, the potion needs to be realigned because the pitch isn't quite right. We need Malcarielle.' Michael could feel the vibration humming through his teeth. It had none of the soothing aspect it had when the potion had first been mixed and this off-key vibration was now running through his friends. No wonder they couldn't think straight.

Malcarielle appeared at Michael's side already singing softly. With his eyes fixed in the shadowland, Michael saw her in a different light. She was reminiscent of the angry faerie queen who had greeted him on the back of a giant ant all that time ago. Ethereal wings beat at her back and her eyes blazed with emerald fire.

She appeared stronger, more inclined to violence as the hot winds of the shadowland blew around her. Michael had time to wonder if the covenant had been created to protect the faerie, or to serve as a way to control them. Malcarielle looked like she needed no protection. Either way, her song was having the desired effect.

Michael turned to see Lorcan at his shoulder. His eyes were smouldering like hot coals. 'Quit playing with your friends. We have no more time for this. I can feel the imbalance in your blood. Regain control or I will remove those causing the distraction.'

The boys all turned towards Lorcan – seven sets of eyes glowing with a spectral light. Lorcan's fingers curled into claws and his lips pulled back to expose teeth that appeared yellow in the light thrown by the streetlamp overhead.

'Not in your lifetime,' Lorcan growled, and a flare of energy rippled out from him.

Michael searched around for his friends, afraid the blast had destroyed them. All seven boys dangled from the limbs of the trees that lined the street, all unconscious. The heat from Lorcan had blackened branches and leaves had curled and dropped to the ground, now nothing more than a pile of smoking embers. The burnt smell of eucalyptus that hung in the air almost covered the stench of singed hair. Michael was just grateful it wasn't the sweet smell of burnt flesh that hung over their heads.

'Get them inside so the faeries can help your uncle realign the potion,' said Lorcan. His hands were clenched angrily at his side. He looked like he wanted to destroy something and in his present state that might just be whatever happened to be in front of him when he finally exploded. Once more he stepped into the shadowland; the distorted swirls of colours seemed to embrace him before he disappeared.

* * *

After Malcarielle had gotten his friends out of the trees, Michael placed them in front of the television and spoke to them a lot about nothing, trying to refocus their minds on more pleasant things while Malcarielle sang to them. The crystal Malcarielle held bathed them all in a calming green light. Michael spoke of many things, shared memories of the good times they'd had playing together. His words were meant to calm his friends, but they helped him a little too. It helped him remember what this fight was about. He had to stop thinking about whether it was fair or not. He needed to focus on what he needed to achieve.

He was off in his own world when Malcarielle placed her hand on his shoulder. He hadn't realised that she'd stopped singing. The gargoyle and a group of water sprites were given instructions and left to themselves to maintain the song.

'Michael, your emotions cause this imbalance,' Malcarielle said softly, compassion wrapped around her every word. 'You need to keep yourself calm, the potion can only do so much.'

'My friends are currently slaves, Malcarielle,' said Michael. 'And I'm doing my very best to control my emotions, unless you have already rescued my sister from the clutches of the evil creature that lives next door. No? Well then, we have a bit of a problem here, don't we?' Michael didn't bother to listen to her reply.

His mood was already heavy as he walked into the kitchen and it took only a moment to realise he'd stepped into the middle of a shitstorm.

'It wasn't enough for you to poison me,' said Lorcan, hulking over Azuradien. He looked human, but he currently stood at a solid seven feet. 'Are you telling me you were not aware of what they were? Did not even suspect?'

'I needed to see if you were in league with them,' Azuradien countered, not at all intimidated by the vampire.

'And is this proof enough?' Lorcan held forward one of his hands, red and swollen. Three of his fingers sat at odd angles. 'Have I passed your test, or were you hoping she might kill me. I'm stronger than you realise, friend.'

As he stared down at Azuradien, Lorcan grabbed each of his broken fingers one by one and pulled slowly and steadily until each bone snapped back into position. He flexed his fingers in front of the faerie king's face, emphasising his point by cracking the knuckle of each joint.

'Maybe I should break one of your fingers for each of mine that was broken. It would seem fair, would it not?' Lorcan grabbed the faerie king's hand and held it before him. 'Tell me this: did you warn the humans? Do they know what lives next door? No, I can see it in your eyes that you did not!'

Azuradien attempted to remove his hand, but Lorcan's grip was like stone. 'Did you fear they would be tempted? You misjudge us all, and because this is the second time you have wronged me, I *will* take your fingers. Their absence can be a reminder of what you lack.'

Lorcan's canine teeth, normally nothing more than slightly pointed, dropped until they resembled the fangs of a jaguar. They were wickedly sharp and curved backwards, as if capable of delivering a dose of poison as well as ripping flesh from the bone.

Michael was about to intervene when Smoke indicated for him to hold.

'I'm sure you would,' Azuradien almost hissed. 'If you could …'

Lorcan's lips curled at Azuradien's words but his eyes did not waver.

The ring of a sword being drawn quietened the room.

Ashul stood before them all, his blade glowing with white-hot energy. 'I am done reasoning with all of you,' he said. His gaze swept the room, paused on Azuradien but came to a stop at Lorcan. 'I am not certain that I could best you, but I know I could lay a lot of pain at your feet before our fight was done. I have the power that was always mine to wield, but it has been tempered in the fires of fear and torment. The bond has changed. We now share what has always been denied to us. I would not test what this change has made me capable of.'

Ashul swung around his blade, but halted its arc, now suspended over the network that Sarah had been able to recreate. The blue of Azuradien's signature shone brightly amongst the tapestry before him. 'I am no Fate and I do not have the power of Atropos and I have no idea of this network's scope. But would you like to test it, test your invulnerability? Your thread of life versus my sword?' Ashul lowered his blade to within centimetres of the blue spark. 'You have made your doubts about the ancient one clear. Test him no more. I will personally respond to any action taken against him as if you had touched one of the blood.'

Azuradien made his signature wink off the grid. 'Ashul, you are far less than you once were,' he said.

'As are you, my friend,' said Ashul. 'You placed us all in jeopardy. If you knew of the disciple's presence, you should have informed us. Don't let your memories of a time past taint your ability to see clearly in the present.' Ashul turned away from the grid. Michael sent a mental question to Ashul about these disciples, but Ashul brushed the thought away, telling him to stay focused on the present.

Michael felt himself growing annoyed both by Azuradien's attitude as well as Ashul's dismissive tone. He whispered quietly into his aunt's ear. He didn't like the way Azuradien always found an out of every difficult situation. Michael wanted his thread back on the tapestry.

Ashley sat in the corner of the room. Since her power had awakened, she was isolating herself more from the group than she used to. She smiled at Michael, either reading his mind or his mood. Either way he felt some of his anger ease. Her eyes flicked to the network and she suppressed a laugh when her mother's hands went to work. With a dainty twist of her fingers, the network shifted slightly until Azuradien's blue signature shone once more amongst the multicolour tapestry before them.

Michael smiled. The faerie king kept trying to control the situation and Michael was glad that he could not control Aunt Sarah's magic. He suspected that his aunt's fingers were just as dangerous as Ashul's sword.

Azuradien's attitude was especially getting under Michael's skin. If being untouchable made someone into such a complete arsehole, then Michael was happy to number in the ranks of the vulnerable, with his sister and the rest of their family.

Michael looked at the coiled blue mass that represented himself on the network, twisted so tightly, but flecked with so many other colours. He could still see his sister's amber striations mixed in amongst his own signature.

They have shielded her from us, but her connection to you is still strong. Take strength from this. Smoke's voice in his mind gave Michael clarity. Dana had found Michael when he was awash in the lake of his own consciousness. Something that he'd been told was impossible. Michael pushed Azuradien and his childish outburst into the background. He was too busy focusing on the network in front of him. They already knew Dana's signature wasn't present… but could they see where it had been in the past?

There was a time that Michael could guarantee Dana's signature would be mixed up with his own more than usual.

'Dad, take the network back to the time when I passed out at soccer. Or later during Lorcan's cleansing,' said Michael, barely glancing up from the network. 'Dana reached me then. I know I heard her, yet she shouldn't have been able to. You've all said as much.'

Ashley sat forward and asked, 'Michael, what are you thinking?'

The multidimensional grid in front of them flickered and blurred. Energy signatures flew around the room like time-lapse photography of a highway at night. Michael felt queasy watching the shifting array of colours, but it was evident to all that Joseph viewed the network differently just by the way his eyes flicked from one point to another. His father couldn't watch Michael playing any first-person shooter video games without feeling like he was going to throw up, yet he could scan this ever-shifting network like he was speed-reading through a newspaper article.

Joseph's face creased in concern as the network stopped flickering. Before Michael had a chance to respond, Joseph muttered under his breath. 'She's not there.'

Nicola frowned and said, 'What do you mean, she's not there?'

'I've scanned forwards and backwards through periods when I know exactly where her position should be. She's just not there.' The network shifted again as Joseph desperately searched for any sign of Dana. Nicola placed a hand on his arm and the maddening shifting of light ceased.

'Uncle Joe, go to the moment of Michael's cleansing,' asked Ashley.

'This is the moment of the cleansing,' said Joseph. He pointed out each individual signature. Michael winced at the confused ball of cobalt blue that depicted him. The mass of energy looked tortured. Although Lorcan's influence couldn't be seen directly, the impact on Michael's aura was evident.

'She's somehow been taken out of the time stream,' said Lorcan with none of his usual amusement.

'That is not possible,' protested Azuradien.

'No. On this we agree,' said Lorcan. 'It should not be possible. Yet the evidence is in front of us.' Lorcan touched the tip of his finger to the twisted ball of light that represented Michael. Michael felt a cold shiver run down his spine as Lorcan's dark indigo twisted through his own blue light. Lorcan's energy was all sharp edges and barbed coils.

'So, you have all the knowledge, Azuradien?' said Lorcan. 'What are we seeing here? Because I see only wisps of the girl wrapped around her family like a shadow soon to fade.'

'Time is not something that can be manipulated in this way. One cannot be removed from the basic structure of the universe. Time can be slowed, yes. But to remove a person completely from the stream, no...' Azuradien shook his head. 'It cannot be done.'

'So you believe it to be a fault in the network?' asked Lorcan. 'A limit in its capabilities?'

Azuradien took a moment to answer, speaking the words with some resignation. 'No, the network is more that we know, not less. It would be able to pick up Dana's signature if she were still present.'

'Again, we agree,' said Lorcan.

Joseph asked with some hesitation, 'Could she be in the shadowland?' Would she appear on the network if she had been taken there?'

'The shadowland is linked to this realm; it is part of the same timeline…' But Joseph hadn't waited for Lorcan's response. The network shifted to the time when Michael had entered the shadowland.

'Michael's signature is still there, distorted, hard to track, but still there,' said Joseph.

'Azuradien, how would Michael have appeared if you'd taken him to the crystal cave in the faerie realm?' Nicola asked.

'That is something altogether different. The faerie realm was created as a means of protection. The greatest powers of faerie spent centuries in its construction. The crystal cave is at the very core of our kingdom.'

'Yes, but how would he have appeared on the network?' Nicola pressed him further. 'We know that time runs differently there, we all experienced that.'

'Are you suggesting she has been taken to the faerie realm?' Azuradien nearly choked on the words.

'Has she?' asked Lorcan.

'No, what I'm suggesting…' Nicola threw a warning look in Lorcan's direction, '… is that there is a place that has similar defences. A place separated from time.'

'Do not the imps have similar powers to your own? Are they not distant cousins to the faerie?' Lorcan allowed his condescension full rein.

'We are nothing alike,' said Azuradien. 'You are trying to discredit us.'

Lorcan smiled at Azuradien with arrogant defiance.

'I care nothing for you or your reputation,' said Lorcan. Michael felt Lorcan's breath as if the words were being whispered into his own ears. 'You damn yourself with each word you utter.'

Ashley was paying no attention to the conversation about hidden realms. She was sitting forward with her head to the side not even looking at the network. 'Go back to the moment when Michael first collapsed,' she said. When the network stopped on the correct moment, Ashley looked to Michael. 'She's frantic here. She wants to keep strong, as if her ability to keep things under control would impact your ability to pull through.' To Joseph, Ashley said, 'I can hardly see her, but I can feel her here. Can you zoom in? I don't know… unravel Michael a bit? I think Michael was onto something. Focus on this moment. She reached out to Michael here and that has left a trace.'

'Michael,' said Lorcan. 'If you get me close enough, I can track the girl.' Lorcan turned to speak to Joseph. 'Listen to your niece, try to separate her signature before it fades further. If she's in a place where time is distorted, every moment that we allow to slip past in mindless debate she may experience an eternity of torment.' This thought hadn't occurred to Michael. The need to get moving was doing nothing for his anxiety levels. 'She's wrapped around each one of you, but her scent is strongest on your son, her dog and,' Lorcan scowled and levelled his gaze at Ashul, 'on the warrior.'

* * *

Dana's eyes burned from watching the blank white space that surrounded her. She had tried shutting her eyes but felt the walls close in the moment she allowed her eyelids to droop. She wasn't certain what she despised more: the claustrophobic conditions or the numbing cold that pressed into her body when the walls contracted around her.

Through nothing more than the desire to oppose her constraints, she periodically pushed herself to her feet and approached the walls. She dug her heels in, braced herself and leant against the wall, resisting the wall's movement as she was slowly forced back into what she thought of as the centre of the room.

The whole process was degrading. She was being treated like a child who needed to be placed back into the naughty corner until she learned her lessons. It hadn't worked when she was younger and she'd be damned if it was going to work now. Gritting her teeth, refusing to utter a sound, she wrapped her hands in the sleeves of her top to prevent her skin from being burnt and then stubbornly pressed against the walls. Slowly but inexorably, the dimensions of her containment constricted until they were crushing her shoulders and hips. The cold leached out of her through any and all points of contact. Sometimes, she sat there for what felt like minutes, other times she could only endure seconds before the aching cold forced her to relent. This time she was going for the record.

It was the snickering of the doll, almost lost amidst the sound of her own breathing, that made her drop her hands. She stopped moving and waited.

Nothing.

The brief sound of the doll's laughter had sent her heart rate through the roof. This small break in her routine was almost a blessing.

It would be the monotony of this place that would break her; she found it maddening. The level of light never changed. If she kicked the wall, the noise it made was so muffled that unless she held her breath, she heard nothing.

She remained standing, wanting to be ready for whatever the doll had in store for her next, refusing to ask the doll what it wanted. She'd been hoping it would reveal itself to tease and taunt her. If it did, she would have at least had that to ignore.

But the doll did not taunt her.

Again, there was nothing.

Nothing to focus on. Nothing to oppose.

Even forcing the walls to close in on her seemed like a childish act of petulance.

Dana lifted her palms to her face, trying to force some water into her dry, stinging eyes. She stood with her feet braced apart so that she could anticipate the wall's closure and drop her hands before she became encased in a custom-made coffin.

The sharp ring of a knife being pulled from a block sung around her.

She spun about in search for the source of the noise, but there was still nothing to see. Dana tried to calm her racing heart because she was finding it difficult to hear anything above the pounding in her ears. Her hearing was so muffled by the properties of this cell, it felt like she was wearing noise-cancelling headphones.

She tried to unblock her ears. Although she felt her ears click, the creak of the tendons in her jaw were somehow louder than when she'd clapped her hands together in front of her face. Yet over and above it all she heard, with crystal clarity, the whoosh of the blade slicing through the air inches from her left ear.

She was unable to move fast enough and the edge of the protruding blade caught against her shoulder. Before she had time to register the pain, the blade had retracted into the wall.

So the game was being stepped up a notch. She took a deep breath, trying to relish the sound for its strength, but instead cringed at her own weakness.

A drop of her blood ran down the wall. She almost laughed to herself: at least she had a small spot of red to focus on now. She wondered how much more of her blood would decorate her prison before the doll made its purpose clear.

She had to believe that torture for torture's sake was not the doll's only intention.

Surely it had to be more than that.

Surely.

Camouflage

Michael had no difficulty finding the variance in the air pressure. He'd noticed the thick heavy quality as soon as they entered the second realm. He was unsure whether he was getting better at detecting the change or whether the change was so significant now that anyone could perceive the difference if they knew what they were looking for.

He could feel the clock ticking.

'Michael, I have sent the bonded to scan ahead,' said Ashul. 'I believe there is little doubt that we are in the right area.' His words were meant to calm him, but Michael was already well aware of where the bonded were at any given time.

The air pressed against Michael's skin in a way that made moving forward draining. On each exhale, he could feel the air pooling around his face, heated from its time within his body. Once he knew what he was looking for, the disturbance was hard to miss.

When Ashul confirmed that a large contingent of imps had massed in an area of the second plane just ahead, Michael was torn between riding towards the force and returning home as per the plan.

'You will not be able to reach her from this realm,' said Lorcan before Michael had time to decide either way. 'This place reeks of imp magic. Her scent is here, but it is also not here.' Lorcan was sniffing the air beside him. His eyes were glowing a dark red.

Michael was ready to protest. But Lorcan continued as if he'd heard Michael's thoughts. 'I have no doubt that your sister is being held in this place,' said Lorcan. 'Her scent is very clear to me, but the avenue to get to her is not. The imps have hidden the entrance somewhere else, somewhere in the first realm. This is much the same way that the faeries have their realm concealed. If we want to get in undetected, we will need the faeries' magic.'

Michael said, 'Are you saying that with all of your power, and that of the bonded, we cannot get past a group of these imps? I know what you're capable of.' He was feeling desperate to act.

'You know nothing of my capabilities,' Lorcan said. 'Believe me, restraint is not something I exercise often. But what I am trying to tell you is that I cannot guarantee your sister's safety if we use force alone to get to her.'

'Ashul, speak to your charge,' said Lorcan through clenched teeth, looking like he would like nothing more than to rip his way through the horde of imps.

'Given enough time, we could overcome the imps,' said Ashul. 'Especially here in the second realm where our power is strongest. But our objective is not to destroy them. We need to secure Dana's safety first. We must find the entrance in the first realm, then work out a way to get past their guard. Michael, trust me in this. They could relocate her if we alert them to our presence.' Ashul then spoke also to Michael through the mental link: *Trust me. I will secure her safety.*

Michael knew he was outnumbered; he also knew they were right.

'Lorcan, can you use this location to find the entrance in the first plane?' asked Michael. He needed to know they were somehow closer to getting Dana out.

'I can.'

Reluctantly, Michael flipped back into the first realm.

* * *

Joseph was staring at Sarah's network, working with Ashley to isolate Dana's essence, trying to find a way to reconnect with his daughter. Since she'd been taken by Marcus, there was a hole inside him where his daughter's energy used to flow. The absence dragged at him, and if this was how he felt when he was still connected to the rest of his family, how must Dana be feeling being completely cut off and alone? Joseph didn't want to think about it, he just needed to be able to let her know that they were all still here. He needed to be able to send her his love.

The network had been expanded so it now covered the entire kitchen and the family room ceiling. Sarah hadn't added any territory. She'd just zoomed in as Ashley had suggested, which sort of worked as amplification for both Joseph and Ashley.

Joseph would run the network backwards then forwards with Ashley telling him where to stop. She didn't watch the network and had admitted to Joseph that she really didn't see much more than a set of multicoloured, interconnecting lines. But there was no doubt that she could feel what was running through the network.

When Ashley felt Dana strongly, she would ask him to stop. She could even tell Joseph who Dana was connected to at the time because she felt Dana's emotions in that moment. Using this method, they had been able to identify a number of times when Dana was interconnected with another. At first glance, her amber signature could not be seen, but with a little bit of careful manipulation, wisps of her essence became visible.

Dana's energy danced around Michael like spun sugar and it was just as fine and delicate. Each time Joseph reached for her pattern, the amber would roll around his fingers like a cold mist. He clenched his hands in frustration. Everybody hovering over his shoulders wasn't helping him.

Ashley moved to his side and offered him a cold can of Coke.

How do you grasp thin air? Joseph thought as he traced his finger through the condensation beading the surface of the can. He rubbed the water between his fingers. *You couldn't, so why would you try?* 'We need Michael, Ashul and Sheba together,' he muttered. 'Then I think we may have a chance.'

Michael had just returned from the second plane. Joseph could hear Michael talking to Ashul in the front of the house, so he called out to him. 'Michael, we need you here.'

Michael came at a run with Ashul a couple of steps behind him. Before Michael got his hopes up, Joseph jumped in. He couldn't stand the hopeful expression on his face when they'd found so little. 'We haven't got much, but we do have a plan. What did you find?'

Joseph listened to the details of what they'd found and understood that they still needed to come up with a way to get past the imps guarding Dana. But they had found where they were keeping Dana and that was a huge step in the right direction.

'We're hoping Azuradien will have some suggestions,' said Michael. 'The bonded can destroy the imps. It doesn't matter if they're in the first or the second realm, they can get to them. There's no subtlety in what they do. The imps will know we're coming and that will put Dana in jeopardy. Shame we don't have a great big wooden horse handy. Have you had any luck? Have you found Dana's signature? Can you reach her?'

'Yes and no,' Joseph said.

Joseph had been looking at the network for so long he sometimes forgot what he was looking at. It had been created to be a representation of their life signatures. By the fact that Ashley could read the emotions of the person based on their signature on the network they knew it was more than just a projection of their energies. Joseph had gotten so wrapped up in what he was seeing on the network that he'd completely forgotten where all of the base information was coming from. He saw Michael on the grid as a tightly bound ball of bright cobalt. When he turned and looked at Michael, that same cobalt was visible dancing around him. It wasn't exactly an aura, but that was the best word he could find to describe it. As he was watching the blue shimmer around Michael, Joseph said, 'But I think I have an idea. As much as it pains me to say it, we also need Azuradien.'

'I expected him to be here,' said Michael. 'Telling you what was possible and what was not. Where is he?'

'The faeries are upstairs, strengthening the resonance of the potion,' said Joseph. 'We had a moment while you were gone when the boys became very agitated.' Joseph paused in case Michael wanted to fill him in on any details. He didn't want to push Michael too far, with him trying to keep emotions in check when his sister was being held captive.

There were two holes in the plaster that stood as evidence to Joseph's own inability to keep it together.

'Anyway,' said Joseph. 'Brent has given them a calming tea. Dave and Tony are looking after them just in case they need to be restrained. Once we get Dana back, we have to find a better way to control their condition.' The boys' equilibrium was the furthest thing from his mind. 'I have an idea about how to trap Dana's signature.' Joseph went to the sliding door and let Sheba in. He didn't need to call for her – she'd been sitting listlessly next to the back door since Dana had been taken.

'I haven't been able to grasp Dana on the network,' said Joseph. 'She's there though. Ashley can feel her, and I can see her if I tease your signature open enough. The problem is that what remains of her essence is gossamer thin. If I try to reach for it, it disperses.' Joseph was scanning the network for a Dana hotspot to show as an example.

'Just like condensation forms on a cold surface, Dana's essence should gravitate and condense – for want of a better term – on you,' said Joseph. 'I'm coming to believe the individual perceives even the smallest of touches on these lines on some level, so I need to be extremely careful.' Joseph placed the three of them in the centre of the network. 'Don't look for her or grasp at anything, let's just see what happens.'

Joseph walked around the edges of the grid, carefully unwinding filaments of amber that laced through so many aspects of the network. When the thin fibres broke apart, Sheba, who was closest, without prompting gently nudged her nose in their direction. Thin wisps of amber swirled around her head and settled in place. Joseph worked through this process many times, sometimes shifting the time frame of the network. Michael, Ashul and Sheba were soon covered in a layer of fine amber cobwebs.

'The boys are…' Nicola said as she entered the room, but she stopped short and gazed in wonder at what was in front of her.

'We have managed to stabilise the boys,' Brent finished for her. 'They're watching a movie upstairs. Azuradien will be down shortly. I know you don't have much time for him, Joseph, but he was an amazing help up there. He has a deftness of touch that we just don't have.'

Sarah's reaction when she saw Michael, Ashul and Sheba covered in a shifting layer of amber mirrored Nicola's. Her mouth opened slightly in wonder and she moved to Ashley's side and hugged her. Tears were welling up in Ashley's eyes. 'I can feel her, Uncle Joe,' said Ashley. 'Not the memory of her, I swear I feel *her*.'

Joseph could feel the difference too, like Dana was about to walk into the room.

'Okay, so now I'm at a loss,' said Joseph. 'If I try to touch the fibres, they'll disintegrate under my fingers.' Joseph sat there, uncertain for the first time since the process had begun.

'If you would allow me, I think I can be of assistance,' said Azuradien. Nobody had heard him enter the room. He no longer strode around like a crazy zealot and seemed genuinely humbled by what they had created with the network.

'Go on,' said Joseph, nodding his assent.

A gentle breeze rose up around the room, seemingly to come from all corners at once. Azuradien raised his hands slightly and his fingers moved like he was conducting a complicated orchestra. With small gestures, the delicate breeze eased the scattered filaments so that they slowly moved to lie in one place.

'Joseph, I believe if touched, these small aspects of Dana will once again disperse,' said Azuradien.

Sarah nodded. 'They are different somehow,' she said. 'I can't tie them to the network. I wish I could.' Her regret was palpable. 'They come from different timelines. If I did anything to anchor them to the network, the integrity of the structure would be compromised.' Sarah didn't need to explain herself; Joseph had already come to a similar conclusion.

'But if they are wrapped back within a single signature…' Azuradien raised his hands with palms up. 'I really do not know what will happen, but I believe it is the best option.'

'I think that could work,' said Sarah, excitement in her voice. She moved to stand next to Joseph.

'Dana's link to Michael is the strongest.' Joseph focused on the section of the network where Michael shone with his cobalt blue light. 'Michael, we're going to need to play with your energy signature a bit. Are you okay with that?'

'Dad, I just want to be able to let Dana know we're coming. Do anything you need to.' Michael responded just as Joseph knew he would.

'Tell me the moment something doesn't feel quite right.' With similar hand gestures to Azuradien's, Joseph coaxed Michael's signature to spread, to expand ever so slightly. He had used this technique to tease out the few amber striations that had existed in different points on the grid, but now he was pushing it a little further. He was trying to open a hole in Michael's signature, one just large enough to coax the gossamer threads of Dana's signature into. On a couple of occasions, Sarah reached forward and gripped Joseph's hand, gently guiding his movements. This was a delicate operation and sweat was already running down Joseph's face. Quick checks on Michael showed that from his end everything was fine. Michael gave a quick thumbs up to continue. When Joseph felt satisfied with the space created, he nodded to Azuradien.

With tiny flicks of his fingers, Azuradien coaxed the amber threads to lift and move towards Michael. Azuradien's touch was so light that Joseph could barely detect the shift in the energy flow around him. The small hairs of the back of Joseph's arms were standing on end. The way Azuradien used the energy was so subtle it didn't register on Sarah's network. And it was this feather light touch that allowed Azuradien to move the thin fibres without destroying them.

It was a slow process. Azuradien executed the task like he was performing microsurgery on a brain. He worked slowly, methodically. And he did not miss one fibre. He gave Joseph a short nod to say he was done. In the centre of Michael's signature where there had been the smallest of holes now there was a twisting ball of amber.

Taking a breath to steady himself, Joseph wiped the sweat off his forehead then carefully allowed Michael's signature to tighten around the amber fibres. Joseph had no idea what to expect. His heart was racing.

When Michael gasped and his hand dropped onto Joseph's shoulder, he nearly had a heart attack.

'I have her, Dad,' said Michael. 'I have Dana.'

Ashley moved to Michael's side and placed her hand on his arm. She spoke quietly, yet everyone in the room heard her, such was the weight of power behind her words. 'We are coming, Dana. We are coming.' Calm determination and reassurance flooded the room. 'Be strong. We love you, and we're coming.'

* * *

Dana had lost all concept of time. She didn't know if she'd been imprisoned for hours or days. It couldn't have been weeks surely. She hadn't been given any food or water and she'd be dead if it had been weeks with no water, wouldn't she?

Her vow of silence hadn't lasted as long as she'd hoped. When the blade had come up through the floor and nicked the edge of her foot, she hissed out an obscenity. Now, she found she was mumbling conversations to herself.

What disturbed Dana the most was her lack of awareness of the duration of this captivity. She looked at the walls. Tiny red dots now marred the previously uniform nondescript surface.

She calculated that if she was hit with every third strike and each strike came roughly every twenty minutes, then she'd been locked away for at least two days, and that did not include the time where the doll had left her confined in the constant shifting space.

It felt so much longer. But she refused to just sit around and be manipulated. She was learning how to dodge the blades. She was sure the doll was suffering from an obvious lack of imagination. Once the blades had started to come, they soon fell into a fairly predictable pattern. High, right, low, high, high, left, and then repeat. There was always some variance to the pattern, but not quite enough.

Dana was able to anticipate each strike, then dodge it mostly. She allowed herself to get nicked every so often, so the doll didn't realise she was onto it. The only problem was orientation. With the constant shifting around, left and right became confused. But there was an easy fix for that. Each 'wall' now had a small letter of identification written in her own blood – smudged and haphazard – seemingly random marks to those not aware of what they were looking for.

She waited for the next low strike, balanced on the balls of her feet. With a sharp hiss, the white blade appeared, barely detectable. Not allowing herself a moment's hesitation, she dropped and landed on the flat of the blade with her left knee. A loud *crack*. She waited, not moving. There was no sound of the blade retracting.

Dana lifted her knee. There was a small cut in her jeans. A long white blade lay on the ground almost invisible against the bright white of the floor.

With extreme care, she used the blade to cut a strip of material from the bottom of her jeans and began fashioning a makeshift handle by wrapping the pieces of fabric around the blade. This was so similar to what she'd done in the forest outside of the faerie realm a lifetime ago, the irony was not lost on her.

Ever so gently, Dana ran the blade along the edge of her cage, looking for a point of weakness. She tried to be quiet, but the action produced a thin screech as she dragged the blade along the corners where the walls joined.

'You don't think I have tried that? You won't find a way out.'

Dana knew Marcus' voice even when it was a whisper. The strange acoustics of the place made his voice bounce around. Panicked, she spun around this way and that, looking first over one shoulder then her other. There was no-one in the room with her.

'Are you being held captive too?'

'No, I just enjoy the solitude, the occasional sharp jab just to keep things interesting.' Even muffled, Dana could hear his sneer. He sounded like he was whispering from right behind her.

'Marcus, what's happening? What do they want?'

'They want what they've always wanted. Power.'

'Who? The doll? Your parents? The imps?'

'All of them. All of you. Don't think you're any better. I've seen how you greedily grasp at the breach, sucking at the energy. You're all the same. Pigs at a trough. You disgust me.'

'Marcus, we're just trying to defend ourselves. The doll needs to be stopped. And you need to get away from your parents.'

The conversation died out for a time. Dana wasn't sure if Marcus would respond again.

When Marcus finally did speak, Dana didn't think the words were for her. 'I'll never be able to get away.' His words were so very quiet. 'You'll never be able to get away.'

Dana tried to speak to Marcus further, but he steadfastly refused to engage with her. She needed to understand why he'd been imprisoned too. It made no sense to her – he was working with the doll, wasn't he?

He'd helped capture her. But he'd also been strung up in his own home with blood being drained from him. She had wondered if it had all been staged. Just part of an elaborate trap, like Ashul had suggested, a manipulation to get them isolated while the imps struck. It was possible. But what was indisputable was that Marcus' parents routinely tortured their own child while he was sleeping. And they'd been doing so for some time. Ashley had been certain of that.

Dana remembered the impact on Michael when the doll had been visiting him for just a few weeks. Marcus had been enduring the torment of his parents for years, long before the doll sunk its claws into him as well. She couldn't help but feel sorry for Marcus. Because it wasn't even close to being the same as what Michael had suffered.

Michael had a family that he could turn to, a family who would do anything to help him. Michael's monster was an evil, otherworldly creature somehow come back into the world. Marcus' demons were far worse – he was being tormented by the ones who were supposed to love and protect him.

Dana was so lost in her thoughts that she forgot to be ready for the next blade strike.

There was a slight displacement of air and a sharp sensation of pain in her left shoulder. It felt like the blade had gone all the way through her, but when she checked, the wound seemed to be only a centimetre or so deep. She kept her hand against her shoulder, wincing slightly, but maintaining the pressure, hoping the bleeding would stop quickly. She refused to look at the cut again. She couldn't afford to faint.

Tears ran down her face. Not for herself, but for the boy who didn't even understand the horror of what had been done to him.

She huddled on the ground, waiting for the next blade to come from the roof. She had both arms wrapped around herself, softly rocking back and forth, wanting to close her eyes and imagine herself some place other than where she was. An image of Michael draping his arm over her shoulder came so sharply into her mind that she felt the weight of his hand wrapping around her. Dana closed her eyes. The feeling of love and reassurance that washed over her was too much: her composure broke.

She was sobbing quietly when she heard Ashley whisper into her mind.

'We are coming, Dana. We are coming!'

'Be strong.'

'We love you, and we're coming.'

* * *

The doll was watching the girl with growing enjoyment. So strong. So resilient. When tested by isolation, she'd pushed back, repeatedly forcing herself to be placed in confinement so crushingly close that most would lose their minds. But the girl saw this as some strange point of contest, a way to rebel. She'd refused to cry out in anger or fear.

When the blades pierced the walls of her cage, her resolve for silence was finally broken. It would have preferred a plea for release, even a cry of pain, but the girl just hissed out an obscenity.

When the girl dropped onto the blade and snapped it from the wall, Anarcus nearly ordered her crushed completely.

Insolent cow.

But It stilled the rage inside, and grudgingly had to admire her resilience. So very different to the husk of a human It had imprisoned next to her. The boy It could understand. He would continue to fight as long as the carrot of power was waved before him. The girl was more difficult to manipulate.

For nothing more than the perverse pleasure It received when humans fought, It allowed the walls to thin just enough for them to hear one another. The conversation did not have the amount of rage that It had anticipated, but the impact on the girl was delightful nevertheless. Her spirit was being slowly crushed by each word that fell from the boy's mouth.

She was finally starting to understand her predicament. It would not be the walls that crushed her, it would be the despair of her situation.

These humans, all that was needed to break them was to isolate them from each other and then their strength faded away, wilting like fruit cut from the vine.

The girl would continue to struggle, using up what little energy remained to her, pointlessly fighting against her captivity. Conversely, her brother could not use his considerable strength for fear of succumbing to the Nachzehrer poison, an unexpected and frustrating turn of events but entertaining in its own way. Any situation could be turned to your advantage if you had had millennia of imprisonment to run through endless scenarios.

The boy being poisoned was an affront that would be rectified in due course, but the unpredictable twist was how it had hamstrung him. His fight to maintain his humanity was weakening not only himself but the bonded as well. As long as this circumstance did not change, the boy would remain neutralised.

The mother would continue to waste her energy fearing for her young. She had the potential to wipe her enemies out if she would just focus on what she had to win and not what she had to lose.

The rest of the blood were weak, their powers defensive at best. It would just pick them off one by one. The warrior would be driven insane with his inability to protect those in his care.

Then, finally, It would have what It required to make the realms one.

Ashul would be kneeling before It and begging for mercy.

It sent another blade towards the girl huddled on the floor, smiling as the edge ran down the muscle of her shoulder. It turned away as the tears ran down the girl's face. She was broken.

It had been easier than expected.

It could now focus on the mother.

* * *

'Okay, we need to get to Dana, and get to her fast.' Michael didn't want to go into the details of the flash of pain he'd felt and the feeling of claustrophobia, of isolation. He didn't want everybody to lose their shit, but he needed them to understand how important it was for them to stop fighting one another and find a way to get to Dana.

Ashul said, 'Azuradien, do you believe you will be able to access the entrance to the imps' realm if we get you close enough to it?' Ashul's manner was abrupt – he'd read all he needed to from Michael's thoughts.

'Their magic is similar to ours—' Azuradien started.

Ashul interrupted by slamming his hands down on the table in a mixture of anger and frustration. 'A yes or no, we need to act quickly,' he said.

'Then, yes,' said the faerie king. 'I may need Nicola's assistance, but I will be able to detect the entrance. With one or both of our magics, we will get you through.'

'But how can we get close enough?' asked Azuradien. 'If the second realm is swarming with imps, I think we can assume the entrance in the first realm will be likewise guarded.' Azuradien looked around the room for insight.

'I can disguise myself, hide behind her scent,' Lorcan replied quickly. Michael appreciated his ability to turn the bullshit off. 'But I think if they smell the girl outside of her cage, it will put them all on guard. I may not get close enough before they realise something is amiss.' Lorcan began pacing the room.

Brent raised his hand to seek some clarification. 'What do you mean you can hide behind her scent?'

Lorcan waved a hand at Brent dismissively. 'I can imitate the scent of all of those I have… sampled.'

'You sampled my daughter?' said Joseph. Sparks were racing over his knuckles.

'She bled into my mouth when the faeries planted the destructive seed in my throat. So yes, I have a sample of her blood in my system, as I do your son's. Can we move on?' Despite remaining in his human appearance, Lorcan still managed to project fury barely held in check.

'How would you "hide" behind her scent? I still don't quite understand.' Brent was following Lorcan back and forth. They paced the room together.

'The imps are near blind,' explained Lorcan. 'They are like magical bats with a basic level of intellect at most.'

'Their intellect is at the same level as that of the faeries,' Azuradien interjected.

'Your point?' Lorcan looked at Azuradien with scorn. When the faerie king didn't bite, he moved on. 'Barely above a base level. They rely on their smell as the faeries rely on their warped view of history. They will ignore what makes logical sense in deference to their sense of smell. Therefore, if I masked my smell as if I were Dana, they would for a time believe that I was in fact Dana.'

'The Nachzehrer have been around the area,' said Ashul. 'Could Michael and I get though if Michael allowed his balance to shift. If he allowed the poison to activate in his blood. Would they think that we were indeed Nachzehrer?'

'The poison would take over your system before you got close enough,' Azuradien said, more calmly than Michael would have expected at such a dangerous suggestion. 'And it wouldn't get Nicola and myself near the entrance.' Azuradien was stroking his beard again. 'But something like that would cloud the waters. Lorcan, you killed a number of imps tonight. Do you have a "sample" of their blood?'

'I am not the monster you think I am,' said Lorcan. 'I would not allow a drop of their blood to pass my lips.' Michael caught the faintest hint of red in Lorcan's eyes.

'Yet the girl's blood you keep in your system to savour at will.'

'Her blood was freely given, as was the boy's,' Lorcan said with quiet menace.

'There is a truckload of dead imps lying around back,' said Michael. 'Can we use that?' Michael was getting desperate. He could see the brief truce between the faeries and Lorcan crumbling. Lorcan shook his head. 'What if we mixed our blood? You have said the faeries are distantly related to the imps. Mix it with some of yours, some of ours. Surely that will keep them guessing long enough for us to get past.' When neither of them spoke, Michael knew he was onto something. 'I think it would work,' said Lorcan. 'The imps would smell their own or a near enough cousin to confuse them for a time. The doll has made all sorts of allegiances. The scent around the area will be confusing. Yes, I think it will work.' Lorcan smiled at Michael with the tips of his teeth clearly visible. 'Your uncle could mix a kind of camouflaging spray to mask our true scents.'

Michael was looking around the room expecting a little more enthusiasm. 'What? What have I missed?'

'The faeries are guarded by a magical protection, as are the bonded,' said Ashul. 'It is what made the bonded invulnerable to the Nachzehrer poison. There is no way to get to the faeries' blood.'

'More of your covenants!' Lorcan growled. 'I remember a time when the faeries fought and *died* for the causes they believed in. I remember a time when the faeries aided the "great mage" as he slew my people! You hide behind this magical shield and your twisted covenant.' Lorcan shook with fury. He'd walked towards the faerie king as he spoke so that only a few centimetres separated them.

'I cannot change the way we are made,' Azuradien said calmly. Malcarielle by his side looked less convinced.

'You, the greatest faerie of your time, cannot override a piddling convention.' Lorcan spat the words in his face. Azuradien shook his head.

'No, but you did once, did you not?' said Lorcan, seeming to be goading the king. 'When your pride got the better of you. When you attempted to strike the killing blow.'

'How do you know these things?' said Azuradien. But before Lorcan could answer, Azuradien said simply, 'I paid the price for my transgression.'

'There is no price to be paid here, old man. No eels to burrow under your skin. Just a life to be saved. And you get to take your best shot at me in the meantime. It's a win-win for you.' Lorcan stood at seven feet, his wings thrashed at the air. Michael could once more see the tendrils of inky smoke rising off his shoulders.

Azuradien held his ground. Malcarielle blazed at his side, almost incandescent with the conflicting emotions that caused her powers to flare.

'No, not you, little one,' said Lorcan as he smiled at Malcarielle. Then, striking as fast as a snake, Lorcan reached forward and grasped Azuradien's arm. He lifted a thin blade he kept in a sheath on his forearm. 'I respect your restraint, I really do. But we don't have the time. The girl suffers for your inflexibility.'

'You cannot breach my protections,' Azuradien said calmly even as Lorcan held his arm.

'Oh, but I can, because the boy can,' said Lorcan. 'I have his memories from that time.'

Before Azuradien could react, Lorcan drew the knife over the scars that marked his forearms. A thin line of blood welled up along Azuradien's skin. Before the shield reactivated, Lorcan grabbed a drinking glass from the bench to catch the thin stream of blood as it dripped from the skin.

He wiped the blade on his pants then handed the blade hilt first to Azuradien.

'Do not cut too deep, old man,' the vampire said. Lorcan offered his own arm for the blade. Too shocked to protest, Azuradien ran the knife along the inside of the vampire's arm. The line was not as clean and straight as the one Lorcan had made. Azuradien's hand was noticeably shaking.

'Now, don't tell me you didn't enjoy that,' said Lorcan as he retrieved his knife from the king. He turned to Brent and held his arm out. 'You might want to be a bit careful with mine, it has a hunger of its own.'

Michael was impressed with his uncle's composure. He paused for only a second.

'Nicola, can I have saline and some vodka for a mixing solution?' asked Brent. 'Any eyedroppers that you have, and a clear glass jug.'

Brent cleared a space on the bench. Michael saw him reach for a pair of disposable gloves from the cupboard under the sink, then settled for a disinfectant wipe for the bench instead. Michael remembered the ease that Lorcan's blood had eaten through the roots of the oak tree, so he understood his uncle's decision to forgo the gloves. They were going to spray this concoction over their bodies anyway. Any thought of handling the blood in a sanitary fashion was already mute.

Brent placed a stainless-steel bowl under Lorcan's arm, now dripping blood.

'I trust that this is not a danger to us,' said Brent, not even looking up. He grabbed the bottle that Nicola placed on the bench and started pouring, then mixing, a collection of ingredients together.

Brent muttered as he worked. He nicked the inside of his own arm and allowed a couple of drops of blood to fall into the solution. After an impatient hand gesture, the glass of the faerie's blood was placed in his hands. He grabbed one eyedropper and measured out a couple of millilitres and added these few drops into the solution. Brent gave the bottle a gentle swirl. The liquid had a light pink tinge with two distinctly separate swirls of red seen through the glass.

With a fresh set of eyedroppers, Brent took a deep breath and withdrew an equal amount of Lorcan's blood, being careful not to knock the bowl. Holding the droppers over the glass, he measured out just one drop. Nothing happened. Brent mumbled, chanting something under his breath. He carefully allowed another drop to fall.

The blood didn't disperse into the liquid, but instead pooled on the top like thick oil. Another drop, and the dark burgundy oil now covered the entire surface of the glass. Brent paused, waiting for something more to happen. He moved the eyedropper back to the stainless-steel bowl but his eyes never left the glass jug in front of him.

Michael felt a little underwhelmed by the whole thing. He wasn't certain what he'd been expecting, but nothing so mundane as this watery mix of pink liquid.

He looked to his uncle and noticed the lines of concentration on Brent's face. He continued to murmur away. The dark liquid on top started to swirl. The faint traces of Azuradien's blood spun away from the darker mass. There was a moment of resistance as the pink swirled first one way then the other. At the rate the vampire's blood was multiplying, the pink wash was soon overwhelmed.

Lorcan shrugged, his mouth curled up into an apologetic smile. 'I am what I am.'

Michael thought he'd understood what the vampire was. But even Lorcan's blood was predatory, those two drops of blood seeking out other traces of life and extinguishing them. Michael had a moment of insight into the hunger that Lorcan must battle just by being near them.

Michael realised that he had some of that very same blood running in his veins. What stopped it from overwhelming him?

Michael also had a zombie infection kept at bay with his own strange method of control. He'd struggled to maintain the balancing act against that infection for the last couple of days, and he was aware that he wouldn't be able to continue to do so for much longer. He was not Lorcan. He was not his mother. Absolute control was something that he could manage only for a short period of time.

Smoke always in his mind, shared her strength with him: *You will manage for as long as you must. Remember, you have achieved something that no other before you can claim.*

Ashul, always in tune with Michael, understood the urgency he was feeling. 'So do we have this camouflage, or not?'

Lorcan sniffed the glass bottle and inclined his head as he extracted a couple of drops of the dark liquid. The vampire turned to Brent. After a brief nod of assent, the liquid was placed on the back of Brent's neck.

Michael felt his vision twisting.

Sheba barked and snapped in Brent's direction. Michael allowed his vision to shift, felt the colour of his eyes change.

Before him still stood his uncle, but shimmering under the surface was a dark-winged silhouette blotting out almost all signs of his humanity. His uncle dwelled somewhere within the dark, leathery-skinned creature, but only traces of him were visible.

Michael smiled. 'We have ourselves some camouflage alright.'

Transformation

Dana had broken off another blade by the time the room turned dark.

She sat with her eyes hooded for at least ten minutes before she was convinced the light level wasn't going to improve. Unless the rules had changed, she didn't really care whether the lights were on or not. She waited patiently – never having been scared of the dark before – and listened to the sounds around her. The swish to her left confirmed that she could still anticipate the direction of the next blade as long as she didn't allow herself to get turned around. She was really quite amazed at how in tune her body was with her surroundings. Dana could feel whether the room was closing in on her: a slight change in temperature would give her as much warning as she needed.

When she detected a shift behind her, she spun in that direction, not because she feared the walls closing in but because she felt warmth, like a breath on the back of her neck. She held her arms up in a defensive position, a blade in each hand, straining to hear something in the darkness. But there were no further sounds, and the warm gust of air did not come again. The weight of holding the blades raised became too much for her, so she dropped her fists down onto her hips.

When the muscles in her legs began to shake, lowering herself slowly to the ground to rest on one knee seemed like the best option. Dana was worried that her legs would start cramping. The question was – how long could she keep going if her muscles were already fatigued. This kind of adrenaline high was unsustainable. With no way to boost her blood sugar, she would soon become slow and lethargic.

As she knelt on the floor, Dana periodically swapped her legs to keep the blood flow going, all the while listening for the swish of the next blade. No longer sure of her position, she didn't move when the warm air once again blew against the back of her neck.

She'd been straining to hear something for so long that the quiet rang in her ears with an intensity all of its own. She counted to herself, and when she reached sixty twice, and heard nothing, she decided to try to reach Marcus again.

'Marcus?' Dana whispered into the dark. Her voice sounded weak to her own ears. She tried again, this time forcing herself to speak at a normal pitch. She placed one of her blades on the ground and tentatively reached forward, suddenly needing to know where the nearest wall was. She had a feeling she was going to have to move quickly and jumping forward and knocking herself out wasn't ideal.

'Marcus, are you still there?'

A coldly detached voice replied, 'And where exactly do you expect I may have gone?' While his words were bitchy, they didn't project the level of disdain she'd come to expect from him.

'What is the purpose of this?' said Dana. 'Is this all just an elaborate setup for the doll's amusement or does it have a reason for doing this?'

'You really don't have any clue. Everything it does has purpose.'

'Will this cage be opened? They'll have to come and check on us at some time? Give us something to drink at least?'

'What makes you think you haven't been checked on?' said Marcus. 'Your captors can smell everything they need to know about you. They'll keep you running at this level until you collapse and then they'll allow you to regain some strength. Then do it all over again.' The despondency in his voice convinced Dana that he was telling the truth more than any pronouncement of sincerity.

'My family is coming,' said Dana. 'They'll get us both out of here.' Dana was saying this as much for herself as for her captors.

'No-one is coming. No-one ever comes,' said Marcus. 'You're locked in a cage, hidden outside of time, on the cusp of two realms.' His voice dropped and he was talking more to himself than to Dana. 'We no longer even exist.'

The back of Dana's neck prickled. She'd felt the strange warmth against her cheek as Marcus was speaking. Keeping her breathing steady, she waited until she couldn't stay still any longer. She tried to ease up onto her feet, unlock her stiff muscles, but she was temporarily unable to move, terrified of what might be in the dark with her. Childhood fears of drawing the attention of the bogeyman floated through her head. If she stayed still and silent, she would be safe. She blinked her eyes repeatedly, trying to force herself to break the paralysis.

'Marcus, my family is coming.' Dana spoke aloud to drive the fear away. She spoke to protest the paralysis that gripped her. She spoke to force her body to respond to her commands.

'And they will get us out,' she said. She pushed herself off the ground and grasped the hilt of one broken blade in both of her hands. While she had been speaking, her left hand had been fumbling around trying to find the second blade. *They will get us out,* she thought, *and if they cannot I will get us both out myself.* The confirmation that something had been in the cage with her was evident by the missing blade. It wasn't just her imagination playing tricks on her, dredging up childhood nightmares. Something had reached next to her leg and removed the knife, its breath warming her face as it did so.

She should feel disgusted that something had been crawling around with her in the dark, close enough to touch her, sniffing at her body, to get a sense of her state of mind, her wellbeing. The damn thing might still be in there with her – this should have made her feel vulnerable, but it did not.

A stupid mistake had been made. Such a stupid mistake. She would be waiting now.

Knowing that there was a way in proved that there was a way out. Next time she would be the one leaving.

* * *

Using his ability to walk in both worlds, Lorcan had been able to find the location of the entrance to the imps' realm without too much fanfare. Once Michael had shown him the location in the second realm, he merely had to place a foot into the first realm and they had details of exactly where the imp had hidden their entrance. Problem solved.

It was decided that everybody was coming. No family member was going to be left behind, not this time. There was no telling whose powers were going to be needed. Dave and Tony were staying at the house to make sure the boys from soccer stayed sedated. A contingent of magical creatures had flocked to the house, and a chorus of near angelic music kept the potion positively aligned.

Malcarielle had also decided to stay, promising Michael that if the boys looked to be in any jeopardy, she would take them directly to the crystal cave in the faerie realm and keep them safe until they found a solution.

Michael was relieved. It was one less thing that he needed to worry about.

Lorcan gripped Michael's arm. 'How are you faring, Michael?' he said. 'Your blood is telling me that the Nachzehrer poison is active.'

'I can keep it contained a while longer,' said Michael. 'But this situation isn't helping. I sense the Nachzehrer want a final reckoning with the doll and that we might be playing right into their hands by going straight towards it. I wouldn't be surprised if we have to fight our way through Nachzehrer as well as imps to get to Dana.' Michael felt a weight lift off his shoulders as he said the words.

'We have only one course of action to take,' said Ashul. 'Whether it is the course our enemy wishes for us or not is irrelevant.' Ashul was checking the tack on Lightning. 'We will do what we must if the Nachzehrer attack.'

Lorcan lifted an eyebrow at Ashul. 'He likes to keep things simple, doesn't he?'

'He's that kind of guy,' said Michael. Ashul shook his head at Michael's banter with Lorcan.

'How many of us can you take at once?' asked Ashul.

'Men, or livestock?' Lorcan asked.

Ashul turned to Lorcan, bristling at the insult. 'Our horses are part of us, do not speak of them so again.'

'They may be part of you, Ashul, but they do add a little extra weight.' Lorcan ducked his head, waiting for Ashul to acknowledge the truth of his words. When Ashul did not react, Lorcan shrugged. 'I would take you and Michael first,' he said. 'The entrance is closer than you think, which makes sense. The doll would want to stay near the rift. I believe your troupe will be able to follow us. It will be quicker than me making fourteen separate journeys.' Ashul nodded his assent to the vampire.

They were standing in a small group on the back lawn of Michael's family's home. Smoke and Lightning were the only other bonded present. The rest of the bonded rode above the cloud level, monitoring the conversation through the mindlink.

'Michael, can you still feel Dana?' said Nicola.

'Yep, it's like her hand's resting on my shoulder.' Michael placed his fingers over the spot that almost tingled with her touch.

'Is she okay?' asked Nicola.

'She's being held prisoner, Mum. She needs us to get her out.'

Nicola hesitated before she replied, looking first to Michael, then at Ashul. 'Yes, let's get going.'

Nicola turned away sharply, but Michael saw the tears pooling in her eyes. 'Mum, we'll get her back.' Nicola nodded at the words, but she still didn't reply.

* * *

It had expected her to be broken by now. When the darkness enveloped her, It expected a crying child. She was blind, yet she was undeterred, with her ridiculous weapons raised. It sent an imp in to torment her, make her jump at every sound. She had spun, ready to attack, and only after a time did she drop to the ground exhausted. When the second imp crept into her little hole, she failed to even react. Good, the fire could only burn for so long.

It had to admit these children of the blood had access to reserves of strength It could almost admire. But in the end, they always broke. It turned away as she lay shaking on the ground. The imps could have their plaything soon and the dried-out husk too.

Anarcus didn't need these children as prisoners any longer. The warrior was on his way. He would soon be vulnerable.

* * *

Was it coincidence or fate that put the entrance to the imps' realm in the same bushland that grew behind their house? How many other strange creatures lived in this particular piece of scrubland? Michael thought back to the creature that had blotted the sky in the shadowland, and the grasping hands too.

And now imps.

To think he used to take runs along the trails that circled the edge of this park.

The worlds are shifting, Smoke said to Michael as she rode through the clouds above. *When you ran these trails, these creatures were far from you. These realms are hidden deep behind many layers of magic.*

'Well, they aren't hidden any longer.' Michael could hear something crawling through the branches above his head. The trees were so much taller here and the canopy so dense it blotted out the stars overhead. *You are no longer truly in the first plane.*

Was this doorway into the second plane any different to what the doll's trying to achieve? Michael asked Smoke, thinking back to the shadowland, how the edges of his vision had blurred and distorted. He didn't need to wait for an answer, realising himself how different the two really were. The imps and faeries created doorways to move from one realm to another. The doll wanted to twist the fabric of existence to merge the two realms together, distorting both, and exposing a place that shouldn't even exist in the process. There was no real comparison.

Ashul spoke from behind his shoulder and Michael jumped. 'We are all here. It is time.'

He turned to face Ashul. 'Really? We're all a little on edge here.' Michael's nerves were twisted tight, he just wanted to get moving. Having something creeping around in the trees overhead was not doing anything for his already strained nerves.

Azuradien and Nicola were trying to sense the exact nature of the magic used to separate the realms, searching the sky to look for any clue to the entrance's exact location.

Lorcan moved to Nicola's side and whispered quietly to her, 'There are a number of imps in the trees overhead. They're aware of our presence but not at this point are they alarmed.' Lorcan stepped carefully, able to move across the ground without disturbance. Michael was relieved to see that he at least had to watch his footing, showing that there were some limits to his abilities. Despite Lorcan's warnings of imps in the trees, Michael noticed that Lorcan seemed more concerned about tripping than he did being attacked by a swarm of imps angry at their territory being invaded. It must feel nice to be so invulnerable.

The movement in the canopy above them increased. The hiss of the imps could be heard as they sprung from one tree to the next.

One after another, the leathery black creatures dropped to the ground with a dull thud. Once on ground-level, their animal grace left them. They scrambled along, pulling themselves forward on the padded knuckles of their scrunched-up wings, nothing more than a lurching crawl.

Up close, in this environment, they appeared like mutated bats, scraping and hobbling over the ground, their wet noses sampling the air. A number of the creatures paused in front of Michael. He kept his body perfectly still while they sniffed at his feet. He was finding it hard to resist the urge to kick the thing, wanting to vent some of his rage at those helping to keep his sister captive. But Smoke's voice in his mind helped him still his trembling muscles. *There will come a reckoning but now is not that time.*

The camouflage spray was working. The imps barely seemed to notice their presence. They were moving as if they had purpose, almost urgently, wasting no time as they pushed past Michael and the others. Then an imp stopped in front of Ashley, sniffing the air as if it had sensed something amiss. Michael could feel the unease baking off her; Ashley's fear made the hairs on the back of his neck stand on end. Michael kept his breathing regular and tried to send some of his calm back through the link towards Ashley.

He wasn't going to let them touch her.

Ashley looked back at Michael, moving only her eyes. Michael felt the knot in his stomach ease as Ashley forced herself to keep calm. After what seemed like minutes, the imp shook its head and began digging at the ground at her feet, kicking up piles of leaves. The other imps were doing the same thing. All around them the ground was being thrown up into the air. Ashley had to turn her face away as dirt was flung in her direction. Somehow, she managed to keep still. The imp closest to her gave a wet snort and then thrust its face into the ground, pushing itself below the surface. It only took a few minutes for all the imps to drop to the ground and work themselves into the hidden tunnels lining the forest floor.

The place was now eerily quiet. No imps remained either in the treetops above, nor snuffling along the ground below.

It was like the imps had never been there. But the holes they had dug were still visible.

They had found the entrance.

* * *

Dana was ready. Her body shook with the tension. She kept her breathing as steady as she could, waiting for the telltale sign of warmth against her skin that signalled *company*. When she felt the hot humid exhale against her left ear, she almost failed to act because a similar brush of warmth was moving the hairs on the top of her head.

She thrust the blade up past her ears, jumping to her feet as she did so. She brought the blade around in a sweep where her head had been a few seconds ago.

The screech as the imp fell at her feet confirmed she'd found her mark.

There was a scrambling over to her left, and she plunged the blade in that direction and was met with resistance. Another imp fell at her feet.

She was panting wildly, trying to keep her breathing steady so she could focus on the sounds of her enemy. Her footing slipped as she moved. The floor was suddenly slick under her and she went down, her head painfully slamming against the floor. Ears ringing and seeing stars, she scampered away, desperately pushing herself backwards to clear her head. She expected the cell walls to close in on her at any moment.

She sat in this crab-like position for minutes, ready to move at the slightest sound.

She blinked her eyes, trying to see something.

Waiting there, again in the dark, she started to perceive that it was lighter above her. She stood on her tiptoes and reached towards the pale round circle above her head, but she could feel nothing. Moving around the room, she examined the walls, trying to find some kind of foothold to get her closer but she already knew there would be none.

She gagged as her hand touched the first body. It was laying against one wall, still warm, still smelling of earth and excrement. She gritted her teeth and fumbled until she found a foot to hold on to and dragged the body so that it lay under the pale circle above her.

She took one breath, then a second. Steeling herself, she stepped onto the mound she'd made for herself, ignoring the feel of warm flesh under foot. She reached for the ceiling, stretching up until the muscles in her legs felt like they were going to cramp. A couple of times she overbalanced as she reached her fingertips towards the opening she knew was above her. She was unable to touch anything, it was just too high. All she felt was a cool draft on her face.

Dana took in a shaky breath. She couldn't believe it: after everything she'd been through, to be left in a stinking hole with two dead imps when her freedom stood just beyond her ability to reach seemed more that unfair.

It seemed unjust!

She scrambled into the corner, kicking at the walls, punching at the darkness.

A breeze blew the hair back from her sticky forehead, cooling skin hot from her exertions. She closed her eyes, unconsciously turning towards the opening she knew existed far above her, wishing herself anywhere but here. The gentle breeze caressed her face, indifferent to her predicament. She positioned herself so that she was under the hole in the roof.

She could hear Marcus' voice, sounding much closer now that her room was no longer secure. 'I told you no-one was coming to save you.'

'I don't need anybody to save me,' said Dana. She tilted her head, allowing the wind to blow around her, sensing the air currents. 'I can save myself.'

She felt energy running through her and understood she had a power of her own. She allowed it to course through her. This energy ran down her muscles, poured into her extremities until her fingers and toes buzzed with a strange vibration just waiting for her direction, waiting for inspiration to give it purpose.

Her skin prickled. There was the sound of cartilage cracking in her ears.

Dana lifted her arms and beat down against the wind with two strokes of her powerful wings.

She flew up towards the exit to her prison. Dana turned her small, lightweight body so that she could skim through the cage's opening, only having to fold her wings to prevent the tips from hitting rough-hewn walls. And she was finally free from that confined space.

She twisted and spiralled – feathers on her face blown back by her speed – banked left then right as she flew through the network of tunnels, following the air currents towards the light, always onwards towards the light.

She screeched out her joy as she flew into the open air.

* * *

'It's Dana!' yelled Michael, virtually screaming at Nicola. 'Oh geez. She's broken out.'

But Nicola already knew her daughter was free. As soon as Dana had cleared the entrance to her prison, she was no longer lost to her. To Nicola she had become a beacon.

'She's out!' Nicola called to Ashul. 'We don't need the bloody imps' entrance any longer. She's in in the second realm.' Nicola's heart was racing, things were moving too quickly. She wanted to savour the joy at her daughter's escape, but Dana wasn't out of danger yet. None of them were safe. And there was so much more that needed to be done this night. The wild magic was ready and waiting, sitting at the bottom of her consciousness like a coiled snake, waiting for the opportunity to strike. Nicola wasted no time in explanation. The ropes of her power wrapped around her family and she dragged them with her as she transitioned into the second realm.

Her methods were not subtle, but they were effective. More importantly, they were fast. They all stood under the uniform grey sky of the second realm.

The light level suddenly dropped as a mass of imps circled above them.

Nicola looked upwards into the heavens, desperate to find Dana.

Almost invisible against the nondescript sky, a light grey falcon could be seen swooping downwards as an imp raked its talons in the falcon's direction.

'Dana?' Nicola whispered as the small bird dove to the right.

Lorcan followed Nicola's gaze and then sniffed, trying to catch her scent. After just a few samples of the air, he nodded, understanding what had occurred. Black smoke coiled from his shoulders.

'I have the air.' Lorcan kicked up from the ground with a grace that belied the creature he became, a creature so much larger than any of the imps. His outstretched wings were fully four metres tip to tip.

Every inch of Lorcan's body was a weapon. Powerful legs with long taloned feet tore at the bodies of the creatures flying towards the falcon. Long clawed hands drew the imps to his mouth where he ripped their throats out before dropping them to the ground.

Lorcan closed the distance between himself and the falcon that was Nicola's daughter. Nicola watched the circling imps above and wished Lorcan good hunting.

'Ashul, Michael, that's Dana flying up there,' said Nicola. 'Protect her. Bring her back safe.'

The two of them were already airborne before the first word had left her mouth. Michael didn't need her help to recognise his sister and she trusted that Ashul would lay down his life to protect her children. She just hoped that he wouldn't have to.

She had to work fast now that she could feel the doll approaching. Just as she knew it would.

'The Nachzehrer are coming,' said Nicola. 'As is the doll. Brent, do you have anything that we can use to light up this area?' Nicola didn't wait for a response. 'Joseph, fireballs in the interim will work. Can you keep a couple going at one time?' Nicola was scanning the ground at her feet, looking for the putrid mud that would herald the Nachzehrer's arrival.

Nicola needed this area to be lit up and she needed to be able to control the light. They couldn't afford for anyone else to be infected by the Nachzehrer's shadow.

The area around them began to glow with the half-dozen white fireballs that Joseph had raised into the air. Being in the second realm, they had access to powers beyond what they had in the first, but Nicola was still amazed by the intensity of the fire burning a few metres above her head.

Brent grabbed a canister from his bandolier and held it above his head. It stayed in his hand for a moment and then lifted into the air, stopping when it was at the same level as Joseph's fireballs. With a few deft flicks of his wrist, one of

Brent's cylinders now accompanied each of the balls of flame. After a brief pause, the canisters began to spin, circling each of the fireballs in a complex orbit.

With a pop, the end of each cannister blew free and a jet of fine powder sprayed out. Joseph's fire ignited the powder and, like the most over-the-top fireworks display ever created, the area was bathed in an incandescent shower of liquid light.

'Let's see how you like this light show, you zombie bastards,' said Joseph, each word forced through gritted teeth. His eyes kept returning to the falcon above his head. He smiled briefly when the talons of the bird ripped through the wing of an imp flying too close. The fireballs flickered briefly as electricity shot upwards from Joseph's hand. The imp with the torn wing fell to the ground, now nothing more than a lump of charcoal. 'Stay away from my kids, bat-face.'

'Azuradien, help Sarah,' Nicola said. Her heart was racing now. 'Create a net to protect us from any shadows that may get through. We don't want anyone else infected.'

Azuradien stepped forth and called up the wind. Sarah, half a pace behind the faerie king, gave the wind form. Gossamer-thin spirals of air rose from the ground, twisting up around the family's ankles and knees. Azuradien called on the powers of faerie, and the fine layer of protection glowed with blue phosphorescence.

Nicola turned away, leaving them to their work. She could feel the protection's embrace as it slowly crept up her body.

'Ashley, sweetie, stay right here beside me,' said Nicola. 'I'm going to need your help when things go shit-shaped.' Nicola was banking everything on some pretty vague assumptions. *But what choice did she have?*

'Aunty Nic, I think we're already at that point.'

The ground at their feet bubbled and spat as pools of mud started to form – the Nachzehrer's arrival was imminent.

Nicola drew what moisture she could from the air and a white vapour swirled up around her feet. She continued until she stood in the middle of a thick fog. Pushing the fog away from her, she forced it to condense. A dome of thickened air formed. She pushed it away from her until the area they stood in was fully encased. The water suspended within her construction glistened, refracting light in all directions, like a thousand strings of tiny diamonds had been strung in the air.

Bands of cold ebbed from the ground, drawing the warmth from Nicola. Heat was being slowly sucked from her by the Nachzehrer lurking below.

Fingers pushed upwards through the thick mud and the temperature dropped further as the Nachzehrer broke the surface. The rotting corpse looked to the sky where Michael battled with the imps.

The zombie face leered at her son with a possessive grin.

Nicola pushed Ashley behind her protectively and stood her ground. She could not allow doubt to creep in. She'd already placed her bets.

A thin layer of ice crackled at the edges of the mud pit, radiating outwards as the Nachzehrer continued absorbing the ambient heat of their environment.

Nicola saw Joseph's fires flicker. The heat that had baked down from above now barely warmed her face. Like the sun going behind a cloud on a hot summer's day, she mourned the loss of the heat's comforting embrace.

'I have come to claim what is mine,' said the Nachzehrer, words bubbling over decaying lips.

'Over my dead body,' said Nicola. She reached into the sleeves of her top and brought out two long kitchen knives. The Nachzehrer could not abide the touch of steel and she needed to keep the zombie king busy until the doll arrived.

'Fight me, and I will never allow you to die,' said the Nachzehrer. 'Once the boy ceases his futile efforts to defy me, you too will join our ranks. I will personally ensure this.' The creature attempted a laugh, but its rotted vocal cords only emitted a husky rumble.

Nicola allowed her fury at the stinking piece of flesh to guide her hand. Her blade sank to the hilt: the zombie dropped into a pile of ash.

And as it fell away, it was replaced by another zombie. The crooked smile of the zombie king formed on this face, lifting the corners of yet another rotting mouth into yet another rictus grin.

Nicola looked up to the sky once more, as if offering a prayer, though she was really checking how Ashul and Lorcan were going while protecting her children. The fight was no even match: the sleeping warriors could handle the imps on their own, but with Lorcan's aid it was a blood bath.

The doll was close. She could feel its unique brand of frenzied energy prickling against her skin. She reached for her magic. The fog solidified until the area surrounding her was encased in a wall of ice.

More zombies crawled up from the pit, bringing with them the overwhelming sick stench of putrefaction. With her shadow dancing in front of her, Nicola walked towards the zombies. Joseph's fire and Brent's pyrotechnics continued to light the sky and it felt as if the sun had once again broken through the clouds.

Nicola allowed herself a moment of hope, she had little else at this moment in time. Hope and a handful of assumptions.

The hooves of the bonded riding through the sky reverberated through her chest. She heard the hunting screech of a falcon above her somewhere accompanied by the beat of heavy wings. She felt the protection Azuradien and Sarah's magic offered her, mapped to her like a second skin. And she felt Ashley's calm certainty that Nicola had everything in hand.

Nicola whispered under her breath, 'You will have to get past a lot!' She did not need the voices of the master to make her words ring with promise.

She closed her eyes, and this time she did say a silent prayer. It was almost time. The doll was waiting in the wings, hoping to enter the fight when they were already weakened by battle. She had no intention of allowing it this luxury. She would have to force its hand. And this was the assumption around which all of her plans had been based. The doll would never allow the Nachzehrer to claim Michael. She knew that as Michael drew closer to the Nachzehrer, the poison in his blood would activate. There was no way he would be able to keep the balance of the disease, not so near to its source. And if she knew this, then so too did the doll.

'You will both need to get through us,' Nicola said through gritted teeth. Her hatred for all that her children had been forced to endure coloured her words. And streaks of wild magic wrapped around the steel blade she plunged into the neck of the nearest zombie crawling before her.

She looked up to the sky where a battle still raged and whispered, 'Remember your promise.'

* * *

Michael had thought it would work. He thought that he would be able to keep the balance until his family found a way to save him. The water around him was clear and crystalline, and the depth near fathomless. But Michael still drifted up towards the surface, like a decaying corpse filled by its own gases – a buoyancy that he could no longer control.

The zombie on the shore smiled as Michael drew closer.

The moment Michael's face broke the lake's surface, the guardian attacked. Titan launched himself at the Nachzehrer, ripping away at dead flesh.

* * *

It watched with complete incomprehension as the field was set for a battle between the mother and the Nachzehrer. Why had she allowed her son to get within striking distance of them? She thought herself so clever, so calculating with her nets of power and her light shields, protecting herself from contamination. It mattered naught if she defeated them. The contamination grew with proximity. If the son came any closer, the infection in his blood would spread at a speed no potion or tonic could keep at bay. And It could not allow that to happen. It had no intention of allowing the diseased ghouls to have so much power.

Anarcus took a moment to marvel at the power at Its disposal, drawn from so many connections It had established.

They should never have allowed It access to so many minds.

* * *

Nicola felt the wave of cold hatred against the skin of her neck and she knew the Anarcus had finally entered the field of battle. A small smile curled at the corner of her lips.

A fist of force punched the air from her lungs as the doll launched its first attack. She found herself facedown in the frozen mud at the Nachzehrer's feet. Her lips smacked into the hard ice, splitting skin open. She spat red-streaked saliva onto the ground and relished the coppery taste.

The doll walked through the wall of ice she had created as if the solidity of the barrier meant nothing to it. The wall remained untouched after it passed through. The power that radiated from the doll was so intense she felt the air rippling around her. Snatches of random thought tickled at the edges of her mind as the doll drew closer. Whispers of emotions tried to take hold. She kept her goal fixed firmly in her mind, locked behind layers of protection where she hoped the doll was unable to reach.

She asked one of the questions that all of her flimsy assumptions had been based upon.

'Ashley, can you feel them? Can you feel the connections?' Nicola yelled above the violently twisted air around her. A Nachzehrer loomed above her, but she was viewing it through a shimmering veil of incandescent blue as the protections Azuradien and Sarah had created activated.

The bonded fighting in the air above her had felt the doll's presence and left the few remaining imps for Lorcan to deal with. She pushed the hair out of her face and looked back over her shoulder as she drew herself to her feet. Lighting had almost made it to the ground. And where Ashul was, Michael wasn't far behind.

'Aunty Nic, I can,' Ashley called back. 'There are so many.'

And there was no more time to delay. The scene had finally been set. The Nachzehrer rose behind her, the doll walked towards her, and her family stood ready to fight by her side.

Past her own panting breaths, Nicola heard the pounding of hooves, so very close now. 'Michael, use the sight!' Nicola shouted this even as tears ran down her face. 'Can you see them?'

'No, Michael!' Ashul's voice boomed, the force of the bonded's power making the words reverberate with command. 'Not so close to the Nachzehrer, not here.' The warrior turned to Nicola in disbelief.

'He must!' Nicola cried out. 'Ashul, I am of the blood and you *will* obey me in this.' She'd turned her back upon the Nachzehrer as she screamed at the warrior, knowing her family would protect her back. 'You made a vow!'

Ashul tried to resist. Through the compulsion of her command, Nicola was able to feel the warrior's attempts to take on the full burden of the infection. And given just one more second, he would have succeeded. But Michael was her son and he listened when she spoke.

Michael could hear the desperation in her voice and he responded almost instantly as she knew he would.

She didn't need to see her son's eyes flare to know he was using the second sight. Nicola had learned to attune herself to his ability since the incident with Mr Stevens.

In front of her, a myriad of pulsating tendrils had sprung from the doll's head. Nicola reached for Ashley's hand and drew her close. There must have been at least a hundred cords radiating up and out into the ether. And now that Nicola could see these cords, Ashley too could feel them. Here in the second realm, their link to Michael was that strong.

But the use of the second sight came at a cost. The delicate balance that Michael had been struggling to maintain had finally been lost. His skin grew pale as the disease he'd kept at bay coursed through his body. His skin took on a waxy texture, but his eyes still shone with the light of the curse. He barely managed to stay in the saddle.

Nicola sobbed but she did not relent, she did not ask him to stop. That card had already been played and there was no going back now.

Ashul's eyes glowed with the same white light as he fell from Lightning's back. The warrior already shared more of the burden than he knew. He just hadn't come to terms with this piece of reality. His connection to Michael was the cause, not the sharing of any Nachzehrer contamination.

Grey cords of corruption ran under the warrior's skin, giving him a sickly pallor. His eyes were yellow, thick tears wept from the corners of his eyes, streaking the too young face. Somehow, he managed to push himself up to his feet, but the struggle was almost beyond him. Lightning leant against Ashul's back, lending him strength. The black coat of the horse was dull and thinning in places; corruption already lined his hide.

The doll reacted exactly as Nicola had anticipated it would. It wanted the warrior more than it wanted Michael, and it would not allow the Nachzehrer to have either of them. With the bonded finally weakened by the Nachzehrer poison running through their bloodstream, the doll prepared to attack.

It was holding nothing back.

Where there had been a hundred threads of power snaking up from the doll's head and neck, suddenly the number had doubled. The black skin of its back rippled and cracked as new connections burst forth. It would draw on every mind that it had linked to.

And while the doll drank in energy, more bonded fell from the sky.

Nicola had banked on so many things. Evil's need to be the most powerful. A son's need to save the day. A dog's love even after death. And a warrior who would not keep a promise if it meant sacrificing his friend.

'Ashley...'

Ashley needed no prompting. She sent out her mental probes, wrapping herself around the cords snaking through the air. Initially tentative, but then with calculated purpose, ephemeral hands reached forward and pulled at the connections. She gained confidence as she went, ripping more and more of the cords from the doll's head.

Grasping, tearing, Ashley was methodical in her work. Her disgust at the doll's insidiousness made Ashley utterly ruthless.

The doll's knees buckled as the first handful of umbilicals were torn from its back and it fell to the ground, its body jerking in pain-racked spasms.

As Ashley continued to rip, she remained calm, serene. She soothed each of the minds that were being given their freedom in such a brutal and violent way.

In a frenzy of outrage, the doll lashed out at the warrior struggling to his feet before him. Its goal was so close that it continued to draw on energy it no longer had access to.

Its skin split and peeled back from the bone.

The Nachzehrer king, seeing the doll interfere with one he had laid claim to, lumbered forward. His decaying hands held the power of his kind, and he lifted the doll high into the air and tossed it to the ground.

Anarcus landed in the mud at the Nachzehrer's feet. The zombie king brought his foot down and pinned Anarcus under the surface of the muck. The twisted smile grew.

Smoke dropped from the sky behind Ashul, and Michael almost fell from her back. Although his eyes shone with the pale white light, they held a jaundice look that had not been there before. Smoke's beautiful grey coat was now marred by the same lines of corruption that infected the rest of the bonded. As Michael slipped from Smoke's back, his legs buckled, but he managed to remain standing.

Ashul placed his hand on Lightning's shoulder and drew his sword from his back.

Michael too drew his blade, mirroring the leader of the bonded.

They stood side by side in defiance of the Nachzehrer. The rest of the troupe struggled to their feet. The pit of stinking mud in the middle of Nicola's makeshift battlefield was now surrounded by the bonded.

All of the bonded's eyes glowed with the same faint white light.

The mud bubbled from where Anarcus and the Nachzehrer king fought. Nicola prepared herself for the arrival of more Nachzehrer, but it was the doll's stringy black hair that rose up first, dripping, thick with mud. The dried-up husks of Nachzehrer lay inanimate around the edges of the pool.

The doll, now larger than before, laughed as mud ran down its face. 'You think I can only drain the living?'

The Nachzehrer king stumbled as the doll began to drain the energy of the zombie hive.

But the white light radiating from the eyes of the bonded made everything easier to see. Ashley reached towards Anarcus. She dropped her hands down in a chopping gesture and the mud fountained up around the doll as it was cut off from its new source of fuel.

The doll blasted cold fury towards Nicola and Ashley, but Ashul threw himself in front of them and took the full impact of the assault.

In bloodlust and rage, the doll sent wave after wave of energy in the warrior's direction.

As each blast rippled off Ashul's chest, energy crackled down his arms and legs and then dispersed amongst the bonded. The bonded lit up with the energy flowing through their bodies – horses and warriors alike – but it soon faded, losing power as it was forced to flow through so many. Just as the pestilence had been shared, so too were the bonded able to share the brunt of the doll's attack.

'You may have been able to defeat one of us,' said Ashul, striding forth, sword held high. 'But you will not be able to defeat all of us.'

But the doll had survived many battles by knowing when to cut and run. The pile of waste at its feet bubbled up violently around it and the doll started to disappear into the ground.

Ashley held firm as she gripped the doll's umbilicals. She would not allow it to slink away. The doll thrashed its head like a dog stung by hornets. It slashed at the last remaining connections, attempting to rip itself free.

Now that Joseph had less Nachzehrer to protect against, he sent a bolt of electricity towards the ground where the doll fought to free itself. Sparks sizzled across the mud's surface and the doll's skin blackened further.

With uncanny speed, the remaining connections from the doll were pulled loose with a sickening wet pop and the doll dropped from sight.

Nicola had been conserving every bit of energy for this last fight. The one that truly mattered. She turned her gaze towards the Nachzehrer that remained in the middle of the stinking pool and dropped the knives she still clenched.

'Your son can share the *symptoms* with these others,' said the Nachzehrer king. 'But he cannot share the infection in his veins. He will die, and he will rise as one of mine. It's inevitable.' The zombie spoke with a calm certainty that chilled Nicola to the bone.

'The vampire can burn the infection from his body!' Nicola screamed at the creature. Nicola felt a beat of wings and knew that Lorcan now stood at her back, a grey falcon resting on his forearm.

'Only your son's death will save those that he has infected. It is the simple beauty of our curse.' Again broken laughter bubbled up from the creature's throat.

Nicola waved her hands. The solid sheets of ice surrounding them smoothed and the diamond shimmer became hard, mirrored surfaces.

Hundreds of eyes reflected outwards from the bridge she'd created. The fragments in the gypsy book helped her in keeping the connection open.

'Well, so be it,' said Nicola. Tears streamed down her face as she wrapped her magic around Michael. 'Lorcan, Ashul, do what is required.'

Michael looked shocked and, for the first time, uncertain about Nicola's strategy.

She rushed forwards and she threw Michael towards the mirror in the ice. The surfaced dimpled as his body struck, then shattered as she followed him through.

Nicola knew the moment Michael's body dropped to the ground in the second plane, now separated from his soul. She had made certain that no connection between body and soul remained, banking everything on the fact that his link to the bonded would keep his body functioning whilst his soul was elsewhere, believing that if she risked leaving even the smallest of connections the curse would not be lifted.

It was as close to death as could be achieved.

There was no certainty in what she was doing. She was running on blind faith and a twisted string of logic, but it was all she had.

Her own soul retained a tenuous connection to her body. She'd ventured into the gypsy book before and knew its ways. She would be able to find her way back when she needed to. She just hoped her son had a body to come back to when the time was right.

She hoped her family understood what was now required, prayed that they forgave her for all that she was risking.

'Baby, I'll protect you,' said Nicola, surrounded once again by the hall of mirrors. She held Michael close as she shielded him from the thousands of voices, each begging to be heard, begging him just as they had her.

* * *

Lorcan nodded at Ashul, and they descended on the remaining Nachzehrer with a swiftness that allowed none to escape. Flashing claws and flaming swords saw the remaining zombies destroyed before any could drop within the safety of the mud's embrace.

The grey falcon glided to land on the ground. She no longer had the will to fly.

Resolution

The site of their last stand looked like the final scene from some B-grade horror movie. Fallen, dismembered zombies and slain imps lay around them everywhere.

Lorcan lifted the boy into his arms and asked for his boon from the faeries, the one request that could not be denied. 'I need access to the crystal cave,' Lorcan stated. 'The boy will not survive the cleansing without its protection.'

Azuradien didn't protest, he simply nodded. 'The boon is granted willingly. But is there any point in the cleansing if the boy's soul is lost?' he asked.

'I trust in the mother,' said Lorcan. 'She has already succeeded in breaking the curse and saved all of those infected by Michael.' Lorcan walked beside Ashul as he carried Michael's body from the field of battle. None of the earlier signs of corruption that had spread through the bonded lined Ashul's face.

Lorcan hoped that the cleansing would not kill the body now that it no longer held a soul. He could feel the combined efforts of the bonded refusing to allow the body to die. It was their link to Michael keeping his heart beating.

Lorcan shook his head. None of that was his concern. Lorcan had been given his part to play. The mother had presumptuously assumed that the vampire would not let the boy die, that he would dutifully carry out his assigned tasks. She had indeed factored all of her plans around Lorcan's ability to cure the boy and around his compliance to that end. Had she even considered for a moment that he would be better served by simply letting the boy wither away? The risk of Michael's emerging powers would be neutralised without the need for any of the boy's blood to be on his hands.

But Nicola had trusted *him*. Not only with her son's life, but with her daughter's also.

'I will save his body,' said Lorcan. 'The mother will have to find a way to guard his soul.'

* * *

Dana led her father down through the pathways to her former prison. The bodies of the two imps she'd killed lay broken on the floor. She looked down without remorse at what she'd been required to do to escape.

'Marcus?' she said quietly, then with more force when he didn't respond: 'Marcus?'

It took her father only a few moments to break down the walls that had separated the two cells, walls that had seemed impenetrable to Dana dissolved effortlessly when blasted with the electricity from Joseph.

Marcus was huddled in one corner of his cell. 'Come to gloat?'

Dana reached down and offered him her hand.

* * *

Michael lay deep within the waters of the lake. His soul had transferred to this place the moment his mother had released them from the book. She made the transition back to her own body easily but then she'd come back from that place before. Michael was finding the journey a little more difficult.

'The danger has passed,' he heard his mother say; her words seemed to come from so very far away. Michael was uncertain if she really spoke to him or if it was just his own imagination. It was irrelevant, the words spoken were true.

The lake's shore was empty save for a black dog sitting patiently by the shore. The Nachzehrer was gone.

'Titan cannot leave until you do.'

Michael understood this also to be true. He took in a deep breath and inhaled the waters of his consciousness.

* * *

Lorcan managed to save the boy. The cleansing had actually been easier without the boy's soul present and having to endure the torture. The bonded shared the burden of the body's turmoil and were strengthened by their ability to do so.

When Lorcan left the confines of the faerie realm, he allowed his rage to boil to the surface. At his full seven feet – indigo wings trembling against his back – he readied himself to unleash all the pent-up fury he no longer felt the need to control.

He had a score to settle.

He searched through the store of scents that he locked away within his blood and found the one he required. Trying not to savour the scent too much – those thoughts were dangerous – he allowed the pheromones to bead against his skin.

Eventually, he found the place he sought. He tore at the ground and was soon racing through the hidden tunnels of the imps' realm.

When he found Dana's cage, his blood boiled at the red drops painting the walls. He settled back into the corner and allowed her scent to rise from his skin until her fragrance once again permeated the room.

He crossed his hands behind his head and waited for the first of the imps to arrive.

'Expecting the girl, were you,' he said. 'Sorry to disappoint.' Lorcan eyes blazed.

The walls soon ran with the ichor of imp blood.

Even Michael, who had seen him in his truest form, wouldn't recognise the beast that delighted in his redecoration.

Soon, another group of imps were attracted by the smell of easy meat.

Lorcan thought to himself: *They really do have a very base level of intellect.*

Epilogue
Family Ties

It was strange to have Marcus living under their roof.

But Nicola wouldn't allow Marcus to return home. Captain Dave ensured that after some discussion with the appropriate people that Marcus could stay within their care since they had declared his home unsafe due to the damage sustained in the recent 'freak storm'.

Marcus had remained withdrawn and unresponsive since they'd rescued him from the imps' cells. He could answer questions, usually with a snide remark, but if they left him alone, he left everyone else alone. Michael couldn't understand what his life must have been like.

Weeks had passed and they had neither seen nor heard from Marcus' parents.

When the doorbell rang late one Saturday night, Michael thought nothing much of it. His mother still had her wardings protecting their home, so no-one got any further than the front door if she didn't want them to. He continued to play his video game as the sound of voices drifted up the stairs. He paused the game only when he didn't recognise the voice of the old woman his mother was speaking to. Curious by nature, Michael wandered downstairs.

Nicola was offering a glass of water to an older woman and a young boy whom Michael assumed was her grandson.

'I'm so sorry to come calling at such a ridiculous time of night. But I could not get Tommy to calm down. He's been so unsettled of late with nightmares and the like. He's always been a sensitive child, having an old woman like me raising him probably makes him a little spoiled but...'

Nicola placed her hand against the woman's arm, offering comfort as well as support. Her hands were shaking so badly Michael thought she would drop the glass of water she had been given. 'Don't worry, I have sensitive children myself. I know what it's like when they get something stuck in their heads.' Nicola gave Michael a sideways glance. The mention of the nightmares had gotten her attention.

Dana, not just also curious by nature – more downright nosey – walked into the room and gave the little boy a casual wave. He smiled brightly at her.

'As I said, my name is Patricia,' the woman said. 'And this is my grandson, Tommy. Since he recently turned eight, he likes to be called Tom.' Nicola smiled in the boy's direction, bending down slightly to be on his level, but the boy had eyes only for Dana.

'I cannot explain what he's been like lately. He wakes crying, screaming about some doll in his dreams. Childish nonsense. But at night when I lay there with him in my arms rocking him to sleep it doesn't feel like nonsense.'

Dana took Tom over to the window and was introducing him to Sheba. The boy was as taken by their dog as he was by Dana. Michael could tell by Dana's posture that she'd been listening keenly to every word since the mention of the doll.

'With today being such a beautiful day, I decided to take him for a drive,' said Patricia. 'We came out this way for a nice picnic. So much wildlife in this area. Tom is quite the explorer. Aren't you, honey?' Patricia held the glass of water in both hands. They were still shaking too badly for her to risk taking a sip.

'Then for the first time that I can remember, he started raving about the doll in the daytime,' said Patricia. 'Said it was hiding, buried deep underground. He could feel it digging, trying to get to him.' Patricia suppressed a sob. 'I couldn't calm him down. What could I do? I bundled everything back into the car and drove home. I have no idea where he gets these thoughts from.'

Michael bent down to speak to Tom. 'Buddy, how long have you been dreaming about this doll for?'

Tommy nodded. 'Years. I've been dreaming about you too. You and the horses.' Michael and Dana shared a look, both surprised by Tommy's comment. 'I could show you where the doll's hiding, if you want. The ants will show me exactly where, if I ask them.' Tommy looked sideways at Michael as if imparting a great secret.

'I'm not sure what's happening,' said Patricia. 'I feel like my daughter would have been able to handle things, but I'm an old woman and I don't understand what's troubling him.'

'May I ask what happened to your daughter?' Nicola asked gently.

'She was killed in a car accident. Tommy was still in the hospital, born four weeks premature. His little lungs couldn't breathe on their own. They were all killed in a freak crash. My daughter, son-in-law, and his older brother.' Patricia raised a tissue to her eyes.

'I'm so sorry for your loss,' said Nicola. She wrapped an arm around the older woman's shoulders. 'You've done a wonderful job; he's a gorgeous child.'

'Marcus?' The old woman spoke barely above a whisper. There were too many emotions underpinning this one word.

'I'm sorry, yes, Marcus. He's the young boy staying with us.' Nicola quickly moved to steady the old woman as she swayed on her feet. She looked like she was about to collapse. Nicola tried to steer her towards the nearest chair but she was frozen on the spot, staring at the doorway where Marcus stood studying their visitors. His expression was as neutral as ever.

Patricia dropped the glass. 'Marcus?' Her knees buckled, and Nicola only just managed to catch her weight before she fell to the floor.

Tommy turned to Dana. 'He's my brother, you know.' The young boy shrugged like he was commenting on nothing more than the weather.

Search for the Seer

Prologue
Brother of Mine

Nicola was speechless. After all that they had recently gone through she would never have suspected that the arrival at her front door of an old woman and her somewhat peculiar grandchild would be the event that stole the words from her mouth. And it wasn't just that she'd lost the ability to think of something to say, her mind had actually gone blank. Or, more accurately, her memories were in freefall, running back over the last six months, trying to find the pieces of the puzzle that she had missed.

That her son, Michael, had become a member of a mythological band of warriors tasked with the protection of the realm, well, she couldn't have been expected to see *that* coming but in all honestly it wasn't that much of a surprise to her either. He'd always been a protector of the underdog, righter of wrongs, always had an affinity with the hero that was willing to push the envelope just that little bit further to save the day. Not exactly breaking the rules but bending and moulding them until they had a level of flexibility that allowed him to achieve whatever goal he had set himself. The ends did not justify the means in Michael's mind, but he never lost sight of the fact that 'the end' was the point.

With a directness that belied the confusion in the room, Michael said what they were all thinking.

'I don't know about you, but I for one did *not* see that coming.' Michael placed his hand on Nicola's shoulder. Her fingers were splayed out against the black granite of the benchtop as if she needed its support.

'Michael, Dana, has there ever been any mention of Marcus having a brother? At school, amongst his friends?' Nicola's voice became stronger as she neared the end of her sentence, her mind beginning to function once again.

She doubted that her children would have heard anything directly, but local gossip sometime hid truth. They lived in the leafier suburbs of Melbourne where things didn't stay personal for long.

'In case you'd forgotten, Mum,' said Michael. 'Until you invited him to live with us, we didn't exactly hang in the same crowds. He and his mates made it their life's work to make mine miserable.'

Michael's sister Dana seemed to be suffering the same inability to think that Nicola had been struggling with just moments before. Her long hair had been pushed behind her ears and she was staring out the kitchen windows as if the answers they needed were sitting in plain sight outside.

'Are you seriously saying you believe that old lady? That she's Marcus' grandmother and that the creepy kid with her is his little brother. I'm not...' Michael next words were cut off by Dana.

'That's definitely his brother,' said Dana. 'Sheba smelt it on him the minute I let her sniff his hand.' Dana's eyes regained focus and they found Nicola's. 'Shouldn't we be more worried about the fact that the little kid seemed pretty confident that he knew where the doll was? Right now, while they are out having a little family reunion, Marcus is having that information given to him.' Dana paused to let the room ponder things for a moment. 'We may have freed Marcus, but let's not forget that Marcus has been working with the doll since the beginning.' Dana raised her hand to forestall Nicola's argument. 'Yes, Mum, I know he'd been coerced, but his "parents" spent years brainwashing that kid using the most *extreme* techniques. Do we really think that kind of reprogramming can just be undone? It's not safe him having that kind of information about the doll.'

Nicola had no doubt that Dana was correct about the brother. They'd all been changed by the rift that was now allowing magic to seep back into the world. Her daughter no less so than her son. Nicola could almost see the animals lurking behind her daughter's eyes. Dana's link to their Doberman, Sheba, had strengthened to such a degree that Nicola doubted if either of them realised that they were constantly communicating. And if Sheba said the two boys were related, who was Nicola to argue.

'Mum, I have to agree with Dana,' said Michael. 'I kind of get your need to give Marcus a safe place to be. But just because we feel sorry for all that has happened to him doesn't mean we can trust him. So far he hasn't spoken to us about *any* of it. Now a grandmother and brother turn up out of the blue. We find out his real parents may be dead. If that is in fact the case, then what the hell is going on? Who has he been living with? That old woman claims his real parents were killed in a car crash. That *Marcus* was killed in a car crash. Well, she's obviously wrong about that. Could she just be delusional?' Michael moved, as he always did lately, to stand beside Dana. 'Fabricating a story because her daughter, I don't know, abandoned her kids.'

Dana lifted her phone so that Michael could see the screen. Dana had found an old newspaper article. The headline left little room for any doubt. *Local family die in tragic crash.*

The old woman wasn't delusional.

'But it says here that all three occupants of the vehicle were killed. No-one survived,' Dana said as she handed her phone over to Nicola. 'Tommy is mentioned by name as being the only surviving member of the family. Every word Patricia said is true.'

'So what the hell's going on?' asked Michael. And who the hell have we allowed to live under our roof?' Michael had begun pacing.

Nicola was about to speak but the skin prickled on the back of her arms as the wardings she'd set over the house triggered. She looked up as Marcus silently opened the door to the kitchen. He seemed to have grown in the short time he'd been living with them. His black hair needed a cut, and he was still too pale, but the dark circles under his eyes no longer looked like bruises. The side of his mouth curled up at the corner. Nicola closed her eyes, for a moment needing to remind herself of all that this boy had endured.

When she looked back towards him, her own features composed, his smirk was gone.

'How did things go? Nicola asked, trying to sound casual.

'He is no brother of mine,' Marcus declared in a cold, detached voice and without saying anything further he turned and left the room.

About the Author

Petra has lived in a world where plans mean little and dreams are the only constant. Diagnosed with ear disease at the age of eight, she turned to books to escape the constant medical procedures that would be a part of her life for two decades. She always had an open view of the world around her, having grown up on stories of her gypsy ancestors, but a near death experience during surgery confirmed what she  had long known: the world has many layers and the people that reside within it have even more.

Petra runs her own Finance IT Consulting business and writes about her strange 'what if' view of the world in any spare moment she has. She is married with two children, and the characters in her books have a tiny bit more than a passing resemblance to her family. All of their strengths are their own and all of their weaknesses are pure fiction.

462

www.ingramcontent.com/pod-product-compliance
Lightning Source LLC
Chambersburg PA
CBHW060723190726
48285CB00001B/46